# Old Celtic Romances

## Tales from Irish Mythology

P. W. Joyce

**DOVER PUBLICATIONS, INC.**
Mineola, New York

*Copyright*

Copyright © 1907 by Longmans, Green, & Co.
All rights reserved under Pan American and International Copyright Conventions.

Published in Canada by General Publishing Company, Ltd., 30 Lesmill Road, Don Mills, Toronto, Ontario.

*Bibliographical Note*

This Dover edition, first published in 2001, is an unabridged republication of the third, expanded edition (1907, Longmans, Green, & Co.) of the work originally published in 1879 by David Nutt, London. This edition includes thirteen tales (two not included in the first edition and one not included in the 1894 second edition).

*Library of Congress Cataloging-in-Publication Data*

Old Celtic romances : tales from Irish mythology / P.W. Joyce.
    p. cm.
  Originally published: London : David Nutt, 1879.
  Includes bibliographical references.
  ISBN 0-486-41609-7 (pbk.)
    1. Epic literature, Irish—Translations into English. 2. Heroes—Ireland—Legends. 3. Mythology, Celtic. 4. Tales—Ireland. 5. Tales, Medieval. I. Joyce, P. W. (Patrick Weston), 1827–1914. II. Title.

PB1421 .J6 2001
891.6'208—dc21

                                                                00-064495

Manufactured in the United States of America
Dover Publications, Inc., 31 East 2nd Street, Mineola, N.Y. 11501

# PREFACE

AMONG the Celtic people of Ireland and the north-west of Scotland, story-telling has always been a favourite amusement. In the olden time, they had professional story-tellers, variously designated according to rank—ollaves, shanachies, poets, bards, etc.—whose duty it was to know by heart a number of old tales, poems, and historical pieces, and to recite them at festive gatherings for the entertainment of the chiefs and their guests. These story-tellers were always well received at the houses of princes and chiefs, and treated with much consideration, and they were often rewarded with costly presents.

To meet the demand for this sort of entertainment, ingenious " men of learning," taking legends or historical events as themes, composed stories from time to time; of which those that struck the popular fancy were caught up and remembered, and handed down from one generation of story-tellers to another. In course of time, a body of romantic literature grew up, consisting chiefly of prose tales.

Some of these tales were founded on historical events, and corresponded closely with what is now called the historical romance; while others were altogether fictitious. But even in the fictitious tales, the main characters are always historical, or such as were considered so. The old ollaves wove their fictions round Conor Mac Nessa and his Red Branch Knights, or Finn and his Fena, or Lugh of the Long Arms and his Dedannans, or Conn the Hundred-fighter, or Cormac Mac Airt; like the Welsh legends of Arthur and his Round Table, or the Arabian romances of Haroun-al-Raschid and his Court.

The greater number of the tales were, as I have said, in prose. But some were in poetry; and in many of the prose tales the leading characters are often made to express themselves in verse, or some striking incident of the story is repeated in a poetical

v

form. Not unfrequently the fragments of verse introduced into a prose tale are quotations from an older poetical version of the same tale; and hence it often happens that while the prose may be plain enough, the poetry is often archaic and obscure.

At some very early period in Ireland—how early we have now no means of determining with certainty—Celtic thought began to be committed to writing; and as everything seems to have been written down that was considered worth preserving, manuscripts accumulated in course of time, and were kept either in monasteries or in the houses of the hereditary professors of learning. But in the dark time of the Danish ravages, and during the troubled centuries that followed the Anglo-Norman invasion, the manuscript collections were gradually dispersed, and a large proportion lost or destroyed. Yet we have remaining—rescued by good fortune from the general wreck—a great body of manuscript literature. Our two most important collections are those in Trinity College and in the Royal Irish Academy, Dublin; where we have manuscripts of various ages, from the year 1100 down to the present century, on every conceivable subject—Annals, History, Biography, Theology, Romance, Legend, Science, etc. These manuscripts, which, it should be remarked, are nearly all copies from older books, contain a vast collection of romantic literature: it may, indeed, be said that there is scarcely one important event in our early history, or one important native personage or native legend, that has not been made the subject of some fanciful story.

The volume I now offer to the notice of the public contains eleven tales, selected and translated from the manuscripts of Trinity College and of the Royal Irish Academy. Some have been already published, with original text and *literal* translation, and are to be found in the Transactions of various literary societies, where, however, they are inaccessible to the general run of readers; and even if they were accessible, they are almost unreadable, the translations having been executed, not for literary, but for linguistic purposes. Others have never been translated or given to the public in any shape or form till now.

Of the whole collection of eleven tales, therefore, it may be said that they are quite new to the general mass of the reading public. And furthermore, this is the first collection of the old Gaelic prose romances that has ever been published in fair English translation.

Scraps and fragments of some of these tales have been given to the world in popular publications, by writers who, not being able to read the originals, took their information from printed books in the English language. But many of these specimens have been presented in a very unfavourable and unjust light—distorted to make them look *funny*, and their characters debased to the mere modern conventional stage Irishman. There is none of this silly and odious vulgarity in the originals of these fine old tales, which are high and dignified in tone and feeling—quite as much so as the old romantic tales of Greece and Rome.

A translation may either follow the very words, or reproduce the life and spirit, of the original; but no translation can do both. If you render word for word, you lose the spirit; if you wish to give the spirit and manner, you must depart from the exact words, and frame your own phrases. I have chosen this latter course. My translation follows the original closely enough in narrative and incident; but so far as mere phraseology is concerned, I have used the English language freely, not allowing myself to be trammelled by too close an adherence to the very words of the text. The originals are in general simple in style; and I have done my best to render them into simple, plain, homely English. In short, I have tried to tell the stories as I conceive the old shanachies themselves would have told them if they had used English instead of Gaelic.

In the originals, the stories run on without break or subdivision; but I have thought it better to divide the longer ones into chapters, with appropriate headings.

In almost all cases I had at my command several copies of the same story, some of them differing in phraseology and in minor points of detail, though agreeing, in the main, in narrative and incident. I found this a considerable advantage, as it gave me more freedom in the choice of expression.

I now give a few particulars concerning these tales, including a short account of the manuscript or manuscripts from which they have been translated.

## THE THREE TRAGIC STORIES OF ERIN

Among the ancient Gaelic tales, three were known as " the three most sorrowful (tales) of story-telling," or " The Three Tragic Stories of Erin "; viz., " The Fate of the Children of Usna," " The Fate of the Children of Lir," and " The Fate of the Children of Turenn."

## THE FATE OF THE CHILDREN OF LIR

Two translations of this tale have been published: one literal, with the Gaelic text, by Professor O'Curry, in the *Atlantis* (Nos. vii and viii); and another, less literal, by Gerald Griffin, in his " Tales of a Jury-Room."

The oldest known copies of the tale are, one in the National University, Dublin, made by Andrew Mac Curtin, a well-known Gaelic scholar and scribe of the county Clare, who lived between 1680 and 1740; one in Trinity College, Dublin, made by Hugh O'Daly, in 1758; and one in the British Museum, made by Richard Tipper of Dublin, in 1718. There is also a very good copy in the Royal Irish Academy (23.C. 26), of which I made considerable use, written in or about 1782, by Peter O'Connell, a good Gaelic scholar of the county Clare. From a comparison of several of these versions, O'Curry made his copy of the text as published in the *Atlantis*.

## THE FATE OF THE CHILDREN OF TURENN

In the Book of Lecan (folio 28), which was compiled by the Mac Firbises, about A.D. 1416, is a short account, partly in prose and partly in verse, of the celebrated eric-fine imposed on the three sons of Turenn, by Lugh of the Long Arms, for killing his father Kian; but this old book does not give the story of the quest for the fine. The full tale, text and literal translation, has been published by O'Curry in the *Atlantis*. There are several good copies in the Royal Irish Academy.

There are references to these three sons of Turenn, and to the manner of their death, in two very old authorities, viz., Cormac's " Glossary " (about A.D. 900); and a poem by Flann of Monasterboice (who died A.D. 1056), a copy of which is in the Book of Leinster, written about A.D. 1130.

In the older references to the sons of Turenn, they are called Brian, Iuchar, Iucharba; but in some comparatively modern copies of the tale the names are a little different—for instance, Peter O'Connell calls them Uar, Iuchar, and Iucharba; and they vary still further in other copies. I have taken advantage of this variety to give the names in a more pronounceable form in my translation.

## THE OVERFLOWING OF LOUGH NEAGH

" Leabhar na hUidhre," or " The Book of the Dun Cow," from which this and the two following tales are taken, is the oldest manuscript of miscellaneous Gaelic literature we possess. It was transcribed from older books by Maelmuire Mac Ceilechair, who died in 1106; and it is now in the Royal Irish Academy, Dublin— or rather, I should say, a large fragment of it, for the book has suffered much mutilation. This venerable book may now be said to be in the hands of the public, as it has been lately reproduced in lithograph facsimile, and published by the Council of the Royal Irish Academy.

The story of " The Overflowing of Lough Neagh " (called in the original " The Destruction of Eocho Mac Mairedo ") has been published, with text and literal translation, by J. O'Beirne Crowe, in the Kilkenny Archaeological Journal (volume for 1870-1).

In this story I have been obliged to make a few transpositions in the order of the incidents, for the narrative in the original is in some places very ill arranged.

It is now nearly eight hundred years since this story was *transcribed* from some old authority into " The Book of the Dun Cow "; and it is singular that the tradition of the formation of Lough Neagh, by the overflow of an enchanted well which was neglected by the woman in charge of it, still remains among the people.

## CONNLA OF THE GOLDEN HAIR, AND
## THE FAIRY MAIDEN

This tale (called in the original " Echtra Condla Cain," " The Adventures of Connla the Comely ") is taken from " The Book of the Dun Cow."

It is one of the many tales that illustrate the ancient and widespread superstition that fairies sometimes take away mortals to their palaces in the fairy forts and pleasant green hills; of which the last story in

this book—" Oisin in Tír na nÓg "—is another example.   This
superstition prevailed in Ireland and the Scottish Highlands as far
back as either history or tradition reaches;  it flourished in full vigour
within my own memory;  and it is scarcely quite extinct—in Ireland
at least—at the present day.   In connection with the antiquity of this
superstition, it must be borne in mind that the present story was
transcribed into " The Book of the Dun Cow " in or about the year
1100, from some older book;  and that it relates to the time of Conn
the Hundred-fighter, king of Ireland, who reigned in the second
century of the Christian era.

## THE VOYAGE OF MAILDUN

Of this tale (which is now given to the public for the first time)
the oldest copy is in " The Book of the Dun Cow " (about the year
1100);  but it is imperfect at both beginning and end—a portion
having been torn away when the book was mutilated at some former
time.   There is a perfect copy in the Yellow Book of Lecan, in Trinity
College, Dublin, and another in the British Museum (MS. Harl.
5280).

After I had made a rough translation of the greater part of this
piece, I discovered a good literal translation in manuscript in the
Royal Irish Academy, made by the late J. O'Beirne Crowe, which
was of great use to me, as it helped to explain some strange terms,
and to clear up some obscure passages.

This voyage would appear from internal evidence to have been
made in the beginning of the eighth century (O'Curry says about
the year 700); for I think it likely that Maildun did actually go on a
voyage, which was afterwards made the framework of the story.
On my translation of this tale, Lord Tennyson founded his poem
" The Voyage of Maeldune."

Of the *Imrama* or voluntary sea expeditions (to which the present
story belongs) there are, according to O'Curry (Lect. MS. Mat. 289),
only four remaining, all very ancient.   Of these the best known is the
" Voyage of St. Brendan," undertaken in the sixth century, which
was at one time celebrated all over Europe.

## THE FAIRY PALACE OF THE QUICKEN TREES

The " Bruighean Caorthainn," or " The Fairy Palace of the
Quicken Trees," which is now translated for the first time, is one of
the most popular of the Gaelic romances.

This is one of a type of stories very common in Gaelic romantic literature:—One or more of the heroes are entrapped by some enchanter and held under a spell in a castle, or a cave, or a dungeon; till, after a series of adventures, they are released by the bravery or mother-wit of some of their companions. " The Chase of Slieve Fuad " and " The Chase of Slieve Cullinn " are two other examples of this class of Gaelic tales.

## THE PURSUIT OF THE GIOLLA DACKER AND HIS HORSE

This is a humorous story of a trick—a very serious practical joke— played by Avarta, a Dedannan enchanter, on sixteen of the Fena, whom he carried off to " The Land of Promise "; and of the adventures of Finn, Dermat O'Dyna, and the others, in their pursuit of Avarta (who had taken the shape of the Giolla Dacker) to recover their companions. It may be regarded as belonging to the same class as the last story.

I think it strange that such a story should not have been noticed before by writers on Gaelic literature; for as a work of imagination, it seems to me a marvellous and very beautiful creation.

The battles fought by the king of Sorca, aided by Finn and his Fena, against the King of the World, are described at much length in the original; but I have cut them down to a very short compass; and I have omitted altogether a long episode towards the end, which travels away from the main story.

## THE PURSUIT OF DERMAT AND GRANIA

This tale is one of those mentioned in the list contained in the Book of Leinster, which was written about A.D. 1130; but though this proves the tale to be an ancient one, I have never come across a copy older than the last century.

I cannot help believing that this fine story originally ended with the death of Dermat; though in all the current versions there is an additional part recounting the further proceedings of Grania and her sons, after the death of the hero. But this part is in every respect inferior to the rest—in language, in feeling, and in play of imagination. It seems to me very clear that it was patched on to the original story by some unskilful hand; and I have accordingly omitted it, and ended the story with the death of Dermat. I have also omitted two short episodes—that of the *cnumh* or reptile of Corca Divna, as a mere excrescence; and Finn's expedition to Scotland for aid against Dermat. And, for the sake of clearness, I have slightly changed the place of that part of the tale which recounts the origin of the Fairy Quicken Tree of Dooros. There are one or two other trifling but very necessary modifications which need not be mentioned here.

### THE CHASE OF SLIEVE CULLINN: THE CHASE OF SLIEVE FUAD: OISIN IN TÍR NA NÓG

In the original Gaelic these are three poetical tales. All three have been printed, with Gaelic text and literal translation, in the Transactions of the Ossianic Society: the two first by the late John O'Daly, and " Oisin in Tír na nÓg " by Professor O'Looney. There are many good copies of these tales in the manuscripts of the Royal Irish Academy; though of not one of them have I seen a copy older than the last century.

### THE FATE OF THE SONS OF USNA

See note on " The Three Tragic Stories of Erin " (page viii).

P. W. JOYCE

## PREFACE TO THE THIRD EDITION.

In this edition there is an additional tale, "The Fate of the Sons of Usna," a notice of which will be found at page viii, above.

LYRE-NA-GRENA, LEINSTER ROAD,
    RATHMINES, 1907.

## Editor's Note, Dover Edition

Although the original Preface correctly states that eleven tales are included in the volume, this edition (2001) includes thirteen tales, six of which consist of several chapters. "The Voyage of the Sons of O'Corra" was added in the second edition (1894). As stated above, "The Fate of the Sons of Usna" was added in the third edition (1907).

# CONTENTS

## The Voyage of Maildun

## The Fairy Palace of the Quicken Trees

# The Fate of the Children of Lir

## OR

### THE FOUR WHITE SWANS

Silent, O Moyle, be the roar of thy water;
  Break not, ye breezes, your chain of repose;
While murmuring mournfully, Lir's lonely daughter
  Tells to the night-star her tale of woes.

MOORE

## CHAPTER I

### BOVE DERG CHOSEN KING OF THE DEDANNANS

AFTER the battle of Tailltenn,* the Dedannans[1]† of the five provinces of Erin assembled in one place of meeting to consider on their state, and to choose a king. For their chiefs said it was better for them to have one king over all, than to be divided, as they were, serving sundry lords and princes.

Now of those who expected the sovereignty for themselves, the following chiefs were the noblest, namely:—Bove Derg, son of the Dagda; his brother Angus, of Brugh on the Boyne, who, however, had no earnest wish to become king, preferring to remain as he was; Ilbrec of Assaroe; Lir of Shee Finnaha; and Midir the Haughty of Bri-Leth.[1]

Then the chief people went into council, all except the five above named; and the decision they came to was to elect Bove Derg, son of the Dagda, king over the whole of the

---

* Now Teltown, on the river Blackwater between Kells and Navan, in Meath.
† The Dedannans were regarded as gods, and as being immortal or semi-immortal.

Dedannan race. When the election was made known, none of
those who were disappointed took the matter to heart except
Lir of Shee Finnaha alone. And when Lir found that the chiefs
had chosen Bove Derg, he was greatly offended, and straightway
left the assembly in anger, without taking leave of anyone, and
without showing any mark of respect or obedience to the new
king.

When the chiefs heard this, they were wroth; and they
said they would follow him to Shee Finnaha,* and slay
him with spear and sword, and burn his house, because he
did not yield obedience to the king they had elected in lawful
council.

But Bove Derg would not permit them to do so. " This man,"
he said, " will defend his territory, and many will be slain; and
I am none the less your king, although he has not submitted to
me."

Matters remained so for a long time. But at last a great
misfortune happened to Lir, for his wife died after an illness of
three days. This weighed heavily on him, and his heart was
weary with sorrow after her. Her death, moreover, was a great
event at that time, and was much spoken of throughout
Erin.

When the tidings reached the mansion of Bove Derg, where
the chief men of the Dedannans were then assembled, the king
said: " As Lir's wife is now dead, my friendship would be of
service to him, if he were willing to accept it. For I have in my
house three maidens, the most beautiful and the best instructed
in all Erin, namely, Eve, Eva, and Alva, my own foster children,
and daughters of Allil of Ara." †

The Dedannans agreed to this, and said that their king had
spoken wisely and truly.

Messengers were accordingly sent to Lir, and they were told
to say to him—

" If thou art willing to submit to the king, he will give thee
for a wife one of his three foster children; and thou shalt have
his friendship for ever."

---

* Shee Finnaha, Lir's residence, is thought to have been situated near the boundary
    of Armagh and Monaghan, not far from Newtown Hamilton.
† Ara, the islands of Aran, in Galway Bay.

It was pleasing to Lir to make this alliance; and accordingly he set out next day from Shee Finnaha with a company of fifty chariots; and they never halted or turned aside till they reached the palace of Bove Derg, on the shore of the Great Lake.* Their arrival gave much joy and happiness to the king and his household; for although Lir did not submit at first to Bove Derg, he was a good man, and was greatly beloved by the king himself and by all his subjects. So Lir and his followers got a kindly welcome; and they were supplied with everything necessary, and were well attended to that night.

Next day, the three daughters of Allil of Ara sat on the same couch with the queen, their foster mother; and the king said to Lir: "Take thy choice of the three maidens, and whichever thou choosest, she shall be thy wife."

"They are all beautiful," said Lir, "and I cannot tell which of them is best; but I will take the eldest, for she must be the noblest of the three."

Then the king said, "Eve is the eldest, and she shall be given to thee if it be thy wish." So Lir chose Eve for his wife, and they were wedded that day.

Lir remained a fortnight in the king's palace, and then departed with his wife to his own house, Shee Finnaha, where he celebrated his marriage by a great royal wedding feast.

## CHAPTER II

### THE CHILDREN OF LIR

IN course of time, Lir's wife bore him two children at a birth, a daughter and a son, whose names were Finola and Aedh. A second time she brought forth twins, two sons, who were named Fiachra and Conn: and she died in giving them birth. This was a cause of great anguish to Lir; and he would almost have died of grief, only that his mind was turned from his sorrow by his great love for his four little children.

---

* Lough Derg, on the Shannon, above Killaloe.

When the news of Eve's death reached the mansion of Bove Derg, the king was in deep grief, and the people of his household raised three great cries of lamentation for her. And when their mourning was ended, the king said—

"We grieve for our foster child, both on her own account, and for the sake of the good man to whom we gave her; for we are thankful for his alliance and his friendship. But our acquaintance shall not be ended, and our alliance shall not be broken; for I will give him her sister to wife, my second foster child, Eva."

Messengers were sent to Lir to Shee Finnaha, to tell him of this; and he consented. So after some time he came to the king's house to espouse her, and they were united; and he brought her home with him to his own house.

The four children grew up under Eva's care. She nursed them with great tenderness, and her love for them increased every day. They slept near their father; and he would often rise from his own bed at the dawn of morning, and go to their beds, to talk with them and to fondle them.

The king, Bove Derg, loved them almost as well as did their father. He went many times every year to Shee Finnaha to see them; and he used to bring them often to his palace, where he kept them as long as he could on each occasion, and he always felt sad when he sent them home.

At this time, too, the Dedannans used to celebrate the Feast of Age[2] at the houses of their chiefs by turns; and whenever it happened that the festival was held at Shee Finnaha, these children were the delight and joy of the Dedannans. For nowhere could four lovelier children be found; so that those who saw them were always delighted with their beauty and their gentleness, and could not help loving them with their whole heart.

## CHAPTER III

### THE FOUR CHILDREN OF LIR ARE TURNED INTO
### FOUR WHITE SWANS BY THEIR STEPMOTHER

Now when Eva saw that the children of Lir received such attention and affection from their father, and from all others that came to his house, she fancied she was neglected on their account; and a poisonous dart of jealousy entered her heart, which turned her love to hatred; and she began to have feelings of bitter enmity for her sister's children.

Her jealousy so preyed on her that she feigned illness, and lay in bed for nearly a year, filled with gall and brooding mischief; and at the end of that time she committed a foul and cruel deed of treachery on the children of Lir.

One day she ordered her horses to be yoked to her chariot, and she set out for the palace of Bove Derg, bringing the four children with her.

Finola did not wish to go, for it was revealed to her darkly in a dream that Eva was bent on some dreadful deed; and she knew well that her stepmother intended to kill her and her brothers that day, or in some other way to bring ruin on them. But she was not able to avoid the fate that awaited her.

When they had gone some distance from Shee Finnaha on their way to the palace, Eva tried to persuade her attendants to kill the children. " Kill them, and you shall be rewarded with all the wordly wealth you may desire; for their father loves me no longer, and has neglected and forsaken me on account of his great love for these children."

But they heard her with horror, and refused, saying: " We will not kill them. Fearful is the deed thou hast contemplated, O Eva; and evil will surely befall thee for having even thought of killing them."

Then she took the sword to slay them herself; but her woman's weakness prevented her, and she was not able to strike them. So they set out once more, and fared on till they came to the shore of Lake Darvra,* where they alighted, and the horses were unyoked.

---

* Lake Darvra, now Lough Derravaragh, in Westmeath.

She led the children to the edge of the lake, and told them to go to bathe; and as soon as they had got into the clear water, she struck them one by one with a druidical[3] fairy wand, and turned them into four beautiful snow-white swans. And she addressed them in these words—

> Out to your home, ye swans, on Darvra's wave;
>   With clamorous birds begin your life of gloom:
> Your friends shall weep your fate, but none can save;
>   For I've pronounced the dreadful words of doom.

After this, the four children of Lir turned their faces to their stepmother; and Finola spoke—

"Evil is the deed thou hast done, O Eva; thy friendship to us has been a friendship of treachery; and thou hast ruined us without cause. But the deed will be avenged; for the power of thy witchcraft is not greater than the druidical power of our friends to punish thee; and the doom that awaits thee shall be worse than ours."

> Our stepmother loved us long ago;
> Our stepmother now has wrought us woe:
> With magical wand and fearful words,
> She changed us to beautiful snow-white birds;
> And we live on the waters for evermore,
> By tempests driven from shore to shore.

Finola again spoke and said: "Tell us now how long we shall be in the shape of swans, so that we may know when our miseries shall come to an end."

"It would be better for you if you had not put that question," said Eva; "but I shall declare the truth to you, as you have asked me. Three hundred years on smooth Lake Darvra; three hundred years on the Sea of Moyle, between Erin and Alban; three hundred years at Irros Domnann* and at Inis Glora on

---

* Irros Domnann; Erris, in the county Mayo. Inis Glora; a small island about five miles west from Belmullet, in the same county.

the Western Sea.  Until the union of Largnen, the prince from
the north, with Decca, the princess from the south; until the
Taillkenn* shall come to Erin, bringing the light of a pure faith;
and until ye hear the voice of the Christian bell.  And neither
by your own power, nor by mine, nor by the power of your
friends, can ye be freed till the time comes."

Then Eva repented what she had done; and she said:
" Since I cannot afford you any other relief, I will allow you
to keep your own Gaelic speech; and ye shall be able to sing sweet,
plaintive, fairy music, which shall excel all the music of the
world, and which shall lull to sleep all that listen to it.  Moreover,
ye shall retain your human reason; and ye shall not be in grief
on account of being in the shape of swans."

And she chanted this lay—

> Depart from me, ye graceful swans;
> The waters are now your home:
> Your palace shall be the pearly cave,
> Your couch the crest of the crystal wave,
> And your mantle the milk-white foam!

> Depart from me, ye snow-white swans
> With your music and Gaelic speech:
> The crystal Darvra, the wintry Moyle,
> The billowy margin of Glora's isle;—
> Three hundred years on each!

> Victorious Lir, your hapless sire,
> His lov'd ones in vain shall call;
> His weary heart is a husk of gore,
> His home is joyless for evermore,
> And his anger on me shall fall!

> Through circling ages of gloom and fear
> Your anguish no tongue can tell;
> Till Faith shall shed her heavenly rays,
> Till ye hear the Taillkenn's anthem of praise,
> And the voice of the Christian bell!

---

* Taillkenn, a name given by the druids to St. Patrick.

Then ordering her steeds to be yoked to her chariot she departed westwards, leaving the four white swans swimming on the lake.

> Our father shall watch and weep in vain;
> He never shall see us return again.
> Four pretty children, happy at home;
> Four white swans on the feathery foam;
> And we live on the waters for evermore,
> By tempests driven from shore to shore.

## CHAPTER IV

### THE FOUR WHITE SWANS ON LAKE DARVRA

WHEN Eva arrived at the house of Bove Derg, the chiefs bade her welcome; and the king asked her why she had not brought the children of Lir to him.

"Because," she replied, "Lir no longer loves thee; and he does not wish to entrust his children to thee, lest thou shouldst harm them."

The king was greatly astonished and troubled at this, and he said: "How can that be? For I love those children better than I love my own."

But he thought in his own mind that Eva had played some treachery on them. And he sent messengers with all speed northwards to Shee Finnaha, to inquire for the children, and to ask that they might be sent to him.

When the messengers had told their errand, Lir was startled; and he asked, "Have the children not reached the palace with Eva?"

They answered, "Eva arrived alone, and she told the king that you refused to let the children come."

A sad and sorrowful heart had Lir when he heard this; and he now felt sure that Eva had destroyed his four lovely children. So, early next morning, his chariot was yoked for him, and he set out with his attendants for the king's palace; and they travelled with all speed till they arrived at the shore of Lake Darvra.

The children of Lir saw the cavalcade approaching; and Finola spoke these words—

I see a mystic warrior band
From yonder brow approach the strand;
I see them winding down the vale,
   Their bending chariots slow advancing;
I see their shields and gilded mail,
   Their spears and helmets brightly glancing.

Ah! well I know that proud array;
I know too well their thoughts to-day:
The Dannan host and royal Lir;
   Four rosy children they are seeking:
Too soon, alas! they find us here,
   Four snowy swans like children speaking!

Come, brothers dear, approach the coast,
To welcome Lir's mysterious host.
Oh, woful welcome! woful day,
   That never brings a bright to-morrow!
Unhappy father, doomed for aye
   To mourn our fate in hopeless sorrow!

When Lir came to the shore, he heard the birds speaking, and, wondering greatly, he asked them how it came to pass that they had human voices.

" Know, O Lir," said Finola, " that we are thy four children, who have been changed into swans and ruined by the witchcraft of our stepmother, our own mother's sister, Eva, through her baleful jealousy."

When Lir and his people heard this, they uttered three long mournful cries of grief and lamentation.

After a time, their father asked them, " Is it possible to restore you to your own shapes? "

" It is not possible," replied Finola. "No man has the power to release us until Largnen from the north and Decca from the south are united. Three hundred years we shall be on Lake Darvra; three hundred years on the sea-stream of Moyle; three hundred years on the Sea of Glora in the west. And we shall not regain our human shape till the Taillkenn comes with his pure faith into Erin, and until we hear the voice of the Christian bell."

And again the people raised three great cries of sorrow.

"As you have your speech and your reason," said Lir, "come now to land, and ye shall live at home, conversing with me and my people."

"We are not permitted to leave the waters of the lake, and we cannot live with our people any more. But the wicked Eva has allowed us to retain our human reason, and our own Gaelic speech; and we have also the power to chant plaintive, fairy music, so sweet that those who listen to us would never desire any other happiness. Remain with us to-night, and we will chant our music for you."

Lir and his people remained on the shore of the lake; and the swans sang their slow, fairy music, which was so sweet and sad, that the people, as they listened, fell into a calm, gentle sleep.

At the glimmer of dawn next morning, Lir arose, and he bade farewell to his children for a while, to seek out Eva.

> The time has come for me to part:—
>   No more, alas! my children dear,
> Your rosy smiles shall glad my heart,
>   Or light the gloomy home of Lir.
>
> Dark was the day when first I brought
>   This Eva in my home to dwell!
> Hard was the woman's heart that wrought
>   This cruel and malignant spell!
>
> I lay me down to rest in vain;
>   For through the livelong, sleepless night,
> My little lov'd ones, pictured plain,
>   Stand ever there before my sight.
>
> Finola, once my pride and joy;
>   Dark Aedh, adventurous and bold;
> Bright Fiachra, gentle, playful boy;
>   And little Conn, with curls of gold;—
>
> Struck down on Darvra's reedy shore,
>   By wicked Eva's magic power:
> Oh, children, children, never more
>   My heart shall know one peaceful hour!

Lir then departed, and travelled south-west till he arrived at the king's palace, where he was welcomed; and Bove Derg began to reproach him, in presence of Eva, for not bringing the children.

"Alas!" said Lir; "it was not by me that the children were prevented from coming. But Eva, your own foster child, the sister of their mother, has played treachery on them; and has changed them by her sorcery into four white swans on Lake Darvra."

The king was confounded and grieved at this news; and when he looked at Eva, he knew by her countenance that what Lir had told him was true; and he began to upbraid her in a fierce and angry voice.

"The wicked deed thou hast committed," said he, "will be worse for thee than for the children of Lir; for their suffering shall come to an end, and they shall be happy at last."

Again he spoke to her more fiercely than before; and he asked her what shape of all others, on the earth, or above the earth, or beneath the earth, she most abhorred, and into which she most dreaded to be transformed.

And she, being forced to answer truly, said, "A demon of the air." *

"That is the form you shall take," said Bove Derg; and as he spoke he struck her with a druidical magic wand, and turned her into a demon of the air. She opened her wings, and flew with a scream upwards and away through the clouds; and she is still a demon of the air, and she shall be a demon of the air till the end of time.

Then Bove Derg and the Dedannans assembled on the shore of the lake, and encamped there; for they wished to remain with the birds, and to listen to their music. The Milesian people † came and formed an encampment there in like manner; for historians say that no music that was ever heard in Erin could be compared with the singing of these swans.

And so the swans passed their time. During the day they conversed with the men of Erin, both Dedannans and Milesians, and discoursed lovingly with their friends and fellow nurselings; and at night they chanted their slow, sweet, fairy music the most delightful that was ever heard by men; so that all who listened to it, even those who were in grief, or sickness, or pain, forgot

---

* Demons of the air were held in great abhorrence by the ancient Irish.
† The Milesian people; the colony who conquered and succeeded the Dedannans.

their sorrows and their sufferings, and fell into a gentle, sweet sleep, from which they awoke bright and happy.

So they continued, the Dedannans and the Milesians, in their encampments, and the swans on the lake, for three hundred years. And at the end of that time, Finola said to her brothers—

"Do you know, my dear brothers, that we have come to the end of our time here; and that we have only this one night to spend on Lake Darvra?"

When the three sons of Lir heard this, they were in great distress and sorrow; for they were almost as happy on Lake Darvra, surrounded by their friends and conversing with them day by day, as if they had been in their father's house in their own natural shapes; whereas they should now live on the gloomy and tempestuous Sea of Moyle, far away from all human society.

Early next morning, they came to the margin of the lake, to speak to their Father and their friends for the last time, and to bid them farewell; and Finola chanted this lay—

### I

Farewell, farewell, our father dear!
    The last sad hour has come:
Farewell, Bove Derg! farewell to all,
    Till the dreadful day of doom! *
We go from friends and scenes beloved,
    To a home of grief and pain;
        And that day of woe
        Shall come and go,
Before we meet again!

### II

We live for ages on stormy Moyle,
    In loneliness and fear;
The kindly words of loving friends
    We never more shall hear.
Four joyous children long ago;
    Four snow-white swans to-day;
        And on Moyle's wild sea
        Our robe shall be
The cold and briny spray.

---

* It must be remembered that the children of Lir had some obscure foreknowledge of the coming of Christianity.

### III

Far down on the misty stream of time,
  When three hundred years are o'er,
Three hundred more in storm and cold,
  By Glora's desolate shore;
Till Decca fair is Largnen's spouse;
  Till north and south unite;
    Till the hymns are sung,
    And the bells are rung,
  At the dawn of the pure faith's light.

### IV

Arise, my brothers, from Darvra's wave,
  On the wings of the southern wind;
We leave our father and friends to-day
  In measureless grief behind.
Ah! sad the parting, and sad our flight
  To Moyle's tempestuous main;
    For the day of woe
    Shall come and go,
  Before we meet again!

The four swans then spread their wings, and rose from the surface of the water in sight of all their friends, till they reached a great height in the air; then resting, and looking downwards for a moment they flew straight to the north, till they alighted on the Sea of Moyle between Erin and Alba.

The men of Erin were grieved at their departure, and they made a law, and proclaimed it throughout the land, that no one should kill a swan in Erin from that time forth.

## CHAPTER V

### THE FOUR WHITE SWANS ON THE SEA OF MOYLE

As to the children of Lir, miserable was their abode and evil their plight on the Sea of Moyle. Their hearts were wrung with sorrow for their father and their friends; and when they looked towards the steep, rocky, far-stretching coasts, and saw the great, dark wild sea around them, they were overwhelmed with fear and despair. They began also to suffer from cold and hunger, so that all the hardships they had endured on Lake Darvra appeared as nothing compared with their suffering on the sea-current of Moyle.

And so they lived, till one night a great tempest fell upon the sea. Finola, when she saw the sky filled with black, threatening clouds, thus addressed her brothers—

" Beloved brothers, we have made a bad preparation for this night; for it is certain that the coming storm will separate us; and now let us appoint a place of meeting, or it may happen that we shall never see each other again."

And they answered, " Dear sister, you speak truly and wisely; and let us fix on Carricknarone, for that is a rock that we are all very well acquainted with."

And they appointed Carricknarone as their place of meeting.

Midnight came, and with it came the beginning of the storm. A wild, rough wind swept over the dark sea, the lightnings flashed, and the great waves rose, and increased their violence and their thunder.

The swans were soon scattered over the waters, so that not one of them knew in what direction the others had been driven. During all that night they were tossed about by the roaring winds and waves, and it was with much difficulty they preserved their lives.

Towards morning the storm abated, and the sea became again calm and smooth; and Finola swam to Carricknarone. But she found none of her brothers there, neither could she see any trace of them when she looked all round from the summit of the rock over the wide face of the sea.

Then she became terrified, for she thought she should never see them again; and she began to lament them plaintively in these words—

> The heart-breaking anguish and woe of this life
> I am able no longer to bear:
> My wings are benumbed with this pitiless frost;
> My three little brothers are scattered and lost;
> And I am left here to despair.

> My three little brothers I never shall see
> Till the dead shall arise from the tomb:
> How I sheltered them oft with my wings and my breast,
> And I soothed their sorrows and lulled them to rest,
> As the night fell around us in gloom!

Ah! where are my brothers, and why have I lived,
This last worst affliction to know?
What now is there left but a life of despair?—
For alas! I am able no longer to bear
This heart-breaking anguish and woe.

Soon after this she looked again over the sea, and she saw
Conn coming towards the rock, with his head drooping, and his
feathers all drenched with the salt spray; and she welcomed him
with joyful heart.

Not long after, Fiachra appeared, but he was so faint with wet
and cold and hardship, that he was scarce able to reach the place
where Finola and Conn were standing; and when they spoke to
him he could not speak one word in return. So Finola placed the
two under her wings, and she said—

"If Aedh were here now, all would be happy with us."

In a little time they saw Aedh coming towards them, with head
erect and feathers all dry and radiant and Finola gave him a
joyful welcome. She then placed him under the feathers of her
breast, while Conn and Fiachra remained under her wings; and
she said to them—

"My dear brothers, though ye may think this night very bad,
we shall have many like it from this time forth."

So they continued for a long time on the Sea of Moyle,
suffering hardships of every kind, till one winter night came upon
them, of great wind and of snow and frost so severe that nothing
they ever before suffered could be compared to the misery of that
night. And Finola uttered these words—

Our life is a life of woe;
No shelter or rest we find:
How bitterly drives the snow;
How cold is this wintry wind!

From the icy spray of the sea,
From the wind of the bleak north east,
I shelter my brothers three,
Under my wings and breast.

Our stepmother sent us here,
And misery well we know:—
In cold and hunger and fear;
Our life is a life of woe!

Another year passed away on the Sea of Moyle; and one night in January, a dreadful frost came down on the earth and sea, so that the waters were frozen into a solid floor of ice all round them. The swans remained on Carricknarone all night, and their feet and their wings were frozen to the icy surface, so that they had to strive hard to move from their places in the morning; and they left the skin of their feet, the quills of their wings, and the feathers of their breasts clinging to the rock.

" Sad is our condition this night, my beloved brothers," said Finola, " for we are forbidden to leave the Sea of Moyle; and yet we cannot bear the salt water, for when it enters our wounds, I fear we shall die of pain."

And she spoke this lay—

> Our fate is mournful here to-day;
>   Our bodies bare and chill,
> Drenched by the bitter, briny spray,
>   And torn on this rocky hill!
>
> Cruel our stepmother's jealous heart
>   That banished us from home;
> Transformed to swans by magic art,
>   To swim the ocean foam.
>
> This bleak and snowy winter day,
>   Our bath is the ocean wide;
> In thirsty summer's burning ray,
>   Our drink the briny tide.
>
> And here 'mid rugged rocks we dwell
>   In this tempestuous bay;
> Four children bound by magic spell;—
>   Our fate is sad to-day!

They were, however, forced to swim out on the stream of Moyle, all wounded and torn as they were; for though the brine was sharp and bitter, they were not able to avoid it. They stayed as near the coast as they could, till after a long time the feathers of their breasts and wings grew again, and their wounds were healed.

After this they lived on for a great number of years, sometimes visiting the shores of Erin, and sometimes the headlands of

Alba. But they always returned to the sea-stream of Moyle, for it was destined to be their home till the end of three hundred years.

One day they came to the mouth of the Bann, on the north coast of Erin, and looking inland, they saw a stately troop of horsemen approaching directly from the south-west. They were mounted on white steeds, and clad in bright-coloured garments, and as they wound towards the shore their arms glittered in the sun.

"Do ye know yonder cavalcade?" said Finola to her brothers.

"We know them not," they replied; "but it is likely they are a party of the Milesians, or perchance a troop of our own people, the Dedannans."

They swam towards the shore, to find out who the strangers were; and the cavalcade on their part, when they saw the swans, knew them at once, and moved towards them till they were within speaking distance.

Now these were a party of the Dedannans; and the chiefs who commanded them were the two sons of Bove Derg, the Dedannan king, namely, Aedh the Keenwitted, and Fergus the Chess-player, with a third part of the Fairy Host.* They had been for a long time searching for the children of Lir along the northern shores of Erin, and now that they had found them, they were joyful; and they and the swans greeted each other with tender expressions of friendship and love. The children of Lir inquired after the Dedannans, and particularly after their father Lir, and Bove Derg, and all the rest of their friends and acquaintances.

"They are all well," replied the chiefs, "and they and the Dedannans in general are now gathered together in the house of your father, at Shee Finnaha, celebrating the Feast of Age, pleasantly and agreeably. Their happiness would indeed be complete, only that you are not with them, and that they know not where you have been since you left Lake Darvra,"

"Miserable has been our life since that day," said Finola, "and no tongue can tell the suffering and sorrow we have endured on the Sea of Moyle."

---

* Fairy host; i.e. the Dedannans. (See note on page 1.)

And she chanted these words—

> Ah, happy is Lir's bright home to-day,
> With mead and music and poet's lay:
> But gloomy and cold his children's home,
> For ever tossed on the briny foam.
>
> Our wreathed feathers are thin and light
> When the wind blows keen through the wintry night:
> Yet oft we were robed, long, long, ago
> In purple mantles and furs of snow.
>
> On Moyle's bleak current our food and wine
> Are sandy sea-weed and bitter brine:
> Yet oft we feasted in days of old,
> And hazel-mead drank from cups of gold.
>
> Our beds are rocks in the dripping caves;
> Our lullaby song the roar of the waves:
> But soft rich couches once we pressed,
> And harpers lulled us each night to rest.
>
> Lonely we swim in the billowy main,
> Through frost and snow, through storm and rain:
> Alas for the days when round us moved
> The chiefs and princes and friends we loved!
>
> My little twin brothers beneath my wings
> Lie close when the north wind bitterly stings,
> And Aedh close nestles before my breast;
> Thus side by side through the night we rest.
>
> Our father's fond kisses, Bove Derg's embrace,
> The light of Mannanan's[1] godlike face,
> The love of Angus[1]—all, all are o'er,
> And we live on the billows for evermore!

After this they bade each other farewell, for it was not permitted to the children of Lir to remain away from the stream of Moyle. As soon as they had parted, the Fairy Cavalcade returned to Shee Finnaha, where they related to the Dedannan chiefs all that had passed, and described the condition of the children of Lir. And the chiefs answered—

"It is not in our power to help them; but we are glad indeed that they are living; and we know that in the end the enchantment will be broken, and that they will be freed from their sufferings."

As to the children of Lir, they returned to their home on the Sea of Moyle, and there they remained till they had fulfilled their term of years.

## CHAPTER VI

### THE FOUR WHITE SWANS ON THE WESTERN SEA

AND when their three hundred years were ended, Finola said to her brothers: " It is time for us to leave this place, for our period here has come to an end."

> The hour has come; the hour has come;
>   Three hundred years have passed:
> We leave this bleak and gloomy home,
>   And we fly to the west at last!
>
> We leave for ever the stream of Moyle;
>   On the clear, cold wind we go;
> Three hundred years round Glora's isle,
>   Where wintry tempests blow!
>
> No sheltered home, no place of rest,
>   From the tempest's angry blast:
> Fly, brothers, fly, to the distant west,
>   For the hour has come at last!

So the swans left the Sea of Moyle, and flew westward till they reached Irros Domnann and the sea round the isle of Glora. There they remained for a long time, suffering much from storm and cold, and in nothing better off than they were on the Sea of Moyle.

It chanced that a young man named Ebric, of good family, the owner of a tract of land lying along the shore, observed the birds and heard their singing. He took great delight in listening to their plaintive music, and he walked down to the shore almost every day, to see them and to converse with them; so that he came to love them very much, and they also loved him. This young man told his neighbours about the speaking swans, so that the matter became noised abroad; and it was he who arranged the story, after hearing it from themselves, and related it as it is related here.

Again their hardships were renewed, and to describe what they suffered on the great open Western Sea would be only to tell over again the story of their life on the Moyle. But one particular night came, of frost so hard that the whole face of the sea, from Irros Domnann to Achill, was frozen into a thick floor of ice; and the snow was driven by a north-west wind. On that night it seemed to the three brothers that they could not bear their sufferings any longer, and they began to utter loud and pitiful complaints. Finola tried to console them, but she was not able to do so, for they only lamented the more; and then she herself began to lament with the others.

After a time, Finola spoke to them and said, " My dear brothers, believe in the great and splendid God of truth, who made the earth with its fruits, and the sea with its wonders; put your trust in Him, and He will send you help and comfort."

" We believe in Him," they said.

" And I also," said Finola, " believe in God, who is perfect in everything, and who knows all things."

And at the destined hour they all believed, and the Lord of heaven sent them help and protection; so that neither cold nor tempest molested them from that time forth, as long as they abode on the Western Sea.

So they continued at the point of Irros Domnann, till they had fulfilled their appointed time there. And Finola addressed the sons of Lir: " My dear brothers, the end of our time here has come; we shall now go to visit our father and our people."

And her brothers were glad when they heard this.

Then they rose lightly from the face of the sea, and flew eastward with joyful hopes, till they reached Shee Finnaha. But when they alighted they found the place deserted and solitary, its halls all ruined and overgrown with rank grass and forests of nettles; no houses, no fire, no mark of human habitation.

Then the four swans drew close together, and they uttered three loud mournful cries of sorrow.

And Finola chanted this lay—

What meaneth this sad, this fearful change,
    That withers my heart with woe?
The house of my father all joyless and lone,
Its halls and its gardens with weeds overgrown—
    A dreadful and strange overthrow!

No conquering heroes, no hounds for the chase,
    No shields in array on its walls,
No bright silver goblets, no gay cavalcades,
No youthful assemblies or high-born maids,
    To brighten its desolate halls!

An omen of sadness—the home of our youth
    All ruined, deserted, and bare.
Alas for the chieftain, the gentle and brave;
His glories and sorrows are stilled in the grave,
    And we left to live in despair!

From ocean to ocean, from age unto age,
    We have lived to the fulness of time;
Through a life such as men never heard of we've passed,
In suffering and sorrow our doom has been cast,
    By our stepmother's pitiless crime!

The children of Lir remained that night in the ruins of the palace —the home of their forefathers, where they themselves had been nursed; and several times during the night they chanted their sad, sweet, fairy music.

Early next morning they left Shee Finnaha, and flew west to Inis Glora, where they alighted on a small lake. There they began to sing so sweetly that all the birds of the district gathered in flocks round them on the lake, and on its shore, to listen to them; so that the little lake came to be called the Lake of the Bird-flocks.

During the day the birds used to fly to distant points of the coast to feed, now to Iniskea of the lonely crane,* now to Achill, and sometimes southwards to Donn's Sea Rocks,† and to many

---

* Iniskea; a little rocky island near the coast of Erris, in Mayo. "The lonely crane of Iniskea" was one of the "Wonders of Ireland." According to an ancient legend, a crane—one lonely bird—has lived on the island since the beginning of the world, and will live there till the day of judgment.

† Donn's Sea Rocks—called in the text *Teach-Dhuinn*, or Donn's House, which is also the present Irish name; a group of three rocks off Kenmare Bay, where Donn, one of the Milesian brothers, was drowned. These remarkable rocks are now called in English the "Bull, Cow, and Calf."

other islands and headlands along the shore of the Western Sea, but they returned to Inis Glora every night.

They lived in this manner till holy Patrick came to Erin with the pure faith; and until Saint Kemoc came to Inis Glora.

The first night Kemoc came to the island, the children of Lir heard his bell at early matin time, ringing faintly in the distance. And they trembled greatly, and started, and ran wildly about; for the sound of the bell was strange and dreadful to them, and its tones filled them with great fear. The three brothers were more affrighted than Finola, so that she was left quite alone; but after a time they came to her, and she asked them—

" Do you know, my brothers, what sound is this? "

And they answered, " We have heard a faint, fearful voice, but we know not what it is."

" This is the voice of the Christian bell," said Finola; " and now the end of our suffering is near; for this bell is the signal that we shall soon be freed from our spell, and released from our life of suffering; for God has willed it."

And she chanted this lay—

> Listen, ye swans, to the voice of the bell,
>   The sweet bell we've dreamed of for many a year;
> Its tones floating by on the night breezes, tell
>   That the end of our long life of sorrow is near!
>
> Listen, ye swans, to the heavenly strain;
>   'Tis the anchoret tolling his soft matin bell:
> He has come to release us from sorrow, from pain,
>   From the cold and tempestuous shores where we dwell!
>
> Trust in the glorious Lord of the sky;
>   He will free us from Eva's druidical spell:
> Be thankful and glad, for our freedom is nigh,
>   And listen with joy to the voice of the bell!

Then her brothers became calm; and the four swans remained listening to the music of the bell, till the cleric had finished his matins.

" Let us sing our music now," said Finola.

And they chanted a low, sweet, plaintive strain of fairy music, to praise and thank the great high King of heaven and earth.

Kemoc heard the music from where he stood; and he listened with great astonishment. But after a time it was revealed to him that it was the children of Lir who sang that music; and he was glad, for it was to seek them he had come.

When morning dawned he came to the shore of the lake, and he saw the four white swans swimming on the water. He spoke to them, and asked them were they the children of Lir.

They replied, " We are indeed the children of Lir, who were changed long ago into swans by our wicked stepmother."

" I give God thanks that I have found you," said Kemoc; " for it is on your account I have come to this little island in preference to all the other islands of Erin. Come ye now to land, and trust in me; for it is in this place that you are destined to be freed from your enchantment."

So they, filled with joy on hearing the words of the cleric, came to the shore, and placed themselves under his care. He brought them to his own house, and, sending for a skilful workman, he caused him to make two bright, slender chains of silver; and he put a chain between Finola and Aedh, and the other chain he put between Fiachra and Conn.

So they lived with him, listening to his instructions day by day, and joining in his devotions. They were the delight and joy of the cleric, and he loved them with his whole heart; and the swans were so happy that the memory of all the misery they had suffered during their long life on the waters caused them neither distress nor sorrow now.

## CHAPTER VII

### THE CHILDREN OF LIR REGAIN THEIR HUMAN SHAPE AND DIE

THE king who ruled over Connacht at this time was Largnen, the son of Colman; and his queen was Decca, the daughter of Finnin,* king of Munster—the same king and queen whom Eva had spoken of in her prophecy long ages before.

---

* These are well-known historical personages, who flourished in the seventh century.

Now word was brought to Queen Decca regarding these wonderful speaking swans, and their whole history was related to her; so that even before she saw them, she could not help loving them, and she was seized with a strong desire to have them herself. So she went to the king, and besought him that he would go to Kemoc and get her the swans. But Largnen said that he did not wish to ask them from Kemoc. Whereupon Decca grew indignant; and she declared that she would not sleep another night in the palace till he had obtained the swans for her. So she left the palace that very hour, and fled southwards towards her father's home.

Largnen, when he found she had gone, sent in haste after her, with word that he would try to procure the swans; but the messengers did not overtake her till she had reached Killaloe. However, she returned with them to the palace; and as soon as she had arrived, the king sent to Kemoc to request that he would send the birds to the queen; but Kemoc refused to give them.

Largnen became very angry at this; and he set out at once for the cleric's house. As soon as he had come, he asked the cleric whether it was true that he had refused to give the swans to the queen. And when Kemoc answered that it was quite true, the king, being very wroth, went up to where the swans stood, and seizing the two silver chains, one in each hand, he drew the birds from the altar, and turned towards the door of the church, intending to bring them by force to the queen; while Kemoc followed him, much alarmed lest they should be injured.

The king had proceeded only a little way, when suddenly the white feathery robes faded and disappeared; and the swans regained their human shape, Finola being transformed into an extremely old woman, and the three sons into three feeble old men, white-haired and bony and wrinkled.

When the king saw this, he started with affright, and instantly left the place without speaking one word; while Kemoc reproached and denounced him very bitterly.

As to the children of Lir, they turned towards Kemoc; and Finola spoke—

" Come, holy cleric, and baptize us without delay, for our death is near. You will grieve after us, O Kemoc; but in truth you are not more sorrowful at parting from us than we are **at** parting from you. Make our grave here and bury us together; and as I often sheltered my brothers when we were swans, so let us be placed in the grave—Conn standing near me at my right side, Fiachra at my left, and Aedh before my face." *

> Come, holy priest, with book and prayer;
>   Baptize and shrive us here:
> Haste, cleric, haste, for the hour has come,
>   And death at last is near!
>
> Dig our grave—a deep, deep grave,
>   Near the church we loved so well;
> This little church, where first we heard
>   The voice of the Christian bell.
>
> As oft in life my brothers dear
>   Were sooth'd by me to rest—
> Fiachra and Conn beneath my wings,
>   And Aedh before my breast.
>
> So place the two on either hand—
>   Close, like the love that bound me;
> Place Aedh as close before my face,
>   And twine their arms around me.
>
> Thus shall we rest for evermore,
>   My brothers dear and I:
> Haste, cleric, haste, baptize and shrive,
>   For death at last is nigh!

Then the children of Lir were baptized, and they died immediately. And when they died, Kemoc looked up; and lo, he saw a vision of four lovely children, with light, silvery wings, and faces all radiant with joy. They gazed on him for a moment; but even as they gazed, they vanished upwards, and he saw them no more. And he was filled with gladness, for he knew they had gone to heaven; but when he looked down on the four bodies lying before him, he became sad and wept.

And Kemoc caused a wide grave to be dug near the little church; and the children of Lir were buried together, as Finola

---

* Among the ancient Celtic nations, the dead were often buried standing up in the grave. It was in this way Finola and her brothers were buried.

had directed—Conn at her right hand, Fiachra at her left, and Aedh standing before her face. And he raised a grave-mound over them, placing a tombstone on it, with their names graved in Ogham;* after which he uttered a lament for them, and their funeral rites were performed.

So far we have related the sorrowful story of the Fate of the Children of Lir.

---

* Ogham, a sort of writing, often used on sepulchral stones.

# The Fate of the
# Children of Turenn

## OR

## THE QUEST FOR THE ERIC-FINE

For the blood that we spilled,
For the hero we killed,
Toil and woe, toil and woe, till the doom is fulfilled!

## CHAPTER I

### THE LOCHLANNS INVADE ERIN

WHEN the Dedannans[1] held sway in Erin, a prosperous free-born king ruled over them, whose name was Nuada of the Silver Hand.[4]

In the time of this king, the Fomorians,[5] from Lochlann,[6] in the north, oppressed the Dedannans, and forced them to pay heavy tributes; namely, a tax on kneading-troughs, a tax on querns, and a tax on baking flags; and besides all this, an ounce of gold for each man of the Dedannans. These tributes had to be paid every year at the Hill of Usna; * and if any one refused or neglected to pay his part, his nose was cut off by the Fomorian tyrants.

At this time a great fair-meeting was held by the king of Ireland, Nuada of the Silver Hand, on the Hill of Usna. Not long had the people been assembled, when they saw a stately band of warriors, all mounted on white steeds, coming towards them from the east; and at their head, high in command over all, rode a young champion, tall and comely, with a countenance as bright and glorious as the setting sun.

---

* The Hill of Usna, in the parish of Conry, in Westmeath, one of the royal residences of Ireland.

This young warrior was Lugh of the Long Arms.[7] He was accompanied by his foster brothers, namely, the sons of Mannanan Mac Lir; and the troop he led was the Fairy Host from the Land of Promise.[8]

Now in this manner was he arrayed. He rode the steed of Mannanan Mac Lir,[8] namely, Enbarr of the Flowing Mane: no warrior was ever killed on the back of this steed, for she was as swift as the clear, cold wind of spring, and she travelled with equal ease on land and on sea. He wore Mannanan's coat of mail: no one could be wounded through it, or above it, or below it. He had on his breast Mannanan's breast-plate, which no weapon could pierce. His helmet had two glittering precious stones set in front, and one behind; and whenever he took it off, his face shone like the sun on a dry day in summer. Mannanan's sword, the Answerer, hung at his left side: no one ever recovered from its wound; and those who were opposed to it in the battle-field were so terrified by looking at it, that their strength left them till they became weaker than a woman in deadly sickness.

This troop came forward to where the king of Erin sat surrounded by the Dedannans, and both parties exchanged friendly greetings.

A short time after this they saw another company approaching, quite unlike the first, for they were grim and fierce and surly looking; namely, the tax-gatherers of the Fomorians, to the number of nine nines, who were coming to demand their yearly tribute from the men of Erin. When they reached the place where the king sat, the entire assembly—the king himself among the rest—rose up before them. For the whole Dedannan race stood in great dread of these Fomorian tax-collectors; so much so that no man dared even to chastise his own son without first seeking their consent.

Then Lugh of the Long Arms spoke to the king and said, " Why have ye stood up before this hateful-looking company, when ye did not stand up for us? "

" We durst not do otherwise," replied the king; " for if even an infant of a month old remained seated before them, they would deem it cause enough for killing us all."

When Lugh heard this he brooded in silence for a little while, and then he said, " Of a truth, I feel a great desire to kill all these men! "

Then he mused again, and after a time, said, " I am strongly urged to kill these men! "

" That deed would doubtless bring great evil on us," said the king, " for then the Fomorians would be sure to send an army to destroy us all."

But Lugh, after another pause, started up, exclaiming, " Long have ye been oppressed in this manner! " and so saying, he attacked the Fomorians, dealing red slaughter among them. Neither did he hold his hand till he had slain them all except nine. These he spared, because they ran with all speed and sat nigh the king, that he might protect them from Lugh's wrath.

Then Lugh put his sword back into its scabbard, and said, " I would slay you also, only that I wish you to go and tell your king, and the foreigners in general, what you have seen."

These nine men accordingly returned to their own country, and they told their tale to the Fomorian people from beginning to end—how the strange, noble-faced youth had slain all the tax-collectors except nine, whom he spared that they might bring home the story.

When they had ended speaking, the king, Balor[9] of the Mighty Blows and of the Evil Eye, asked the chiefs, " Do ye know who this youth is? "

And when they answered, " No," Kethlenda,[9] Balor's queen, said: " I know well who the youth is: he is the Ildana,* Lugh of the Long Arms, the son of your daughter and mine; and it has been long foretold that when he should appear in Erin, our sway over the Dedannans should come to an end."

Then the chief people of the Fomorians held council; namely, Balor of the Mighty Blows, and his twelve sons, and his queen Kethlenda of the Crooked Teeth; Ebb and Sencab, the grandsons of Neid; Sotal of the Large Heels; Luath the Long-bodied; Luath the Story-teller; Tinna the Mighty, of Triscadal; Loskenn of the Bare Knees; Lobas, the druid; besides the nine prophetic poets and philosophers of the Fomorians.

After they had debated the matter for some time, Bres, the son of Balor, arose and said, " I will go to Erin with seven great battalions of the Fomorian army, and I will give battle to the

---

* Lugh of the Long Arms is often called The Ildana, *i.e.* the Man of many sciences, to signify his various accomplishments.

Ildana, and I will bring his head to you to our palace of Berva." [6]

The Fomorian chiefs thought well of this proposal, and it was agreed to.

So the ships were got ready for Bres; abundant food and drink and war stores were put into them, their seams were calked with pitch, and they were filled with sweet-smelling frankincense. Meantime the two Luaths, that is to say, Luath the Story-teller and Luath of the Long Body, were sent all over Lochlann to summon the army. And when all the fighting men were gathered together, they arrayed themselves in their battle-dresses, prepared their arms, and set out for Erin.

Balor went with them to the harbour where they were to embark, and when they were about to go on board, he said to them—

" Give battle to the Ildana, and cut off his head. And after ye have overcome him and his people, put your cables round this island of Erin, which gives us so much trouble, and tie it at the sterns of your ships; then sail home, bringing the island with you, and place it on the north side of Lochlann, whither none of the Dedannans will ever follow it."

Then, having hoisted their many-coloured sails and loosed their moorings, they sailed forth from the harbour into the great sea, and never slackened speed or turned aside from their course till they reached the harbour of Eas-Dara.* And as soon as they landed, they sent forth an army through West Connacht, which wasted and spoiled the whole province.

## CHAPTER II

### THE MURDER OF KIAN

Now the king of Connacht at that time was Bove Derg, the son of the Dagda, a friend to Lugh of the Long Arms. It chanced that Lugh was then at Tara,† and news was brought to him that the Fomorians had landed at Eas-Dara, and were spoiling and wasting the province. He immediately got ready his steed, Enbarr

---

* Eas-Dara, now Ballysodare, in the county Sligo.
† Tara, in Meath, the chief seat of the kings of Ireland.

of the Flowing Mane; and early in the morning, when the point of night met the day, he went to the king and told him that the foreigners had landed, and that they had wasted and plundered the province of Bove Derg.

"I shall give them battle," said Lugh, "and I wish to get from you some help of men and arms."

"I will give no help," said the king; "for I do not wish to avenge a deed that has not been done against myself."

When Lugh heard this reply he was wroth, and departing straightway from Tara, he rode westward. He had not travelled long when he saw at a distance three warriors, fully armed, riding towards him. Now these were three brothers, the sons of Canta: namely, Kian and Cu and Kethen; and Kian was Lugh's father. And they saluted each other, and conversed together for a time

"Why art thou abroad so early?" they said.

"Cause enough have I," replied Lugh; "for the Fomorians have landed in Erin, and have wasted the province of Bove Derg, the son of the Dagda. It is well indeed that I have met you, for I am about to give them battle, and I wish now to know what aid I shall get from you."

"We will go into the battle with you," they said, "and each of us will ward off from you a hundred of the Fomorian warriors."

"That, indeed, is good help," said Lugh, "but, for the present, I wish you to go to the several places throughout Erin where the Fairy Host are abiding, and summon them all to me."

The three brothers accordingly separated, Cu and Kethen going south, while Lugh's father, Kian, turned his face northwards and rode on till he came to Moy Murthemna.* He had not been long travelling over the plain when he saw three warriors, clad in armour and fully armed, coming towards him. These were three Dedannan chiefs, the sons of Turenn, and their names were Brian, Ur, and Urcar. Now these three and the three sons of Canta were at deadly feud with each other, on account of an old quarrel, and whenever they met there was sure to be a fight for life or death.

As soon as Kian saw these three, he said: "If my two brothers were now with me, we should have a brave fight; but as they are not, and as I am only one against three, it is better to avoid the

---

* Moy Murthemna, a plain in the county of Louth.

combat." So saying, he looked round, and seeing near him a herd of swine, he struck himself with a golden druidical[3] wand, and changed himself into a pig; and he quickly joined the herd.

No sooner had he done so than Brian, the eldest of the sons of Turenn, said to his brothers: " Tell me, my brothers, do you know what has become of the warrior that we saw just now approaching us on the plain? "

" We saw him," said they, " but we know not whither he has gone."

" You deserve great blame," said he, " that you are not more watchful while traversing the country during this time of war. Now I know what has happened to this warrior; he has changed himself, by a druidical spell, into a pig; and he is now among yonder herd. And whoever he may be, of this be sure—he is no friend of ours."

" This is an unlucky matter," said they; " for as these pigs belong to one of the Dedannans, it would be wrong for us to kill them; and even if we should do so, the enchanted pig might escape after all."

" But," answered Brian, " I think I can manage to distinguish any druidical beast from a natural one; and if you had attended well to your learning, you would be able to do the same."

Saying this, he struck his brothers one after the other with his golden druidical wand, and turned them into two fleet, slender, sharp-nosed hounds. The moment he had done so they put their noses to the earth, and, yelping eagerly, set off towards the herd on the trail of their enemy. When they had come near, the druidical pig fell out from the herd, and made towards a thick grove that grew hard by; but Brian was there before him, and drove his spear through his chest.

The pig screamed and said: "You have done an ill deed to cast your spear at me, for you know well who I am."

" Your voice, methinks, is the voice of a man," said Brian, " but I know not who you are."

And the pig answered: "I am Kian, the son of Canta; and now I ask you to give me quarter."

Ur and Urcar, who had regained their shape and come up, said: "We will give you quarter indeed, and we are sorry for what has happened to you."

But Brian, on the other hand, said: "I swear by the gods of the air, that if your life returned to you seven times, I would take it from you seven times."

"Then," said Kian, "as you will not grant me quarter, allow me first to return to my own shape."

"That we will grant you," said Brian, "for I often feel it easier to kill a man than to kill a pig."

Kian accordingly took his own shape, and then he said: "You indeed, ye sons of Turenn, are now about to slay me; but even so, I have outwitted you. For if you had slain me in the shape of a pig, you would have to pay only the eric-fine[10] for a pig; whereas, now that I am in my own shape, you shall pay the full fine for a man. And there never yet was killed, and there never shall be killed, a man for whom a greater fine shall be paid, than you will have to pay for me. The weapons with which I am slain shall tell the deed to my son; and he will exact the fine from you."

"You shall not be slain with the weapons of a warrior," said Brian; and so saying, he and his brothers laid aside their arms, and smote him fiercely and rudely with the round stones of the earth, till they had reduced his body to a disfigured mass; and in this manner they slew him.

They then buried him a man's height in the earth; but the earth, being angry at the fratricide,* refused to receive the body, and cast it up on the surface. They buried him a second time, and again the body was thrown up from beneath the clay. Six times the sons of Turenn buried the body of Kian a man's height in the earth, and six times did the earth cast it up, refusing to receive it.

But when they had buried him the seventh time, the earth refused no longer, and the body remained in the grave.

Then the sons of Turenn prepared to go forward after Lugh of the Long Arms to the battle. But as they were leaving the grave, they thought they heard a faint, muffled voice coming up from the ground beneath their feet—

The blood you have spilled,
The hero you've killed,
Shall follow your steps till your doom be fulfilled!

---

* Fratricide; Gaelic, *fionghal*, the murder of a relative. The sons of Turenn and the sons of Canta appear to have been related to each other.

## CHAPTER III

### DEFEAT AND FLIGHT OF THE LOCHLANNS

Now as to Lugh. After parting from his father, he journeyed westward till he reached Ath Luain,* thence to Roscomáin, and over Moy-Lurg to the Curlew Hills, and to the mountain of Kesh-Corran, till he reached the " Great Plain of the Assembly," where the foreigners were encamped, with the spoils of Connacht around them.

As he drew nigh to the Fomorian encampment, Bres, the son of Balor, arose and said—

" A wonderful thing has come to pass this day; for the sun, it seems to me, has risen in the west."

" It would be better that it were so," said the druids,[3] " than that matters should be as they are."

" What else can it be, then? " asked Bres.

" The light you see," replied the druids, " is the brightness of the face, and the flashing of the weapons of Lugh of the Long Arms, our deadly enemy, he who slew our tax-gatherers, and who now approaches."

Then Lugh came up peacefully and saluted them.

" How does it come to pass that you salute us," said they, " since you are, as we know well, our enemy? "

" I have good cause for saluting you," answered Lugh, " for only one half of my blood is Dedannan. The other half comes from you; for I am the son of the daughter of Balor of the Mighty Blows, your king. And now I come in peace, to ask you to give back to the men of Connacht all the milch cows you have taken from them."

" May ill luck follow thee," said one of the Fomorian leaders, in a voice loud and wrathful, " until thou get one of them, either a milch cow or a dry cow! "

And the others spoke in a like strain.

---

* *Ath Luain*, Athlone; *Roscomáin*, Roscommon; *Moy-Lurg*, a plain in the county Roscommon; Curlew Hills, a range of hills in Roscommon; Kesh-Corran, a mountain in Sligo. The " Great Plain of the Assembly " must have been near Ballysodare, in Sligo.

Then Lugh put a druidical spell upon the plundered cattle; and he sent all the milch cows home, each to the door of her owner's house, throughout all that part of Connacht that had been plundered. But the dry cows he left, so that the Fomorians might be cumbered, and that they might not leave their encampment till the Fairy Host should arrive to give them battle.

Lugh tarried three days and three nights near them, and at the end of that time the Fairy Host arrived, and placed themselves under his command. They encamped near the Fomorians, and in a little time Bove Derg, son of the Dagda, joined them with twenty-nine hundred men.

Then they made ready for the fight. The Ildana put on Mannanan's coat of mail and his breast-plate; he took also his helmet, which was called Cathbharr, and it glittered in the sun with dazzling brightness; he slung his broad, dark-blue shield from his shoulder at one side; his long, keen-edged sword hung at his thigh; and lastly, he took his two long, heavy-handled spears, which had been tempered in the poisonous blood of adders. The other kings and chiefs of the men of Erin arrayed their men in battle ranks; hedges of glittering spears rose high above their heads; and their shields, placed edge to edge, formed a firm fence around them.

Then at the signal they attacked the Fomorians, and the Fomorians, in no degree dismayed, answered their onset. At first a cloud of whizzing javelins flew from rank to rank across the open space, and as the warriors rushed together in closer conflict, their spears were shivered in their hands. Then they drew their gold-hilted swords, and fought foot to foot and shield to shield, so that a forest of bright flashes rose high above their helmets, from the clashing of their keen-tempered weapons.

In the midst of the fight, Lugh looked round, and seeing at some distance, Bres, surrounded by his Fomorian warriors, dealing havoc and death among the Dedannans, he rushed through the press of battle, and attacked first Bres's guards so fiercely that in a few moments twenty of them fell beneath his blows.

Then he struck at Bres himself, who, unable to withstand his furious onset, cried aloud—

" Why should we be enemies, since thou art of my kin? Let there be peace between us, for nothing can withstand thy blows.

Let there be peace, and I will undertake to bring my Fomorians to assist thee at Moytura,[11] and I will promise never again to come to fight against thee."

And Bres swore by the sun and the moon, by the sea and land, and by all the elements, to fulfil his engagement; and on these conditions Lugh granted him his life.

Then the Fomorians, seeing their chief overcome, dropped their arms, and sued for quarter. The Fomorian druids and men of learning next came to Lugh to ask him to spare their lives; and Lugh answered them—

" So far am I from wishing to slay you, that in truth, if you had taken the whole Fomorian race under your protection, I would have spared them."

And after this, Bres, the son of Balor, returned to his own country with his druids, and with those of his army who had escaped from the battle.

## CHAPTER IV

### THE ERIC-FINE ON THE SONS OF TURENN FOR THE SLAYING OF KIAN

TOWARDS the close of the day, when the battle was ended, Lugh espied two of his near friends; and he asked them if they had seen his father, Kian, in the fight. And when they answered, " No," Lugh said—

" My father is not alive; for if he lived he would surely have come to help me in the battle. And now I swear that neither food nor drink will I take till I have found out who has slain him, and the manner of his death."

Then Lugh set out with a small chosen band of the Fairy Host, and he halted not till he reached the place where he had parted from his father. And from that he travelled on to the plain of Murthemna, where Kian had been forced to take the shape of a pig to avoid the sons of Turenn, and where they had slain him.

When he had come near to the very spot, he walked some little way before his companions, and the stones of the earth spoke beneath his feet, and said—

" Here thy father lies, O Lugh. Grievous was Kian's strait when he was forced to take the shape of a pig on seeing the three sons of Turenn; and here they slew him in his own shape! "

> The blood that they spilled,
> The hero they killed,
> Shall darken their lives till their doom be fulfilled!

Lugh stood for a while silent, pondering on these words. But as his companions came up, he told them what had happened; and having pointed out the spot from which the voice came, he caused the ground to be dug up. There they found the body, and raised it to the surface; and when they had examined it, they saw that it was covered all over with gory wounds and bruises.

Then Lugh spoke after a long silence. "A cruel and merciless death has my beloved father suffered at the hands of the sons of Turenn! "

He kissed his father's face three times, and again spoke, grieving: "Ill fare the day on which my father was slain! Woeful is this deed to me, for my eyes see not, my ears hear not, and my heart's pulse has ceased to beat, for grief. Why, O ye gods whom I worship, why was I not present when this deed was done? Alas! an evil thing has happened, for the Dedannans have slain their brother Dedannan. Ill shall they fare of this fratricide, for its consequences shall follow them, and long shall the crime of brother against brother continue to be committed in Erin! "

And he spoke this speech—

> A dreadful doom my father found
>   On that ill-omened even-tide;
> And here I mourn beside the mound,
>   Where, whelmed by numbers, Kian died—
> This lonely mound of evil fame,
> That long shall bear the hero's name!
>
> Alas! an evil deed is done,
>   And long shall Erin rue the day:
> There shall be strife 'twixt sire and son,
>   And brothers shall their brothers slay;
> Vengeance shall smite the murderers too,
> And vengeance all their race pursue!

The light has faded from mine eyes;
    My youthful strength and power have fled.
Weary my heart with ceaseless sighs;
    Ambition, hope, and joy are dead;
And all the world is draped in gloom—
The shadow of my father's tomb!

Then they placed the hero again in the grave, and they raised a tomb over him with his name graved in Ogham; after which his lamentation lays were sung, and his funeral games were performed.

When these rites were ended, Lugh said to his people: "Go ye now to Tara, where the king of Erin sits on his throne with the Dedannans around him; but do not make these things known till I myself have told them."

So Lugh's people went straightway to Tara, as he had bade them; but of the murder of Kian they said naught. Lugh himself arrived some time after, and was received with great honour, being put to sit high over the others, at the king's side; for the fame of his mighty deeds at the battle of the Assembly Plain had been noised over the whole country, and had come to the ears of the king.

After he was seated, he looked round the hall, and saw the sons of Turenn in the assembly. Now these three sons of Turenn exceeded all the champions in Tara in comeliness of person, in swiftness of foot, and in feats of arms; and, next to Lugh himself, they were the best and bravest in the battles against the Fomorians; wherefore they were honoured by the king beyond most others.

Lugh asked the king that the chain of silence* should be shaken; and when it was shaken, and when all were listening in silence, he stood up and spoke—

"I perceive, ye nobles of the Dedannan race, that you have given me your attention, and now I have a question to put to each man here present: What vengeance would you take of the man who should knowingly and of design kill your father?"

They were all struck with amazement on hearing this, and the king of Erin said—

"What does this mean? For that your father has not been killed, this we all know well!"

---

* Chain of silence; a chain, probably hung with little bells, which the lord of a
mansion shook when he wished to get silence and attention.

" My father has indeed been killed," answered Lugh; "and I see now here in this hall those who slew him. And furthermore, I know the manner in which they put him to death, even as they know it themselves."

The Sons of Turenn, hearing all this, said nothing; but the king spoke aloud and said—

" If any man should wilfully slay my father, it is not in one hour or in one day I would have him put to death; but I would lop off one of his members each day, till I saw him die in torment under my hands! "

All the nobles said the same, and the sons of Turenn in like manner.

" The persons who slew my father are here present, and are joining with the rest in this judgment," said Lugh; " and as the Dedannans are all now here to witness, I claim that the three who have done this evil deed shall pay me a fitting eric-fine for my father. Should they refuse, I shall not indeed transgress the king's law nor violate his protection; but of a certainty they shall not leave this hall of Micorta* till the matter is settled."

And the king of Erin said: "If I had killed your father, I should be well content if you were willing to accept an eric-fine from me."

Now the sons of Turenn spoke among themselves; and Ur and Urcar said, "It is of us Lugh speaks this speech. He has doubtless found out that we slew his father; and it is better that we now acknowledge the deed, for it will avail us naught to hide it."

Brian, however, at first set his face against this, saying that he feared Lugh only wanted an acknowledgment from them in presence of the other Dedannans, and that afterwards he might not accept a fine. But the other two were earnest in pressing him, so that he consented, and then he spoke to Lugh:

" It is of us thou speakest all these things, Lugh; for it has been said that we three have been at enmity with the three sons of Canta. Now, as to the slaying of thy father Kian, let that matter rest; but we are willing to pay an eric-fine for him, even as if we had killed him."

---

* Micorta; the name of the great banqueting hall of Tara.

" I shall accept an eric-fine from you," said Lugh, " though ye indeed fear I shall not. I shall now name before this assembly the fine I ask, and if you think it too much, I shall take off a part of it.

" The first part of my eric-fine is three apples; the second part is the skin of a pig; the third is a spear; the fourth, two steeds and a chariot; the fifth, seven pigs; the sixth, a hound-whelp; the seventh, a cooking-spit; and the eighth, three shouts on a hill. That is my eric, and if ye think it too much, say so now, that I may remit a part; but if not, then it will be well that ye set about paying it."

" So far," said Brian, " we do not deem it too great. It seems, indeed, so small that we fear there is some hidden snare in what you ask, which may work us mischief."

" I do not deem my eric too small," said Lugh; " and now I engage here, before the assembled Dedannans, that I will ask no more, and that I will seek no further vengeance for my father's death. But, as I have made myself answerable to them for the faithful fulfilment of my promise, I demand the same guarantee from you, that you also be faithful to me."

" Alas that you should doubt our plighted word! " said the sons of Turenn. " Are we not ourselves sufficient guarantee for the payment of an eric-fine greater even than this? "

" I do not deem your word sufficient guarantee," answered Lugh, " for often have we known great warriors like you to promise a fine before all the people, and afterwards to go back of their promise."

And the sons of Turenn consented, though unwillingly, for they grieved that their word should be doubted. So they bound themselves on either side: Lugh not to increase his claims; and the sons of Turenn, on their part, to pay him the full fine. And the king of Erin and Bove Derg, son of the Dagda, and the nobles of the Dedannans in general, were witnesses and sureties of this bond.

Then Lugh stood up and said, " It is now time that I give you a full knowledge of this eric-fine.

" The three apples I ask are the apples of the Garden of Hisberna,* in the east of the world, and none others will I have.

---

* The Garden of the Hesperides.

There are no apples in the rest of the world like them, for their beauty and for the secret virtues they possess. Their colour is the colour of burnished gold; they have the taste of honey; and if a wounded warrior or a man in deadly sickness eat of them, he is cured immediately. And they are never lessened by being eaten, being as large and perfect at the end as at the beginning. Moreover any champion that possesses one of them may perform with it whatsoever feat he pleases, by casting it from his hand, and the apple will return to him of itself. And though you are three brave warriors, ye sons of Turenn, methinks you will not find it easy to bring away these apples; for it has been long foretold that three young champions from the Island of the West would come to take them by force, so that the king has set guards to watch for your coming.

" The pig's skin I seek from you belongs to Tuis, the King of Greece. When the pig was alive, every stream of water through which she walked was turned into wine for nine days, and all sick and wounded people that touched her skin were at once cured, if only the breath of life remained. Now the king's druids told him that the virtue lay, not in the pig herself, but in her skin; so the king had her killed and skinned, and he has her skin now. This, too, ye valiant champions, is a part of my eric-fine which you will find it hard to get, either by force or by friendship.

" The spear I demand from you is the venomed spear of Pezar, king of Persia. Its name is Slaughterer. In time of peace, its blazing, fiery head is kept always in a great cauldron of water, to prevent it from burning down the king's palace; and in time of war, the champion who bears it to the battle-field can perform any deed he pleases with it. And it will be no easy matter to get this spear from the king of Persia.

" The two steeds and the chariot belong to Dobar, king of Sigar.* The chariot exceeds all the chariots in the world for beauty of shape and goodliness of workmanship. The two noble steeds have no equal for strength and fleetness, and they travel with as much ease on sea as on land.

" The seven pigs I demand are the pigs of Asal, the king of the Golden Pillars. Whoever eats a part of them shall not suffer

---

* Sigar, *i.e.* Sicily.

from ill-health or disease; and even though they should be killed and eaten to-day, they will be alive and well to-morrow.

" The hound-whelp belongs to the king of Iroda,* and his name is Failinis. He shines as brightly as the sun in a summer sky; and every wild beast of the forest that sees him falls down to the earth powerless before him.

" The cooking-spit belongs to the warlike women of the island of Fincara. They are thrice fifty in number, and woe to the champion who approaches their house; for each of them is a match for three good warriors in single combat; and they never yet gave a cooking-spit to any one without being overcome in battle.

" The hill on which I require you to give three shouts is the Hill of Midkena, in the north of Lochlann.[6] Midkena and his sons are always guarding this hill, for they are under geasa[12] not to allow any one to shout on it. Moreover, it was they that instructed my father in championship and feats of arms, and they loved him very much; so that even if I should forgive you his death they would not. And, though you should be able to procure all the rest of the eric-fine, you will not, I think, succeed in this, for they will be sure to avenge on you my father's death.

" And this, ye sons of Turenn, is the eric-fine I demand from you! "


## CHAPTER V

### THE SONS OF TURENN OBTAIN MANNANAN'S CANOE, " THE WAVE-SWEEPER "

THE sons of Turenn were so astounded on hearing this eric-fine that they spoke not one word; but rising up, they left the meeting, and repaired to the house of their father Turenn.

He heard their story to the end, and then said: "Your tidings are bad, my sons, and I fear me you are doomed to meet your death in seeking what the Ildana asks. But the doom is a just one, for it was an evil thing to kill Kian. Now as to this eric-fine: it cannot be obtained by any living man without the help of either

---

\* Iroda was the name given by the Irish to some country in the far north of Europe, probably Norway.

Lugh himself or of Mannanan Mac Lir;[8] but if Lugh wishes to aid you, ye shall be able to get it. Go ye now, therefore, and ask him to lend you Mannanan's steed, Enbarr of the Flowing Mane. If he wishes you to get the full eric-fine, he will lend you the steed; otherwise he will refuse, saying that she does not belong to him, and that he cannot lend what he himself has got on loan. Then, if ye obtain not the steed, ask him for the loan of Mannanan's canoe, the Wave-sweeper, which would be better for you than the steed; and he will lend you that, for he is forbidden to refuse a second request."

So the sons of Turenn returned to Lugh, and having saluted him, they said—

" It is not in the power of any man to obtain this eric-fine without thy own aid, O Lugh; we ask thee therefore, to lend us Mannanan's steed, Enbarr of the Flowing Mane."

" That steed is not my own," said Lugh, " and I cannot lend that which I have myself obtained on loan."

" If that be so," said Brian, " then I pray thee lend us Mannanan's canoe, the Wave-sweeper."

" I shall lend you that," replied Lugh. "It lies at Brugh of the Boyne; * and ye have my consent to take it."

So they came again to their father, and this time Ethnea, their sister, was with him; and they told them that Lugh had given them the canoe.

" I have much fear," said Turenn, " that it will avail you little against the dangers of your quest. Nevertheless, Lugh desires to obtain that part of the eric that will be useful to him at the battle of Moytura,[11] and so far he will help you. But in seeking that which is of no advantage to him, namely, the cooking-spit, and the three shouts on Midkena's Hill, therein he will give you no aid, and he will be glad if ye perish in your attempts to obtain it."

They then set out for Brugh of the Boyne, accompanied by their sister Ethnea, leaving Turenn lamenting after them. The canoe they found lying in the river; and Brian went into it and said—

" It seems to me that only one other person can sit here along with me," and he began to complain very bitterly of its smallness.

---

* Brugh of the Boyne, the palace of Angus, the great Dedannan magician, was situated on the north shore of the Boyne, not far from Slane.

He ceased, however, at the bidding of Ethnea, who told him that the canoe would turn out large enough when they came to try it, and that it was under strict command not to let any one grumble at its smallness. And she went on to say—

" Alas, my beloved brothers, it was an evil deed to slay the father of Lugh of the Long Arms, and I fear you will suffer much woe and hardship on account of it."

ETHNEA:

The deed was a dark one, a deed full of woe,
    Your brother Dedannan to slay;
And hard and relentless the heart of your foe,
The bright-faced Ildana, that forced you to go,
    This eric of vengeance to pay!

THE BROTHERS:

Oh, cease, sister Ethnea, cease thy sad wail;
    Why yield to this terror and gloom?
Long, long shall the poets remember the tale,
For our courage and valour and swords shall prevail,
    Or win us a glorious tomb!

ETHNEA:

Then search ye, my brothers, go search land and sea;
    Go search ye the isles of the East—
Alas, that the cruel Ildana's decree
Has banished my three gentle brothers from me,
    On this fearful and perilous quest!

## CHAPTER VI

### THE APPLES OF THE GARDEN OF HISBERNA

AFTER this the three brothers entered the canoe, which they now found large enough to hold themselves and their arms, and whatsoever else they wished to bring; for this was one of its secret gifts. They then bade their sister farewell, and, leaving her weeping on the shore, they rowed swiftly till they had got beyond the beautiful shores and bright harbours of Erin, out on the open sea.

Then the two younger brothers said, " Now our quest begins: what course shall we take? "

Brian answered, " As the apples are the first part of the fine, we shall seek them first."

And then he spoke to the canoe: "Thou canoe of Mannanan, thou Sweeper of the waves, we ask thee and we command thee, that thou sail straightway to the Garden of Hisberna! "

The canoe was not unmindful of the voice of its master, and obeyed the command without delay, according to its wont. It took the shortest way across the deep sea-chasms, and, gliding over the green-sided waves more swiftly than the clear, cold wind of March, it stayed not in its course till it reached the harbour near the land of Hisberna.

Brian now spoke to his brothers: "Be sure that this quest is a perilous one, since we know that the best champions of the country, with the king at their head, are always guarding the apples. And now in what manner, think you, is it best for us to approach the garden? "

" It seems to us," answered his brothers, " that we had better go straight and attack these champions, and either bring away the apples, or fall fighting for them. For we cannot escape the dangers that lie before us; and if we are doomed to fall in one of these adventures, it may, perchance, be better for us to die here than to prolong our hardships."

But Brian answered: "Not so, my brothers; for it becomes a warrior to be prudent and wary as well as brave. We should now act so that the fame of our skill and valour may live after us, and that future men may not say, ' These sons of Turenn did not deserve to be called brave champions, for they were senseless and rash, and sought their own death by their folly.' In the present case, then, what I counsel is this: Let us take the shape of strong, swift hawks; and as we approach the garden, have ye care of the light, sharp lances of the guards, which they will certainly hurl at us: avoid them actively and cunningly, and when the men have thrown all, let us swoop down and bring away an apple each."

They approved this counsel; and Brian, striking his two brothers and himself with a druidical magic wand, all three were changed into three beautiful hawks. Then, flying swiftly to the garden, they began to descend in circles towards the tops of the trees; but the sharp-eyed guards perceived them, and with a great shout they threw showers of venomous darts at them. The hawks, however, mindful of Brian's warning, watched the spears with keen glances, and escaped them every one, until the guards had thrown all their light weapons. Then, swooping suddenly down on the trees, the two younger brothers carried off an apple each, and Brian two, one between his talons and the other in his beak; and the three rose again into the air without wound or hurt of any kind. Then, directing their course westward, they flew over the wide sea with the speed of an arrow.

The news spread quickly through the city, how three beautiful hawks had carried off the apples; and the king and his people were in great wrath. Now the king had three daughters, very skilful in magic and cunning in counsel; and they forthwith transformed themselves into three swift-winged, sharp-taloned griffins, and pursued the hawks over the sea. But the hawks, when they saw they were pursued, increased their speed, and flew like the wind, and left their pursuers so far behind that they appeared to the griffins like three specks on the sky. Then the angry griffins let fly from their eyes, and from their open beaks, bright flashes of flame straight forward, which overtook and blinded the hawks, and scorched them, so that they could bear the heat no longer.

" Evil is our state now," said Ur and Urcar, " for these sheets of flame are burning us, and we shall perish if we do not get relief."

" I will try whether I cannot relieve you," said Brian; and with that he struck his brothers and himself with his golden druidical wand; and all three were instantly turned into swans. The swans dropped down on the sea; and when the griffins saw the hawks no longer straight before them, they gave up the chase. And the sons of Turenn went safely to their canoe, bringing the apples with them.

## CHAPTER VII

### THE GIFTED SKIN OF THE PIG

AFTER resting a little while, they held council as to their next journey; and what they resolved on was to go to Greece, to seek the skin of the pig, and to bring it away, either by consent or by force. So they went into the canoe, and Brian spoke—

" Thou canoe of Mannanan, thou Sweeper of the Waves, we ask thee and we command thee that thou sail with us straightway to Greece! "

And the canoe, obeying as before, glided swiftly and smoothly over the waves, till the sons of Turenn landed near the palace of the king of Greece.

" In what shape, think you, should we go to this court? " said Brian.

" We think it best," answered the others, " to go in our own shapes; that is to say, as three bold champions."

" Not so," said Brian. " It seems best to me that we should go in the guise of learned poets from Erin; for poets are held in much honour and respect by the great nobles of Greece."

" It is, indeed, hard for us to do that," answered his brothers, " for as to poems, we neither have any, nor do we know how to compose them."

However, as Brian would have it so, they consented, though unwillingly; and, tying up their hair after the manner of poets, they knocked at the door of the palace. The door-keeper asked who was there.

" We are skilful poets from Erin," said Brian, " and we have come to Greece with a poem for the king."

The door-keeper went and gave the message.

" Let them be brought in," said the king, " for it is to seek a good and bountiful master whom they may serve faithfully that they have come so far from Erin."

The sons of Turenn were accordingly led into the banquet hall, where sat the king surrounded by his nobles; and, bowing low, they saluted him; and he saluted them in return, and welcomed them. They sat at the table among the company, and joined the feast at once, drinking and making merry like the others; and they thought they had never seen a banquet hall so grand, or a household so numerous and mirthful.

At the proper time the king's poets arose, according to custom, to recite their poems and their lays for the company. And when they had come to an end, Brian, speaking low, said to his brothers: " As we have come as poets, it is meet that we should practise the poetic art like the others; therefore now arise, and recite a poem for the king."

" We have no poems." they replied, " and we do not wish to practise any art except the art we have learned and practised from our youth, namely, to fight like brave champions, and to take by valour and force of arms that which we want, if we be stronger than our enemies, or to fall in battle if they be the stronger."

" That is not a pleasant way of making poetry," said Brian; and with that he arose and requested attention for his poem. And when they sat listening, he said—

> To praise thee, O Tuis, we've come to this land:
> Like an oak among shrubs, over kings thou dost stand:
> Thy bounty, great monarch, shall gladden the bard;
> And the *Imnocta-fessa* I claim as reward.
>
> Two neighbours shall war, with an O to an O;
> A bard unrequited—how dreadful a foe!
> Thy bounty shall add to thy wealth and thy fame;
> And the *Imnocta-fessa* is all that I claim.

" Your poem would doubtless be thought a very good one," said the king, " if we were able to judge of it; but it is unlike all other poems I have ever heard, for I do not in the least understand its sense."

" I will unfold its sense," said Brian.

> To praise thee, O Tuis, we've come to this land:
> Like an oak among shrubs, over kings thou dost stand:

" This means that as the oak excels all the other trees of the forest, so dost thou excel all the other things of the world for greatness, nobility, and generosity.

" ' *Imnocta-fessa.*' *Imnocta* means ' skin,' and *fessa* ' a pig.'
That is to say, thou hast, O king, the skin of a pig, which I
desire to get from thee as a guerdon for my poetry.

> Two neighbours shall war, with an O to an O;
> A bard unrequited—how dreadful a foe!

"*O* means ' an ear '; that is to say, thou and I shall be ear to
ear fighting with each other for the skin, if thou give it not of
thy own free will.

" And that, O king, is the sense of my poem."

" Thy poem would have been a very good one," said the
king, " and I would have given it due meed of praise if my pig's
skin had not been mentioned in it. But it is a foolish request
of thine, O ferdana,* to ask for that skin; for, even though all
the poets and men of science of Erin, and all the nobles of the
whole world were to demand it from me, I would refuse it.
Nevertheless, thou shalt not pass unrewarded, for I will give
thee thrice the full of the skin of red gold—one for thyself, and
one for each of thy brothers."

" Thy ransom is a good one, O king," said Brian, " but I
am a near-hearted and suspicious man, and I pray thee let me
see with my eyes thy servants measure the gold, lest they deal
unfairly with me."

The king agreed to this; so his servants went with the three
sons of Turenn to the treasure-room, and one of them drew
forth the skin from its place, to measure the gold. As soon as
Brian caught sight of it, he sprang suddenly towards the servant,
and, dashing him to the ground with his right hand, he snatched
the skin with his left, and bound it hastily over his shoulders.

Then the three drew their keen swords, and rushed into the
banquet hall. The king's nobles, seeing how matters stood,
surrounded and attacked them; but the sons of Turenn, nothing
daunted by the number of their foes, hewed down the foremost
and scattered the rest, so that scarce one of the whole party
escaped death or deadly wounds.

Then at last Brian and the king met face to face, nor was
either slow to answer the challenge of the other. They fought

---

* Ferdana, a poet; literally, " a man of verse."

as great champions fight, and it was long doubtful which should prevail; but the end of the combat was that the king of Greece fell by the overpowering valour of Brian, the son of Turenn.

After this victory, the three brothers rested in the palace till they had regained their strength, and healed up their wounds by means of the apples and the pig's skin; and at the end of three days and three nights they found themselves able to undertake the next adventure.

## CHAPTER VIII

### THE BLAZING SPEAR OF THE KING OF PERSIA

So, after holding council, they resolved to go to seek the spear of the king of Persia; and Brian reminded his brothers that now, as they had the apples and the skin to aid them, it would be all the easier to get the spear, as well as the rest of the fine.

Leaving now the shores of Greece with all its blue streams, they went on board the canoe, which, at Brian's command, flew across the wide seas; and soon they made land near the palace of Pezar, king of Persia. And seeing how they had fared so well in their last undertaking, they resolved to put on the guise of poets this time also.

And so they put the poet's tie on their hair, and, passing through the outer gate, they knocked at the door of the palace. The door-keeper asked who they were, and from what country they had come.

" We are poets from Erin," answered Brian, " and we have brought a poem for the king."

So they were admitted and brought to the presence of the king, who seated them among the nobles of his household; and they joined in the drinking and the feasting and the revelry.

The king's poets now arose, and chanted their songs for the king and his guests. And when the applause had ceased, Brian, speaking softly, said to his brothers—

" Arise, now, and chant a poem for the king."

But they answered: "Ask us not to do that which we are unable to do; but if you wish us to exercise the art we have learned from our youth, we shall do so, namely, the art of fighting and overcoming our foes."

" That would be an unusual way of reciting poetry," said Brian; " but I have a poem for the king, and I shall now chant it for him."

So saying, he stood up; and when there was silence, he recited this poem—

> In royal state may Pezar ever reign,
> Like some vast yew tree, monarch of the plain;
> May Pezar's mystic javelin, long and bright,
> Bring slaughter to his foes in every fight!
>
> When Pezar fights and shakes his dreadful spear,
> Whole armies fly and heroes quake with fear:
> What shielded foe, what champion can withstand
> The blazing spear in mighty Pezar's hand!

" Your poem is a good one," said the king, " but one thing in it I do not understand, namely, why you make mention of my spear."

" Because," answered Brian, " I wish to get that spear as a reward for my poem."

" That is a very foolish request," said the king, " for no man ever escaped punishment who asked me for my spear. And as to your poetry, the highest reward I could now bestow on you, and the greatest favour these nobles could obtain for you, is that I should spare your life."

Thereupon Brian and his brothers started up in great wrath and drew their swords, and the king and his chiefs drew their swords in like manner; and they fought a deadly fight. But Brian, at last, drawing forth one of his apples, and taking sure aim, cast it at the king and struck him on the forehead; so that Pezar fell, pierced through the brain.

After this Brian fought on more fiercely than before, dealing destruction everywhere around him; but when the chiefs saw that their king had fallen, they lost heart and fled through the doors, till at length none remained in the banquet hall but the three sons of Turenn.

Then they went to the room where the spear was kept; and they found it with its head down deep in a great cauldron of water, which hissed and bubbled round it. And Brian, seizing it boldly in his hand, drew it forth; after which the three brothers left the palace and went to their canoe.

## CHAPTER IX

### THE CHARIOT AND STEEDS OF THE KING OF SIGAR

RESTING now for some days from their toil, they resolved to seek the steeds and chariot of the king of Sigar; for this was the next part of the Ildana's eric-fine. So they commanded the canoe; and the canoe, obedient to their behest, glided swiftly and smoothly over the green waves till they landed in Sigar. Brian bore the great, heavy, venomed spear in his hand; and the three brothers were of good heart, seeing how they had succeeded in their last quest, and that they had now three parts of the fine.

" In what shape think you we should go to this court?" said Brian.

" How should we go," answered the others, " but in our own shapes, namely, as three hostile champions, who have come to get the chariot and steeds, either by force or by good will?"

" That is not what seems best to me," said Brian. " My counsel is, that we go as soldiers from Erin, willing to serve for pay; and should the king take us into his service, it is likely we shall find out where the chariot and steeds are kept."

His brothers having agreed to this, the three set out for the palace.

It happened that the king was holding a fair-meeting on the broad, level green before the palace; and when the three warriors came near, the people made way for them. They bowed low to the king; and he asked them who they were, and from what part of the world they had come.

" We are valiant soldiers from Erin," they answered, " seeking for service and pay among the great kings of the world."

"Do you wish to enter my service?" asked the king: and they answered, "Yes." So they made a covenant with each other—the king to place them in a post of honour and trust, and they to serve him faithfully, and to name their own reward. Whereupon the brothers entered the ranks of the king's bodyguard.

They remained in the palace for a month and a fortnight, looking round and carefully noting everything; but they saw nothing of the chariot and steeds. At the end of that time Brian said to his brothers—

"It fares ill with us here, my brothers; for we know nothing of the chariot and steeds at this hour, more than when we first came hither."

The others said this was quite true, and asked if he meant to do anything in the matter.

"This is what I think we should do," answered Brian. "Let us put on our travelling array, and take our arms of valour in our hands; and in this fashion let us go before the king, and tell him that unless he shows us the chariot and steeds, we shall leave his service."

This they did without delay; and when they had come before the king, he asked them why they came to his presence so armed and in travelling gear.

"We will tell thee of that, O king," answered Brian. "We are valiant soldiers from Erin, and into whatsoever lands we have travelled, we have been trusted with the secret counsels of the kings who have taken us into their service; and we have been made the guardians of their rarest jewels and of all their gifted arms of victory. But as to thee, O king, thou hast not so treated us since we came hither; for thou hast a chariot and two steeds which exceed all the chariots and steeds in the world, and yet we have never seen them."

"A small thing it is that has caused you to prepare for departure," said the king; "and there is, moreover, no need that you should leave my service; for I would have shown you those steeds the day you came, had I only known that you wished it. But ye shall see them now; for I have never had in my service soldiers from a distant land in whom I and my people have placed greater trust than we have placed in you."

He then sent for the steeds, and had them yoked to the chariot—those steeds that were as fleet as the clear, cold wind of March, and which travelled with equal speed on land and on sea.

Brian, viewing them narrowly, said aloud: "Hear me, O king of Sicily. We have served thee faithfully up to this time; and now we wish to name our own pay, according to the covenant thou hast made with us. The guerdon we demand is yonder chariot and steeds; these we mean to have, and we shall ask for nothing more."

But the king, in great wrath, said: "Foolish and luckless men! Ye shall certainly die because you have dared to ask for my steeds!"

And the king and his warriors drew their swords, and rushed towards the sons of Turenn to seize them.

They, on the other hand, were not taken unaware; and a sore fight began. And Brian, watching his opportunity, sprang with a sudden bound into the chariot, and, dashing the charioteer to the ground, he seized the reins in his left hand; then, raising the venomed spear of Pezar in his right, he smote the king with its fiery point in the breast, so that he fell dead. And the three brothers dealt red slaughter among the king's guards, till those who were not slain scattered and fled in all directions. So they fared in this undertaking.

## CHAPTER X

### THE SEVEN PIGS OF THE KING OF THE GOLDEN PILLARS

AFTER resting till their wounds were healed, Ur and Urcar asked where they should go next.

"We shall go," said Brian, "to Asal, the king of the Golden Pillars, to ask him for his seven pigs; for this is the next part of the Ildana's eric-fine."

So they set out; and the canoe brought them straightway to the land of the Golden Pillars, without delay and without mishap. As they drew nigh to the harbour, they saw the shore lined with men all armed. For the fame of the deeds of these great champions had begun to be noised through many lands; how they had been forced to leave Erin by the hard sentence of the Ildana; and how they were seeking and bearing away the most precious and gifted jewels of the world to pay the fine. Wherefore the king of the Golden Pillars had armed his people, and had sent them to guard the harbours.

The king himself came down to the beach to meet them. As soon as they had come within speaking distance, he bade them stay their course; and then he asked them, in an angry and chiding tone, if they were the three champions from Erin, who had overcome and slain so many kings.

Brian answered: "Be not displeased with us, O king, for in all this matter we are not to blame. The Ildana has demanded a fine which we perforce must pay; for we have promised, and the Dedannans are our guarantee. If the kings to whom he sent us had given us peaceably the precious things we demanded, we would gladly have departed in peace; but as they did not, we fought against them, unwillingly indeed and overthrew them; for no one has as yet been able to withstand us."

"Tell me now," said the king, "what has brought you to my country?"

"We have come for thy seven pigs," answered Brian; "for they are a part of the fine."

"And in what manner do you think ye shall get them?" asked the king.

Brian answered: "Thou hast heard, O king, how the Ildana has brought us to these straits, and we must pay him the fine, every jot, or else we shall die at the hands of our people. Thou, perchance, wilt have pity on our hardship, and give us these pigs in token of kindness and friendship, and if so we shall be thankful; but if not, then we will fight for them, and either bring them away by force, after slaying thee and thy people, or fall ourselves in the attempt."

Hearing this, the king and his people went into council; and after debating the matter at full length, they thought it best to give the pigs peaceably, seeing that no king, however powerful, had as yet been able to withstand the sons of Turenn.

The three champions wondered greatly when this was told to them; for in no other country had they been able to get any part of the fine without battle and hardship, and without leaving much of their blood behind them. So they were now very glad; and thanked Asal and his people.

The king then brought them to his palace, and gave them a kind welcome; and they were supplied with food and drink to their hearts' desire, and slept on soft, downy beds. So they rested after all their weary journeys and toils.

When they arose next morning, they were brought to the king's presence, and the pigs were given to them; and Brian addressed the king in these words—

> The prizes we've brought to this land,
>    We have won them in conflict and blood;
> But the gift we have sought at thy hand,
>    That gift thou hast freely bestowed.
>
> The red spear rewarded our deeds,
>    When Pezar the mighty we slew;
> And the fight for the chariot and steeds,
>    Ah, long shall the Sigarites rue!
>
> Great Asal! in happier days,
>    When our deeds bring us glory and fame;
> Green Erin shall echo thy praise,
>    And her poets shall honour thy name!

## CHAPTER XI

### THE HOUND-WHELP OF THE KING OF IRODA

" WHITHER do you go next, ye sons of Turenn?" asked Asal.

" We go," answered Brian, " to Iroda, for Failinis, the king's hound-whelp."

" Then grant me this boon," said the king, " namely, that ye let me go with you to Iroda. For my daughter is the king's wife; and I will try to prevail on him that he give you the hound-whelp freely and without battle."

This they agreed to. But the king wished that they should go in his own ship; so it was got ready, and they went on board with all their wealth; and it is not told how they fared till they reached the borders of Iroda. The shores were covered with fierce, armed men, who were there by orders of the king to guard the harbour; and these men shouted at the crew, warning them to come no farther; for they knew the sons of Turenn, and well they knew what they came for.

Asal then requested the three champions to remain where they were for a time, while he went on shore to talk with his son-in-law. Accordingly he landed, and went to the king, who, after he had welcomed him, asked what had brought the sons of Turenn to his country.

" They have come for your hound-whelp," answered Asal.

And the king of Iroda said: "It was an evil counsel you followed, when you came with these men to my shores; for to no three champions in the world have the gods given such strength or such good luck as that they can get my hound-whelp, either by force or by my own free will."

" It will be unwise to refuse them," replied Asal. " They have overpowered and slain many great kings; for they have gifted arms that no warrior, however powerful, can withstand; and behold, I have come hither to tell you what manner of men these are, that you might be advised by me, and give them your hound-whelp in peace."

So he pressed him earnestly; but his words were only thrown away on the king of Iroda, who spoke scornfully of the sons of Turenn, and refused Asal's request with wrathful words.

Asal, much troubled at this, went and told the sons of Turenn how matters stood. And they, having without delay put on their battle-dress, and taken their arms in their hands, challenged the king of Iroda and his people. Then began a very fierce and bloody battle; for though nothing could stand before the sons of Turenn, yet the warriors of Iroda were many and very brave. So they fought till the two younger brothers became separated from Brian, and he was quite surrounded. But as he wielded the dreadful spear of Pezar, with its blazing, fiery point, his enemies fell back dismayed, and the ranks were broken before him, so that those who crossed his path stood in a gap of danger.

At length he espied the king of Iroda, where he fought hedged round by spears; and he rushed through the thick of

the battle straight towards him, striking down spears and swords
and men as he went. And now these two valiant warriors fought
hand to hand a stout and watchful and fierce battle—for the
others fell back by the king's command; and it was long before
any advantage was gained on either side. But though to those
who looked on, Brian seemed the more wrathful of the two, yet
he held back his hand, so as not to slay his foe; and this it was,
indeed, that prolonged the combat, for he sought to tire out
the king. At length, watching his opportunity, Brian closed
suddenly, and, seizing the king in his strong arms, he lifted him
clean off the ground, and bore him to where Asal stood. Then,
setting him down, he said—

"Behold thy son-in-law; it would have been easier to kill
him three times over than to bring him to thee once!"

When the people saw their king a prisoner, they ceased
fighting; and the end of all was that peace was made, and the
hound-whelp was given over to the sons of Turenn. Then they
took their leave, and left the shores of Iroda in friendship with
the king and with Asal his father-in-law.

## CHAPTER XII

### RETURN OF THE SONS OF TURENN
### WITH PART OF THE ERIC-FINE

Now we shall speak of Lugh of the Long Arms. It was revealed
to him that the sons of Turenn had obtained all those parts of
the fine which he wanted for the battle of Moytura;[11] but that
they had not yet got the cooking-spit, or given the three shouts
on Midkena's Hill. So he sent after them a druidical spell,
which, falling on them soon after they had left Iroda, caused
them to forget the remaining part of the fine, and filled them
with a longing desire to return to their native home. Accordingly,
they went on board their canoe; and the canoe glided swiftly
over the waves to Erin.

At this time Lugh was with the king at a fair-meeting on the plain before Tara; and it was made known to him secretly that the sons of Turenn had landed at Brugh of the Boyne. He left the assembly anon, telling no one; and he went direct to Caher-Crofinn* at Tara, and, closing the gates and doors after him, he put on his battle array, namely, the smooth Greek armour of Mannanan Mac Lir, and the enchanted mantle of the daughter of Flidas.

Soon after, the sons of Turenn were seen approaching; and as they came forward, the multitude flocked out to meet them, gazing with wonder at the many marvellous things they had brought. When the three champions had come to the royal tent, they were joyfully welcomed by the king and by the Dedannans in general; and then the king spoke kindly to them, and asked if they had brought the eric-fine.

" We have obtained it after much hardship and danger," they replied; " and now we wish to know where Lugh is, that we may hand it over to him."

The king told them that Lugh was at the assembly; but when they sent to search for him, he was nowhere to be found.

" I can tell where he is," said Brian. " It has been made known to him that we have arrived in Erin, bringing with us gifted arms that none can withstand; and he has gone to one of the strongholds of Tara, to avoid us, fearing we might use these venomed weapons against himself."

Messengers were then sent to Lugh to tell him that the sons of Turenn had arrived, and to ask him to come forth to the meeting, that they might give him the fine.

But he answered: " I will not come to the meeting yet; but go ye back, and tell the sons of Turenn to give the fine to the king for me."

The messengers returned with this answer; and the sons of Turenn gave to the king for Lugh all the wonderful things they had brought, keeping, however, their own arms; after which the whole company went into the palace.

When Lugh was told how matters stood, he came to where the king and all the others were; and the king gave him the

---

* Caher-Crofinn, otherwise called Rath-ree, the principal fortress at Tara.

fine. Then Lugh, looking narrowly at everything that had been given up to him, said—

" Here, indeed, is an eric enough to pay for any one that ever yet was slain, or that shall be slain to the end of time. But yet there is one kind of fine that must be paid to the last farthing, namely, an eric-fine; for of this it is not lawful to hold back even the smallest part. And moreover, O king, thou and the Dedannans whom I see here present, are guarantees for the full payment of my eric-fine. Now I see here the three apples, and the skin of the pig, and the fiery-headed spear, and the chariot and steeds, and the seven pigs, and the hound-whelp; but where, ye sons of Turenn, is the cooking-spit of the women of Fincara? And I have not heard that ye have given the three shouts on Midkena's Hill."

On hearing this, the sons of Turenn fell into a faintness like the faintness before death. And when they had recovered they answered not one word, but left the assembly and went to their father's house. To him and their sister Ethnea they told all that had befallen them; and how they should set out on another quest, as they had forgotten part of the eric-fine through the spells of Lugh.

At this Turenn was overwhelmed with grief; and Ethnea wept in great fear and sorrow. And so they passed that night. Next day, they went down to the shore, and their father and sister went with them to their ship, and bade them farewell.

## CHAPTER XIII

### THE COOKING-SPIT OF THE WOMEN OF FINCARA

THEN they went on board their ship—for they had Mannanan's canoe no longer—and they sailed forth on the green billowy sea to search for the Island of Fincara. For a whole quarter of a year they wandered hither and thither over the wide ocean, landing on many shores and inquiring of all they met; yet they were not able to get the least tidings of the island.

At last, they came across one very old man, who told them that he had heard of the Island of Fincara in the days of his youth; and that it lay not on the surface, but down deep in the waters, for it was sunk beneath the waves by a spell in times long past.[13]

Then Brian put on his water-dress, with his helmet of transparent crystal on his head, and, telling his brothers to await his return, he leaped over the side of the ship, and sank at once out of sight. He walked about for a fortnight down in the green salt sea, seeking for the Island of Fincara; and at last he found it.

There were many houses on the island; but one he saw larger and grander than the rest. To this he straightway bent his steps, and found it open. On entering, he saw in one large room a great number of beautiful ladies, busily employed at all sorts of embroidery and needlework; and in their midst was a long, bright cooking-spit lying on a table.

Without speaking a word, he walked straight to the table, and, seizing the spit in one hand, he turned round and walked towards the door. The women neither spoke nor moved, but each had her eyes fixed on him from the moment he entered, admiring his manly form, his beauty, and his fearlessness; but when they saw him about to walk off with the spit, they all burst out laughing; and one, who seemed chief among them, said:

" Thou hast attempted a bold deed, O son of Turenn! Know that there are thrice fifty warlike women here, and that the weakest among us would be able of herself to prevent thee taking this cooking-spit, even if thy two brothers were here to help thee. But thou art a brave and courageous champion, else thou wouldst not have attempted, unaided, to take it by force, knowing the danger. And for thy boldness and valour, and for the comeliness of thy person, we will let thee take this one, for we have many others besides."

So Brian, after thanking them, brought away the spit joyfully, and sought his ship.

Ur and Urcar waited for Brian in the same spot the whole time, and when he came not, they began to fear that he would return no more. With these thoughts they were at last about to leave the place, when they saw the glitter of his crystal helmet down deep in the water, and immediately after he came to the surface with the cooking-spit in his hand. They brought him on board, and now all felt very joyful and courageous of heart.

# CHAPTER XIV

### THE THREE SHOUTS ON MIDKENA'S HILL

THE three brothers next sailed away towards the north of Lochlann, and never abated speed till they moored their vessel near the Hill of Midkena, which rose smooth and green over the sea-shore. When Midkena saw them approaching, he knew them at once, and, coming towards them armed for battle, he addressed them aloud.

" You it was that slew Kian, my friend and pupil; and now come forth and fight, for you shall not leave these shores till you answer for his death."

Brian, in no degree daunted by the fierce look and threatening speech of Midkena, sprang ashore, and the two heroes attacked each other with great fury. When the three sons of Midkena heard the clash of arms, they came forth, and, seeing how matters stood, they rushed down to aid their father; but just as they arrived at the shore, Midkena fell dead, cloven through helmet and head by the heavy sword of Brian.

And now a fight began, three on each side; and if men were afar off, even in the land of Hisberna, in the east of the world, they would willingly come the whole way to see this battle, so fierce and haughty were the minds of those mighty champions, so skilful and active were they in the use of their weapons, so numerous and heavy were their blows, and so long did they continue to fight without either party giving way. The three sons of Turenn were at last dreadfully wounded—wounded almost to death. But neither fear nor weakness did this cause them, for their valour and their fury arose all the more for their wounds, and with one mighty onset they drove their spears through the bodies of their foes; and the sons of Midkena fell before them into the long sleep of death.

But now that the fight was ended, and the battle-fury of the victors had passed off—now it was that they began to feel the effects of their wounds. They threw themselves full length on the blood-stained sward, and long they remained without moving or speaking a word, as if they were dead; and a heavy curtain of darkness fell over their eyes.

At last Brian, raising his head, spoke to his brothers to know if they lived, and when they answered him feebly, he said:

" My dear brothers, let us now arise and give the three shouts on the hill while there is time, for I feel the signs of death."

But they were not able to rise.

Then Brian, gathering all his remaining strength, stood up and lifted one with each hand, while his own blood flowed plentifully; and then they raised three feeble shouts on Midkena's Hill.

## CHAPTER XV

### RETURN AND DEATH OF THE SONS OF TURENN

MAKING no further delay, he led them to their ship, and they set sail for Erin. While they were yet far off, Brian, gazing over the sea towards the west, suddenly cried out:

" Lo, I see Ben Edair* yonder, rising over the waters; and I see also Dun Turenn farther towards the north."

And Ur answered from where he reclined with Urcar on the deck: " If we could but get one sight of Ben Edair methinks we should regain our health and strength; and as thou lovest us and as thou lovest thy own renown, my brother, come and raise our heads and rest them on thy breast, that we may see Erin

---

* Howth Hill, near Dublin. Dun Turenn, the fortress of their father Turenn.

once more.　　After that, we shall welcome either life or death."

### UR:

O brother, torch of valour, strong of hand,
　　Come, place our weary heads upon thy breast;
And let us look upon our native land,
　　Before we sink to everlasting rest!

### BRIAN:

Beloved sons of Turenn, woe is me!
　　My wounds are deep, my day of strength is past;
Yet not for this I grieve, but that I see
　　Your lives, my noble brothers, ebbing fast!

### UR:

Would we could give our lives to purchase thine;
　　Ah, gladly would we die to ease thy pain!
For art thou not the pride of Turenn's line,
　　The noblest champion of green Erin's plain?

### BRIAN:

That mighty Dannan healer, Dianket; *
　　Or Midac, who excelled his sire in skill;
The maiden-leech, Armedda, mightier yet,
　　Who knew the herbs to cure, the herbs to kill:

Oh, were they here; or had we now at hand
　　Those gifted apples from the distant East;
Then might we hope to reach our native land,
　　And live again in joy and peace and rest!

### UR:

Brother, methinks could we but see once more
　　Ben Edair's slopes, or Bregia's dewy plain,
Tailltenn, or Brugh's mystic mansion hoar,
　　Our blood would course in health and strength again.

---

* Dianket, the great Dedannan physician.  His son Midac and his daughter Armedda were still more skilful than their father.

*Bregia*, the plain lying between the Liffey and the Boyne.

*Tailltenn*, now Teltown, on the Blackwater, about midway between Navan and Kells, in Meath.  Here annual meetings were held from the most ancient times, on the first of August, and for some days before and after, at which games were celebrated, like the Olympic games of Greece.

*Brugh* on the Boyne, where Angus or Mac Indoc, the great Dedannan enchanter, had his " mystic mansion hoar."

> Or let us once behold our father's home,
> Or winding Liffey down by Ahaclee,
> Old Frevan's hill, or Tara's regal dome;
> Then welcome death or life, whiche'er may be!

So Brian raised their heads and rested them on his breast, and they gazed on the rocky cliffs and green slopes of Ben Edair while the ship wafted them slowly towards land.

Soon after this they landed on the north side of Ben Edair, from which they made their way slowly to Dun Turenn. And when they had reached the green in front of the house, Brian cried out—

"Father, dear father, come forth to thy children!"

Turenn came forth and saw his sons all wounded and pale and feeble.

And Brian said: "Go, beloved father—go quick to Tara, and quickly return. Bring this cooking-spit to Lugh, and tell him that we have given the three shouts on Midkena's Hill. Say that we have now paid the full eric-fine, and bring back from him the apples of the Garden of Hisberna, to heal our wounds, else we die."

BRIAN:

> Father, our wounds are deadly; nought can save
> Thy children's lives but Lugh's friendly hand:
> Go, seek him, father—fare thee fast—and crave
> The healing apples from Hisberna's land!

TURENN:

> In vain, my sons, ye seek to fly your doom;
> The stern Ildana's mind too well I know:
> Alas! far liefer would he see your tomb,
> Than all the treasures all this world could show!

BRIAN:

> But he is just; and though his sire we slew,
> Have we not paid full eric for the deed?
> The great Ildana is our kinsman too,
> And will relent in this our time of need.

> Then go, my father, thou art swift and strong;
> Speed like the wind—why linger here to mourn?
> Go straight to Lugh's home, nor tarry long;
> Or, father, we shall die ere thou return!

---

*Ahaclee*, Ath Cliath (Dublin).
*Tara*, in Meath, the chief seat of the Irish kings.

Turenn set out and travelled like the wind till he reached
Tara, where he found Lugh.

He gave him the cooking-spit, and said: "Behold, my three
sons have now paid thee the full eric-fine, for they have given
the three shouts on Midkena's Hill. But they are wounded even
unto death; and now give me, I pray thee, the apples from the
Garden of Hisberna, to cure them, else they die."

But Lugh refused, and turned away from Turenn.

Turenn hastened back to his sons with a sorrowful heart,
and told them that he had failed to get the apples.

Then Brian said: "Take me with thee to Tara. I will see
him, and perchance he may have pity on us, and give us the
apples."

And it was done so. But when Brian begged for the apples,
Lugh said—

"I will not give them to thee. If thou shouldst offer me
the full of the whole earth of gold, I would not give them to
thee. Thou and thy brothers committed a wicked and pitiless
deed when you slew my father. For that deed you must suffer,
and with nothing short of your death shall I be content."

> For the blood that you spilled,
>   For the hero you killed—
> The deed is avenged, and your doom is fulfilled!

Brian turned away and went back to his brothers, and, lying
down between them, his life departed; and his brothers died
at the same moment.

Then their father and their sister stood hand in hand over
their bodies, lamenting. And Turenn spoke this lay—

> Oh, pulseless is my heart this woeful hour,
>   My strength is gone, my joy for ever fled;
> Three noble champions, Erin's pride and power,
>   My three fair youths, my children, cold and dead!
>
> Mild Ur, the fair-haired; Urcar, straight and tall;
>   The kings of Banba* worthy both to be;
> And Brian, bravest, noblest, best of all,
>   Who conquered many lands beyond the sea:

---

* Banba, one of the ancient names of Ireland.

Lo, I am Turenn, your unhappy sire,
  Mourning with feeble voice above your grave;
No life, no wealth, no honours I desire;
  A place beside my sons is all I crave!

After this, Turenn and Ethnea fell on the bodies of the three young heroes and died.

And they were all buried in one grave.

This is the story of the Fate of the Children of Turenn.

# The Overflowing of Lough Neagh

*AND*

## THE STORY OF LIBAN THE MERMAID

IN the days of old a good king ruled over Mumha,* whose name was Marid Mac Carido. He had two sons, Ecca and Rib. Ecca was restless and unruly, and in many ways displeased the king; and he told his brother Rib that he had made up his mind to leave his home, and win lands for himself in some far off part of the country. Rib tried hard to dissuade him; but though this delayed his departure for a while, he was none the less bent on going.

At last, Ecca, being wrought upon by his stepmother Ebliu (from whom Slieve Eblinne† was afterwards named), did a grievous wrong to his father, and fled from Mumha with all his people; and his brother Rib and his stepmother Ebliu went with him. Ten hundred men they were in all, besides women and children; and they turned their faces towards the north.

After they had travelled for some time, their druids³ told them that it was not fated for them to settle in the same place; and accordingly, when they had come to the Pass of the two Pillar Stones, they parted.

Rib and his people turned to the west, and they journeyed till they came to the plain of Arbthenn. And there the water of a fountain burst forth over the land, and drowned them all; and a great lake was formed, which to this day is called the Lake of Rib.‡

---

* Mumha, *i.e.* Munster.
† Slieve Eblinne, now Slieve Eelim or Slieve Phelim, in Tipperary, sometimes called the Twelve Hills of Evlinn. " Eblinne " is the genitive of " Ebliu."
‡ Now Lough Ree, on the Shannon.

Ecca continued his journey northwards; and he and his people fared slowly on till they came near to Brugh of the Boyne, the palace of Mac Indoc, where they were fain to rest. No sooner had they halted, than a tall man came forth from the palace, namely, Angus Mac Indoc of the Brugh, son of the Dagda, and commanded them to leave the place without delay. But they, being spent with the toil of travel, heeded not his words, and, pitching their tents, they rested on the plain before the palace. Whereupon, Angus being wroth that his commands were unheeded, killed all their horses that night.

Next day, he came forth again, and he said to them, " Your horses I slew last night; and now, unless ye depart from this place, I will slay your people to-night."

And Ecca said to him, " Much evil hast thou done to us already, for thou hast killed all our horses. And now we cannot go, even though we desire it, for without horses we cannot travel."

Then Angus brought to them a very large horse in full harness, and they put all their goods on him. And when they were about to go, he said to them—

" Beware that ye keep this great steed walking continually; not even a moment's rest shall ye give him, otherwise he will certainly be the cause of your death."

After this they set out again, on a Sunday in the mid-month of autumn, and travelled on till they reached the Plain of the Grey Copse,* where they intended to abide. They gathered then round the great steed to take their baggage off him, and each was busy seeing after his own property, so that they forgot to keep the horse moving. And the moment he stood still, a magic well sprang up beneath his feet.

Now Ecca, when he saw the well spring up, was troubled, remembering Angus's warning. And he caused a house to be built round it, and near it he built his palace, for the better security. And he chose a woman to take care of the well, charging her strictly to keep the door locked, except when the people of the palace came for water.

---

* The Plain of the Grey Copse, according to the legend, was the name of the plain now covered by Lough Neagh.

After that the King of Ulaidh,* that is to say, Muridach, the son of Fiaca Findamnas (who was grandson of Conal Carna of the Red Branch[15]) came against Ecca to drive him forth from Ulaidh. But Ecca made a stout fight, so that he won the lordship of half of Ulaidh from Muridach. And after that his people settled down on the Plain of the Grey Copse.

Now Ecca had two daughters, Ariu and Liban, of whom Ariu was the wife of Curnan the Simpleton. And Curnan went about among the people, foretelling that a lake would flow over them from the well, and urging them earnestly to make ready their boats.

> Come forth, come forth, ye valiant men; build boats, and
>     build ye fast!
> I see the water surging out, a torrent deep and vast;
> I see our chief and all his host o'erwhelmed beneath the wave;
> And Ariu, too, my best beloved, alas! I cannot save.
>     But Liban east and west shall swim
>     Long ages on the ocean's rim,
>     By mystic shores and islets dim,
>         And down in the deep sea cave!

And he ceased not to warn all he met, repeating this verse continually; but the people gave no heed to the words of the Simpleton.

Now the woman who had charge of the well, on a certain occasion forgot to close the door, so that the spell was free to work evil. And immediately the water burst forth over the plain, and formed a great lake, namely the Lake of the Copse. And Ecca and all his family and all his folk were drowned, save only his daughter Liban, and Conang, and Curnan the Simpleton. And they buried Ariu, and raised a mound over her, which is called from her Carn-Arenn.

Of Conang nothing more is told. But as to Curnan, he died of grief after his wife Ariu; and he was buried in a mound, which is called Carn-Curnan to this day in memory of him.

And thus the great Lake of the Copse was formed, which is now called Lough Necca,† in memory of Ecca, the son of Marid. And it was the overflow of this lake which, more than all other causes, scattered the Ultonians over Erin.

---

* Ulaidh, *i.e.* Ulster.
† Lough Necca, now Lough Neagh.

Now as to Liban. She also was swept away like the others; but she was not drowned. She lived for a whole year with her lap-dog, in her chamber beneath the lake, and God protected her from the water. At the end of the year she was weary; and when she saw the speckled salmon swimming and playing all round her, she prayed and said—

"O my Lord, I wish I were a salmon, that I might swim with the others through the clear green sea!"

And at the words she took the shape of a salmon, except her face and breast, which did not change. And her lap-dog was changed to an otter, and attended her afterwards whithersoever she went, as long as she lived in the sea.

And so she remained swimming about from sea to sea for three hundred years; that is to say, from the time of Ecca, the son of Marid, to the time of Comgall of Bangor.

Now on one occasion, Comgall sent Beoc, the son of Indli, from Bangor to Rome, to talk with Gregory* concerning some matters of order and rule. And when Beoc's curragh[17] was sailing over the sea, he and his crew heard sweet singing in the waters beneath them, as it were the chanting of angels.

And Beoc, having listened for a while, looked down into the water, and asked what the chant was for, and who it was that sang.

And Liban answered, "I am Liban, the daughter of Ecca, son of Marid; and it is I who sang the chant thou hast heard."

"Why art thou here?" asked Beoc.

And she replied, "Lo, I have lived for three hundred years beneath the sea; and I have come hither to fix a day and a place of meeting with thee. I shall now go westward; and I beseech thee, for the sake of the holy men of Dalriada,† to come to Inver Ollarba‡ to meet me, on this same day at the end of a year. Say also to Comgall and to the other holy men of Bangor, all that I say to thee. Come with thy boats and thy fishing-nets, and thou shalt take me from the waters in which I have lived."

* Gregory, i.e. Pope Gregory.
† Dalriada, the old name of a territory which included the southern half of the county Antrim and a part of Down.
‡ Inver Ollarba, i.e. the inver, or mouth of the river Ollarba, which was the ancient name of the Larne Water, in Antrim.

"I shall not grant thee the boon thou askest," said Beoc, "unless thou give me a reward."

"What reward dost thou seek?" asked Liban.

"That thou be buried in one grave with me in my own monastery," answered Beoc.

"That shall be granted to thee," said Liban.

Beoc then went on his way to Rome. And when he had returned, he related to Comgall and to the other saints of the monastery at Bangor, the story of the mermaid. And now the end of the year was nigh.

Then they made ready their nets, and on the day appointed they went in their boats to Inver Ollarba, a goodly company of the saints of Erin. And Liban was caught in the net of Fergus of Miluc*: and her head and shoulders were those of a maiden, but she had the body of a fish.

Now the boat in which she was brought to land was kept half-full of sea water, in which she remained swimming about. And many came to see her; and all were filled with wonder when they saw her strange shape and heard her story.

Among the rest came the chief of the tribe of Hua-Conang, wearing a purple cloak; and she kept gazing at him earnestly. The young chief, seeing this, said to her—

"Dost thou wish to have this cloak? If so, I will give it to thee willingly."

But she answered, "Not so: I desire not thy cloak. But it brings to my mind my father Ecca; for on the day he was drowned, he wore a cloak of purple like thine. But may good luck be on thee for thy gentleness, and on him who shall come after thee in thy place; and in every assembly where thy successor sits, may he be known to all without inquiry."

After that there came up a large-bodied, dark-visaged, fierce hero, and killed her lap-dog. Whereupon she was grieved; and she told him that the heroism of himself and his tribe should be stained by the baseness of their minds, and that they should not be able to defend themselves against injuries till they should do penance, by fasting, for her sake.

---

* Miluc, or Meelick, the name of an ancient ecclesiastical establishment in the county Antrim.

Then the warrior repented what he had done, and humbled himself before her.

And now there arose a contention about her, as to whom she should belong. Comgall said she was his, forasmuch as she was caught in his territory. But Fergus urged that she belonged to him by right, as it was in his net she was taken. And Beoc said he had the best right of all to her, on account of the promise she had made to him.

And as no one could settle the dispute, these three saints fasted and prayed that God would give a judgment between them, to show who should own Liban.

And an angel said to one of the company: "Two wild oxen will come hither to-morrow from Carn-Arenn, that is to say, from the grave-mound of Liban's sister, Ariu. Yoke a chariot to them, and place the mermaid in it; and into whatsoever territory they shall bring her, she shall remain with the owner thereof."

The oxen came on the morrow, as the angel had foretold. And when they were yoked, and when Liban was placed in the chariot, they brought her straightway to Beoc's church, namely to Tec-Da-Beoc.

Then the saints gave her a choice—either to die immediately after baptism, and go to heaven; or to live on earth as long as she had lived in the sea, and then to go to heaven after these long ages. And the choice she took was to die immediately. Whereupon Comgall baptized her; and he gave her the name of Murgen, that is, " Sea-born ", or Murgelt, that is " Mermaid."

And she is counted among the holy virgins, and held in honour and reverence, as God ordained for her in heaven; and wonders and miracles are performed through her means at Tec-Da-Beoc.

# Connla of the
# Golden Hair

*AND*

## THE FAIRY MAIDEN

CONNLA of the Golden Hair was the son of Conn the Hundred-fighter.[18] One day as he stood with his father on the royal Hill of Usna, he saw a lady a little way off, very beautiful, and dressed in strange attire. She approached the spot where he stood; and when she was near, he spoke to her, and asked who she was, and from what place she had come.

The lady replied, "I have come from the Land of the Living[19]—a land where there is neither death nor old age, nor any breach of law. The inhabitants of earth call us Aes-shee,[19] for we have our dwellings within large, pleasant, green hills. We pass our time very pleasantly in feasting and harmless amusements, never growing old; and we have no quarrels or contentions."

The king and his company marvelled very much; for though they heard this conversation, no one saw the lady except Connla alone.

"Who is this thou art talking to, my son?" said the king.

And anon she answered for the youth: "Connla is speaking with a lovely, noble-born young lady, who will never die, and who will never grow old. I love Connla of the Golden Hair, and I have come to bring him with me to Moy-mell,[19] the plain of never-ending pleasure. On the day that he comes with me he shall be made king; and he shall reign for ever in Fairyland, without weeping and without sorrow. Come with me, O gentle Connla of the ruddy cheek, the fair, freckled neck, and the

74

golden hair! Come with me, beloved Connla, and thou shalt retain the comeliness and dignity of thy form, free from the wrinkles of old age, till the awful day of judgment! "

> Thy flowing golden hair, thy comely face,
> Thy tall majestic form of peerless grace,
> That show thee sprung from Conn's exalted race.

King Conn the Hundred-fighter, being much troubled, called then on his druid,[3] Coran, to put forth his power against the witchery of the banshee.[19]

" O Coran of the mystic arts and of the mighty incantations, here is a contest such as I have never been engaged in since I was made king at Tara—a contest with an invisible lady who is beguiling my son to Fairyland by her baleful charms. Her cunning is beyond my skill, and I am not able to withstand her power; and if thou, Coran, help not, my son will be taken away from me by the wiles and witchery of a woman from the fairy hills."

Coran, the druid, then came forward, and began to chant against the voice of the lady. And his power was greater than hers for that time, so that she was forced to retire.

As she was going away she threw an apple to Connla, who straightway lost sight of her; and the king and his people no longer heard her voice.

The king and the prince returned with their company to the palace; and Connla remained for a whole month without tasting food or drink, except the apple. And though he ate of it each day, it was never lessened, but was as whole and perfect in the end as at the beginning. Moreover, when they offered him aught else to eat or drink, he refused it; for while he had his apple he did not deem any other food worthy to be tasted. And he began to be very moody and sorrowful, thinking of the lovely fairy maiden.

At the end of the month, as Connla stood by his father's side among the nobles, on the Plain of Arcomin, he saw the same lady approaching him from the west. And when she had come near, she addressed him in this manner:

" A glorious seat, indeed, has Connla among wretched, short-lived mortals, awaiting the dreadful stroke of death! But now, the ever-youthful people of Moy-mell, who never feel old age, and who fear not death, seeing thee day by day among thy friends, in the assemblies of thy Fatherland, love thee with a strange love; and they will make thee king over them if thou wilt come with me."

When the king heard the words of the lady, he commanded his people to call the druid again to him.

" Bring my druid, Coran, to me; for I see that the fairy lady has this day regained the power of her voice."

At this the lady said: " Valiant Conn, fighter of a hundred, the faith of the druids has come to little honour among the upright, mighty, numberless people of this land.    When the righteous law shall be restored, it will seal up the lips of the false, black demon; and his druids shall no longer have power to work their guileful spells."

Now the king observed, and marvelled greatly, that whenever the lady was present, his son never spoke one word to any one, nay, even though they addressed him many times.    And when the lady had ceased to speak, the king said—

" Connla, my son, has thy mind been moved by the words of the lady? "

Connla spoke then, and replied: " Father, I am very unhappy; for though I love my people beyond all, yet I am filled with sadness on account of this lady! "

When Connla had said this, the maiden again addressed him, and chanted these words in a very sweet voice—

### THE CHANT OF THE FAIRY MAIDEN TO CONNLA OF THE GOLDEN HAIR

I

A land of youth, a land of rest,
  A land from sorrow free;
It lies far off in the golden west,
  On the verge of the azure sea.
A swift canoe of crystal bright,
  That never met mortal view—
We shall reach the land ere fall of night,
  In that strong and swift canoe:

We shall reach the strand
Of that sunny land,
From druids and demons free;
The land of rest,
In the golden west,
On the verge of the azure sea!


II

A pleasant land of winding vales, bright streams, and verdurous plains,
Where summer all the live-long year, in changeless splendour reigns;
A peaceful land of calm delight, of everlasting bloom;
Old age and death we never know, no sickness, care, or gloom;
The land of youth,
Of love and truth,
From pain and sorrow free;
The land of rest,
In the golden west,
On the verge of the azure sea!


III

There are strange delights for mortal men in that island of the west;
The sun comes down each evening in its lovely vales to rest:
And though far and dim
On the ocean's rim
It seems to mortal view,
We shall reach its halls
Ere the evening falls,
In my strong and swift canoe:
And ever more
That verdant shore
Our happy home shall be;
The land of rest,
In the golden west,
On the verge of the azure sea!


IV

It will guard thee, gentle Connla of the flowing golden hair,
It will guard thee from the druids, from the demons of the air;
My crystal boat will guard thee, till we reach that western shore,
Where thou and I in joy and love shall live for evermore:
From the druid's incantation,
From his black and deadly snare,
From the withering imprecation
Of the demon of the air,
It will guard thee, gentle Connla of the flowing golden hair:
My crystal boat will guard thee, till we reach that silver strand
Where thou shalt reign in endless joy, the king of the Fairy-land!

When the maiden had ended her chant, Connla suddenly walked away from his father's side, and sprang into the curragh, the gleaming, straight-gliding, strong, crystal canoe. The king and his people saw them afar off and dimly, moving away over the bright sea towards the sunset. They gazed sadly after them, till they lost sight of the canoe over the utmost verge; and no one can tell whither they went, for Connla was never again seen in his native land.

# The
# Voyage of Maildun

*An account of
the adventures of Maildun and his crew,
and of the wonderful things they saw during their voyage
of three years and seven months, in their curragh,
on the western sea.*

## CHAPTER I

### MAILDUN'S CHILDHOOD AND YOUTH. HE BEGINS HIS VOYAGE IN QUEST OF THE PLUNDERERS WHO SLEW HIS FATHER

THERE was once an illustrious man of the tribe of Owenacht*
of Ninus, Allil Ocar Aga by name, a goodly hero, and lord of
his own tribe and territory. One time, when he was in his
house unguarded, a fleet of plunderers landed on the coast and
spoiled his territory. The chief fled for refuge to the church of
Dooclone; but the spoilers followed him thither, slew him, and
burned the church over his head.

Not long after Allil's death, a son was born to him. The
child's mother gave him the name of Maildun; and, wishing to
conceal his birth, she brought him to the queen of that country,
who was her dear friend. The queen took him to her, and gave
out that he was her own child, and he was brought up with the
king's sons, slept in the same cradle with them, and was fed
from the same breast and from the same cup. He was a very

---

* There were several tribes named Owenacht in the south of Ireland. This
 particular tribe, the Owenacht of Ninus, owned territory in the north-west of
 the county Clare, opposite the Islands of Aran.

lovely child; and the people who saw him thought it doubtful if there was any other child living at the time equally beautiful.

As he grew up to be a young man, the noble qualities of his mind gradually unfolded themselves. He was high-spirited and generous, and he loved all sorts of manly exercises. In ball-playing, in running and leaping, in throwing the stone, in chess-playing, in rowing, and in horse-racing, he surpassed all the youths that came to the king's palace, and won the palm in every contest.

One day, when the young men were at their games, a certain youth among them grew envious of Maildun; and he said, in an angry and haughty tone of voice:

" It is a cause of much shame to us that we have to yield in every game, whether of skill or of strength, whether on land or on water, to an obscure youth, of whom no one can tell who is his father or his mother, or what race or tribe he belongs to."

On hearing this, Maildun ceased at once from play; for until that moment he believed that he was the son of the king of the Owenacht, and of the queen who had nursed him. And going anon to the queen, he told her what had happened; and he said to her—

" If I am not thy son, I will neither eat nor drink till thou tell me who my father and mother are."

She tried to soothe him, and said, " Why do you worry yourself searching after this matter? Give no heed to the words of this envious youth. Am I not a mother to you? And in all this country, is there any mother who loves her son better than I love you?"

He answered, " All this is quite true. Yet I pray thee let me know who my parents are."

The queen then, seeing that he would not be put off, brought him to his mother, and put him into her hands. And when he had spoken with her, he asked her to tell him who his father was.

" You are bent on a foolish quest, my child," she said, " for even if you knew all about your father, the knowledge would bring neither advantage nor happiness to you, for he died before you were born."

" Even so," he replied, " I wish to know who he was."

So his mother told him the truth, saying, " Your father was Allil Ocar Aga, of the tribe of Owenacht of Ninus."

Maildun then set out for his father's territory; and his three foster-brothers, namely, the king's three sons, who were noble and handsome youths like himself, went with him. When the people of his tribe found out that the strange youth was the son of their chief, whom the plunderers had slain years before, and when they were told that the three others were the king's sons, they gave them all a joyful welcome, feasting them, and showing them much honour; so that Maildun was made quite happy, and soon forgot all the abasement and trouble he had undergone.

Some time after this, it happened that a number of young people were in the churchyard of Dooclone—the same church in which Maildun's father had been slain—exercising themselves in casting a hand-stone. The game was to throw the stone clear over the charred roof of the church that had been burned; and Maildun was there contending among the others. A foul-tongued fellow named Brickna, a servant of the people who owned the church, was standing by; and he said to Maildun:

" It would better become you to avenge the man who was burned to death here, than to be amusing yourself casting a stone over his bare, burnt bones."

" Who was he? " inquired Maildun.

" Allil Ocar Aga, your father," replied the other.

" Who slew him? " asked Maildun.

" Plunderers from a fleet slew him and burned him in this church," replied Brickna. "And the same plunderers are still sailing in the same fleet."

Maildun was disturbed and sad after hearing this. He dropped the stone that he held in his hand, folded his cloak round him, and buckled on his shield. And he left the company and began to inquire of all he met, the road to the plunderers' ships. For a long time he could get no tidings of them; but at last some persons, who knew where the fleet lay, told him that it was a long way off, and that there was no reaching it except by sea.

Now Maildun was resolved to find out these plunderers, and to avenge on them the death of his father. So he went without delay into Corcomroe,* to the druid[3] Nuca, to seek his advice about building a curragh, and to ask also for a charm to protect him, both while building it, and while sailing on the sea afterwards.

The druid gave him full instructions. He told him the day he should begin to build his curragh, and the exact day on which he was to set out on his voyage; and he was very particular about the number of the crew, which, he said, was to be sixty chosen men, neither more nor less.

So Maildun built a large triple-hide curragh,[17] following the druid's directions in every particular; chose his crew of sixty, among whom were his two friends, Germane and Diuran Lekerd; and on the day appointed put out to sea.

When he had got only a very little way from the land, he saw his three foster-brothers running down to the shore, signalling and calling out to him to return and take them on board; for they said they wished to go with him.

" We shall not turn back," said Maildun; " and you cannot come with us; for we have already got our exact number."

" We will swim after you in the sea till we are drowned, if you do not return for us," replied they; and so saying, the three plunged in and swam after the curragh.

When Maildun saw this, he turned his vessel towards them, and took them on board rather than let them be drowned.

## CHAPTER II

### THE FIRST ISLAND. TIDINGS OF THE PLUNDERERS

THEY sailed that day and night, as well as the whole of next day, till darkness came on again; and at midnight they saw two small bare islands, with two great houses on them near the shore. When they drew near, they heard the sounds of merriment and laughter, and the shouts of revellers intermingled with the loud voices of warriors boasting of their deeds. And

---

*Corcomroe, an ancient territory, now a barony in the north-west of the county Clare.

listening to catch the conversation, they heard one warrior say to another—

"Stand off from me, for I am a better warrior than thou; it was I who slew Allil Ocar Aga, and burned Dooclone over his head; and no one has ever dared to avenge it on me. Thou hast never done a great deed like that!"

"Now surely," said Germane and Diuran to Maildun, "Heaven has guided our ship to this place! Here is an easy victory. Let us now sack this house, since God has revealed our enemies to us, and delivered them into our hands!"

While they were yet speaking, the wind arose, and a great tempest suddenly broke on them. And they were driven violently before the storm, all that night and a part of next day, into the great and boundless ocean; so that they saw neither the islands they had left nor any other land; and they knew not whither they were going.

Then Maildun said: "Take down your sail and put by your oars, and let the curragh drift before the wind in whatsoever direction it pleases God to lead us"; which was done.

He then turned to his foster-brothers, and said to them: "This evil has befallen us because we took you into the curragh, thereby violating the druid's directions; for he forbade me to go to sea with more than sixty men for my crew, and we had that number before you joined us. Of a surety more evil will come of it."

His foster-brothers answered nothing to this, but remained silent.

## CHAPTER III

### THE ISLAND OF THE MONSTROUS ANTS

FOR three days and three nights they saw no land. On the morning of the fourth day, while it was yet dark, they heard a sound to the north-east; and Germane said—

"This is the voice of the waves breaking on the shore."

As soon as it was light they saw land and made towards it. While they were casting lots to know who should go and explore the country, they saw great flocks of ants coming down to the beach, each of them as large as a foal. The people judged by their numbers, and by their eager and hungry look, that they were bent on eating both ship and crew; so they turned their vessel round and sailed quickly away.

> Their multitudes countless, prodigious their size;
> 　Were never such ants seen or heard of before.
> They struggled and tumbled and plunged for the prize,
> And fiercely the famine-fire blazed from their eyes,
> 　As they ground with their teeth the red sand of the shore!

## CHAPTER IV

### THE TERRACED ISLE OF BIRDS

AGAIN for three days and three nights they saw no land. But on the morning of the fourth day they heard the murmur of the waves on the beach; and as the day dawned, they saw a large high island, with terraces all round it, rising one behind another. On the terraces grew rows of tall trees, on which were perched great numbers of large, bright-coloured birds.

When the crew were about to hold council as to who should visit the island and see whether the birds were tame, Maildun himself offered to go. So he went with a few companions; and they viewed the island warily, but found nothing to hurt or alarm them; after which they caught great numbers of the birds and brought them to their ship.

> A shield-shaped island, with terraces crowned,
> And great trees circling round and round:
> From the summit down to the wave-washed rocks,
> There are bright-coloured birds in myriad flocks—
> Their plumes are radiant; but hunger is keen;
> 　　So the birds are killed,
> 　　Till the curragh is filled,
> And the sailors embark on the ocean green!

## CHAPTER V

### A MONSTER

THEY sailed from this, and on the fourth day discovered a large, sandy island, on which, when they came near, they saw a huge, fearful animal standing on the beach, and looking at them very attentively. He was somewhat like a horse in shape; but his legs were like the legs of a dog; and he had great, sharp claws of a blue colour.

Maildun, having viewed this monster for some time, liked not his look; and, telling his companions to watch him closely, for that he seemed bent on mischief, he bade the oarsmen row very slowly towards land.

The monster seemed much delighted when the ship drew nigh the shore, and gambolled and pranced about with joy on the beach, before the eyes of the voyagers; for he intended to eat the whole of them the moment they landed.

" He seems not at all sorry to see us coming," said Maildun, " but we must avoid him and put back from the shore."

This was done. And when the animal observed them drawing off, he ran down in a great rage to the very water's edge, and digging up large, round pebbles with his sharp claws, he began to fling them at the vessel; but the crew soon got beyond his reach, and sailed into the open sea.

A horrible monster, with blazing eyes,
In shape like a horse and tremendous in size,
    Awaiting the curragh, they saw;
        With big bony jaws
        And murderous claws,
    That filled them with terror and awe:
        How gleeful he dances,
        And bellows and prances,
    As near to the island they draw;
        Expecting a feast—
        The bloodthirsty beast—
    With his teeth like the edge of a saw:
        Then he ran to the shore,
        With a deafening roar,
    Intending to swallow them raw:
        But the crew, with a shout,
        Put their vessel about,
    And escaped from his ravenous maw!

# CHAPTER VI

### THE DEMON HORSE-RACE

AFTER sailing a long distance, they came in view of a broad, flat island. It fell to the lot of Germane to go and examine it, and he did not think the task a pleasant one. Then his friend Diuran said to him—

"I will go with you this time; and when next it falls to my lot to visit an island, you shall come with me." So both went together.

They found the island very large; and some distance from the shore they came to a broad green race-course, in which they saw immense hoof-marks, the size of a ship's sail, or of a large dining-table. They found nut-shells, as large as helmets, scattered about; and although they could see no one, they observed all the marks and tokens that people of huge size were lately employed there at sundry kinds of work.

Seeing these strange signs, they became alarmed, and went and called their companions from the boat to view them. But the others, when they had seen them, were also struck with fear, and all quickly retired from the place and went on board their curragh.

When they had got a little way from the land, they saw dimly, as it were through a mist, a vast multitude of people on the sea, of gigantic size and demoniac look, rushing along the crests of the waves with great outcry. As soon as this shadowy host had landed, they went to the green, where they arranged a horse-race.

The horses were swifter than the wind; and as they pressed forward in the race, the multitudes raised a mighty shout like thunder, which reached the crew as if it were beside them. Maildun and his men, as they sat in their curragh, heard the strokes of the whips and the cries of the riders; and though the race was far off, they could distinguish the eager words of the spectators:—"Observe the grey horse!" "See that chestnut horse!" "Watch the horse with the white spots!" "My horse leaps better than yours!"

After seeing and hearing these things, the crew sailed away from the island as quickly as they were able, into the open ocean, for they felt quite sure that the multitude they saw was a gathering of demons.

A spacious isle of meadowy plains, with a broad and sandy shore:
Two bold and trusty spies are sent, its wonders to explore.
Mysterious signs, strange, awful sights, now meet the wanderers' eyes:
Vast hoof-marks, and the traces dire of men of monstrous size:
And lo! on the sea, in countless hosts, their shadowy forms expand;
They pass the affrighted sailors by, and like demons they rush to land;
They mount their steeds, and the race is run, in the midst of hell's uproar:
Then the wanderers quickly raise their sails, and leave the accursed shore.

# CHAPTER VII

### THE PALACE OF SOLITUDE

THEY suffered much from hunger and thirst this time, for they
sailed a whole week without making land; but at the end of
that time they came in sight of a high island, with a large and
very splendid house on the beach near the water's edge. There
were two doors—one turned inland, and the other facing the
sea; and the door that looked towards the sea was closed with
a great flat stone. In this stone was an opening, through which
the waves, as they beat against the door every day, threw
numbers of salmon into the house.

The voyagers landed, and went through the whole house
without meeting any one. But they saw in one large room an
ornamented couch, intended for the head of the house, and in
each of the other rooms was a larger one for three members of
the family: and there was a cup of crystal on a little table
before each couch. They found abundance of food and ale,
and they ate and drank till they were satisfied, thanking God
for having relieved them from hunger and thirst.

Aloft, high towering o'er the ocean's foam,
The spacious mansion rears its glittering dome.
Each day the billows, through the marble door,
Shoot living salmon floundering on the floor.
Couches that lure the sailors to recline,
Abundant food, brown ale, and sparkling wine;
Tables and chairs in order duly placed,
With crystal cups and golden goblets graced.
But not a living soul the wanderers found;
'Twas silence all and solitude profound.
They eat and drink, give thanks, then hoist their sail,
And skim the deep once more, obedient to the gale.

## CHAPTER VIII

### THE ISLAND OF THE WONDERFUL APPLE TREE

AFTER leaving this, they suffered again from hunger, till they came to an island with a high hill round it on every side. A single apple tree grew in the middle, very tall and slender, and all its branches were in like manner exceedingly slender, and of wonderful length, so that they grew over the hill and down to the sea.

When the ship came near the island, Maildun caught one of the branches in his hand. For three days and three nights the ship coasted the island, and during all this time he held the branch, letting it slide through his hand, till on the third day he found a cluster of seven apples on the very end. Each of these apples supplied the travellers with food and drink for forty days and forty nights.

## CHAPTER IX

### THE ISLAND OF BLOODTHIRSTY QUADRUPEDS

A BEAUTIFUL island next came in view, in which they saw, at a distance, multitudes of large animals shaped like horses. The voyagers, as they drew near, viewed them attentively, and soon observed that one of them opened his mouth and bit a great piece out of the side of the animal that stood next to him, bringing away skin and flesh. Immediately after, another did the same to the nearest of his fellows. And, in short, the voyagers saw that all the animals in the island kept worrying and tearing each other from time to time in this manner; so that the ground was covered far and wide with the blood that streamed from their sides.

> In needless strife they oft contend,
> A cruel, mutual-mangling brood;
> Their flesh with gory tusks they rend,
> And crimson all the isle with blood.

## CHAPTER X

### AN EXTRAORDINARY MONSTER

THE next island had a wall all round it. When they came near the shore, an animal of vast size, with a thick, rough skin, started up inside the wall, and ran round the island with the swiftness of the wind. When he had ended his race, he went to a high point, and standing on a large, flat stone, began to exercise himself according to his daily custom, in the following manner. He kept turning himself completely round and round in his skin, the bones and flesh moving, while the skin remained at rest.

When he was tired of this exercise, he rested a little; and he then began turning his skin continually round his body, down at one side and up at the other like a mill-wheel; but the bones and flesh did not move.

After spending some time at this sort of work, he started and ran round the island as at first, as if to refresh himself. He then went back to the same spot, and this time, while the skin that covered the lower part of his body remained without motion, he whirled the skin of the upper part round and round like the movement of a flat-lying millstone. And it was in this manner that he spent most of his time on the island.

Maildun and his people, after they had seen these strange doings, thought it better not to venture nearer. So they put out to sea in great haste. The monster, observing them about to fly, ran down to the beach to seize the ship; but finding that they had got out of his reach, he began to fling round stones at them with great force and an excellent aim. One of them struck Maildun's shield and went quite through it, lodging in the keel of the curragh; after which the voyagers got beyond his range and sailed away.

> In a wall-circled isle a big monster they found,
>    With a hide like an elephant, leathery and bare;
> He threw up his heels with a wonderful bound,
> And ran round the isle with the speed of a hare.

But a feat more astounding has yet to be told:
    He turned round and round in his leathery skin;
His bones and his flesh and his sinews he rolled—
    He was resting outside while he twisted within!

Then, changing his practice with marvellous skill,
    His carcase stood rigid and round went his hide;
It whirled round his bones like the wheel of a mill—
    He was resting within while he twisted outside!

Next, standing quite near on a green little hill,
    After galloping round in the very same track,
While the skin of his belly stood perfectly still,
    Like a millstone he twisted the skin of his back!

But Maildun and his men put to sea in their boat,
    For they saw his two eyes looking over the wall;
And they knew by the way that he opened his throat,
    He intended to swallow them, curragh and all! *

# CHAPTER XI

### THE ISLE OF RED-HOT ANIMALS

Not daring to land on this island, they turned away hurriedly, much disheartened, not knowing whither to turn or where to find a resting-place. They sailed for a long time, suffering much from hunger and thirst, and praying fervently to be relieved from their distress. At last, when they were beginning to sink into a state of despondency, being quite worn out with toil and hardship of every kind, they sighted land.

It was a large and beautiful island, with innumerable fruit trees scattered over its surface, bearing abundance of gold-coloured apples. Under the trees they saw herds of short, stout animals, of a bright red colour, shaped somewhat like pigs; but

---

* The verse in the original is quite serious; but I could not resist the temptation to give it a humorous turn.

coming nearer, and looking more closely, they perceived with astonishment that the animals were all fiery, and that their bright colour was caused by the red flames which penetrated and lighted up their bodies.

The voyagers now observed several of them approach one of the trees in a body, and striking the trunk all together with their hind legs, they shook down some of the apples and ate them. In this manner the animals employed themselves every day, from early morning till the setting of the sun, when they retired into deep caves, and were seen no more till next morning.

Numerous flocks of birds were swimming on the sea, all round the island. From morning till noon, they continued to swim away from the land, farther and farther out to sea; but at noon they turned round, and from that to sunset they swam back towards the shore. A little after sunset, when the animals had retired to their caves, the birds flocked in on the island, and spread themselves over it, plucking the apples from the trees and eating them.

Maildun proposed that they should land on the island and gather some of the fruit, saying that it was not harder or more dangerous for them than for the birds; so two of the men were sent beforehand to examine the place. They found the ground hot under their feet, for the fiery animals, as they lay at rest, heated the earth all around and above their caves; but the two scouts persevered notwithstanding, and brought away some of the apples.

When morning dawned, the birds left the island and swam out to sea; and the fiery animals, coming forth from their caves, went among the trees as usual, and ate the apples till evening. The crew remained in their curragh all day; and as soon as the animals had gone into their caves for the night, and the birds had taken their place, Maildun landed with all his men. And they plucked the apples till morning, and brought them on board, till they had gathered as much as they could stow into their vessel.

## CHAPTER XII

### THE PALACE OF THE LITTLE CAT

AFTER rowing for a long time, their store of apples failed them, and they had nothing to eat or drink; so that they suffered sorely under a hot sun, and their mouths and nostrils were filled with the briny smell of the sea. At last they came in sight of land—a little island with a large palace on it. Around the palace was a wall, white all over, without stain or flaw, as if it had been built of burnt lime, or carved out of one unbroken rock of chalk; and where it looked towards the sea it was so lofty that it seemed almost to reach the clouds.

The gate of this outer wall was open, and a number of fine houses, all snowy white, were ranged round on the inside, enclosing a level court in the middle, on which all the houses opened. Maildun and his people entered the largest of them, and walked through several rooms without meeting with any one. But on reaching the principal apartment, they saw in it a small cat, playing among a number of low, square, marble pillars, which stood ranged in a row; and his play was leaping continually from the top of one pillar to the top of another. When the men entered the room, the cat looked at them for a moment, but returned to his play anon, and took no further notice of them.

Looking now to the room itself, they saw three rows of precious jewels ranged round the wall from one door-jamb to the other. The first was a row of brooches of gold and silver, with their pins fixed in the wall, and their heads outwards; the second, a row of torques of gold and silver; and the third, a row of great swords, with hilts of gold and silver.

Round the room were arranged a number of couches, all pure white and richly ornamented. Abundant food of various kinds was spread on tables, among which they observed a boiled ox and a roast hog; and there was many large drinking-horns, full of good, intoxicating ale.

" Is it for us that this food has been prepared? " said Maildun to the cat.

The cat, on hearing the question, ceased from playing, and looked at him; but he recommenced his play immediately. Whereupon Maildun told his people that the dinner was meant for them; and they all sat down, and ate and drank till they were satisfied, after which they rested and slept on the couches.

When they awoke, they poured what was left of the ale into one vessel; and they gathered the remnants of the food to bring them away. As they were about to go, Maildun's eldest foster-brother asked him—

" Shall I bring one of those large torques away with me? "

" By no means," said Maildun. " It is well that we have got food and rest. Bring nothing away, for it is certain that this house is not left without some one to guard it."

The young man, however, disregarding Maildun's advice, took down one of the torques and brought it away. But the cat followed him, and overtook him in the middle of the court, and, springing on him like a blazing, fiery arrow, went through his body and reduced it in a moment to a heap of ashes. He then returned to the room, and, leaping up on one of the pillars, sat upon it.

Maildun turned back, bringing the torque with him, and, approaching the cat, spoke some soothing words; after which he put the torque back to the place from which it had been taken. Having done this, he collected the ashes of his foster-brother, and, bringing them to the shore, cast them into the sea. They all then went on board the curragh, and continued their voyage, grieving for their lost companion, but thanking God for His many mercies to them.


## CHAPTER XIII

### AN ISLAND THAT DYED BLACK AND WHITE

ON the morning of the third day, they came to another island, which was divided into two parts by a wall of brass running across the middle. They saw two great flocks of sheep, one on each side of the wall; and all those at one side were black, while those at the other side were white.

A very large man was employed in dividing and arranging the sheep; and he often took up a sheep and threw it with much ease over the wall from one side to the other. When he threw over a white sheep among the black ones, it became black immediately; and in like manner, when he threw a black sheep over, it was instantly changed to white.

The travellers were very much alarmed on witnessing these doings; and Maildun said—

"It is very well that we know so far. Let us now throw something on shore, to see whether it also will change colour; if it does, we shall avoid the island."

So they took a branch with black-coloured bark and threw it towards the white sheep, and no sooner did it touch the ground than it became white. They then threw a white-coloured branch on the side of the black sheep, and in a moment it turned black.

"It is very lucky for us," said Maildun, "that we did not land on the island, for doubtless our colour would have changed like the colour of the branches."

So they put about with much fear, and sailed away.

# CHAPTER XIV

### THE ISLAND OF THE BURNING RIVER

ON the third day, they came in view of a large, broad island, on which they saw a herd of gracefully shaped swine; and they killed one small porkling for food. Towards the centre rose a high mountain, which they resolved to ascend, in order to view the island; and Germane and Diuran Lekerd were chosen for this task.

When they had advanced some distance towards the mountain, they came to a broad, shallow river; and sitting down on the bank to rest, Germane dipped the point of his lance into the water, which instantly burned off the top, as if the lance had been thrust into a furnace. So they went no farther.

On the opposite side of the river, they saw a herd of animals like great hornless oxen, all lying down; and a man of gigantic size near them: and Germane began to strike his spear against his shield, in order to rouse the cattle.

" Why are you frightening the poor young calves in that manner? " demanded the big shepherd, in a tremendous voice.

Germane, astonished to find that such large animals were nothing more than calves, instead of answering the question, asked the big man where the mothers of those calves were.

" They are on the side of yonder mountain," he replied.

Germane and Diuran waited to hear no more; but, returning to their companions, told them all they had seen and heard; after which the crew embarked and left the island.

## CHAPTER XV

### THE MILLER OF HELL

THE next island they came to, which was not far off from the last, had a large mill on it; and near the door stood the miller, a huge-bodied, strong, burly man. They saw numberless crowds of men and horses laden with corn, coming towards the mill; and when their corn was ground they went away towards the west. Great herds of all kinds of cattle covered the plain as far as the eye could reach, and among them many wagons laden with every kind of wealth that is produced on the ridge of the world. All these the miller put into the mouth of his mill to be ground; and all, as they came forth, went westwards.

Maildun and his people now spoke to the miller, and asked him the name of the mill, and the meaning of all they had seen on the island. And he, turning quickly towards them, replied in few words—

" This mill is called the Mill of Inver-tre-Kenand, and I am the miller of hell. All the corn and all the riches of the world that men are dissatisfied with, or which they complain of in any way, are sent here to be ground; and also every precious article, and every kind of wealth, which men try to conceal from God. All these I grind in the Mill of Inver-tre-Kenand, and send them afterwards away to the west."

He spoke no more, but turned round and busied himself again with his mill. And the voyagers, with much wonder and awe in their hearts, went to their curragh and sailed away.*

# CHAPTER XVI

### THE ISLE OF WEEPING

AFTER leaving this, they had not been long sailing when they discovered another large island, with a great multitude of people on it. They were all black, both skin and clothes, with black head-dresses also; and they kept walking about, sighing and weeping and wringing their hands, without the least pause or rest.

It fell to the lot of Maildun's second foster-brother to go and examine the island. And when he went among the people, he also grew sorrowful, and fell to weeping and wringing his hands, with the others. Two of the crew were sent to bring him back; but they were unable to find him among the mourners; and, what was worse, in a little time they joined the crowd, and began to weep and lament like all the rest.

Maildun then chose four men to go and bring back the others by force, and he put arms in their hands, and gave them these directions—

---

* The incident of the big miller occurs in the Voyage of the Sons of O'Corra, as well as in the Voyage of Maildun. The two accounts are somewhat different; and I have combined both here.

" When you land on the island, fold your mantles round your faces, so as to cover your mouths and noses, that you may not breathe the air of the country; and look neither to the right nor to the left, neither at the earth nor at the sky, but fix your eyes on your own men till you have laid hands on them."

They did exactly as they were told, and having come up with their two companions, namely, those who had been sent after Maildun's foster-brother, they seized them and brought them back by force. But the other they could not find. When these two were asked what they had seen on the island, and why they began to weep, their only reply was—

" We cannot tell; we only know that we did what we saw the others doing."

And after this the voyagers sailed away from the island leaving Maildun's second foster-brother behind.

## CHAPTER XVII

### THE ISLE OF THE FOUR PRECIOUS WALLS

THE next was a high island, divided into four parts by four walls meeting in the centre. The first was a wall of gold; the second, a wall of silver; the third, a wall of copper; and the fourth, a wall of crystal. In the first of the four divisions were kings; in the second, queens; in the third, youths; and in the fourth, young maidens.

When the voyagers landed, one of the maidens came to meet them, and leading them forward to a house, gave them food. This food, which she dealt out to them from a small vessel, looked like cheese, and whatever taste pleased each person best, that was the taste he found on it. And after they had eaten till they were satisfied, they slept in a sweet sleep, as if gently intoxicated, for three days and three nights. When they awoke on the third day, they found themselves in their curragh on the open sea; and there was no appearance in any direction either of the maiden or of the island.

## CHAPTER XVIII

### THE PALACE OF THE CRYSTAL BRIDGE

THEY came now to a small island, with a palace on it, having a copper chain in front, hung all over with a number of little silver bells. Straight before the door there was a fountain, spanned by a bridge of crystal, which led to the palace. They walked towards the bridge, meaning to cross it, but every time they stepped on it they fell backwards flat on the ground.

After some time, they saw a very beautiful young woman coming out of the palace, with a pail in her hand; and she lifted a crystal slab from the bridge, and, having filled her vessel from the fountain, she went back into the palace.

"This woman has been sent to keep house for Maildun," said Germane.

"Maildun indeed!" said she, as she shut the door after her.

After this they began to shake the copper chain, and the tinkling of the silver bells was so soft and melodious that the voyagers gradually fell into a gentle, tranquil sleep, and slept so till next morning. When they awoke, they saw the same young woman coming forth from the palace, with the pail in her hand; and she lifted the crystal slab as before, filled her vessel, and returned into the palace.

"This woman has certainly been sent to keep house for Maildun," said Germane.

"Wonderful are the powers of Maildun!" said she, as she shut the door of the court behind her.

They stayed in this place for three days and three nights, and each morning the maiden came forth in the same manner, and filled her pail. On the fourth day, she came towards them, splendidly and beautifully dressed, with her bright yellow hair bound by a circlet of gold, and wearing silver-work shoes on her small, white feet. She had a white mantle over her shoulders, which was fastened in front by a silver brooch studded with gold; and under all, next her soft, snow-white skin, was a garment of fine white silk.

"My love to you, Maildun, and to your companions," she said; and she mentioned them all, one after another, calling each by his own proper name. "My love to you," said she. "We knew well that you were coming to our island, for your arrival has long been foretold to us."

Then she led them to a large house standing by the sea, and she caused the curragh to be drawn high up on the beach. They found in the house a number of couches, one of which was intended for Maildun alone, and each of the others for three of his people. The woman then gave them, from one vessel, food which was like cheese; first of all ministering to Maildun, and then giving a triple share to every three of his companions; and whatever taste each man wished for, that was the taste he found on it. She then lifted the crystal slab at the bridge, filled her pail, and dealt out drink to them; and she knew exactly how much to give, both of food and of drink, so that each had enough and no more.

"This woman would make a fit wife for Maildun," said his people. But while they spoke, she went from them with her pail in her hand.

When she was gone, Maildun's companions said to him, "Shall we ask this maiden to become thy wife?"

He answered, "What advantage will it be to you to ask her?"

She came next morning, and they said to her, "Why dost thou not stay here with us? Wilt thou make friendship with Maildun; and wilt thou take him for thy husband?"

She replied that she and all those that lived on the island were forbidden to marry with the sons of men; and she told them that she could not disobey, as she knew not what sin or transgression was.

She then went from them to her house; and on the next morning, when she returned, and after she had ministered to them as usual, till they were satisfied with food and drink, and were become cheerful, they spoke the same words to her.

"To-morrow," she replied, "you will get an answer to your question"; and so saying, she walked towards her house, and they went to sleep on their couches.

When they awoke next morning, they found themselves lying in their curragh on the sea, beside a great high rock; and when they looked about, they saw neither the woman, nor the palace of the crystal bridge, nor any trace of the island where they had been sojourning.

## CHAPTER XIX

### THE ISLE OF SPEAKING BIRDS

ONE night, soon after leaving this, they heard in the distance, towards the north-east, a confused murmur of voices, as if from a great number of persons singing psalms. They followed the direction of the sound, in order to learn from what it proceeded; and at noon the next day, they came in view of an island, very hilly and lofty. It was full of birds, some black, some brown, and some speckled, who were all shouting and speaking with human voices; and it was from them that the great clamour came.

## CHAPTER XX

### THE AGED HERMIT, AND THE HUMAN SOULS

AT a little distance from this they found another small island, with many trees on it, some standing singly, and some in clusters, on which were perched great numbers of birds. They also saw an aged man on the island, who was covered thickly all over with long, white hair, and wore no other dress. And when they landed, they spoke to him, and asked him who he was and what race he belonged to.

" I am one of the men of Erin," he replied. " On a certain day, a long, long time ago, I embarked in a small curragh, and put out to sea on a pilgrimage; but I had got only a little way from shore, when my curragh became very unsteady, as if it were about to overturn. So I returned to land, and, in order to steady my boat, I placed under my feet at the bottom, a number of green surface sods, cut from one of the grassy fields of my own country, and began my voyage anew. Under the guidance of God, I arrived at this spot; and He fixed the sods in the sea for me, so that they formed a little island. At first I had barely room to stand; but every year, from that time to the present, the Lord has added one foot to the length and breadth of my island, till in the long lapse of ages it has grown to its present size. And on one day in each year, He has caused a single tree to spring up, till the island has become covered with trees. Moreover, I am so old that my body, as you see, has become covered with long, white hair, so that I need no other dress.

"And the birds that ye see on the trees," he continued, "these are the souls of my children, and of all my descendants, both men and women, who are sent to this little island to abide with me according as they die in Erin. God has caused a well of ale to spring up for us on the island; and every morning the angels bring me half a cake, a slice of fish, and a cup of ale from the well; and in the evening the same allowance of food and ale is dealt out to each man and woman of my people. And it is in this manner that we live, and shall continue to live till the end of the world; for we are all awaiting here the day of judgment."

Maildun and his companions were treated hospitably on the island by the old pilgrim for three days and three nights; and when they were taking leave of him, he told them that they should all reach their own country except one man.

## CHAPTER XXI

### THE ISLAND OF THE BIG BLACKSMITHS

WHEN they had been for a long time tossed about on the waters, they saw land in the distance. On approaching the shore, they heard the roaring of a great bellows, and the thundering sound of smiths' hammers striking a large glowing mass of iron on an anvil; and every blow seemed to Maildun as loud as if a dozen men had brought down their sledges all together.

When they had come a little nearer, they heard the big voices of the smiths in eager talk.

" Are they near? " asked one.

" Hush! silence! " says another.

" Who are they that you say are coming? " inquired a third.

" Little fellows, that are rowing towards our shore in a pigmy boat," says the first.

When Maildun heard this, he hastily addressed the crew—

" Put back at once, but do not turn the curragh: reverse the sweep of your oars, and let her move stern forward, so that those giants may not perceive that we are flying! "

The crew at once obey, and the boat begins to move away from the shore, stern forward, as he had commanded.

The first smith again spoke. " Are they near enough to the shore? " said he to the man who was watching.

" They seem to be at rest," answered the other, " for I cannot perceive that they are coming closer, and they have not turned their little boat to go back."

In a short time the first smith asks again, " What are they doing now? "

" I think," said the watcher, " they are flying; for it seems to me that they are now farther off than they were a while ago."

At this the first smith rushed out of the forge—a huge burly giant—holding, in the tongs which he grasped in his right hand, a vast mass of iron sparkling and glowing from the furnace; and, running down to the shore with long, heavy strides, he flung the red-hot mass with all his might after the curragh. It fell a little short, and plunged down just near the prow, causing the whole sea to hiss and boil and heave up around the boat. But they plied their oars, so that they quickly got beyond his reach, and sailed out into the open ocean.

## CHAPTER XXII

### THE CRYSTAL SEA

AFTER a time, they came to a sea like green crystal. It was so calm and transparent that they could see the sand at the bottom quite clearly, sparkling in the sunlight. And in this sea they saw neither monsters, nor ugly animals, nor rough rocks; nothing but the clear water and the sunshine and the bright sand. For a whole day they sailed over it, admiring its splendour and beauty.

# CHAPTER XXIII

## A LOVELY COUNTRY BENEATH THE WAVES

AFTER leaving this they entered on another sea, which seemed like a clear, thin cloud; and it was so transparent, and appeared so light, that they thought at first it would not bear up the weight of the curragh.

Looking down, they could see, beneath the clear water, a beautiful country, with many mansions surrounded by groves and woods. In one place was a single tree; and, standing on its branches, they saw an animal fierce and terrible to look upon.

Round about the tree was a great herd of oxen grazing, and a man stood near to guard them, armed with shield and spear and sword; but when he looked up and saw the animal on the tree, he turned anon and fled with the utmost speed. Then the monster stretched forth his neck, and, darting his head downward, plunged his fangs into the back of the largest ox of the whole herd, lifted him off the ground into the tree, and swallowed him down in the twinkling of an eye; whereupon the whole herd took to flight.

When Maildun and his people saw this, they were seized with great terror; for they feared they should not be able to cross the sea over the monster, on account of the extreme mist-like thinness of the water; but after much difficulty and danger they got across it safely.

# CHAPTER XXIV

## AN ISLAND GUARDED BY A WALL OF WATER

WHEN they came to the next island, they observed with astonishment that the sea rose up over it on every side, steep and high, standing, as it were, like a wall all round it. When the people of the island saw the voyagers, they rushed hither and thither, shouting: "There they are, surely! There they come again for another spoil! "

Then Maildun's people saw great numbers of men and women, all shouting and driving vast herds of horses, cows, and sheep. A woman began to pelt the crew from below with large nuts; she flung them so that they alighted on the waves round the boat, where they remained floating; and the crew gathered great quantities of them and kept them for eating.

When they turned to go away, the shouting ceased: and they heard one man calling aloud, " Where are they now? " and another answering him, " They are gone away! "

From what Maildun saw and heard at this island, it is likely that it had been foretold to the people that their country should some day be spoiled by certain marauders; and that they thought Maildun and his men were the enemies they expected.

# CHAPTER XXV

### A WATER-ARCH IN THE AIR

ON the next island they saw a very wonderful thing, namely, a great stream of water which, gushing up out of the strand, rose into the air in the form of a rainbow, till it crossed the whole island and came down on the strand at the other side. They walked under it without getting wet; and they hooked down from it many large salmon. Great quantities of salmon of a very great size fell also out of the water over their heads down on the ground; so that the whole island smelled of fish, and it became troublesome to gather them on account of their abundance.

From the evening of Sunday till the evening of Monday, the stream never ceased to flow, and never changed its place, but remained spanning the island like a solid arch of water. Then the voyagers gathered the largest of the salmon, till they had as much as the curragh would hold; after which they sailed out into the great sea.

## CHAPTER XXVI

### THE SILVER PILLAR OF THE SEA

THE next thing they found after this was an immense silver pillar standing in the sea. It had eight sides, each of which was the width of an oar-stroke of the curragh, so that its whole circumference was eight oar-strokes. It rose out of the sea without any land or earth about it, nothing but the boundless ocean; and they could not see its base deep down in the water, neither were they able to see the top on account of its vast height.

A silver net hung from the top down to the very water, extending far out at one side of the pillar; and the meshes were so large that the curragh in full sail went through one of them. When they were passing through it, Diuran struck the mesh with the edge of his spear, and with the blow cut a large piece off it.

" Do not destroy the net," said Maildun, " for what we see is the work of great men."

" What I have done," answered Diuran, " is for the honour of my God, and in order that the story of our adventures may be more readily believed; and I shall lay this silver as an offering on the altar of Armagh, if I ever reach Erin."

That piece of silver weighed two ounces and a half, as it was reckoned afterwards by the people of the church of Armagh.

After this they heard some one speaking on the top of the pillar, in a loud, clear, glad voice; but they knew neither what he said, nor in what language he spoke.

## CHAPTER XXVII

### AN ISLAND STANDING ON ONE PILLAR

THE island they saw after this was named Encos*; and it was so called because it was supported by a single pillar in the middle. They rowed all round it, seeking how they might get into it; but could find no landing-place. At the foot of the

---

* Encos means " one foot."

pillar, however, down deep in the water, they saw a door securely closed and locked, and they judged that this was the way into the island. They called aloud, to find out if any persons were living there; but they got no reply. So they left it, and put out to sea once more.

## CHAPTER XXVIII

### THE ISLAND QUEEN DETAINS THEM WITH HER MAGIC THREAD-CLEW

THE next island they reached was very large. On one side rose a lofty, smooth, heath-clad mountain, and all the rest of the island was a grassy plain. Near the sea-shore stood a great high palace, adorned with carvings and precious stones, and strongly fortified with a high rampart all round. After landing, they went towards the palace, and sat to rest on the bench before the gateway leading through the outer rampart; and, looking in through the open door, they saw a number of beautiful young maidens in the court.

After they had sat for some time, a rider appeared at a distance, coming swiftly towards the palace; and on a near approach, the travellers perceived that it was a lady, young and beautiful and richly dressed. She wore a blue, rustling silk head-dress; a silver-fringed purple cloak hung from her shoulders; her gloves were embroidered with gold-thread; and her feet were laced becomingly in close-fitting scarlet sandals. One of the maidens came out and held her horse, while she dismounted and entered the palace; and soon after she had gone in, another of the maidens came towards Maildun and his companions and said—

"You are welcome to this island. Come into the palace; the queen has sent me to invite you, and is waiting to receive you."

They followed the maiden into the palace; and the queen bade them welcome, and received them kindly. Then, leading them into a large hall in which a plentiful dinner was laid out, she bade them sit down and eat. A dish of choice food and a crystal goblet of wine were placed before Maildun; while a single dish and a single drinking-bowl, with a triple quantity of meat and drink, were laid before each three of his companions. And having eaten and drunk till they were satisfied, they went to sleep on soft couches till morning.

Next day, the queen addressed Maildun and his companions—

"Stay now in this country, and do not go a-wandering any longer over the wide ocean from island to island. Old age or sickness shall never come upon you; but you shall be always as young as you are at present, and you shall live for ever a life of ease and pleasure."

"Tell us," said Maildun, "how you pass your life here."

"That is no hard matter," answered the queen. "The good king who formerly ruled over this island was my husband, and these fair young maidens that you see are our children. He died after a long reign, and as he left no son, I now reign, the sole ruler of the island. And every day I go to the Great Plain, to administer justice and to decide causes among my people."

"Wilt thou go from us to-day?" asked Maildun.

"I must needs go even now," she replied, "to give judgments among the people; but as to you, you will all stay in this house till I return in the evening, and you need not trouble yourselves with any labour or care."

They remained in that island during the three months of winter. And these three months appeared to Maildun's companions as long as three years, for they began to have an earnest desire to return to their native land. At the end of that time, one of them said to Maildun—

"We have been a long time here. Why do we not return to our own country?"

"What you say is neither good nor sensible," answered Maildun, "for we shall not find in our own country anything better than we have here."

But this did not satisfy his companions, and they began to murmur loudly. "It is quite clear," said they, "that Maildun loves the queen of this island; and as this is so, let him stay here; but as for us, we will return to our own country."

Maildun, however, would not consent to remain after them, and he told them that he would go away with them.

Now, on a certain day, not long after this conversation, as soon as the queen had gone to the Great Plain to administer justice, according to her daily custom, they got their curragh ready and put out to sea. They had not gone very far from land when the queen came riding towards the shore; and, seeing how matters stood, she went into the palace and soon returned with a ball of thread in her hand.

Walking down to the water's edge, she flung the ball after the curragh, but held the end of the thread in her hand. Maildun caught the ball as it was passing, and it clung to his hand; and the queen, gently pulling the thread towards her, drew back the curragh to the very spot from which they had started in the little harbour. And when they had landed, she made them promise that if ever this happened again, some one should always stand up in the boat and catch the ball.

The voyagers abode on the island, much against their will, for nine months longer. For every time they attempted to escape, the queen brought them back by means of the clew, as she had done at first, Maildun always catching the ball.

At the end of the nine months, the men held council, and this is what they said—

"We know now that Maildun does not wish to leave the island; for he loves this queen very much, and he catches the ball whenever we try to escape, in order that we may be brought back to the palace."

Maildun replied: "Let some one else attend to the ball next time, and let us try whether it will cling to his hand."

They agreed to this, and, watching their opportunity, they again put off towards the open sea. The queen arrived, as usual, before they had gone very far and flung the ball after them as before. Another man of the crew caught it, and it clung as firmly to his hand as to Maildun's; and the queen began to draw the curragh towards the shore. But Diuran, drawing his sword, cut off the man's hand, which fell with the ball into the sea; and the men gladly plying their oars, the curragh resumed her outward voyage.

When the queen saw this, she began to weep and lament, wringing her hands and tearing her hair with grief; and her maidens also began to weep and cry aloud and clap their hands, so that the whole palace was full of grief and lamentation. But none the less did the men bend to their oars, and the curragh sailed away; and it was in this manner that the voyagers made their escape from the island.

# CHAPTER XXIX

### THE ISLE OF INTOXICATING WINE-FRUITS

THEY were now a long time tossed about on the great billows, when at length they came in view of an island with many trees on it. These trees were somewhat like hazels, and they were laden with a kind of fruit which the voyagers had not seen before, extremely large, and not very different in appearance from apples, except that they had a rough, berry-like rind.

After the crew had plucked all the fruit off one small tree, they cast lots who should try them, and the lot fell on Maildun. So he took some of them, and, squeezing the juice into a vessel, drank it. It threw him into a sleep of intoxication so deep that he seemed to be in a trance rather than in a natural slumber, without breath or motion, and with the red foam on his lips. And from that hour till the same hour next day, no one could tell whether he was living or dead.

When he awoke next day, he bade his people to gather as much of the fruit as they could bring away with them; for the world, as he told them, never produced anything of such surpassing goodness. They pressed out the juice of the fruit till they had filled all their vessels; and so powerful was it to produce intoxication and sleep, that, before drinking it, they had to mix a large quantity of water with it to moderate its strength.

## CHAPTER XXX

### THE ISLE OF THE MYSTIC LAKE

THE island they came to next was larger than most of those they had seen. On one side grew a wood of yew trees and great oaks; and on the other side was a grassy plain, with one small lake in the midst. A noble-looking house stood on the near part of the plain, with a small church not far off; and numerous flocks of sheep browsed over the whole island.

The travellers went to the church, and found in it a hermit, with snow-white beard and hair, and all the other marks of great old age. Maildun asked who he was, and whence he had come.

He replied: "I am one of the fifteen people, who, following the example of our master, Brendan of Birra,[20] sailed on a pilgrimage out into the great ocean. After many wanderings, we settled on this island, where we lived for a long time; but my companions died one after another, and of all who came hither, I alone am left."

The old pilgrim then showed them Brendan's satchel,[21] which he and his companions had brought with them on their pilgrimage; and Maildun kissed it, and all bowed down in veneration before it. And he told them that as long as they remained there, they might eat of the sheep and of the other food of the island; but to waste nothing.

One day, as they were seated on a hill, gazing out over the sea, they saw what they took to be a black cloud coming towards them from the south-west. They continued to view it very closely as it came nearer and nearer; and at last they perceived with amazement that it was an immense bird, for they saw quite plainly the slow, heavy flapping of his wings. When he reached the island, he alighted on a little hillock over the lake; and they felt no small alarm, for they thought, on account of his vast size, that if he saw them, he might seize them in his talons, and carry them off over the sea. So they hid themselves under trees and in the crannies of rocks; but they never lost sight of the bird, for they were bent on watching his movements.

He appeared very old, and he held in one claw a branch of a tree, which he had brought with him over the sea, larger and heavier than the largest full-grown oak. It was covered with fresh, green leaves, and was heavily laden with clusters of fruit, red and rich-looking like grapes, but much larger.

He remained resting for a time on the hill, being much wearied after his flight, and at last he began to eat the fruit off the branch. After watching him for some time longer, Maildun ventured warily towards the hillock, to see whether he was inclined to mischief; but the bird showed no disposition to harm him. This emboldened the others, and they all followed their chief.

The whole crew now marched in a body round the bird, headed by Maildun, with their shields raised; and as he still made no stir, one of the men, by Maildun's directions, went straight in front of him, and brought away some of the fruit from the branch which he still held in his talons. But the bird went on plucking and eating his fruit, and never took the least notice.

On the evening of that same day, as the men sat looking over the sea to the south-west, where the great bird first appeared to them, they saw in the distance two others, quite as large, coming slowly towards them from the very same point. On they came, flying at a vast height, nearer and nearer, till at last they swooped down and alighted on the hillock in front of the first bird, one on each side.

Although they were plainly much younger than the other, they seemed very tired, and took a long rest. Then, shaking their wings, they began picking the old bird all over, body, wings and head, plucking out the old feathers and the decayed quill points, and smoothing down his plumage with their great beaks. After this had gone on for some time, the three began plucking the fruit off the branch, and they ate till they were satisfied.

Next morning, the two birds began at the very same work, picking and arranging the feathers of the old bird as before; and at midday they ceased, and began again to eat the fruit, throwing the stones and what they did not eat of the pulp into the lake, till the water became red like wine. After this the old bird plunged into the lake and remained in it, washing himself, till evening, when he again flew up on the hillock, but perched on a different part of it, to avoid touching and defiling himself with the old feathers and the other traces of age and decay, which the younger birds had removed from him.

On the morning of the third day, the two younger birds set about arranging his feathers for the third time; and on this occasion they applied themselves to their task in a manner much more careful and particular than before, smoothing the plumes with the nicest touches, and arranging them in beautiful lines and glossy tufts and ridges. And so they continued without the least pause till midday, when they ceased. Then, after resting for a little while, they opened their great wings, rose into the air, and flew away swiftly towards the south-west, till the men lost sight of them in the distance.

Meantime the old bird, after the others had left, continued, to smooth and plume his feathers till evening; then, shaking his wings, he rose up, and flew three times round the island, as if to try his strength. And now the men observed that he had lost all the appearances of old age: his feathers were thick and glossy, his head was erect and his eye bright, and he flew with quite as much power and swiftness as the others. Alighting for the last time on the hillock, after resting a little, he rose again, and turning his flight after the other two, to the point from which he had come, he was soon lost to view, and the voyagers saw no more of him.

It now appeared very clear to Maildun and his companions that this bird had undergone a renewal of youth from old age, according to the word of the prophet, which says, " Thy youth shall be renewed as the eagle." Diuran, seeing this great wonder, said to his companions—

" Let us also bathe in the lake, and we shall obtain a renewal of youth like the bird."

But they said, " Not so, for the bird has left the poison of his old age and decay in the water."

Diuran, however, would have his own way; and he told them he was resolved to try the virtue of the water, and that they might follow his example or not, whichever they pleased. So he plunged in and swam about for some time, after which he took a little of the water and mixed it in his mouth; and in the end he swallowed a small quantity. He then came out perfectly sound and whole; and he remained so ever after, for as long as he lived he never lost a tooth or had a grey hair, and he suffered not from disease or bodily weakness of any kind. But none of the others ventured in.

The voyagers, having remained long enough on this island, stored in their curragh a large quantity of the flesh of the sheep; and after bidding farewell to the ancient cleric, they sought the ocean once more.

> Now once again, when winds and tide combine,
> The flying curragh cleaves the crested brine.
> Far to the west an island rose to view,
> With verdant plains, clear streams, and mountains blue.
> An aged hermit, bred in Erin's land,
> Welcomed and blessed the chieftain and his band;
> Brought food and drink, and bade them rest awhile,
> And view the wonders of that lovely isle.
>   Lo, from the sea, three birds of monstrous size,
> With vast wings slowly moving, cleave the skies;
> And as they nearer drew, the sailors saw
> One held a fruit branch firmly in his claw.
> Down by the clear, mysterious lake they light,
> Eat from the branch, and rest them from their flight.
>   The aged bird, with plumes decayed and thin,
> Paused on the brink awhile, then, plunging in,
> He bath'd and smooth'd his feathers o'er and o'er,
> Shook his great wings and rested on the shore.
>   Now while the other two his plumes arrange,
> Through all his frame appears a wondrous change:
> His eyes grow bright, his head erect and bold,
> His glossy plumage shines like burnished gold;
> Free from old age, his glorious form expands;
> In radiant youth and beauty proud he stands!
>   Such was the gift that lake of wonder gave;
> Such was the virtue of its mystic wave.

# CHAPTER XXXI

## THE ISLE OF LAUGHING

THEY next came to an island with a great plain extending over its whole surface. They saw a vast multitude of people on it, engaged in sundry youthful games, and all continually laughing. The voyagers cast lots who should go to examine the island; and the lot fell upon Maildun's third foster-brother.

The moment he landed he went among the others and joined in their pastimes and in their laughter, as if he had been among them all his life. His companions waited for him a very long time, but were afraid to venture to land after him; and at last, as there seemed no chance of his returning, they left him and sailed away.

## CHAPTER XXXII

### THE ISLE OF THE BLEST

THEY came now to a small island with a high rampart of fire all round it; and that rampart revolved continually round the island. There was one large open door in the rampart; and whenever the door, in its revolution, came in front of them, they could see almost the whole island through it, and all that was therein.

And this is what they saw: A great number of people, beautiful and glorious-looking, wearing rich garments adorned and radiant all over, feasting joyously, and drinking from embossed vessels of red gold which they held in their hands. The voyagers heard also their cheerful, festive songs; and they marvelled greatly, and their hearts were full of gladness at all the happiness they saw and heard. But they did not venture to land.

## CHAPTER XXXIII

### THE HERMIT OF THE SEA-ROCK

A LITTLE time after leaving this, they saw something a long way off towards the south, which at first they took to be a large white bird floating on the sea, and rising and falling with the waves; but on turning their curragh towards it for a nearer view, they found that it was a man. He was very old, so old that he was covered all over with long, white hair, which grew from his body; and he was standing on a broad, bare rock, and kept continually throwing himself on his knees, and never ceased praying.

When they saw that he was a holy man, they asked and received his blessing; after which they began to converse with him; and they inquired who he was, and how he had come to that rock. Then the old man gave them the following account:—

" I was born and bred in the island of Tory.* When I grew up to be a man, I was cook to the brotherhood of the monastery; and a wicked cook I was; for every day I sold part of the food entrusted to me, and secretly bought many choice and rare things with the money. Worse even than this I did; I made secret passages underground into the church and into the houses belonging to it, and I stole from time to time great quantities of golden vestments, book-covers adorned with brass and gold, and other holy and precious things.

" I soon became very rich, and had my rooms filled with costly couches, with clothes of every colour, both linen and woollen, with brazen pitchers and cauldrons, and with brooches and armlets of gold. Nothing was wanting in my house, of furniture and ornament, that a person in a high rank of life might be expected to have; and I became very proud and overbearing.

" One day, I was sent to dig a grave for the body of a rustic that had been brought from the mainland to be buried on the island. I went and fixed on a spot in the little graveyard; but as soon as I had set to work, I heard a voice speaking down deep in the earth beneath my feet—

" ' Do not dig this grave! '

" I paused for a moment, startled; but, recovering myself, I gave no further heed to the mysterious words, and again I began to dig. The moment I did so, I heard the same voice, even more plainly than before—

" ' Do not dig this grave! I am a devout and holy person, and my body is lean and light; do not put the heavy, pampered body of that sinner down upon me! '

" But I answered, in the excess of my pride and obstinacy: ' I will certainly dig this grave; and I will bury this body down on you! '

---

* Tory Island, off the coast of Donegal, where there was a monastery dedicated to St. Columcille.

" ' If you put that body down on me, the flesh will fall off your bones, and you will die, and be sent to the infernal pit at the end of three days; and, moreover, the body will not remain where you put it.'

" ' What will you give me,' I asked, ' if I do not bury the corpse on you? '

" ' Everlasting life in heaven,' replied the voice.

" ' How do you know this; and how am I to be sure of it? ' I inquired.

" And the voice answered me: ' The grave you are digging is clay. Observe now whether it will remain so, and then you will know the truth of what I tell you. And you will see that what I say will come to pass, and that you cannot bury that man on me, even if you should try to do so.'

" These words were scarce ended, when the grave was turned into a mass of white sand before my face. And when I saw this, I brought the body away, and buried it elsewhere.

" It happened, some time after, that I got a new curragh made, with the hides painted red all over; and I went to sea in it. As I sailed by the shores and islands, I was so pleased with the view of the land and sea from my curragh that I resolved to live altogether in it for some time; and I brought on board all my treasures—silver cups, gold bracelets, and ornamented drinking-horns, and everything else, from the largest to the smallest article.

" I enjoyed myself for a time, while the air was clear and the sea calm and smooth. But one day, the winds suddenly arose and a storm burst upon me, which carried me out to sea, so that I quite lost sight of land, and I knew not in what direction the curragh was drifting. After a time, the wind abated to a gentle gale, the sea became smooth, and the curragh sailed on as before, with a quiet, pleasant movement.

" But suddenly, though the breeze continued to blow, I thought I could perceive that the curragh ceased moving, and, standing up to find out the cause, I saw with great surprise an old man not far off, sitting on the crest of a wave.

" He spoke to me; and, as soon as I heard his voice, I knew it at once, but I could not at the moment call to mind where I had heard it before. And I became greatly troubled, and began to tremble, I knew not why.

" ' Whither art thou going? ' he asked.

" ' I know not,' I replied; ' but this I know, I am pleased with the smooth, gentle motion of my curragh over the waves.'

" ' You would not be pleased,' replied the old man, ' if you could see the troops that are at this moment around you.'

" ' What troops do you speak of? ' I asked.

" And he answered: ' All the space round about you, as far as your view reaches over the sea, and upwards to the clouds, is one great towering mass of demons, on account of your avarice, your thefts, your pride, and your other crimes and vices.'

" He then asked, ' Do you know why your curragh has stopped? '

" I answered, ' No '; and he said, ' It has been stopped by me; and it will never move from that spot till you promise me to do what I shall ask of you.'

" I replied that perhaps it was not in my power to grant his demand.

" ' It is in your power,' he answered. ' And if you refuse me, the torments of hell shall be your doom.'

" He then came close to the curragh, and, laying his hands on me, he made me swear to do what he demanded.

" ' What I ask is this,' said he; ' that you throw into the sea this moment all the ill-gotten treasures you have in the curragh.'

" This grieved me very much, and I replied, ' It is a pity that all these costly things should be lost.'

" To which he answered: ' They will not go to loss; a person will be sent to take charge of them. Now do as I say.'

" So, greatly against my wishes, I threw all the beautiful precious articles overboard, keeping only a small wooden cup to drink from.

" ' You will now continue your voyage,' he said, ' and the first solid ground your curragh reaches, there you are to stay.'

" He then gave me seven cakes and a cup of watery whey as food for my voyage; after which the curragh moved on, and I soon lost sight of him. And now I all at once recollected that the old man's voice was the same as the voice that I had heard come from the ground when I was about to dig the grave for the body of the rustic. I was so astonished and troubled at this discovery, and so disturbed at the loss of all my wealth, that I threw aside my oars, and gave myself up altogether to the winds and currents, not caring whither I went; and for a long time I was tossed about on the waves, I knew not in what direction.

" At last it seemed to me that my curragh ceased to move; but I was not sure about it, for I could see no sign of land. Mindful, however, of what the old man had told me, that I was to stay wherever my curragh stopped, I looked round more carefully; and at last I saw, very near me, a small rock level with the surface over which the waves were gently laughing and tumbling. I stepped on to the rock; and the moment I did so, the waves seemed to spring back, and the rock rose high over the level of the water; while the curragh drifted by and quickly disappeared, so that I never saw it after. This rock has been my abode from that time to the present day.

" For the first seven years, I lived on the seven cakes and the cup of whey given me by the man who had sent me to the rock. At the end of that time the cakes were all gone; and for three days I fasted, with nothing but the whey to wet my mouth. Late in the evening of the third day, an otter brought me a salmon out of the sea; but though I suffered much from hunger, I could not bring myself to eat the fish raw, and it was washed back again into the waves.

" I remained without food for three days longer; and in the afternoon of the third day, the otter returned with the salmon. And I saw another otter bring firewood; and when he had piled it up on the rock, he blew it with his breath till it took fire and lighted up. And then I broiled the salmon and ate till I had satisfied my hunger.

" The otter continued to bring me a salmon every day, and in this manner I lived for seven years longer. The rock also grew larger and larger daily, till it became the size you now see it. At the end of seven years, the otter ceased to bring me my salmon, and I fasted for three days. But at the end of the third day, I was sent half a cake of fine wheaten flour and a slice of fish; and on the same day my cup of watery whey fell into the sea, and a cup of the same size, filled with good ale, was placed on the rock for me.

"And so I have lived, praying and doing penance for my sins to this hour. Each day my drinking-vessel is filled with ale, and I am sent half a wheat-flour cake and a slice of fish; and neither rain nor wind, nor heat, nor cold, is allowed to molest me on this rock."

This was the end of the old man's history. In the evening of that day, each man of the crew received the same quantity of food that was sent to the old hermit himself, namely, half a cake and a slice of fish; and they found in the vessel as much good ale as served them all.

The next morning he said to them: "You shall all reach your own country in safety. And you, Maildun, you shall find in an island on your way, the very man that slew your father; but you are neither to kill him nor take revenge on him in any way. As God has delivered you from the many dangers you have passed through, though you were very guilty, and well deserved death at His hands; so you forgive your enemy the crime he committed against you."

After this they took leave of the old man and sailed away.

## THE OLD HERMIT'S STORY

The storms may roar and the seas may rage,
    But here, on this bare, brown rock,
I pray and repent and I tell my beads,
    Secure from the hurricane's shock.

For the good, kind God, in pity to me,
    Holds out His protecting hand;
And cold nor heat nor storm nor sleet,
    Can molest me where I stand.

I robbed the churches and wronged the poor,
    And grew richer day by day;
But now on this bare, brown ocean rock,
    A heavy penance I pay.

A bloated sinner died unshrived,
    And they brought his corse to me—
" Go, dig the grave and bury the dead,
    And pray for the soul set free."

I dug the grave, but my hands were stayed
    By a solemn and fearful sound,
For the feeble tones of a dead man's voice
    Came up from the hollow ground!

*The dead monk speaks up from the grave—*

> Place not that pampered corse on mine,
>     For my bones are weak and thin;
> I cannot bear the heavy weight
>     Of a body defiled by sin.
>
> I was a meek and holy man;
>     I fasted and watched and prayed;
> A sinner's corse would defile the clay
>     Where my wasted body is laid.

*The old hermit continues his story—*

> The voice then ceased, and I heard no more
>     Its hollow, beseeching tone;
> Then I closed the grave, and left the old monk
>     To rest in his coffin alone.
>
> My curragh sailed on the western main,
>     And I saw, as I viewed the sea,
> A withered old man upon a wave;
>     And he fixed his eyes on me.
>
> He spoke, and his voice my heart's blood froze,
>     And I shook with horror and fear:
> 'Twas the very voice of the dead old monk
>     That sounded in mine ear!

*The dead monk speaks again—*

> Far from my grave the sinner's corse
>     In unhallowed clay lies deep;
> And now in my coffin, undefiled,
>     For ever in peace I sleep.
>
> Go, live and pray on the bare, brown rock,
>     Far out in the stormy sea;
> A heavy penance for heavy crimes,
>     And heaven at last for thee!

*The old hermit ends his story—*

> And here I live from age to age;
>     I pray and repent and fast;
> An otter brings me food each day,
>     And I hope for heaven at last.
>
> The tempests roar and the billows rage,
>     But God holds forth His hand,
> And cold nor heat nor storm nor sleet,
>     Can harm me where I stand.

## CHAPTER XXXIV

### SIGNS OF HOME

SOON after they saw a beautiful verdant island, with herds of oxen, cows, and sheep browsing all over its hills and valleys; but no houses nor inhabitants were to be seen. And they rested for some time on this island, and ate the flesh of the cows and sheep.

One day, while they were standing on a hill, a large falcon flew by; and two of the crew, who happened to look closely at him, cried out, in the hearing of Maildun—

" See that falcon! He is surely like the falcons of Erin! "

" Watch him closely," cried Maildun, " and observe exactly in what direction he is flying! "

And they saw that he flew to the south-east, without turning or wavering.

They went on board at once; and, having unmoored, they sailed to the south-east after the falcon. After rowing the whole day, they sighted land in the dusk of the evening, which seemed to them like the land of Erin.

## CHAPTER XXXV

### MAILDUN MEETS HIS ENEMY, AND ARRIVES HOME

ON a near approach, they found it was a small island; and now they recognised it as the very same island they had seen in the beginning of their voyage, in which they had heard the man in the great house boast that he had slain Maildun's father, and from which the storm had driven them out into the great ocean.

They turned the prow of their vessel to the shore, landed, and went towards the house. It happened that at this very time the people of the house were seated at their evening meal; and Maildun and his companions, as they stood outside, heard a part of their conversation.

Said one to another, "It would not be well for us if we were now to see Maildun."

"As to Maildun," answered another, "it is very well known that he was drowned long ago in the great ocean."

"Do not be sure," observed a third; "perchance he is the very man that may waken you up some morning from your sleep."

"Supposing he came now," asks another, "what should we do?"

The head of the house now spoke in reply to the last question; and Maildun at once knew his voice.

"I can easily answer that," said he. "Maildun has been for a long time suffering great afflictions and hardships; and if he were to come now, though we were enemies once, I should certainly give him a welcome and a kind reception."

When Maildun heard this he knocked at the door, and the door-keeper asked who was there; to which Maildun made answer: "It is I, Maildun, returned from all my wanderings."

The chief of the house then ordered the door to be opened; and he went to meet Maildun, and brought himself and his companions into the house. They were joyfully welcomed by the whole household; new garments were given to them; and they feasted and rested, till they forgot their weariness and their hardships.

They related all the wonders God had revealed to them in the course of their voyage, according to the word of the sage who says, "It will be a source of pleasure to remember these things at a future time."

After they had remained here for some days, Maildun returned to his own country. And Diuran Lekerd took the five half-ounces of silver he had cut down from the great net at the Silver Pillar, and laid it, according to his promise, on the high altar of Armagh.

# The Fairy Palace
# of the Quicken Trees *

## CHAPTER I

### COLGA, KING OF LOCHLANN, INVADES ERIN, AND IS SLAIN

ONCE upon a time, a noble, warlike king ruled over Lochlann,[6] whose name was Colga of the Hard Weapons. On a certain occasion, this king held a meeting of his chief people, on the broad, green plain before his palace of Berva.[6] And when they were all gathered together, he spoke to them in a loud, clear voice, from where he sat high on his throne; and he asked them whether they found any fault with the manner in which he ruled them, and whether they knew of anything deserving of blame in him as their sovereign lord and king. They replied, as if with the voice of one man, that they found no fault of any kind.

Then the king spoke again and said, " You see not as I see. Do you not know that I am called King of the Four Tribes of Lochlann, and of the Islands of the Sea? And yet there is one island which acknowledges not my rule."

And when they had asked which of the islands he meant, he said—

" That island is Erin of the green hills. My forefathers, indeed, held sway over it, and many of our brave warriors died there in fight. There fell the great king, Balor of the Mighty Blows;[9] his son Bres[9] also; and his queen, Kethlenda of the Crooked Teeth;[9] there, too, fell Irann and Slana, sisters of the king; and many others that I do not name. But though our hosts at last subdued the land and laid it under tribute, yet they

---

\* The quicken tree, or quickbeam, or mountain ash, or roantree; Gaelic, *caorthainn*. Many mystic virtues were anciently attributed to this tree.

held it not long; for the men of Erin arose and expelled our
army, regaining their ancient freedom.

" And now it is my desire that we once more sail to Erin
with a fleet and an army, to bring it under my power, and take,
either by consent or by force, the tributes that are due to me
by right. And we shall thereafter hold the island in subjection
till the end of the world." The chiefs approved the counsel of
the king, and the meeting broke up.

Then the king made proclamation, and sent his swift scouts
and couriers all over the land, to muster his fighting men, till
he had assembled a mighty army in one place.

And when they had made ready their curve-sided, white-
sailed ships, and their strong, swift-gliding boats, the army
embarked. And they raised their sails and plied their oars; and
they cleft the billowy, briny sea; and the clear, cold winds
whistled through their sails; and they made neither stop nor
stay, till they landed on the shore of the province of Ulaidh.*

The King of Ireland at that time was Cormac Mac Airt,[22]
the grandson of Conn the Hundred-fighter.[18] And when Cormac
heard that a great fleet had come to Erin, and landed an army
of foreigners, he straightway sent tidings of the invasion to
Allen† of the green hill-slopes, where lived Finn,[23] and the noble
Fena[23] of the Gaels.

When the king's messengers had told their tale, Finn
despatched his trusty, swift-footed couriers to every part of Erin
where he knew the Fena dwelt; and he bade them to say that
all should meet him at a certain place, near that part of the
coast where the Lochlann army lay encamped. And he himself
led the Fena of Leinster northwards to join the muster.

They attacked the foreigners, and the foreigners were not
slow to meet their onset; and the Fena were sore pressed in
that battle, so that at one time the Lochlanns were like to prevail.

Oscar, the son of Oisin,[23] when he saw his friends falling all
round him, was grieved to the heart; and he rested for a space
to gather his wrath and his strength. Then, renewing the fight,
he rushed with fury towards the standard of Colga, the Lochlann
king, dealing havoc and slaughter among those foreigners that

---

* Ulaidh, *i.e.*, Ulster.
† The Hill of Allen, in the county Kildare, where Finn had his palace.

stood in his track. The king saw Oscar approach, and met him; and they fought a deadly battle hand-to-hand. Soon their shields were rent, their hard helmets were dinted with sword-blows, their armour was pierced in many places, and their flesh was torn with deep wounds. And the end of the fight was, that the king of the foreigners was slain by Oscar, the son of Oisin.

When the Lochlanns saw their king fall, they lost heart, and the battle went against them. But they fought on nevertheless, till evening, when their army entirely gave way, and fled from the field. And of all the nobles and princes and mighty chiefs who sailed to Erin on that expedition, not one was left alive, except the youngest son of the king, whose name was Midac. Him Finn spared on account of his youth; with intent to bring him up in his own household.

After the Fena had rested for a time, and buried their dead, they turned their faces southward, and marched slowly towards Allen, bringing their sick and wounded companions. And Finn placed Midac among the household of Allen, treating him honourably, and giving him servants and tutors. Moreover, he enlisted him in the Fena, and gave him a high post as befitted a prince.

## CHAPTER II

### MIDAC, THE SON OF COLGA, MEDITATES REVENGE

AFTER this things went on as before, while Midac grew up towards manhood, and hunted and feasted with the Fena, and fought with them when they fought. But he never lost an opportunity of making himself acquainted with all their haunts and hunting-grounds, their palaces and fortresses, and in particular with their manner of carrying on war.

It happened one day that Finn and some of his leading chiefs were in council, considering sundry matters, especially the state and condition of the Fena; and each chief was commanded by Finn to speak, and give his opinion or advice on anything that he deemed weighty enough to be debated by the meeting.

And after many had spoken, Conan Maol, the son of Morna, stood up and said:

"It seems to me, O king, that you and I and the Fena in general are now in great danger. For you have in your house, and mixing with your people, a young man who has good cause of enmity towards you; that is to say, Midac, the son of the king of Lochlann. For was it not by you that his father and brothers and many of his friends were slain? Now I notice that this young prince is silent and distant, and talks little to those around him. Moreover, I see that day after day he takes much pains to know all matters relating to the Fena; and as he has friends in Lochlann, mighty men with armies and ships, I fear me the day may come when this prince will use his knowledge to our destruction."

The king said that all this was quite true, and he asked Conan to give his opinion as to what should be done.

"What I advise in the matter is this," said Conan, "that Midac be not allowed to abide any longer in the palace of Allen. But as it is meet that he should be treated in a manner becoming a prince, let him be given a tract of land for himself in some other part of Erin, with a home and a household of his own. Then shall we be freed from his presence, and he can no longer listen to our counsels, and learn all our secrets and all our plans."

This speech seemed to Finn and the other chiefs reasonable and prudent, and they agreed to follow the advice of Conan Maol.

Accordingly Finn sent for the prince, and said to him:

"Thou knowest, Midac, that thou hast been brought up from boyhood in my household, and that thou hast been dealt with in every way as becomes a prince. Now thou art a man, and standest in no further need of instruction, for thou hast learned everything needful for a prince and for a champion of the Fena; and it is not meet that thou shouldst abide longer in the house of another. Choose, therefore, the two cantreds that please thee best in all Erin, and they shall be given to thee and to thy descendants for ever as a patrimony. There thou shalt build houses and a homestead for thyself, and I will help thee with men and with cattle and with all things else necessary."

Midac listened in silence; and when the king had done speaking, he replied in a cold and distant manner and in few words, that the proposal was reasonable and proper, and pleased him well. And thereupon he chose the rich cantred of Kenri on the Shannon, and the cantred of the Islands lying next to it on the north, at the other side of the river.

Now Midac had good reasons for choosing these two territories beyond all others in Erin. For the river opens out between them like a great sea, in which are many islands and sheltered harbours, where ships might anchor in safety; and he hoped to bring a fleet and an army into Erin some day, to avenge on Finn and the Fena the defeats they had inflicted on his countrymen, and above all, the death of his father and brothers. And being bent on treachery, he could not have chosen in all Erin a territory better suited for carrying out his secret designs.

So these two cantreds were bestowed on Midac. Finn gave him also much cattle and wealth of all kinds; so that when his houses were built, and when he was settled in his new territory, with his servants and his cattle and his wealth all round him, there was no brughaidh* in Erin richer or more prosperous than he.

For fourteen years Midac lived in his new home, growing richer every year. But the Fena knew nothing of his way of life, for he kept himself apart, and none of his old acquaintances visited him. And though he was enrolled in the ranks of the Fena, he never, during all that time, invited one of them to his house, or offered them food or drink or entertainment of any kind.

One day, Finn and the Fena went to hunt in the district of Fermorc,† and over the plains of Hy Conall Gavra.† And when all was arranged and the chase about to begin, Finn himself, and a few of his companions, went to the top of the hill of Knockfierna‡ to see the sport; while the main body of the Fena scattered themselves over the plain with their dogs and attendants, to start the deer and the wild boars and all the other game of the forest.

---

* Brughaidh, a sort of local officer, who was allowed a tract of land free, on condition that he maintained a large establishment as a house of public hospitality. Many of the brughaidhs were very rich.

† Fermorc and Hy Conall Gavra are now the baronies of Upper and Lower Connello, in the county Limerick.

‡ Knockfierna, a conspicuous hill, celebrated for its fairy lore, near Croom, in the county Limerick; very near Kenri, Midac's territory.

Then Finn's people pitched their tents, and made soft couches of rushes and heather, and dug cooking-places;[24] for they intended the hill to be the resting-place of all who chose to rest, till the chase was ended.

After Finn and his companions had sat for some time on the hill, they saw a tall warrior coming towards them, armed in full battle array. He wore a splendid coat of mail of Lochlann workmanship, and over it a mantle of fine satin dyed in divers colours. A broad shield hung on his left shoulder, and his helmet glittered in the morning sun like polished silver. At his left side hung a long sword, with golden hilt and enamelled sheath; and he held in his right hand his two long, polished, death-dealing spears. His figure and gait were wonderfully majestic, and as he came near, he saluted the king in stately and courteous words.

Finn returned the salutation, and spoke with him for a while; and at length he asked him whence he had come, and if he had brought any tidings.

"As to the place I came from," he answered, "that need not be spoken of; and for news, I have nothing to tell except that I am a ferdana,* and that I have come to thee, O king of the Fena, with a poem."

"Methinks, indeed," replied Finn, "that conflict and battle are the poetry you profess; for never have I seen a hero more noble in mien and feature."

"I am a ferdana nevertheless," answered the stranger, "and if thou dost not forbid me, I will prove it by reciting a poem I have brought for thee."

"A mountain-top is not the place for poetry," said Finn; "and moreover, there is now no opportunity either for reciting or listening. For I and these few companions of mine have come to sit here that we may view the chase, and listen to the eager shouts of the men, and the sweet cry of the hounds.

"But if you are, as you say," continued Finn, "a ferdana, remain here with us till the chase is ended; and then you shall come with me to one of our palaces, where I shall listen to your poem, and bestow on you such gifts as are meet for a poet of your rank."

---

* Ferdana, a poet.

But the strange champion answered: "It is not my wish to go to your palace; and I now put you under geasa,[12] which true heroes do not suffer, that you listen to my poem, and that you find out and explain its meaning."

"Well then," said Finn, "let there be no further delay; repeat your poem."

So the hero recited the following verse:—

> I saw a house by a river's shore,
> Famed through Erin in days of yore,
> Radiant with sparkling gems all o'er,
> Its lord deep skilled in magical lore;
> No conqueror ever defiled its floor;
> No spoiler can rive its golden store;
> Fire cannot burn its battlements hoar;
> Safe it stands when the torrents pour;
> Feasting and joy for evermore,
> To all who enter its open door!
> > Now if thou hast learned a champion's lore,
> > Tell me the name of that mansion hoar,
> > With roof of crystal and marble floor—
> > The mansion I saw by the river's shore.

"I can explain that poem," said Finn. "The mansion you saw is Brugh of the Boyne, the fairy palace of Angus, the Dedannan prince, son of the Dagda, which is open to all who wish to partake of its feasts and its enjoyments. It cannot be burned by fire, or drowned by water, or spoiled by robbers, on account of the great power of its lord and master; for there is not now, and there never was, and there never shall be, in Erin, a man more skilled in magic arts than Angus of the Brugh."

"That is the sense of my poem," said the stranger; "and now listen to this other, and explain it to me if thou canst."

> I saw to the south a bright-faced queen,
> With couch of crystal and robe of green;
> A numerous offspring, sprightly and small,
> Plain through her skin you can see them all;
> Slowly she moves, and yet her speed
> Exceeds the pace of the swiftest steed!
> > Now tell me the name of that wondrous queen,
> > With her couch of crystal and robe of green.*

---

\* The poets were much given to proposing poetical puzzles of this kind; and it was considered a mark of superior education, and of great acuteness in a champion to be able to explain them.

" I understand the sense of that poem also," said Finn. " The queen you saw is the river Boyne, which flows by the south side of the palace of Brugh. Her couch of crystal is the sandy bed of the river; and her robe of green the grassy plain of Bregia,* through which it flows. Her children, which you can see through her skin, are the speckled salmon, the lively, pretty trout, and all the other fish that swim in the clear water of the river. The river flows slowly indeed, but its waters traverse the whole world in seven years, which is more than the swiftest steed can do."

" These are my poems," said the champion; " and thou hast truly explained their meaning."

" And now," said Finn, " as I have listened to thy poetry and explained it, tell us, I pray thee, who thou art and whence thou hast come; for I marvel much that so noble a champion should live in any of the five provinces of Erin without being known to me and my companions."

Then Conan Maol spoke. " Thou art, O king, the wisest and most far-seeing of the Fena, and thou hast unravelled and explained the hard poetical puzzles of this champion. Yet, on the present occasion, thou knowest not a friend from a foe; for this man is Midac, whom thou didst bring up with much honour in thine own house, and afterwards made rich, but who is now thy bitter enemy, and the enemy of all the Fena. Here he has lived for fourteen years, without fellowship or communication with his former companions. And though he is enrolled in the order of the Fena, he has never, during all that time, invited thee to a banquet, or come to see any of his old friends, or given food or entertainment to any of the Fena, either master or man."

Midac answered, " If Finn and the Fena have not feasted with me, that is none of my fault; for my house has never been without a banquet fit for either king or chief; but you never came to partake of it. I did not, indeed, send you an invitation; but that you should not have waited for, seeing that I was one of the Fena, and that I was brought up in your own household. However, let that pass. I have now a feast ready, in all respects

---

* Bregia or Magh Breagh, the ancient name of the plain extending from the Liffey northwards to the borders of the county Louth.

worthy of a king; and I put you under geasa that you and the
chiefs that are here with you, come this night to partake of it.
I have two palaces, and in each there is a banquet. One is the
Palace of the Island, which stands on the sea; and the other
is the Palace of the Quicken Trees, which is a little way off
from this hill; and it is to this that I wish you to come."

Finn consented; and Midac, after he had pointed out the
way to the Palace of the Quicken Trees, left them, saying he
would go before, so that he might have things in readiness when
they should arrive.

## CHAPTER III

### FINN IS ENTRAPPED BY MIDAC, AND HELD BY ENCHANTMENT
### IN THE PALACE OF THE QUICKEN TREES

FINN now held council with his companions, and they agreed
that the king's son, Oisin, and five other chiefs, with their
followers, should tarry on the hill till the hunting party returned,
while Finn went to the palace with the rest.

And it was arranged that Finn should send back word
immediately to the party on the hill, how he fared; and that
Oisin and the others were to follow him to the palace when the
hunting party had returned.

Those that remained with Oisin were Dermat O'Dyna;
Fatha Conan, the son of the son of Conn; Kylta Mac Ronan;
Ficna, the son of Finn; and Innsa, the son of Swena Selga.

And of those who went with Finn to the Palace of the
Quicken Trees, the chief were Gall Mac Morna; Dathkeen the
Strong-limbed; Mac Lugha of the Red Hand; Glas Mac Encarda
from Beara; the two sons of Aedh the Lesser, son of Finn;
Racad and Dalgus, the two kings of Leinster; Angus Mac
Bresal Bola; and the two leaders of the Connacht Fena,
namely, Mac-na-Corra, and Corr the Swift-footed.

As Finn and his party came nigh to the palace, they were
amazed at its size and splendour; and they wondered greatly
that they had never seen it before. It stood on a level green,

which was surrounded by a light plantation of quicken trees, all covered with clusters of scarlet berries. At one side of the little plain, very near the palace, was a broad river, with a rocky bank at the near side, and a steep pathway leading down to a ford.

But what surprised them most was that all was lonely and silent—not a living soul could they see in any direction; and Finn, fearing some foul play, would have turned back, only that he bethought him of his geasa and his promise. The great door was wide open, and Conan went in before the others; and after viewing the banqueting hall, he came out quite enraptured with what he had seen. He praised the beauty and perfect arrange-ment of everything, and told his companions that no other king or chief in all Erin had a banqueting hall to match the hall of Midac, the son of Colga. They all now entered, but they found no one—neither host nor guests nor attendants.

As they gazed around, they thought they had never seen a banquet hall so splendid. A great fire burned brightly in the middle, without any smoke, and sent forth a sweet perfume, which filled the whole room with fragrance, and cheered and delighted the heroes. Couches were placed all round, with rich coverlets and rugs, and soft, glossy furs. The curved walls were of wood,* close-jointed and polished like ivory; and each board was painted differently from those above and below; so that the sides of the room, from floor to roof, were all radiant with a wonderful variety of colours.

Still seeing no one, they seated themselves on the couches and rugs. Presently a door opened, and Midac walked into the room. He stood for a few moments before the heroes, and looked at them one after another, but never spoke one word; then, turning round, he went out and shut the great door behind him.

Finn and his friends were much surprised at this; however, they said nothing, but remained resting as they were for some time, expecting Midac's return. Still no one came, and at length Finn spoke—

" We have been invited here, my friends, to a banquet; and it seems to me very strange that we should be left so long without attendance, and without either food or drink. Perhaps, indeed, Midac's attendants have made some mistake, and that

---

* The houses of the ancient Irish were circular, and generally made of wood.

the feast intended for this palace has been prepared in the Palace of the Island. But I wonder greatly that such a thing should have happened."

" I see something more wonderful than that," said Gall Mac Morna; " for lo, the fire, which was clear and smokeless when we first saw it, and which smelled more sweetly than the flowers of the plain, now fills the hall with a foul stench, and sends up a great cloud of black, sooty smoke! "

" I see something more wonderful than that," said Glas Mac Encarda; " for the boards in the walls of this banquet hall, which were smooth and close-jointed and glorious all over with bright colours when we came, are now nothing but rough planks, clumsily fastened together with tough quicken tree withes, and as rude and unshapen as if they had been hacked and hewed with a blunt axe! "

" I see something more wonderful than that," said Foilan, the son of Aedh the Lesser; "for this palace, which had seven great doors when we came in, all wide open, and looking pleasantly towards the sunshine, has now only one small, narrow door, close fastened, and facing straight to the north! "

" I see something more wonderful than that," said Conan Maol; "for the rich rugs and furs and the soft couches, which were under us when we sat here first, are all gone, not as much as a fragment or a thread remaining; and we are now sitting on the bare, damp earth, which feels as cold as the snow of one night! " *

Then Finn again spoke. " You know, my friends, that I never tarry in a house having only one door. Let one of you then, arise, and break open that narrow door, so that we may go forth from this foul, smoky den! "

" That shall be done," cried Conan; and, so saying, he seized his long spear, and, planting it on the floor, point downwards, he attempted to spring to his feet. But he found that he was not able to move, and turning to his companions, he cried out with a groan of anguish: " Alas, my friends! I

---

* " As cold as the snow of one night; " " As white as the snow of one night," are usual comparisons in Gaelic. The first night's snow seems particularly cold and white when you see it in the morning on account of the contrast with the green fields of the day before.

see now something more wonderful than all; for I am firmly
fixed by some druidical spell to the cold clay floor of the
Palace of the Quicken Trees! "

And immediately all the others found themselves, in like
manner, fixed where they sat. And they were silent for a time,
being quite confounded and overwhelmed with fear and anguish.

At length Gall spoke, and said, " It seems clear, O king,
that Midac has planned this treachery, and that danger lies
before us. I wish, then, that you would place your thumb
under your tooth of knowledge,[25] and let us know the truth;
so that we may at once consider as to the best means of
escaping from this strait."

Whereupon Finn placed his thumb under his tooth of
knowledge, and mused for a little while. Then suddenly with-
drawing his thumb, he sank back in his seat and groaned aloud.

" May it be the will of the gods," said Gall, " that it is the
pain of thy thumb that has caused thee to utter that groan! "

" Alas! not so," replied Finn. " I grieve that my death is
near, and the death of these dear companions! For fourteen
years has Midac, the son of the king of Lochlann, been plotting
against us; and now at last he has caught us in this treacherous
snare, from which I can see no escape.

" For in the Palace of the Island there is, at this moment,
an army of foreigners, whom Midac has brought hither for our
destruction. Chief over all is Sinsar of the Battles, from Greece,
the Monarch of the World, who has under his command sixteen
warlike princes, with many others of lesser note. Next to Sinsar
is his son, Borba the Haughty, who commands also a number
of fierce and hardy knights.

" There are, besides, the three kings of the Island of the
Torrent, large-bodied and bloodthirsty, like three furious dragons,
who have never yet yielded to an enemy on the field of battle.
It is these who, by their sorcery, have fixed us here; for this
cold clay that we sit on is part of the soil of the enchanted
Island of the Torrent, which they brought hither, and placed
here with foul spells. Moreover, the enchantment that binds us
to this floor can never be broken unless the blood of these kings
be sprinkled on the clay. And very soon some of Sinsar's
warriors will come over from the Palace of the Island, to slay

us all, while we are fixed here helpless, and unable to raise a hand in our own defence."

Full of alarm and anguish were the heroes when they heard these tidings. And some began to shed bitter tears in silence, and some lamented aloud. But Finn again spoke and said—

"It becomes us not, my friends, being heroes, to weep and wail like women, even though we are in danger of death; for tears and lamentations will avail us nothing. Let us rather sound the Dord-Fian,* sweetly and plaintively, according to our wont, that it may be a comfort to us before we die."

So they ceased weeping, and, joining all together, they sounded the Dord-Fian in a slow, sad strain.

## CHAPTER IV

### INNSA, FINN'S FOSTER-SON, DEFENDS THE FORD LEADING TO THE PALACE OF THE QUICKEN TREES

Now let us speak of Oisin, and the party who tarried with him on the hill of Knockfierna. When he found that his father Finn had not sent back a messenger as he had promised, though the night was now drawing nigh, he began to fear that something was wrong; and he said to his companions—

"I marvel much that we have got no news from the king of how he and his companions have fared in the Palace of the Quicken Trees. It is clear to me that he would have fulfilled his promise to send us word, if he had not been hindered by some unforeseen difficulty. Now, therefore, I wish to know who will go to the palace and bring me back tidings."

Ficna, the son of Finn, stood forth and offered to go; and Finn's foster-son, Innsa, the son of Swena Selga, said he would go with him.

They both set out at once, and as they travelled with speed, they soon reached the plain on which stood the Palace of the

---

* Dord-Fian, or Dord-Fiansa, a sort of musical war-cry, usually performed by several persons in chorus.

Quicken Trees; and now the night was darkening around them.
As they came near to the palace, they marvelled to hear the
loud, slow strains of the Dord-Fian; and Innsa exclaimed
joyfully—

"Things go well with our friends, seeing that they are
amusing themselves with the Dord-Fian!"

But Ficna, who guessed more truly how things really stood,
replied—

"It is my opinion, friend, that matters are not so pleasant
with them as you think; for it is only in time of trouble or
danger that Finn is wont to have the Dord-Fian sounded in a
manner so slow and sad."

While they talked in this wise, it chanced that the Dord-Fian
ceased for a little space; and Finn, hearing the low hum of
conversation outside, asked was that the voice of Ficna. And
when Ficna answered, "Yes", Finn said to him—

"Come not nearer, my son; for this place teems with
dangerous spells. We have been decoyed hither by Midac, and
we are all held here by the foul sorcery of the three kings of
the Island of the Torrent."

And thereupon Finn told him the whole story of the treachery
that had been wrought on them, from beginning to end; and
he told him also that nothing could free them but the blood of
those three kings sprinkled on the clay.

Then he asked who the second man was whom he had heard
conversing with Ficna; and when he was told that it was Innsa,
the son of Swena Selga, he addressed Ficna earnestly—

"Fly, my son, from this fatal place! Fly, and save my
foster-child from the treacherous swords of the foreigners; for
they are already on their way hither!"

But Innsa quickly answered, "That I will never do. It would,
indeed, be an ungrateful return to a kind foster-father, to leave
thee now in deadly strait, and seek my own safety."

And Ficna spoke in a like strain.

Then Finn said, "Be it so, my sons; but a sore trial awaits
you. Those who come hither from the Palace of the Island must
needs pass the ford under the shadow of these walls. Now this
ford is rugged and hard to be crossed; and one good man,
standing in the steep, narrow entrance at the hither side, might

dispute the passage for a time against many. Go now, and defend this ford; and haply some help may come in time."

So both went to the ford. And when they had viewed it carefully, Ficna, seeing that one man might defend it for a short time almost as well as two, said to Innsa—

" Stay thou here to guard the ford for a little time, while I go to the Palace of the Island to see how the foreigners might be attacked. Haply, too, I may meet with the party coming hither, and decoy them on some other track."

And Innsa consented; and Ficna set out straightway for the Palace of the Island.


Now as to the Palace of the Island. When Midac returned in the morning, and told how Finn and his people were held safe in the Palace of the Quicken Trees, the foreigners were in great joy. And they feasted and drank and were merry till evening; when an Irla* of the King of the World spoke in secret to his brother, and said—

" I will go now to the Palace of the Quicken Trees, and I will bring hither the head of Finn the son of Cumhal; and I shall gain thereby much renown, and shall be honoured by the King of the World."

So he went, bringing with him a goodly number of his own knights; and nothing is told of what befell them till they arrived at the brink of the ford under the Palace of the Quicken Trees. Looking across through the darkness, the Irla thought he saw a warrior standing at the other brink; and he called aloud to ask who was there, and whether he belonged to the noble or the ignoble races of the world.

And when Innsa answered that he belonged to the household of Finn, the son of Cumhal, the Irla said—

" Lo, we are going to the Palace of the Quicken Trees, to bring Finn's head to the King of the World; and thou shalt come with us and lead us to the door."

" That, indeed," replied Innsa, " would be a strange way for a champion to act who has been sent hither by Finn to guard this

---

* Irla, *i.e.*, an earl, a chief.

ford. I will not allow any foe to pass—of that be sure; and I warn you that you come not to my side of the ford!"

At this the Irla said to his knights, "Force the ford: then shall we see if yonder hero can fight as well as he threatens."

And at the word, they rushed through the water, as many as could find room. But only one or two at a time could attack: and the young champion struck them down right and left as fast as they came up, till the ford became encumbered with their bodies.

And when the conflict had lasted for a long time, and when they found that they could not dislodge him, the few that remained retired across the ford; and Innsa was fain to rest after his long combat.

But the Irla, seeing so many of his knights slain, was mad with wrath; and, snatching up his sword and shield, he attacked Innsa; and they fought a long and bloody fight.

Now the Irla was fresh and strong, while Innsa was weary and sore wounded; and at length the young hero fell in the ford, and the Irla beheaded him, and, exulting in his victory, brought the head away.

Finn and his companions, as they sat in miserable plight in the Palace of the Quicken Trees, heard the clash of arms at the ford, and the shouts and groans of warriors; and after a time all was still again; and they knew not how the fight had ended.

And now the Irla, thinking over the matter, deemed it unsafe to go to the Palace of the Quicken Trees without a larger body of knights; so he returned towards the Palace of the Island, intending to bring Innsa's head to the King of the World. When he came within a little distance of the palace, he met Ficna, who was then on his way back to the ford; and seeing that he was coming from the Palace of the Island, he deemed that he was one of the knights of the King of the World.

Ficna spoke to him, and asked whither he had come.

"I come," replied the Irla, "from the ford of the Palace of the Quicken Trees. There, indeed, on our way to the palace, to slay Finn the son of Cumhal, we were met by a young champion, who defended the ford and slew my knights. But he fell at length beneath my sword; and, lo, I have brought his head for a triumph to the King of the World!

Ficna took the head tenderly, and kissed the cheek thrice, and said, sorrowing—

" Alas, dear youth! only this morning I saw the light of valour in those dim eyes, and the bloom of youth on that faded cheek! "

Then turning wrathfully to the Irla, he asked—

" Knowest thou to whom thou hast given the young warrior's head? "

And the Irla replied, " Hast thou not come from the Palace of the Island, and dost thou not belong to the host of the King of the World? "

" I am not one of his knights," answered Ficna; " and neither shalt thou be, after this hour! "

Whereupon they drew their swords, and fought where they stood; and the foreign Irla fell by the avenging sword of Ficna, the son of Finn. Ficna beheaded him and returned to the ford, bringing the head, and also the head of Innsa. And when he had come to the ford, he made a grave of green sods on the bank, in which he laid the body and the head of Innsa, sometimes grieving for the youth, and sometimes rejoicing that his death had been avenged.

Then he went on to the Palace of the Quicken Trees, bringing the Irla's head; and when he had come nigh the door, he called aloud to Finn, who, impatient and full of anxious thoughts, asked—

" Tell us, Ficna, who fought the battle at the ford, and how it has ended."

" Thine own foster-son, Innsa, defended the ford against many foes, whose bodies now encumber the stream."

" And how is it now with my foster-son? " asked Finn.

" He died where he fought," replied Ficna; " for at the end, when he was weary and sore wounded, the foreign Irla attacked him, and slew him."

" And thou, my son, didst thou stand by and see my nursling slain? "

" Truly I did not," answered Ficna. " Would that I had been there, and I would have defended and saved him! And even now he is well avenged; for I met the Irla soon after, and lo, I have brought thee his head. Moreover, I buried thy nursling tenderly in a grave of green sods by the ford."

And Finn wept and said, " Victory and blessings be with thee, my son! Never were children better than mine. Before I saw them, few were my possessions and small my consideration in Erin; but since they have grown up around me, I have been great and prosperous, till I fell by treachery into this evil plight. And now, Ficna, return and guard the ford, and peradventure our friends may send help in time."

So Ficna went and sat on the brink of the ford.

## CHAPTER V

### FICNA, THE SON OF FINN, DEFENDS THE FORD

Now at the Palace of the Island, another Irla, whose name was Kironn, brother to him who had been slain by Ficna, spoke to some of his own followers—

" It is long since my brother left for the Palace of the Quicken Trees; I fear me that he and his people have fared ill in their quest. And now I will go to seek for them."

And he went, bringing a company of knights well armed; and when they had come to the ford, they saw Ficna at the far side. Kironn called out and asked who he was, and asked also who had made such a slaughter in the ford.

Ficna answered, " I am one of the household champions of Finn the son of Cumhal, and he has sent me here to guard this ford. As to the slaughter of yonder knights, your question stirs my mind to wrath and I warn you, if you come to this side of the ford, you will get a reply, not in words, but in deeds."

Then Kironn and his men rushed through the water, blind with rage, and struck wildly at Ficna. But the young hero watchfully parried their strokes and thrusts; and one after another they fell beneath his blows, till only a single man was left, who ran back with all speed to the Palace of the Island to tell the tale. And Ficna sat down on the brink, covered all over with wounds, and weary from the toil of battle.

When these tidings were brought to the palace, Midac was very wroth, and he said, " These men should not have gone to force the ford without my knowledge; for they were far too few in number, and neither were they bold and hardy enough to meet Finn's valiant champions. I know these Fena well, and it is not to me a matter of surprise that the Irla and his people fell by them.

" But I will now go with a choice party of my own brave men; and I will cross the ford despite their guards, and slay Finn and all his companions in the Palace of the Quicken Trees.

" Moreover, there is one man among them, namely, Conan Maol,[23] who of all the men of Erin has the largest appetite, and is fondest of choice eating and drinking. To him will I bring savoury food and delicious drink, not, indeed, to delight him with eating and drinking, but that I may torment him with the sight and smell of what he cannot taste."

So, having got the food, he set out with a chosen band; and when he had arrived at the ford, he saw a warrior at the far side. He asked who he was, and finding that it was Ficna, he spoke guilefully to him.

" Dear art thou to me, Ficna, dearer even than all the rest of Finn's household; for during the time I lived among the Fena, you never used me ill, or lifted a hand to either man or dog belonging to me."

But Ficna spurned his smooth words, and replied, " While you lived among the Fena, there was not a man among them that had less to do with you than I. But this I know, that you were treated kindly by all, especially by my father Finn, and you have repaid him by ingratitude and treachery."

When Midac heard this speech he was filled with wrath, and no longer hiding his evil mind, he ordered Ficna with threats to leave the ford. But Ficna laughed with scorn, and replied—

" The task is easy, friend Midac, to dislodge a single champion; and surely it is a small matter to you whether I stand in this narrow pass or abandon my post. Come forward, then, you and your knights; but here I will remain to receive you. I only regret you did not come sooner, while my blood was hot, and before my wounds grew stiff, when you would have got a better welcome! "

Then Midac ordered forward his knights, and they ran eagerly across the ford. But Ficna overthrew them with a mighty onset like a hawk among a flight of small birds, or like a wolf among a flock of sheep. When Midac saw this, he buckled on his shield and took his sword. Then, treading warily over the rough rocks, and over the dead bodies of his knights, he confronted Ficna, and they attacked each other with deadly hate and fury.

We shall now speak of those who remained on Knockfierna. When Oisin found that the two heroes did not return as soon as he expected, he thus addressed his companions—

" It seems to me a long time, my friends, since Ficna and Innsa went to the Palace of the Quicken Trees; methinks if they have sped successfully they should have long since come back with tidings of Finn and the others."

And one of his companions answered, " It is plain that they have gone to partake of the feast, and it fares so well with them that they are in no haste to leave the palace."

But Dermat O'Dyna of the Bright Face spoke and said, " It may be as you say, friend, but I should like to know the truth of the matter. And now I will go and find out why they tarry, for my mind misgives me that some evil thing has happened."

And Fatha Conan said he would go with him.

So the two heroes set out for the Palace of the Quicken Trees; and when they were yet a good way off from the ford they heard the clash of arms. They paused for a moment, breathless, to listen, and then Dermat exclaimed—

" It is the sound of single combat, the combat of mighty heroes; it is Ficna fighting with the foreigners, for I know his war-shout. I hear the clash of swords and the groans of warriors; I hear the shrieks of the ravens over the fairy-mansions, and the howls of the wild men of the glens! Hasten, Fatha, hasten, for Ficna is in sore strait, and his shout is a shout for help! "

And so they ran like the wind till they reached the hill-brow over the river; and, looking across in the dim moonlight, they saw the whole ford heaped with the bodies of the slain, and the two heroes fighting to the death at the far side. And at the first glance they observed that Ficna, being sore wounded, was yielding and sheltering behind his shield, and scarce able to ward off the blows of Midac.

Then Fatha cried out, " Fly, Dermat, fly! Save our dear companion! Save the king's son from death."

And Dermat, pausing for a moment, said, as if communing with himself—

" This is surely an evil plight: for if I run to the other side, the foreigner, being the more enraged for seeing me, will strike with greater fury, and I may not overtake the prince alive; and if I cast my spear, I may strike the wrong man ! "

But Fatha, overhearing him, said, " Fear not, Dermat, for you never yet threw an erring cast of a spear! "

Then Dermat, putting his finger in the silken loop of his spear, threw a deadly cast with unerring aim, and struck Midac, so that the iron spear-head went right through his body, and the length of a warrior's hand beyond.

" Woe to the man," exclaimed Midac—" woe to him whom that spear reaches: for it is the spear of Dermat O'Dyna! "

And now his wrath increased, and he struck at Ficna more fiercely than before.

Dermat shouted to him to hold his hand and not slay the king's son; and as he spoke he rushed down the slope and across the ford, to save the young hero. But Midac, still pressing on with unabated strength and fury, replied—

" Had you wished to save the prince's life, you should have spared mine: now that I have been wounded to death by your spear, Finn shall never see his son alive! "

Even as he spoke, he raised his sword for a mighty blow; and just as Dermat, shouting earnestly, was closing on them, he struck the prince lifeless to the earth, but fell down himself immediately after.

Dermat came up on the instant, and looked sadly at his friend lying dead. Then, addressing Midac, he said—

" If I had found thee dead, I would have passed thee untouched; but now that I have overtaken thee alive, I must needs behead thee, for thy head will be to Finn a worthy eric[10] for his son."

And so saying, he struck off Midac's head with one sweep of his heavy sword.

Dermat now repaired to the Palace of the Quicken Trees, leaving Fatha to watch the ford till his return. And when he had come near, he called aloud and struck the door with his heavy spear, for his wrath had not yet left him; but the door yielded not.

Finn knew the voice, and called out impatiently, " Do not try to enter here, Dermat, for this place is full of foul spells. But tell us first, I pray thee, who fought that long and bitter fight; for we heard the clash of arms and the shouts of warriors, but we know nothing more."

" Thy noble son, Ficna," returned Dermat, " fought single-handed against the foreigners."

" And how fares it with my son after that battle? "

" He is dead," answered Dermat; " first sore wounded by many foes whom he slaughtered, and afterwards slain by Midac, the son of Colga. But thy son is avenged; for though I came to the ford indeed too late to save him, I have slain Midac, and here I have brought thee his head as an eric."

And for a long time Dermat heard no more.

At last Finn spoke again and said—

" Victory and blessings be with you, Dermat, for often before did you relieve the Fena from sore straits. But never have we been in such plight as this. For here we sit spell-bound, and only one thing can release us, the blood of the three fierce kings of the Island of the Torrent sprinkled on this clay. Meantime, unless the ford be well defended, the foreigners will come and slay us. In you, Dermat, we trust, and unless you aid us well and faithfully now, we shall of a certainty perish. Guard the ford till the rising of the sun, for then I know the Fena will come to aid you."

" I and Fatha will of a certainty keep the enemy at bay," replied Dermat; and he bade them farewell for a time, and was about to return to the ford: but Conan Maol, with a groan, said—

" Miserable was the hour when I came to this palace, and cold and comfortless is the clay on which I sit—the clay of the Island of the Torrent. But worst of all to be without food and drink so long. And while I sit here, tormented with hunger and thirst, there is great plenty of ale and wine and of rich savoury food yonder in the Palace of the Island. I am not able to bear this any longer; and now, Dermat, I beseech you to bring me from the palace as much food as I can eat and a drinking-horn of wine."

" Cursed be the tongue that spoke these selfish words! " said Dermat. " A host of foreigners are now seeking to compass your death, with only Fatha and myself to defend you. Surely this is work enough for two good men! And now it seems I must abandon my post, and undertake a task of much danger, to get food for the gluttonous Conan Maol! "

"Alas, Dermat-na-mban! " [23] replied Conan, " if it were a lovely maiden, with bright eyes and golden hair, who made this little request, quickly and eagerly you would fly to please her, little recking of danger or trouble. But now you refuse me, and the reason is not hard to see. For you formerly crossed me four times in my courtships; and now it likes you well to see me die of hunger in this dungeon! "

" Well, then," said Dermat, " cease your upbraiding, and I will try to bring you food; for it is better to face danger than to suffer the revilings of your foul tongue."

So saying, he went back to the ford to Fatha, where he stood watching; and after he had told him how matters stood, he said to him—

" I must needs go to the Palace of the Island, to get food for Conan Maol; and you shall guard the ford till I return."

But Fatha told him that there was food and drink enough at the other side of the ford, which Midac had brought from the palace, and urged him to bring a good meal of this to Conan.

" Not so," said Dermat. " He would taunt me with bringing him food taken from the hands of dead men; and though one may recover from his blow, it is not so easy to recover from the venom of his tongue." *

So he left Fatha at the ford, and repaired to the Palace of the Island.

As he drew nigh, he heard the noise of feasting and revelry, and the loud talk and laughter of men deep in drink. Walking tiptoe, he peered warily through the open door, and saw the chiefs and the knights sitting at the tables; with Sinsar of the Battles and his son Borba high seated over all. He saw also many attendants serving them with food and drink, each holding in his hand a large ornamented drinking-horn, filled with wine.

---

* A satirical allusion to Conan's well-known cowardice.

Dermat entered the outer door softly, and stood in a dark part of the passage near the door, silent and stern, with sword drawn, watching his opportunity. And after a time one of the attendants, unsuspecting, passed close to him; when Dermat, with a swift, sure blow, struck off his head. And he snatched the drinking-horn from the man's hand before he fell, so that not a drop of the wine was spilled.

Then, laying the drinking-horn aside for a moment, he walked straight into the hall, and taking up one of the dishes near where the king sat, he went out through the open door, bringing with him both dish and drinking-horn. And amidst the great crowd, and the drinking, and the noise, no one took the least notice of him, so that he got off without hindrance or harm of any kind.

When he reached the ford, he found Fatha lying fast asleep on the bank. He wondered very much that he could sleep in the midst of such a slaughter; but knowing that the young warrior was worn out with watching and toil, he left him lying asleep, and went to the Palace of the Quicken Trees with the food for Conan.

When he had come to the door, he called aloud to Conan and said, " I have here a goodly meal of choice food: how am I to give it to thee? "

Conan said, " Throw it towards me through yonder little opening."

Dermat did so; and as fast as he threw the food, Conan caught it in his large hands, and ate it up ravenously. And when it was all gone, Dermat said—

" I have here a large drinking-horn of good wine: how am I to give it to thee? "

Conan answered, " There is a place behind the palace where, from a rock, you may reach the lower parapet with a light, airy bound. Come from that straight over me, and break a hole in the roof with your spear, through which you can pour the wine down to me."

Dermat did so; and as he poured down the wine, Conan, with upturned face, opened his great mouth and caught it, and swallowed it every drop.

After this Dermat came down and returned to the ford, where he found Fatha still asleep; and he sat beside him, but did not awaken him.

## CHAPTER VI

### DERMAT O'DYNA SLAYS THE THREE KINGS OF THE ISLAND OF THE TORRENT, BREAKS THE SPELL WITH THEIR BLOOD, AND FREES FINN

TIDINGS were brought to the Palace of the Island that Midac and all whom he led were slain at the ford; and the three kings of the Island of the Torrent said—

" The young king of Lochlann did wrong to make this attempt without asking our counsel; and had we known of the thing we would have hindered him. For to us belongs the right to behead Finn and his companions, since it is the spell-venom of the clay which we brought from the Island of the Torrent that holds them bound in the Palace of the Quicken Trees. And now, indeed, we will go and slay them all."

So they set out with a strong party, and soon reached the ford. Looking across in the dim light, they saw Dermat, and called aloud to ask who he was.

" I am Dermat O'Dyna," he replied, " one of Finn's champions. He has sent me to guard this ford, and whoever you are, I warn you not to cross! "

Then they sought to beguile Dermat, and to win him over by smooth words.

" It is a pleasure to us to meet you, Dermat; for we are old friends of yours. We are the three kings of the Island of the Torrent, your fellow-pupils in valour and all heroic feats. For you and we lived with the same tutors from the beginning; and you never learned a feat of arms that we did not learn in like manner. Leave the ford, then, that we may pass on to the Palace of the Quicken Trees."

But Dermat answered in few words. " Finn and his companions are under my protection till morning; and I will defend the ford as long as I am alive! "

And he stood up straight and tall like a pillar, and scowled across the ford.

A number of the foreigners now rushed towards Dermat, and raging in a confused crowd, assailed him. But the strong hero met them as a rock meets the waves, and slew them with ease as they came within the range of his sword. Yet still they pressed on, others succeeding those that fell; and in the midst of the rage of battle, Fatha started up from his sleep, awakened by the crashing of weapons and the riving of shields.

He gazed for a moment, bewildered, at the combatants, and, seeing how matters stood, he was wroth with Dermat for not awakening him; so that he ran at him fiercely with drawn sword. But Dermat stepped aside, and, being angry, thus addressed him—

" Slake thy vengeance on our foes for the present: for me, the swords of the foreigners are enough, methinks, without thine to aid them! "

Then Fatha turned and attacked the foe, and his onset was even more deadly than that of Dermat; so that they fell before him to the right and left on the ford.

And now at last the three kings, seeing so many of their men falling, advanced slowly towards Dermat; and Dermat, unterrified, stood in his place to meet them. And their weapons clashed and tore through their shields, and the fight was long and furious; till at last the champion-pride and the battle-fury of Dermat arose, so that the three dragon-like kings fell slain one by one before him, on that ford of red slaughter.

And now, though smarting with wounds, and breathless, and weary, Dermat and Fatha remembered Finn and the Fena; and Dermat called to mind what Finn had told him as to how the spell was to be broken. So the struck off the heads of the three kings, and, followed by Fatha, he ran with them, all gory as they were, to the Palace of the Quicken Trees.

As they drew nigh to the door, Finn, knowing their voices and their footsteps, called aloud anxiously to ask how it fared with the combatants at the ford. " For," he said, " the crashing and the din of that battle exceeded all we have yet heard, and we know not how it has ended."

Dermat answered, " King of the Fena, Fatha and I have slain the three kings of the Island of the Torrent; and lo, here we have their heads all bloody; but how am I to bring them to thee? "

" Victory and blessings be with you, Dermat; you and Fatha have fought a valiant fight, worthy of the Fena of Erin! Now sprinkle the door with the blood."

Dermat did so, and in a moment the door flew wide open with a crash. And inside they saw the heroes in sore plight, all pale and faint, seated on the cold clay round the wall. Dermat and Fatha, holding the gory heads by the hair, sprinkled the earth under each with the blood, beginning with Finn, and freed them one by one; and the heroes, as they found the spell broken, sprang to their feet with exulting cries. And they thanked the gods for having relieved them from that perilous strait, and they and the two heroes joyfully embraced each other.

But danger still threatened, and they now took counsel what they should do; and Finn, addressing Dermat and Fatha, said—

" The venom of these foul spells has withered our strength, so that we are not able to fight; but at sunrise they will lose their power, and we shall be strong again. It is necessary, therefore, that you still guard the ford, and at the rising of the sun we shall relieve you."

So the two heroes went to the ford, and Fatha returned with food and drink for Finn and the others.


After the last battle at the ford, a few who had escaped brought back tidings to the King of the World and his people, that the three kings of the Island of the Torrent had fallen by the hands of Dermat and Fatha. But they knew not that Finn and the others had been released.

Then arose the king's son, Borba the Haughty, who, next to the king himself, was mightiest in battle of all the foreign host. And he said—

" Feeble warriors were they who tried to cross this ford. I will go now and avenge the death of our people on these Fena, and I will bring hither the head of Finn the son of Cumhal, and place it at my father's feet."

So he marched forth without delay, with a large body of chosen warriors, till he reached the edge of the ford. And although Dermat and Fatha never trembled before a foe, yet when they saw the dark mass drawing nigh, and heard the heavy tread and clank of arms, they dreaded that they might be dislodged and overpowered by repeated attacks, leaving Finn and the rest helpless and unprotected. And each in his heart longed for the dawn of morning.

No parley was held this time, but the foreigners came straight across the ford—as many abreast as could find footing. And as they drew near, Dermat spoke to Fatha—

" Fight warily, my friend: ward the blows of the foremost, and be not too eager to slay, but rather look to thy own safety. It behoves us to nurse our strength and prolong the fight, for the day is dawning, and sunrise is not far off ! "

The foreigners came on, many abreast; but their numbers availed them naught, for the pass was narrow; and the two heroes, one taking the advancing party to the right, and the other to the left, sometimes parried and sometimes slew, but never yielded an inch from where they stood.

And now at last the sun rose up over the broad plain of Kenri; and suddenly the withering spell went forth from the bones and sinews of the heroes who sat at the Palace of the Quicken Trees, listening with anxious hearts to the clash of battle at the ford. Joyfully they started to their feet, and, snatching up their arms, hastened down to the ford with Finn at their head; but one they sent, the swiftest among them, to Knockfierna, to take the news to Oisin.

Dermat and Fatha, fighting eagerly, heeded not that the sun had risen, though it was now indeed glittering before their eyes on the helmets and arms of their foes. But as they fought, there rose a great shout behind them; and Finn and Gall and the rest ran down the slope to attack the foreigners.

The foreigners, not in the least dismayed, answered the attack; and the fight went on till Gall Mac Morna and Borba the Haughty met face to face in the middle of the ford, and they fought a hard and deadly combat. The battle-fury of Gall at length arose, so that nothing could stand before him, and, with one mighty blow, he cleft the head from the body of Borba.

And now the foreigners began to yield: but they still continued to fight, till a swift messenger sped to the Palace of the Island, and told the great king, Sinsar of the Battles, that his son was dead, slain by Gall; and that his army was sore pressed by the Fena, with Finn at their head.

When the people heard these tidings, they raised a long and sorrowful cry of lamentation for the king's son; but the king himself, though sorrow filled his heart, showed it not. And he arose and summoned his whole host; and, having arranged them in their battalions and in their companies under their princes and chiefs, he marched towards the battle-field, desiring vengeance on the Fena more than the glory of victory.

## CHAPTER VII

### THE FIGHT AT THE FORD, WITH THE FOREIGN ARMY

ALL the Fena who had gone to the chase from Knockfierna had returned, and were now with Oisin, the son of Finn. And the messenger came slowly up the hillside, and told them, though with much difficulty, for he was weary and breathless, the whole story from beginning to end, of Finn's enchantment, and of the battles at the ford, and how their companions at that moment stood much in need of aid against the foreigners.

Instantly the whole body marched straight towards the Palace of the Quicken Trees, and arrived on the hill-brow over the ford just as the King of the World and his army were approaching from the opposite direction.

And now the fight at the ford ceased for a time, while the two armies were put in battle array; and on neither side was there any cowardice or any desire to avoid the combat.

The Fena were divided into four battalions. The active, bright-eyed Clann Baskin marched in front of the first battalion; the fierce, champion-like Clann Morna led the second; the strong, sanguinary Mic-an-Smoil brought up the third; and the fourth was led forward by the fearless, venomous Clann O'Navnan.

And they marched forward, with their silken banners, each banner-staff in the hand of a tall, trusty hero; their helmets glittering with precious gems; their broad, beautiful shields on their left shoulders; with their long, straight, deadly lances in their hands; and their heavy, keen-edged swords hanging at the left side of each. Onward they marched; and woe to those who crossed the path of that host of active, high-minded champions, who never turned their backs on an enemy in battle!

And now at last the fight began with showers of light, venomous missiles; and many a hero fell even before the combatants met face to face. Then they drew their long, broad-bladed swords, and the ranks closed and mingled in deadly strife. It would be vain to attempt a description of that battle, for it was hard to distinguish friend from foe. Many a high-souled hero fell wounded and helpless, and neither sigh nor groan of pain escaped them; but they died, encouraging their friends to vengeance with voice and gesture.

The great king Finn himself moved tall and stately from battalion to battalion, now fighting in the foremost ranks, and now encouraging his friends and companions, his mighty voice rising clear over the clash of arms and the shouts of the combatants. And wherever he moved, there the courage of the Fena rose high, and their valour and their daring increased, so that the ranks of their foes fell back thinned and scattered before them.

Oscar, resting for a moment from the toil of battle, looked round, and espied the standard of the King of the World, where he stood guarded by his best warriors, to protect him from the danger of being surrounded and outnumbered by his foes; and the young hero's wrath was kindled when he observed that the Fena were falling back dismayed wherever that standard was borne.

Rushing through the opposing ranks like a lion maddened by dogs, he approached the king; and the king laughed a grim laugh of joy when he saw him, and ordered his guards back; for he was glad in his heart, expecting to revenge his son's death by slaying with his own hand Finn's grandson, who was most loved of all the youthful champions of the Fena. Then these two great heroes fought a deadly battle; and many a warrior stayed his hand to witness this combat. It seemed as if both should fall; for each inflicted on the other many wounds. The king's rage knew no bounds at being so long withstood, for at first sight he despised Oscar for his youth and beauty; and he made an onset that caused Oscar's friends, as they looked on, to tremble; for during this attack the young hero defended himself, and no more.

But now, having yielded for a time, he called to mind the actions and the fame of his forefathers, and attacked the king in turn, and, with a blow that no shield or buckler could withstand, he swept the head from the king's body.

Then a great shout went up from the Fena, and the foreigners instantly gave way; and they were pursued and slaughtered on every side. A few threw away their arms and escaped to the shore, where, hastily unmooring their ships, they sailed swiftly away to their own country, with tidings of the death of their king and the slaughter of their army.

# The Pursuit of the Giolla Dacker and his Horse

## CHAPTER I

### ARRIVAL OF THE GIOLLA DACKER AND HIS HORSE

ONE day in the beginning of summer, Finn, the son of Cumhal, the son of Trenmore O'Baskin,[23] feasted the chief people of Erin at Allen[23] of the broad hill-slopes.  And when the feast was over, the Fena reminded him that it was time to begin the chase through the plains and the glens and the wilderness of Erin.

For this was the manner in which the Fena were wont to spend their time.  They divided the year into two parts.  During the first half, namely, from Bealtaine to Samhain,* they hunted each day with their dogs; and during the second half, namely, from Samhain to Bealtaine, they lived in the mansions and the betas† of Erin; so that there was not a chief or a great lord or a keeper of a house of hospitality in the whole country that had not nine of the Fena quartered on him during the winter half of the year.

Finn and his chiefs now held council as to which of the provinces of Erin they should begin with; and they chose Munster for the first chase.

Next day they set out, both dogs and men; and they travelled through Offaly, and by one side of Fera-call, and to Brosna of Slieve Bloma, and by the Twelve Mountains of Evlinn, till they came to Collkilla, which is now called Knockainy.

---

* *Bealtaine*, the first of May; *Samhain*, the first of November.
† Beta, a house of public hospitality.

Brosna, a small river rising in the Slieve Bloma, or Slieve Bloom mountains, which flows by Birr, and falls into the Shannon near Banagher.

Knockainy, a small hill much celebrated in fairy lore, in the county Limerick. It appears from the text that it was more anciently called Collkilla, or hazel-wood.

The chase was then set in order, and they scattered themselves over the broad plains of Munster. They began at Ardpatrick, and they hunted over Kenn-Avrat of Slieve-Keen, and over Coill-na-drua, which is now called the district of Fermoy; over the fruitful lands of Lehan, and over the confines of Fermorc, which is now called Hy Conall Gavra. Then south to the patrimony of Curoi Mac Dara, and by the shores of Loch Lein; afterwards along the blue-streamy Suir, by Caher-Dun-Isca, over the great plain of Femin, and across the speckled summit of Slievenamon; all over East Munster and West Munster, as far as Balla-Gavran on the one side, and on the other across the Shannon to Cratloe, near Limerick of the blue waters.

In short, there was not a plain or a valley, a wood or a brake, a mountain or a wilderness, in the two provinces of Munster, that they did not hunt over on that occasion.

Now it chanced at one time during the chase, while they were hunting over the plain of Cliach,* that Finn went to rest on the hill of Collkilla, which is now called Knockainy; and he had his hunting-tents pitched on a level spot near the summit. Some of his chief heroes tarried with him; namely, his son Oisin; the valiant Oscar, the son of Oisin; Gall Mac Morna of the Mighty Deeds; Finn's shield-bearer, Skeabrac; Kylta Mac Ronan; Dermat O'Dyna of the Bright Face; Ligan Lumina the Swift-footed; Conan Maol of the Foul Tongue; and Finn Ban Mac Bresal.

---

Ardpatrick, a beautiful hill, with a remarkable church ruin and graveyard on its summit, two miles from Kilfinane, county Limerick.

Kenn-Avrat was the ancient name of Seefin mountain, two miles from Ardpatrick. Slieve-Keen, the old name of the hill of Carrigeennamroanty, near Seefin.

Lehan, the ancient name of the district round Castlelyons, in the county Cork.

Curoi Mac Dara, a celebrated chief who flourished in the time of the Red Branch Knights of Ulster, viz., in the first century of the Christian era. Curoi had his residence on a mountain near Tralee, still called Caherconree (the fortress of Curoi), and his " patrimony " was South Munster. The remains of Curoi's great stone fortress are still to be seen on Caherconree.

Loch Lein, the Lakes of Killarney.

Caher-Dun-Isca, now the town of Caher, on the Suir, in Tipperary

Femin was the name of the great plain lying to the south and west of the mountain of Slievenamon, near Clonmel.

Balla-Gavran, or the pass of Gavran, an ancient road, which ran by Gavran (now Gowran), in the county Kilkenny.

* Cliach, the old name of the plain lying round Knockainy.

When the king and his companions had taken their places on the hill, the Fena unleashed their gracefully shaped, sweet-voiced hounds through the woods and sloping glens. And it was sweet music to Finn's ear, the cry of the long-snouted dogs, as they routed the deer from their covers, and the badgers from their dens; the pleasant, emulating shouts of the youths; the whistling and signalling of the huntsmen; and the encouraging cheers of the mighty heroes, as they spread themselves through the glens and woods, and over the broad, green plain of Cliach.

Then did Finn ask who of all his companions would go to the highest point of the hill directly over them, to keep watch and ward, and to report how the chase went on. For, he said, the Dedannans[1] were ever on the watch to work the Fena mischief by their druidical spells, and more so during the chase than at other times.

Finn Ban Mac Bresal stood forward and offered to go: and, grasping his broad spears, he went to the top, and sat viewing the plain to the four points of the sky. And the king and his companions brought forth the chess-board and chess-men,[26] and sat them down to a game.

Finn Ban Mac Bresal had been watching only a little time, when he saw on the plain to the east, a Fomor* of vast size coming towards the hill, leading a horse. As he came nearer, Finn Ban observed that he was the ugliest-looking giant his eyes ever lighted on. He had a large, thick body, bloated and swollen out to a great size; clumsy, crooked legs; and broad, flat feet, turned inwards. His hands and arms and shoulders were bony and thick and very strong-looking; his neck was long and thin; and while his head was poked forward, his face was turned up, as he stared straight at Finn Mac Bresal. He had thick lips, and long, crooked teeth; and his face was covered all over with bushy hair.

He was fully armed; but all his weapons were rusty and soiled and slovenly looking. A broad shield of a dirty, sooty colour, rough and battered, hung over his back; he had a long, heavy, straight sword at his left hip; and he held in his left hand two thick-handled, broad-headed spears, old and rusty, and seeming as if they had not been handled for years. In his right hand he

---

* Fomor, a gigantic warrior, a giant; its primitive meaning is "a sea-robber," commonly called a Fomorian. (See note 5 at the end.)

held an iron club, which he dragged after him, with its end on the ground; and, as it trailed along, it tore up a track as deep as the furrow a farmer ploughs with a team of oxen.

The horse he led was even larger in proportion than the giant himself, and quite as ugly. His great carcase was covered all over with tangled, scraggy hair, of a sooty black; you could count his ribs, and all the points of his big bones through his hide; his legs were crooked and knotty; his neck was twisted; and as for his jaws, they were so long and heavy that they made his head look twice too large for his body.

The giant held him by a thick halter, and seemed to be dragging him forward by main force, the animal was so lazy and so hard to move. Every now and then, when the beast tried to stand still, the giant would give him a blow on the ribs with his big iron club, which sounded as loud as the thundering of a great billow against the rough-headed rocks of the coast. When he gave him a pull forward by the halter, the wonder was that he did not drag the animal's head away from his body; and, on the other hand, the horse often gave the halter such a tremendous tug backwards that it was equally wonderful how the arm of the giant was not torn away from his shoulder.

Now it was not an easy matter to frighten Finn Ban Mac Bresal; but when he saw the giant and his horse coming straight towards him in that wise, he was seized with such fear and horror that he sprang from his seat, and, snatching up his arms, he ran down the hill-slope with his utmost speed towards the king and his companions, whom he found sitting round the chess-board, deep in their game.

They started up when they saw Finn Ban looking so scared; and, turning their eyes towards where he pointed, they saw the big man and his horse coming up the hill. They stood gazing at him in silent wonder, waiting till he should arrive; but although he was no great way off when they first caught sight of him, it was a long time before he reached the spot where they stood, so slow was the movement of himself and his horse.

When at last he had come up, he bowed his head, and bended his knee, and saluted the king with great respect.

Finn addressed him; and after having given him leave to speak, he asked him who he was, and what was his name; from which of the three chief divisions of the world he had come, and whether he belonged to one of the noble or ignoble races; also what was his profession or craft, and why he had no servant to attend to his horse—if, indeed, such an ugly old spectre of an animal could be called a horse at all.

The big man made answer and said, " King of the Fena, I will answer everything you ask me, as far as lies in my power. Whether I come of a noble or of an ignoble race, that, indeed, I cannot tell, for I know not who my father and mother were. As to where I came from, I am a Fomor of Lochlann[6] in the north; but I have no particular dwelling-place, for I am continually travelling about from one country to another, serving the great lords and nobles of the world, and receiving wages for my service.

" In the course of my wanderings I have often heard of you, O king, and of your greatness and splendour and royal bounty; and I have come now to visit you, and to ask you to take me into your service for one year; and at the end of that time I shall fix my own wages, according to my custom.

" You ask me also why I have no servant for this great horse of mine. The reason of that is this: at every meal I eat, my master must give me as much food and drink as would be enough for a hundred men; and whosoever the lord or chief may be that takes me into his service, it is quite enough for him to have to provide for me, without having also to feed my servant.

" Moreover, I am so very heavy and lazy that I should never be able to keep up with a company on march if I had to walk; and this is my reason for keeping a horse at all.

" My name is the Giolla Dacker,* and it is not without good reason that I am so called. For there never was a lazier or worse servant than I am, or one that grumbles more at doing a day's work for his master. And I am the hardest person in the whole world to deal with; for, no matter how good or noble I may think my master, or how kindly he may treat me, it is hard words and foul reproaches I am likely to give him for thanks in the end.

" This, O Finn, is the account I have to give of myself, and these are my answers to your questions."

---

* Giolla Dacker means " a slothful fellow "—a fellow hard to move, hard to manage, hard to have anything to do with.

" Well," answered Finn, " according to your own account, you are not a very pleasant fellow to have anything to do with; and of a truth there is not much to praise in your appearance. But things may not be so bad as you say; and, anyhow, as I have never yet refused any man service and wages, I will not now refuse you."

Whereupon Finn and the Giolla Dacker made covenants, and the Giolla Dacker was taken into service for a year.

Then the big man turned to Conan Maol, and asked him whether the foot-service or the horse-service had the better pay among the Fena; and Conan answered that the horsemen had twice as much pay as the footmen.

" If that be so," replied the Giolla Dacker, "I will join the horse-service, as I have a fine steed of my own; and indeed, if I had known this before, I would certainly have come hither on horseback, instead of walking.

" And now, as to this same horse of mine, I find I must attend to him myself, as I see no one here worthy of putting a hand near him. So I will lead him to the nearest stud, as I am wont to do, and let him graze among your horses. I value him greatly, however, and it would grieve me very much if any harm were to befall him; so, I put him under your protection, O king, and under the protection of all the Fena that are here present."

At this speech the Fena all burst out laughing, to see the Giolla Dacker showing such concern for his miserable, worthless old skeleton of a horse.

However, the big man, giving not the least heed to their merriment, took the halter off the horse's head, and turned him loose among the horses of the Fena.

But now, this same wretched-looking old animal, instead of beginning to graze, as every one thought he would, ran in among the horses of the Fena, and began straightway to work all sorts of mischief. He cocked his long, hard, switchy tail straight out like a rod, and, throwing up his hind legs, he kicked about on this side and on that, maiming and disabling several of the horses. Sometimes he went tearing through the thickest of the herd, butting at them with his hard, bony forehead; and he opened out his lips with a vicious grin, and tore all he could lay hold on with his sharp, crooked teeth, so that none were safe that came in his way either before or behind. And the end of it was, that not an animal of the whole herd escaped without having a leg broken, or an eye knocked out, or his ribs fractured, or his ear bitten off, or the side of his face torn open, or without being in some other way cut or maimed beyond cure.

At last he left them, and was making straight across to a small field where Conan Maol's horses were grazing by themselves, intending to play the same tricks among them. But Conan, seeing this, shouted in great alarm to the Giolla Dacker, to bring away his horse, and not let him work any more mischief; and threatening, if he did not do so at once, to go himself and knock the brains out of the vicious old brute on the spot.

But the Giolla Dacker took the matter quite cool; and he told Conan that he saw no way of preventing his horse from joining the others, except some one put the halter on him and held him, which would, of course, he said, prevent the poor animal from grazing, and would leave him with a hungry belly at the end of the day.

He said, moreover, that as he had no horse-boy, and must needs do everything for himself, he thought it quite time enough to look after his horse when he had to make ready for a journey. " But," said he to Conan, " there is the halter; and if you are in any fear for your own animals, you may go yourself and bring him away from the field."

Conan was in a mighty rage when he heard this; and as he saw the big horse just about to cross the fence, he snatched up the halter, and running forward with long strides he threw it over the animal's head and thought to lead him back. But in a moment the horse stood stock still, and his body and legs became as stiff as if they were made of wood; and though Conan pulled and tugged with might and main, he was not able to stir him an inch from his place.

He gave up pulling at last, when he found it was no use; but he still kept on holding the halter, while the big horse never made the least stir, but stood as if he had been turned into stone; the Giolla Dacker all the time looking on quite unconcernedly, and the others laughing at Conan's perplexity. But no one offered to relieve him.

At last Fergus Finnvel, the poet, spoke to Conan, and said, " I never would have believed, Conan Maol, that you could be brought to do horse-service for any knight or noble in the whole world; but now, indeed, I see that you have made yourself a horse-boy to an ugly foreign giant, so hateful-looking and low-born that not a man of the Fena would have anything to say to him. As you have, however, to mind this old horse in order to save your own, would it not be better for you to mount him, and revenge yourself for all the trouble he is giving you, by riding him across the country, over the hill-tops, and down into the deep glens and valleys, and through stones and bogs and all sorts of rough places, till you have broken the heart in his big, ugly body?"

Conan, stung by the cutting words of the poet, and by the jeers of his companions, jumped upon the horse's back, and began to beat him mightily with his heels, and with his two big, heavy fists, to make him go; but the horse seemed not to take the least notice and never stirred.

" I know the reason he does not go," said Fergus Finnvel. "He has been accustomed to carry a horseman far heavier than you, that is to say, the Giolla Dacker; and he will not move till he has the same weight on his back."

At this Conan Maol called out to his companions, and asked which of them would mount with him, and help to avenge the damage done to their horses.

" I will go," said Coil Croda the Battle Victor, son of Criffan; and up he went. But the horse never moved.

Dara Donn Mac Morna next offered to go, and mounted behind the others; and after him Angus Mac Airt Mac Morna. And the end of it was, that fourteen men of the Clann Baskin and Clann Morna[23] got up along with Conan; and all began to thrash the horse together, with might and main. But they were none the better of it, for he remained standing stiff and immovable as before. They found, moreover, that their seat was not at all an easy one—the animal's back was so sharp and bony.

## CHAPTER II

### CONAN AND FIFTEEN OF THE FENA ARE CARRIED OFF BY THE GIOLLA DACKER'S HORSE

WHEN the Giolla Dacker saw the Fena beating his horse at such a rate, he seemed very angry, and addressed the king in these words—

" King of the Fena, I now see plainly that all the fine accounts I heard about you and the Fena are false, and I will not stay in your service—no, not another hour. You can see for yourself the ill usage these men are giving my horse without cause; and I leave you to judge whether any one could put up with it—any one who had the least regard for his horse. The time is, indeed, short since I entered your service, but I now think it a great deal too long; so pay me my wages, and let me go my ways."

But Finn said, " I do not wish you to go; stay on till the end of your year, and then I will pay you all I promised you."

" I swear," answered the Giolla Dacker, " that if this were the very last day of my year, I would not wait till morning for my wages, after this insult. So, wages or no wages, I will now seek another master; but from this time forth I shall know what to think of Finn Mac Cumhal and his Fena! "

With that the Giolla Dacker stood up as straight as a pillar, and, turning his face towards the south-west, he walked slowly away.

When the horse saw his master leaving the hill, he stirred himself at once and walked quietly after him, bringing the fifteen men away on his back. And when the Fena saw this they raised a loud shout of laughter, mocking them.

The Giolla Dacker, after he had walked some little way, looked back, and seeing that his horse was following, he stood for a moment to tuck up his skirts. Then, all at once changing his pace, he set out with long, active strides; and if you know what the speed of a swallow is, flying across a mountain-side, or the dry, fairy wind of a March day sweeping over the plains, then you can understand the swiftness of the Giolla Dacker, as he ran down the hill-side towards the south-west.

Neither was the horse behindhand in the race; for, though he carried a heavy load, he galloped like the wind after his master, plunging and bounding forward with as much freedom as if he had nothing at all on his back.

The men now tried to throw themselves off; but this, indeed, they were not able to do, for the good reason that they found themselves fastened firmly, hands and feet and all, to the horse's back.

And now Conan, looking round, raised his big voice, and shouted to Finn and the Fena, asking them were they content to let their friends be carried off in that manner by such a horrible, foul-looking old spectre of a horse.

Finn and the others, hearing this, seized their arms and started off in pursuit. Now the way the Giolla Dacker and his horse took was first through Fermorc,* which is at the present day called Hy Conall Gavra; next over the wide, heathy summit of Slieve Lougher; from that to Corca Divna; and they ran along by Slieve Mish, till they reached Cloghan Kincat, near the deep green sea.

During all this time Finn and his people kept them in view, but were not able to overtake them; and Ligan Lumina, one of the swiftest of the Fena, kept ahead of the others.

The horse now passed by Cloghan Kincat without in the least abating his speed; and when he had arrived on the beach, even at the very water's edge, Ligan overtook him, and caught him by the tail with his two hands, intending to hold him till the rest of the Fena came up. He gave a mighty pull back; but the horse, not in the least checked by this, made no more ado but plunged forward through the waves, dragging Ligan after him hanging at his tail. And Ligan now found that he could neither help his friends nor free himself, for his two hands clung fast to the tail of the horse.

And so the great horse continued his course without stop or stay, bringing the sixteen Fena with him through the sea. Now

---

* Fermorc, now the baronies of Connello, in Limerick. Slieve Lougher, a celebrated mountain near Castleisland, in Kerry. Corca Divna, now the barony of Corkaguiny, the long peninsula lying west of Tralee, and containing the town of Dingle, and the mountain range of Slieve Mish. Cloghan Kincat, now called Cloghan, a small village on the northern coast of the peninsula.

this is how they fared in the sea, while the horse was rushing
swiftly farther and farther to the west: they had always a dry, firm
strand under them, for the waters retired before the horse while
behind them was a wild, raging sea, which followed close after,
and seemed ready every moment to topple over their heads. But
though the billows were tumbling and roaring all round, neither
horse nor riders were wetted by as much as a drop of brine or a
dash of spray.

# CHAPTER III

### PURSUIT

Now as to Finn and the others. They stood on the bank over the
the beach, watching the horse and men till they lost sight of them
in the sea afar off; and then they sat down, weary after their long
chase, and full of sadness for the loss of their companions.

After a long silence, Finn spoke and asked the chiefs what they
thought best to be done. But they replied that he was far beyond
them all in knowledge and wisdom; and they told him they would
follow whatsoever counsel he and Fergus Finnvel, the poet, gave
them. Then Finn told Fergus to speak his mind; and Fergus
said—

" My counsel is that we go straightway to Ben Edair,* where
we shall find a ship ready to sail. For our forefathers, when they
wrested the land from the gifted, bright-complexioned Dedannans,
bound them by covenant to maintain this ship for ever, fitted with
all things needful for a voyage, even to the smallest article, as one
of the privileges of Ben Edair; so that if at any time one of the
noble sons of Gael Glas† wished to sail to distant lands from Erin,
he should have a ship lying at hand in the harbour ready to begin
his voyage."

They agreed to this counsel, and turned their steps without
delay northwards towards Ben Edair. They had not gone far when

* Ben Edair, now Howth Hill, near Dublin.
† Gael Glas, the traditional ancestor of the Gaels.

they met two noble-looking youths, fully armed, and wearing over their armour beautiful mantles of scarlet silk, fastened by brooches of gold. The strangers saluted the king with much respect; and the king saluted them in return. Then, having given them leave to converse, he asked them who they were, whither they had come, and who the prince or chief was that they served. And the elder answered—

" My name is Feradach, and my brother's name is Foltlebar; and we are the two sons of the king of Innia. Each of us professes an art; and it has long been a point of dispute between us, which art is the better, my brother's or mine. Hearing that there is not in the world a wiser or more far-seeing man than thou art, O king, we have come to ask thee to take us into thy service among thy household troops for a year, and at the end of that time to give judgment between us in this matter."

Finn asked them what were the two arts they professed.

" My art," answered Feradach, " is this: If at any time a company of warriors need a ship, give me only my joiner's axe and my crann-tavall,* and I am able to provide a ship for them without delay. The only thing I ask them to do is this—to cover their heads close, and keep them covered, while I give the crann-tavall three blows of my axe. Then I tell them to uncover their heads; and lo, there lies the ship in harbour, ready to sail! "

Then Foltlebar spoke and said, " This, O king, is the art I profess: On land I can track the wild duck over nine ridges and nine glens, and follow her without being once thrown out, till I drop upon her in her nest. And I can follow up a track on sea quite as well as on land, if I have a good ship and crew."

Finn replied, " You are the very men I want; and I now take you both into my service. At this moment I need a good ship and a skilful pilot more than any two things in the whole world. And though our own track-men, namely, the Clann Navin, are good, yet we now need some one still more skilful, to follow the Giolla Dacker through unknown seas."

Then the two brothers asked Finn what strait he was in at that moment, and why he wanted a ship and pilot so much. Whereupon Finn told them the whole story of the Giolla Dacker's doings

---

* Crann-tavall, a sort of sling for projecting stones, made of an elastic piece of wood, and strung somewhat like a cross-bow.

from beginning to end. "And we are now," said he, "on our way to Ben Edair, to seek a ship, that we may follow this giant and his horse, and rescue our companions."

Then Feradach said, " I will get you a ship—a ship that will sail as swiftly as a swallow can fly! "

And Foltlebar said, " I will guide your ship in the track of the Giolla Dacker till ye lay hands on him, in whatsoever quarter of the world he may have hidden himself ! "

And so they turned back to Cloghan Kincat. And when they had come to the beach, Feradach told them to cover their heads; and they did so. Then he struck three blows of his axe on the crann-tavall; after which he bade them look. And lo, they saw a ship, fully fitted out with oars and sails, and with all things needed for a long voyage, riding before them in the harbour!

Then Kylta Mac Ronan went to the top of a high hill; and, turning his face inland, he uttered three mighty shouts, which were taken up by the people of the next valley, and after them by those of the next valley beyond. And so the signal spread, till a shout of alarm was heard in every plain and hill-side, glen and valley, wood and wilderness, in the two provinces of Munster. And when the Fena heard these shouts, they ceased anon from their sports and pastimes; for they knew their king was in danger or strait of some kind. And they formed themselves into ranks and troops and battalions, and began their march; and it is not told how they fared till they reached Cloghan Kincat.

Finn told them the whole story of the Giolla Dacker and his horse, and how he had carried away Conan and fifteen others to some far-off island in the Western Ocean. He also showed them the ship, and told them that he himself and a chosen band of the Fena were about to sail westward in quest of their friends.

And Oisin asked him how many of the chief men of the Fena he wished to take with him.

Finn replied, " I foresee that this will be a perilous quest; and I think all the chiefs here present few enough to bring with me."

"Say not so, O king," said Oisin. "Too many have gone already, and some must be left behind to guard the country, and to keep order. If fifteen good men go with you, and that you find the others, the whole party will be a match for any foe you are like to meet in these western lands."

And Oscar and Gall Mac Morna spoke in like manner.

To this Finn agreed. Then he picked out fifteen men, the bravest and best, the most dexterous at the sword, and the swiftest of foot among the Fena.

The question then arose, who should lead the Fena in the king's absence; and what they agreed on was that Oisin should remain behind and take command, as he was the eldest and bravest and wisest of the king's sons.

Of those who were chosen to go with Finn, the chief men were Dermat O'Dyna; Gall Mac Morna; Oscar, the son of Oisin; Aedh Beg, the son of Finn; Fergus Finnvel, the poet; the three sons of Encarda; and Feradach and Foltlebar, the two sons of the king of Innia.

So the king and his party took leave of Oisin and the rest. And sad, indeed, were they on both sides; for no one knew how far the king might have to sail among unknown seas and islands, or how long he should be away from Erin, or the spells and dangers he and his men might encounter in this pursuit.

Then they went on board, and launched their ship on the cold, bright sea; and Foltlebar was their pilot and steersman. And they set their sail and plied their slender oars, and the ship moved swiftly westward till they lost sight of the shores of Erin; and they saw nothing all round them but a wide girdle of sea. After some days' sailing, a great storm came from the west, and the black waves rose up against them, so that they had much ado to keep their vessel from sinking. But through all the roaring of the tempest, through the rain and blinding spray, Foltlebar never stirred from the helm or changed his course, but still kept close on the track of the Giolla Dacker.

At length the storm abated, and the sea grew calm. And when the darkness had cleared away, they saw to the west, a little way off, a vast rocky cliff towering over their heads to such a height that its head seemed hidden among the clouds. It rose up sheer from the very water, and looked at that distance as smooth as glass, so that at first sight there seemed no way to reach the top.

Foltlebar, after examining to the four points of the sky, found the track of the Giolla Dacker as far as the cliff, but no farther. And he accordingly told the heroes that he thought it was on the top of that rock the giant lived; and that, anyhow, the horse must have made his way up the face of the cliff with their companions.

When the heroes heard this they were greatly cast down and puzzled what to do; for they saw no way of reaching the top of the rock; and they feared they should have to give up the quest and return without their companions. And they sat down and looked up at the cliff, with sorrow and vexation in their hearts.

## CHAPTER IV

### DERMAT O'DYNA, IN QUEST OF THE GIOLLA DACKER, ENCOUNTERS THE WIZARD-CHAMPION AT THE WELL

WHEN now they had been silent for a time, Fergus Finnvel, the poet, arose and said—

" My friends, we have here amongst us one who has been fostered and taught from the child to the man by Mannanan Mac Lir[8] in Fairyland, and by Angus,[1] the wisest of the Dedannans, at Brugh of the Boyne. He has been carefully trained by both in everything a warrior should learn, and in much druidical lore besides; so that he is skilled beyond us all in manly arts and champion-feats. But now it seems that all his arts and accomplishments go for nought, seeing that he is unable to make use of them just at the time that we stand most in need of them. On the top of that rock, doubtless, the Giolla Dacker lives, and there he holds Conan and the others in bondage; and surely this hero, who now sits idly with us here in our ship, should be able to climb up the face of that cliff, and bring us back tidings of our dear friends and companions."

When Dermat O'Dyna heard this speech, his cheek grew red with shame, and he made this reply—

" It is of me you have spoken these words, Fergus. Your reproaches are just; and though the task is hard, I will attempt to follow the track of the Giolla Dacker, and find out some tidings of our friends."

So saying, Dermat arose, and girded on his armour, and put on his glittering helmet. He hung his sword at his left hip; and he took his two long, deadly spears, one in each hand, namely, the Crannboi and the Ga-derg; and the battle-fury of a warrior descended on him, so that he looked a dreadful foe to meet in single combat.

Then, leaning on the handles of his spears, after the manner of skilful champions, he leaped with a light, airy bound on the nearest shelf of rock. And using his spears and his hands, he climbed from ledge to ledge, while his companions watched him anxiously from below; till, after much toil, he measured the soles of his two feet on the green sod at the top of the rock. And when, recovering breath, he turned round and looked at his companions in the ship far below, he started back with amazement and dread at the dizzy height.

He now looked inland, and saw a beautiful country spread out before him:—a lovely, flowery plain straight in front, bordered with pleasant hills, and shaded with groves of many kinds of trees. It was enough to banish all care and sadness from one's heart to view this country, and to listen to the warbling of the birds, the humming of the bees among the flowers, the rustling of the wind through the trees, and the pleasant voices of the streams and waterfalls.

Making no delay, Dermat set out to walk across the plain. He had not been long walking when he saw, right before him, a great tree laden with fruit, overtopping all the other trees of the plain. It was surrounded at a little distance by a circle of pillar-stones; and one stone, taller than the others, stood in the centre near the tree. Beside this pillar-stone was a spring well, with a large, round pool as clear as crystal; and the water bubbled up in the centre, and flowed away towards the middle of the plain in a slender stream.

Dermat was glad when he saw the well; for he was hot and thirsty after climbing up the cliff. He stooped down to take a drink; but before his lips touched the water, he heard the heavy tread of a body of warriors, and the loud clank of arms, as if a whole host were coming straight down on him. He sprang to his feet and looked round; but the noise ceased in an instant, and he could see nothing.

After a little while he stooped again to drink; and again, before he had wet his lips, he heard the very same sounds, nearer and louder than before. A second time he leaped to his feet; and still he saw no one. He knew not what to think of this; and as he stood wondering and perplexed, he happened to cast his eyes on the tall pillar-stone that stood on the brink of the well; and he saw on its top a large, beautiful drinking-horn, chased with gold and enamelled with precious stones.

" Now surely," said Dermat, " I have been doing wrong. It is, no doubt, one of the virtues of this well that it will not let any one drink of its waters except from the drinking-horn."

So he took down the horn, dipped it into the well, and drank without hindrance, till he had slaked his thirst.

Scarcely had he taken the horn from his lips, when he saw a tall wizard-champion* coming towards him from the east, clad in a complete suit of mail, and fully armed with shield and helmet, sword and spear. A beautiful scarlet mantle hung over his armour, fastened at his throat by a golden brooch; and a broad circlet of sparkling gold was bended in front across his forehead, to confine his yellow hair, and keep it from being blown about by the wind.

As he came nearer, he increased his pace, moving with great strides; and Dermat now observed that he looked very wrathful. He offered no greeting, and showed not the least courtesy; but addressed Dermat in a rough, angry voice.

" Surely, Dermat O'Dyna, Erin of the green plains should be wide enough for you; and it contains abundance of clear, sweet water in its crystal springs and green bordered streams, from which you might have drunk your fill. But you have come into my island without my leave, and you have taken my drinking-horn, and have drunk from my well; and this spot you shall never leave till you have given me satisfaction for the insult."

So spoke the wizard-champion, and instantly advanced on Dermat with fury in his eyes. But Dermat was not the man to be terrified by any hero or wizard-champion alive. He met the foe half-way; and now, foot to foot, and knee to knee, and face to face, they began a fight, watchful and wary at first but soon hot

---

* The original word, which I have translated " wizard-champion," is *gruagach*. This word literally means " a hairy fellow "; and it is often used in the sense of " giant ". But in these romantic tales it is commonly used to signify a champion who has always something of the supernatural about him, yet not to such a degree as to shield him completely from the valour of a great mortal hero like Dermat O'Dyna.

and vengeful, till their shields and helmets could scarce withstand their strong thrusts and blows. Like two enraged lions fighting to the death, or two strong serpents intertwined in deadly strife, or two great opposing billows thundering against each other on the ocean border; such was the strength and fury and determination of the combat of these two heroes.

And so they fought through the long day, till evening came, and it began to be dusk; when suddenly the wizard-champion sprang outside the range of Dermat's sword, and leaping up with a great bound, he alighted in the very centre of the well. Down he went through it, and disappeared in a moment before Dermat's eyes, as if the well had swallowed him up. Dermat stood on the brink, leaning on his spear, amazed and perplexed, looking after him in the water; but whether the hero had meant to drown himself, or that he had played some wizard trick, Dermat knew not.

He sat down to rest, full of vexation that the wizard-champion should have got off so easily. And what chafed him still more was that the Fena knew nought of what had happened, and that when he returned, he could tell them nothing of the strange hero; neither had he the least token or trophy to show them after his long fight.

Then he began to think what was best to be done; and he made up his mind to stay near the well all night, with the hope of finding out something further about the wizard-champion on the morrow.

He walked towards the nearest point of a great forest that stretched from the mountain down to the plain on his left; and as he came near, a herd of speckled deer ran by among the trees. He put his finger into the silken loop of his spear, and, throwing it with an unerring cast, brought down the nearest of the herd.

Then, having lighted a fire under a tree, he skinned the deer and fixed it on long hazel spits to roast, having first, however, gone to the well and brought away the drinking-horn full of water. And he sat beside the roasting deer to turn it and tend the fire, waiting impatiently for his meal; for he was hungry and tired after the toil of the day.

When the deer was cooked, he ate till he was satisfied, and drank the clear water of the well from the drinking-horn; after which he lay down under the shade of the tree, beside the fire, and slept a sound sleep till morning.

Night passed away and the sun rose, bringing morning with its abundant light. Dermat started up, refreshed after his long sleep, and, repairing to the forest, he slew another deer, and fixed it on hazel spits to roast at the fire as before. For Dermat had this custom, that he would never eat of any food left from a former meal.

And after he had eaten of the deer's flesh and drunk from the horn, he went towards the well. But though his visit was early, he found the wizard-champion there before him, standing beside the pillar-stone, fully armed as before, and looking now more wrathful than ever. Dermat was much surprised; but before he had time to speak the wizard-champion addressed him—

" Dermat O'Dyna, you have now put the cap on all your evil deeds. It was not enough that you took my drinking-horn and drank from my well: you have done much worse than this, for you have hunted on my grounds, and have killed some of my speckled deer. Surely there are many hunting-grounds in Erin of the green plains, with plenty of deer in them; and you need not have come hither to commit these robberies on me. But now for a certainty you shall not go from this spot till I have taken revenge for all these misdeeds."

And again the two champions attacked each other, and fought during the long day, from morning till evening. And when the dusk began to fall, the wizard-champion leaped into the well, and disappeared down through it, even as he had done the day before.

The selfsame thing happened on the third day. And each day, morning and evening, Dermat killed a deer, and ate of its flesh, and drank of the water of the well from the drinking-horn.

On the fourth morning, Dermat found the wizard-champion standing as usual by the pillar-stone near the well. And as each morning he looked more angry than on the morning before, so now he scowled in a way that would have terrified any one but Dermat O'Dyna.

And they fought during the day till the dusk of evening. But now Dermat watched his foe narrowly; and when he saw him about to spring into the well, he closed on him and threw his arms round him. The wizard-champion struggled to free himself, moving all the time nearer and nearer to the brink; but Dermat held on, till at last both fell into the well.  Down they went, clinging to each other, Dermat and the wizard-champion;  down, down, deeper and deeper they went;  and Dermat tried to look round, but nothing could he see save darkness and dim shadows. At length there was a glimmer of light;  then the bright day burst suddenly upon them;  and presently they came to the solid ground, gently and without the least shock.

## CHAPTER  V

### DERMAT O'DYNA IN TIR-FA-THONN*

At the very moment they reached the ground, the wizard-champion, with a sudden effort, tore himself away from Dermat's grasp and ran forward with great speed.  Dermat leaped to his feet;  and he was so amazed at what he saw around him that he stood stock still and let the wizard-champion escape: a lovely country, with many green-sided hills and fair valleys between, woods of red yew trees, and plains laughing all over with flowers of every hue.

Right before him, not far off, lay a city of great tall houses with glittering roofs;  and on the side nearest to him was a royal palace, larger and grander than the rest.  On the level green in front of the palace were a number of knights, all armed, and amusing themselves with various warlike exercises of sword and shield and spear.

Straight towards this assembly the wizard-champion ran; which, when Dermat saw, he set of in pursuit, hoping to overtake him.  But the wizard-champion had too long a start, and when he reached the exercise green, the knights opened to the right and left, leaving a broad way through which he rushed.  He never halted or looked behind till he had got inside the palace gate; and the moment he had passed in, the knights closed their ranks, and stood facing Dermat with threatening looks and gestures.

Nothing daunted, Dermat held on his pace towards them;  and now those of the front rank started forward with spears and

---

* Tir-fa-thonn, literally " the country beneath the wave." (See note 13 at the end.)

swords, intending to crush him at once, and hew his body to mincemeat. But it was not terror nor weakness nor a desire of flight that this produced in Dermat, for his battle-fury was on him; and he rushed through them and under them and over them, as a hawk rushes among a flight of sparrows, or like a whale through a shoal of little fishes, or like a raging wolf among a flock of sheep, or like a vast billow among a fleet of small vessels, or like a great brown torrent rushing down the steep side of a mountain, that sweeps everything headlong before it. So did Dermat cleave a wide laneway through the hosts, till, from a solid band of warriors, he turned them into a scattered crowd, flying in all directions. And those that did not fall by his hand, ran hither and thither, some to hide themselves in the thick forests and remote, wooded glens of the surrounding country; while others rushed in through the outer gate of the palace, and shut themselves up in the strongest part of the fortress, neither did they deem themselves safe till they had shot home every bolt, and securely fastened every strong iron lock.

At last not a living soul remained on the green, and Dermat sat down, weary after his battle-toil, and smarting all over with wounds. He was grieved and downcast also, for he knew not where he was, and he saw no chance that he should be able either to find any tidings of the friends he was in search of, or to return to his companions in the ship.

At length, being quite overcome with weariness, he fell into a deep sleep. After sleeping for some time, he was awakened by a smart blow. He started up, and saw a young man standing over him, tall, and of a commanding appearance, with long, golden hair, and a manly open countenance. Now this young man had come to Dermat, and finding him asleep in such a dangerous place, he struck him with the flat of his sword to awaken him. In an instant Dermat sprang to his feet and seized his arms; but the youth addressed him in a friendly voice, and said—

"Dermat O'Dyna, put up your arms; I am no enemy, and I have come, not to harm, but to serve you. This, indeed, is a strange place for you to fall asleep, before the very door of the castle, and within sight of your enemies. Come now with me, and I will give you a better place to sleep in, where you will also get a welcome and kindly entertainment."

This speech pleased Dermat very much; and he thanked the young man and went with him. After walking for some time, they came to a large splendid house, and passing through the outer gate they entered the banqueting hall. There they found a noble company of twelve score and ten knights, and almost as many beautiful ladies, with their long hair falling on their shoulders, shining like the golden flower of the marsh-flag, and gentle and modest in their looks and conversation. They wore mantles of scarlet satin, and each mantle was fastened in front by a brooch of burnished gold.

The company sat at tables round the walls of the banquet hall, some feasting, some playing chess, and some listening to the music of harps. When the two heroes entered, all the knights and ladies rose and received them with much respect, and they welcomed Dermat and invited him to join their entertainment. But the young prince—for he was in truth a prince—pointing to Dermat's clothes and arms, all soiled and stained, told them that he had endured much toil that day, and that he wanted rest and refreshment.

He then brought Dermat away, and ordered the attendants to prepare a bath in a great cauldron. He put soothing balsams and healing herbs into it with his own hands, and when Dermat had bathed he was immediately healed of his wounds, and he came forth refreshed and cheerful. The prince then directed that his clothes should be put aside, and had him clad in rich garments like the others.

Dermat now joined the company, and ate and drank, for he had taken neither food nor drink since he had made his meal on the deer early that morning near the well; after which he talked and was cheerful with the others. Then rose up the harpers, and the professors of divers arts and sciences, and one after another they played their sweet music, and recited their poems and their tales of the heroes of the olden time. And when they had ended, the knights gave them gifts of gold and silver and jewels. At last the company broke up, and Dermat was shown to a bed richly ornamented, and soft with the red feathers of wild fowl, and soon he fell into a sound sleep after his long day's adventures.

Now Dermat marvelled much at all he saw and heard; and he knew not what place he was in, or who the people were that had treated him with such kindness. So next morning, when the

company had again assembled, he stood up, and addressed the
prince with gentle words and modest demeanour; and this is what
he said—

" I am much surprised, O prince, at what I have seen, and at
all that has befallen me in this land. Though I am here a stranger,
thou hast shown me much kindness, and these noble knights and
ladies have permitted me to join their sports, and have treated
me with much gentleness and consideration. I wish to know, then,
who thou art, O prince, and what country this is, of which I have
never before heard, and who is the king thereof. Tell me also, I
pray thee, the name of the champion who fought with me for four
days at the well, till at last he escaped from me at the palace."

The prince replied, " I will tell you all, Dermat, as you have
asked, concealing nothing. This country is Tir-fa-thonn. The
champion who fought with you is called the Knight of the
Fountain, and that very champion is king of this land. I am the
brother of the king, and my name is the Knight of Valour. Good
reason indeed have I to be kind to you, Dermat O'Dyna, for
though you do not remember me, I spent a year and a day in the
household of Finn the son of Cumhal.

" A part of this kingdom belongs by right to me. But the king
and his son have seized on my patrimony, and have banished me
from the palace, forcing me to live here in exile with a few of my
faithful followers.

" It is my intention, however. to make war on the king for my
part of the kingdom; and right glad I am that you have come
hither, for I would rather have you on my side than all the other
Fena put together, for your nobleness of mind and your valour
in battle.

" I have here in my household seven score and ten heroes, all
champions of great deeds; and if you consent to aid me, these
shall be placed under your command. By day you shall fight
against the king of Tir-fa-thonn and his son, and by night you shall
feast and rest and sleep with me in this palace. If you enter into
friendship with me and fight on my side, well I know that I shall
win back my right without delay."

Dermat agreed to this. So he and the Knight of Valour made
a covenant; and, placing hand in hand, they pledged themselves
to observe faithfully the conditions of the league of friendship.

## CHAPTER VI

### FINN, IN QUEST OF DERMAT, FIGHTS MANY BATTLES

As to Finn Mac Cumhal and those that remained behind with him in the ship, I will now relate what befell them.

It was now many days since Dermat had left them, and they marvelled much that he did not return with tidings of the Giolla Dacker. At length, when they began to be alarmed, the two sons of the king of Innia offered to go in search of him; but Finn said no, for that they should all go together.

So Feradach and Foltlebar took all the cables and ropes they could find in the ship, and tied them end to end in hard, sure knots, till they had a rope long enough to reach from the top of the rock to the bottom. Then they clambered up the steep face of the cliff, bringing with them the end of the rope; and one by one they drew up Finn and the rest. And when they looked round, they were as much surprised and delighted as Dermat was at the look of the country.

Foltlebar now made a search, and soon found the track of Dermat; and the whole party set out to walk across the plain, Foltlebar leading the way. Having travelled some distance they saw the great fruit tree afar off; and, turning to the left, they found a place where a fire had been lighted, and near it the remains of several meals of deer's flesh. By this they knew that it was here Dermat had slept, for all were well aware of his custom not to eat of what was left from a meal.

They then went towards the tree, and there they found the traces of deadly combat—the ground all trampled and ploughed up, and a broken spear handle lying at the brink of the well. While they stood pondering on these things, with anxious hearts, they saw a horseman at a distance, speeding towards them across the plain. In a little while he came up and reined in.

He was a young man of majestic mien, fair and noble of countenance; and he rode a beautiful chestnut steed, with a bridle of twisted gold, and a saddle of surpassing splendour, ornamented all over with gold and jewels.

He alighted and saluted Finn and the Fena, and told them they were welcome to his country, for that he was king; and he put his hand on Finn's neck and kissed his cheek three times. Then he invited them to go with him, saying that the Plain of the Fountain was a comfortless resting-place after a long journey.

Finn's heart was glad at this, for he and his companions were weary; and they set out to walk across the plain with the young king. Having walked a good distance, they came in sight of a noble palace, with tall towers and carved front. As they came near, they were met by a company of knights on the level green in front, who welcomed them with gentle words. And so they passed into the palace. A bath was prepared, and they bathed and were refreshed after their toils. Then they sat down to supper; and while they ate and drank, the harpers played for them, and the poets told their tales and sang their songs.

They slept that night in the palace; and next day they mingled with the knights on the green, and took part in their games and pastimes. In the evening they sat down to a feast. The people of the palace were ranged at tables according to rank and inheritance, every man in his proper place.

Then the feast went on; and abundance of the newest food and of the oldest drink was served out; and they ate of the savoury food, and drank of the sparkling wines and of the strong ales, till they became merry and gently intoxicated. And Finn could not call to mind that he ever saw an entertainment in the house of either king or chief better ordered. In this manner they were feasted and entertained for three days and three nights.

At the end of that time a meeting was held by the king on the palace green. And Finn stood up and said—

" Tell me, I pray thee, thy name and the name of this country, which I have never seen before, or even heard of."

" This country," replied the king, " is called Sorca, of which I am king; and although you know us not, we know you well, for the fame of your deeds has reached even to this land. But now I wish to know why you have come hither; also the reason why you have brought so few companions, and where the rest have tarried."

Then Finn told him the whole story from beginning to end; how the Giolla Dacker and his great horse had carried off sixteen of their chief men. " And," added Finn, " I and these fifteen companions of mine are now in quest of them."

The king replied, "This is a dangerous undertaking; and you and your fifteen men, valiant even as you are, are too few to venture into unknown lands, where you may meet with many enemies. Now my knights are brave and generous, and they love battle and adventure. Wherefore I will place a band of them under your command, who will follow you whithersoever you go, and who will not be behindhand even with the Fena in facing hardship and danger."

Finn stood up to thank the king; but before he had time to speak, they saw a messenger speeding towards them across the plain from the north-west, breathless, and begrimed all over with mud and dust. When he had come in presence of the company, he bowed low to the king, and, standing up, waited impatient for leave to speak.

The king asked him what news he had brought and he replied:

" Bad and direful news I have for thee, O king. A foreign fleet has come to our shores, which seems to cover all the sea, even as far as the eye can reach; and until the stars of heaven are counted, and the sands of the sea, and the leaves of the woods, the hosts that are landing from their black ships shall not be numbered. Even already they have let loose their plunderers over the country, who are burning and spoiling the farmsteads and the great mansions; and many noble heroes and keepers of houses of hospitality, and many people of the common sort, have been slain by them. Some say that it is the King of the World and his host, who, after conquering every country he has yet visited, has come now to ravage this land with fire and sword and spear, and bring it under his power; but I know not if this be true. And this, O king, is the news I bring thee."

When the messenger had ended, the king spoke nought, though his countenance, indeed, showed trouble; but he looked earnestly at Finn. Finn understood this to mean that the king sought his help; and, with clear voice, he spoke.

" Thou hast been generous to me and my people in our day of need, O king of Sorca; and now thou shalt not find the Fena lacking in grateful memory of thy kindness. We will, for a time, give up the pursuit of the Giolla Dacker, and we will place ourselves under thy command, and help thee against these marauders. Neither do I fear the outcome of this war; for many a time have we met these foreigners on the shores of Erin and elsewhere, and they have always yielded to us in the battle-field."

The king of Sorca was glad of heart when he heard these words; and he sent his swift scouts all over the country to gather his fighting men. And when all had come together, he arranged them in fighting order, and marched towards the shore where the foreigners were spoiling the land. And they met the plundering parties, and drove them with great slaughter back to their ships, retaking all the spoils.

Then they formed an encampment on the shore, with ramparts and deep ditches and long rows of pointed stakes all round. And each day a party of the foreigners landed, led by one of their captains, who were met by an equal number of the men of Sorca, led by one of the Fena; and each time they were driven back to their ships, after losing their best men.

When this had continued for many days, the King of the World called a meeting of the chiefs of his army, and asked their counsel as to what should be done. And they spoke as one man, that their best chiefs had fallen, and that they were in worse case now for overcoming the men of Sorca than they were at first; that their sages and prophets had declared against them; and that they had met with ill luck from the day of their arrival. And the advice they gave the king was to depart from the shores of Sorca, for there seemed no chance of conquering the country as long as the Fena were there to help the king.

So the king ordered the sails to be set, and he left the harbour in the night with his whole fleet, without bringing the king of Sorca under subjection, and without imposing tribute on the people.


## CHAPTER VII

### FINN AND DERMAT MEET

WHEN the people of Sorca and the Fena arose next morning, not a ship was in sight; and they began to rejoice greatly, finding themselves freed from this invasion. And while the king and Finn, with the chiefs and people, stood eagerly conversing on all these matters, they saw a troop at a distance coming towards them, with banners and standards and arms glittering in the morning sun. Now they wondered much who these might be; and Finn desired that some one might go and bring back tidings.

So Fergus Finnvel went with a few followers, and when he was yet a good way off, he knew Dermat O'Dyna at the head of the troop, and ran forward with joy to meet him. And they embraced, even as brothers embrace who meet after being long parted. Then they came towards the assembly; and when the Fena saw Dermat they shouted with joy and welcome. And Dermat embraced them one by one, with glad heart, beginning with Finn.

Then Finn inquired from Dermat all particulars, what places he had visited since the day he had climbed up the rock, and whether he had heard any news of their lost companions; and he asked him also who were they—those valiant-looking fighting men—he had brought with him.

Dermat told him of all his adventures from first to last—of his long combat at the well with the Knight of the Fountain, of his descent to Tir-fa-thonn, and how the Knight of Valour had entertained him hospitably in his palace. He related also how he headed the men of the Knight of Valour, and made war on the king of Tir-fa-thonn (who was also called the Knight of the Fountain, the wizard-champion who fought with Dermat at the well), whom he slew, and defeated his army.

"And now," he continued, bringing forth the Knight of Valour from among the strange host, "this is he who was formerly called the Knight of Valour, but who is now the king of Tir-fa-thonn. Moreover, this king has told me, having himself found it out by his druidical art, that it was Avarta the Dedannan (the son of Illahan of the Many-coloured Raiment) who took the form of the Giolla Dacker, and who brought the sixteen Fena away to the Land of Promise,[8] where he now holds them in bondage."

Finn and the young king then put hand in hand and made convenants of lasting friendship with each other. And the Fena were much rejoiced that they had at last got some tidings of their lost companions.

## CHAPTER VIII

CONAN AND HIS COMPANIONS
FOUND AND RESCUED

Now after they had rested some days in the palace of the king of Sorca, Fergus Finnvel told Finn that it was time to begin once more their quest after Conan and the others. They held council, therefore; and the resolution they came to was to return to the rock at the spot where they had turned aside from the track of the Giolla Dacker, and to begin their search anew from that. And when both the king of Sorca and the king of Tir-fa-thonn would have sent men with them, Finn thanked them, but said that the small party of Fena he had with him were quite enough for that adventure.

So they took leave of the two kings, and went back to the rock, and Foltlebar at once found the track. He traced it from the very edge of the rock across the plain to the sea at the other side; and they brought round their ship and began their voyage. But this time Foltlebar found it very hard to keep on the track; for the Giolla Dacker, knowing that there were not in the world men more skilled in following up a quest than the Fena, took great pains to hide all traces of the flight of himself and his horse; so that Foltlebar was often thrown out; but he always recovered the track after a little time.

And so they sailed from island to island, and from bay to bay, over many seas and by many shores, ever following the track, till at length they arrived at the Land of Promise. And when they had made the land, and knew for a certainty that this was indeed the Land of Promise, they rejoiced greatly; for in this land Dermat O'Dyna had been nurtured by Mannanan Mac Lir of the Yellow Hair.

Then they held council as to what was best to be done; and Finn's advice was that they should burn and spoil the country, in revenge of the outrage that had been done to his people. Dermat, however, would not hear of this. And he said:

" Not so, O king. The people of this land are of all men the most skilled in druidic art; and it is not well that they should be at feud with us. Let us rather send to Avarta a trusty herald, to demand that he should set our companions at liberty. If he does so, then we shall be at peace; if he refuse, then shall we proclaim war against him and his people, and waste this land with fire and sword, till he be forced, even by his own people, to give us back our friends."

This advice was approved by all. And then Finn said—

" But how shall heralds reach the dwelling of this enchanter; for the ways are not open and straight, as in other lands, but crooked and made for concealment, and the valleys and plains are dim and shadowy, and hard to be traversed? "

But Foltlebar, nothing daunted by the dangers and the obscurity of the way, offered to go with a single trusty companion; and they took up the track and followed it without being once thrown out, till they reached the mansion of Avarta. There they found their friends amusing themselves on the green outside the palace walls; for, though kept captive in the island, yet were they in no wise restrained, but were treated by Avarta with much kindness. When they saw the heralds coming towards them, their joy knew no bounds; they crowded round to embrace them, and asked them many questions regarding their home and their friends.

At last Avarta himself came forth, and asked who these strangers were; and Foltlebar replied—

" We are of the people of Finn Mac Cumhail, who has sent us as heralds to thee. He and his heroes have landed on this island, guided hither by me; and he bade us tell thee that he has come to wage war and to waste this land with fire and sword, as a punishment for that thou hast brought away his people by foul spells, and even now keepest them in bondage."

When Avarta heard this, he made no reply, but called a council of his chief men, to consider whether they should send back to Finn an answer of war or of peace. And they, having much fear of the Fena, were minded to restore Finn's people, and to give him his own award in satisfaction for the injury done to him; and to invite Finn himself and those who had come with him to a feast of joy and friendship in the house of Avarta.

Avarta himself went with Foltlebar to give this message. And after he and Finn had exchanged friendly greetings, he told them what the council had resolved; and Finn and Dermat and the others were glad at heart. And Finn and Avarta put hand in hand, and made a league of friendship.

So they went with Avarta to his house, where they found their lost friends; and, being full of gladness, they saluted and embraced each other. Then a feast was prepared; and they were feasted for three days, and they ate and drank and made merry.

On the fourth day, a meeting was called on the green to hear the award. Now it was resolved to make amends on the one hand to Finn, as king of the Fena, and on the other, to those who had been brought away by the Giolla Dacker. And when all were gathered together, Finn was first asked to name his award; and this is what he said—

" I shall not name an award, O Avarta; neither shall I accept an eric from thee. But the wages I promised thee when we made our convenant at Knockainy, that I will give thee. For I am thankful for the welcome thou hast given us here; and I wish that there should be peace and friendship between us for ever."

But Conan, on his part, was not so easily satisfied; and he said to Finn—

" Little hast thou endured, O Finn, in all this matter; and thou mayst well waive thy award. But hadst thou, like us, suffered from the sharp bones and the rough carcase of the Giolla Dacker's monstrous horse, in a long journey from Erin to the Land of Promise, across wide seas, through tangled woods, and over rough-headed rocks, thou wouldst then, methinks, name an award."

At this, Avarta, and the others who had seen Conan and his companions carried off on the back of the big horse, could scarce keep from laughing; and Avarta said to Conan—

" Name thy award, and I will fulfil it every jot: for I have heard of thee, Conan, and I dread to bring the gibes and taunts of thy foul tongue on myself and my people."

" Well then," said Conan, " my award is this: that you choose fifteen of the best and noblest men in the Land of Promise, among whom are to be your own best beloved friends; and that you cause them to mount on the back of the big horse, and that you yourself take hold of his tail. In this manner you shall fare to Erin, back again by the selfsame track the horse took when he brought us hither—through the same surging seas, through the same thick thorny woods, and over the same islands and rough rocks and dark glens."

Now Finn and his people were rejoiced exceedingly when they heard Conan's award—that he asked from Avarta nothing more than like for like. For they feared much that he might claim treasure of gold and silver, and thus bring reproach on the Fena.

Avarta promised that everything required by Conan should be done, binding himself in solemn pledges. Then the heroes took their leave; and having launched their ship on the broad, green sea, they sailed back by the same course to Erin. And they marched to their camping-place at Knockainy, where they rested in their tents.

Avarta then chose his men. And he placed them on the horse's back and he himself caught hold of the tail; and it is not told how they fared till they made harbour and landing-place at Cloghan Kincat. They delayed not, but straightway journeyed over the selfsame track as before, till they reached Knockainy.

Finn and his people saw them afar off coming towards the hill with great speed; the Giolla Dacker, quite as large and as ugly as ever, running before the horse; for he had let go the tail at Cloghan Kincat. And the Fena could not help laughing heartily when they saw the plight of the fifteen chiefs on the great horse's back; and they said with one voice that Conan had made a good award that time.

When the horse reached the spot from which he had at first set out, the men began to dismount. Then the Giolla Dacker, suddenly stepping forward, held up his arm and pointed earnestly over the heads of the Fena towards the field where the horses were standing; so that the heroes were startled, and turned round every man to look. But nothing was to be seen except the horses grazing quietly inside the fence.

Finn and the others now turned round again, with intent to speak to the Giolla Dacker and bring him and his people into the tents; but much did they marvel to find them all gone. The Giolla Dacker and his great horse and the fifteen nobles of the Land of Promise had disappeared in an instant; and neither Finn himself nor any of his chiefs ever saw them afterwards.

# The Pursuit of Dermat and Grania

## CHAPTER I

### FINN, THE SON OF CUMHAL, SEEKS THE PRINCESS GRANIA TO WIFE

ON a certain day, Finn, the son of Cumhal, rose at early morn in Allen of the broad hill-slopes, and, going forth, sat him down on the green lawn before the palace, without companion or attendant. And two of his people followed him, namely, Oisin his son, and Dering the son of Dobar O'Baskin.

Oisin spoke to him and asked, " Why, O king, hast thou come forth so early? "

" Cause enough have I indeed," replied Finn, " for I am without a wife since Manissa, the daughter of Garad of the Black Knee, died; and who can enjoy sweet sleep when his life is lonely like mine, with no wife to comfort and cheer him? This, my friends, is the cause of my early rising."

And Oisin said, " Why should you be without a wife if you desire one? For there is not, within the sea-circle of green Erin, a maiden that we will not bring you, either by consent or by force, if you only turn the light of your eyes on her."

Then Dering spoke and said, " I know where there is a maiden, who in all respects is worthy to be thy wife."

And when Finn asked who she was, Dering replied—

" The maiden is Grania, daughter of king Cormac,[22] the son of Art, the son of Conn the Hundred-fighter; the most beautiful, the best instructed, and the most discreet in speech and manner of all the maidens of Erin."

" There has been strife between me and Cormac for a long time," said Finn, " and it may happen that he will not give me

186

his daughter in marriage. But go you to Tara in my name, you and Oisin, and ask the maiden for me: if the king should refuse, so let it be; but I can better bear a refusal to you than to myself."

" We will go," said Oisin, " but it is better that no man know of our journey till we return."

So the two heroes took leave of Finn and went their way; and nothing is told of what befell them till they reached Tara. It chanced that the king was at this time holding a meeting; and the chiefs and great nobles of Tara were assembled round him. And when the two warriors arrived, they were welcomed, and the meeting was put off for that day; for the king felt sure that it was on some business of weight they had come.

After they had eaten and drunk, the king, sending away all others from his presence, bade the two chiefs tell their errand. So Oisin told him they had come to seek his daughter Grania in marriage for Finn the son of Cumhal.

Then the king said, " In all Erin there is scarce a young prince or noble who has not sought my daughter in marriage; and she has refused them all. And it is on me that the ill feeling and reproach caused by her refusals have fallen; for she has ever made me the bearer of her answers. Wherefore now you shall come to my daughter's presence, and I will not mention the matter to her till she give you an answer from her own lips: so shall I be blameless if she refuse.

So they went to the apartments of the women, at the sunny side of the palace. And when they had entered the princess's chamber, the king sat with her on the couch and said—

" Here, my daughter, are two of the people of Finn the son of Cumhal, who have come to ask thee as a wife for him."

And Grania, giving, indeed, not much thought to the matter, answered, " I know not whether he is worthy to be thy son-in-law; but if he be, why should he not be a fitting husband for me? "

The two messengers were satisfied with this answer, and retired. And Cormac made a feast for them; and they ate and drank and made merry with the chiefs and nobles of the palace; after which the king bade them tell Finn to come at the end of a fortnight to claim his bride.

So the two heroes returned to Allen, and told how they had fared in their quest. And as all things come at last to an end, so this fortnight wore slowly away; and at the end of the time, Finn, having collected round him the chief men of the seven standing battalions of the Fena to be his guard, marched to Tara. The king received him with great honour, and welcomed the Fena, and they were feasted with the nobles of Erin in the great banquet hall of Micorta. And the king sat on his throne to enjoy the feast with his guests, having Finn on his right hand, and on his left the queen, Etta, the daughter of Atan of Corca; and Grania sat next the queen, her mother, on the left. And all the others sat according to their rank and patrimony.

## CHAPTER II

### DERMAT O'DYNA SECRETLY ESPOUSES THE PRINCESS GRANIA

Now while the feast went on, it chanced that Dara of the Poems, one of Finn's druids, sat near Grania. And he recited for her many lays about the deeds of her forefathers; after which a pleasant conversation arose between them. And when they had talked for some time, she asked him—

" What means all this feasting? And why has Finn come with his people on this visit to my father the king? "

Dara was surprised at this question, and answered, " If thou dost not know, it is hard for me to know."

And Grania answered, " I wish, indeed, to learn from you what has brought Finn to Tara."

" It is strange to hear thee ask this question," said the druid. " Knowest thou not that he has come to claim thee for his wife? "

Grania was silent for a long time after hearing this. And again she spoke—

" If, indeed, Finn had sought me for his son Oisin, or for the youthful Oscar, there would be nothing to wonder at; but I marvel much that he seeks me for himself, seeing that he is older than my father."

Then Grania meditated in silence; and after a time she said to the druid—

" This is a goodly company, but I know not one among them, except only Oisin, the son of Finn. Tell me now who is that warrior on the right of Oisin."

" That knightly warrior," answered the druid, " is Gall Mac Morna the Terrible in Battle."

" Who is the youthful champion to the right of Gall? " asked Grania.

" That is Oscar, the son of Oisin," said the druid.

" Who is the graceful and active-looking chief sitting next Oscar? " asked the princess.

" That is Kylta Mac Ronan the Swift-footed," said the druid.

" Next to Kylta Mac Ronan sits a champion with fair, freckled skin, raven-black curls, a gentle, handsome, manly countenance, and soft voice: pray who is he? "

" That is Dermat O'Dyna of the Bright Face, the favourite of maidens, and beloved of all the Fena for his high-mindedness, his bravery, and his generous disposition."

" Who is he sitting at Dermat's shoulder? " asked Grania.

" That is Dering, the son of Dobar O'Baskin," replied the druid; " a valiant champion, and also a druid and a man of science."

Then Grania called her handmaid, and said to her, " Bring me the large jewelled, gold-chased drinking-horn that lies in my chamber."

The handmaid brought the drinking-horn; and Grania, having filled it to the brim, said—

" Take it now to Finn from me, and tell him that I desire him to drink from it."

The handmaiden did so, and Finn took a full draught. He passed the drinking-horn to the king, and the king drank; and after him the queen. Then again Grania bade the handmaid bring it to Carbri of the Liffey, the king's son; and she ceased not till all she wished to drink had drunk from the gold-chased horn. And after a little time, those who had drunk fell into a deep sleep, like the sleep of death.

Then the princess rose from her seat, and, walking softly across the hall, sat down near Dermat O'Dyna; and with downcast eyes and low voice, she said—

" Wilt thou, Dermat, return my love if I give it to thee? "

Dermat heard her at first with amazement and alarm. Then for a moment, even before he was aware, his heart leaped with joy; but when he bethought him of his duty to his chief, he hardened his mind, and answered with cold looks and words—

" The maiden who is betrothed to Finn, I will not love; and even if I were so minded, I dare not."

And with eyes still cast down, Grania said, " I know well it is thy duty, and not thy heart, that prompts thee to speak so. Thou seest how it is with me; and I am forced to speak more boldly than a maiden should. Finn has come to ask me for his wife; but he is an old man, even older than my father, and I love him not. But I love thee, Dermat, and I beseech thee to save me from this hateful marriage. And, lest thou think that my love for thee is only a passing fancy, hear now what befell.

" On a day when a hurling match was played on the green of Tara, between Mac Lugha and the Fena on the one side, and Carbri of the Liffey and the men of Tara on the other, I sat high up at the window of my sunny chamber to see the game. Thou didst remain sitting with some others that day, not meaning to take part in the play. But at last, when the game began to go against thy friends, I saw thee start up; and, snatching the hurley from the man nearest to thee, thou didst rush into the thick of the crowd; and before sitting down thou didst win the goal three times on the men of Tara. At that hour my eyes and my heart were turned to thee; and well I knew thee to-day in this banquet hall, though I knew not thy name till the druid told me. At that same hour, too, I gave thee my love—what I never gave, and never will give, to any other."

Then was Dermat sore troubled. He strove with himself, but strove in vain; for he could not help loving the princess with his whole heart. Yet none the less did he hide his thoughts; for his duty to his chief prevailed. And with looks and words cold and stern, he replied—

" I marvel greatly that thou hast not given thy love to Finn, who deserves it much better than any other man alive. And still more do I marvel that thou hast lighted on me beyond all the princes and nobles of Tara; for truly there is not one among them less worthy of thy love than I. But that thou shouldst be my wife, by no means can this be; for even were I to consent, there is not in Erin a fastness or a wilderness, however strong or remote, that could shelter us from Finn's vengeance."

Then Grania said, " I read thy thoughts; and I know thou art striving against what thy heart prompts. And now, O Dermat, I place thee under geasa,[12] and under the bonds of heavy druidical spells—bonds that true heroes never break through, that thou take me for thy wife before Finn and the others awaken from their sleep; and save me from this hateful marriage."

And Dermat, still unyielding, replied, " Evil are those geasa thou hast put on me; and evil, I fear, will come of them. But dost thou not know, princess, that whenever Finn sleeps at Tara, it is one of his privileges to have in his own keeping the keys of the great gates; so that even if we so willed it, we should not be able to leave the fortress? "

" There is a wicket gate leading out from my apartments," said Grania, " and through that we shall pass forth."

" That I cannot do," answered Dermat; " for it is one of my geasa[12] never to enter a king's mansion, or leave it, by a wicket gate."

And Grania answered, " I have heard it said that every true champion, who has been instructed in all the feats that a warrior should learn, can bound over the highest rampart of a fort by means of the handles of his spears; and well I know that thou art the most accomplished champion among the Fena. I will now pass out through the wicket gate; and even if thou dost not follow, I will fly alone from Tara."

And so she went forth from the banquet hall.

Then Dermat, much doubting how to act, spoke to his friends and asked counsel of them. And first he addressed Oisin, the son of Finn, and asked him how he should deal with the heavy geasa-bonds that had been laid on him by the princess; and what he should do in the case.

" You are blameless in regard to these bonds," answered Oisin; " and I counsel you to follow Grania; but guard yourself well against the wiles of Finn."

" O dear friend Oscar," spoke Dermat again, " what think you is best for me to do, seeing that these heavy geasa-bonds have been put on me? "

"I say you should follow Grania," answered Oscar; "for he, indeed, is but a pitiful champion who fears to keep his bonds."

"What counsel do you give me, Kylta?" said Dermat to Kylta Mac Ronan.

"I say," answered Kylta, "that I would gladly give the world's wealth that the princess had given me her love; and I counsel you to follow her."

Last of all, Dermat spoke to Dering, the son of Dobar O'Baskin, and said, "Give me your judgment in this hard matter, friend Dering."

And Dering answered, "If you espouse Grania, I foresee that your death will come of it, which grieves me even to think of; but even so, I counsel you to follow the princess rather than break through your geasa."

And Dermat, doubting even still, asked for the last time, "Is this, my friends, the counsel you all give?"

And they all answered, "Yes," as with the voice of one man.

Then Dermat arose and put on his armour and his helmet; and he took his shield, and his two heavy spears, and his sword. And with tears he bade farewell to his dear companions; for well he knew that it would be long before they should meet again; and he foresaw trouble and danger.

Then he went forth to where the steep side of the inner mound overlooked the outer rampart; and, placing his two spears point downwards, and leaning on them after the manner of skilful champions, with two light, airy bounds he cleared rampart and ditch, and measured the length of his two feet on the level green outside. And there the princess met him; and he said to her, with voice and manner still distant and stern—

"Evil will certainly come of this espousal, O princess, both to thee and to me. Far better would it be for thee to choose Finn and to pass me by; for now we shall wander without home or rest, fleeing from his wrath. Return, then, princess, return even now through the wicket gate, for the sleepers have not yet awakened; and Finn shall never learn what has happened."

But Grania, gentle and sad indeed, but quite unmoved, replied, "I will never return; and until death takes me I will not part from thee."

Then at last Dermat yielded and strove no longer; and putting off his sternness of manner and voice, he spoke gently to the princess and said—

" I will hide my thoughts from thee no more, Grania. I will be thy husband, all unworthy of thee as I am; and I will guard thee and defend thee to the death from Finn and his hirelings."

And they plighted their faith, and vowed solemn vows to be faithful to each other as man and wife for ever.

## CHAPTER III

### FLIGHT AND PURSUIT

THEN Grania showed Dermat the fenced meadow where her father's horses grazed, and bade him yoke two horses to a chariot. And when he had done so, he and Grania sat in the chariot and travelled with all speed westward, till they reached Ath Luain.*

And when they had come to the ford, Dermat said, " Finn will doubtless pursue us, and it will be all the easier for him to follow our track, that we have the horses."

And Grania answered, " As we are now so far from Tara, we may leave the chariot and horses here, and I will fare on foot henceforward."

So they alighted from the chariot; and Dermat, leading one of the horses across, left them both some distance above the ford, one at each side of the river. And he took up Grania in his strong arms, and brought her tenderly across the ford, so that not even the sole of her foot, or the skirt of her mantle was wetted. Then they walked against the stream for a mile, and turned south-west, till they reached the Wood of the two Tents.†

In the midst of the wood, where it was thickest, Dermat lopped off branches and wove a hut, where they rested. And he

---

* Ath Luain, Athlone, on the Shannon. In ancient times the river had to be crossed by a ford.

† The Wood of the two Tents was situated in the territory of Clanrickard, in County Galway.

brought Grania the wild animals of the wood to eat, and gave
her the water of a clear spring to drink.

As to Finn, the son of Cumhal, I will now tell what befell
him. When the king and his guests arose from their sleep at
early dawn next morning, they found Dermat and Grania gone;
and a burning jealousy seized on Finn, and his rage was so great
that for a time all his strength left him. Then he sent for his
tracking-men, namely, the Clann Navin; and he commanded
them forthwith to follow the track of Dermat and Grania. This
they did with much ease as far as Ath Luain, while Finn and
the others followed after; but when they had come to the ford,
they lost the track. Whereupon Finn, being now indeed easily
kindled to wrath, told them that unless they took up the track
again speedily, he would hang every man of the Clann Navin on
the edge of the ford.

So the trackers, being sore afraid, searched upwards against
the stream, and found the two horses where they had been left,
one on each side of the river. And going on a mile further,
they came to the spot where Dermat and Grania had turned
from the river; and there they lighted on the south-west track,
Finn and the Fena still following. And when the Clann Navin
had pointed out to Finn the direction of the track, he said—

"Well do I know now where we shall find Dermat and
Grania; for of a certainty they have hidden themselves in the
Wood of the two Tents."

Now it chanced that Oisin, and Oscar, and Kylta, and Dering
were present when Finn spoke these words; and they were
troubled, for they loved Dermat. And going aside, they held
council among themselves, and Oisin spoke—

"There is much likelihood, friends, that Finn speaks truth;
for he is far-seeing, and judges not hastily. It is needful, therefore,
that we send Dermat warning, lest he be taken unawares. My
counsel is that you, Oscar, find out Finn's hound, Bran, and tell
him to go to the Wood of the two Tents with a warning to
Dermat; for Bran does not love his own master Finn better
than he loves Dermat."

So Oscar called Bran secretly, and told him what he should
do. Bran listened, with sagacious eye and ears erect, and
understood Oscar's words quite well. Then, running back to

the rear of the host, so that Finn might not see him, he followed the track without once losing it, till he arrived at the Wood of the two Tents. There he found Dermat and Grania asleep in their hut, and he put his head into Dermat's bosom.

Dermat started up from his sleep, and seeing Bran, he awakened Grania, and said—

" Here is Bran, Finn's hound; he has come to warn me that Finn himself is near."

And Grania trembled and said, " Let us take the warning, then, and fly! "

But Dermat answered, " I will not leave this hut; for however, long we fly, we cannot escape from Finn; and it is not worse to fall into his hands now than at any other time. But they shall not come into this fastness unless I permit them."

Then great fear fell on Grania; but, seeing Dermat gloomy and downcast, she urged the point no further.

Again Oisin spoke to his three companions and said, " I fear me that Bran may not have been able to baffle Finn, or that some other mischance may have hindered him from finding Dermat; so we must needs send him another warning. Bring hither, therefore, Fergor, Kylta's errand-man."

And Kylta brought forward Fergor.

Now this Fergor had a voice so loud that his shout was heard over the three nearest cantreds.

So they caused him to give three shouts that Dermat might hear. And Dermat heard Fergor's shouts, and, awakening Grania from her sleep, said to her—

" I hear the shout of Fergor, Kylta's errand-man. And he is with Kylta, and Kylta is with Finn; and I know that my friends have sent me this warning, as a sign that Finn himself is coming."

And again Grania trembled and said, " Let us take this warning and fly! "

But Dermat answered, " I will not fly; and we shall not leave this wood till Finn and the Fena overtake us."

And Grania was in great fear; but this time Dermat looked gloomy and stern, and she pressed the matter no further.

# CHAPTER IV

## THE FASTNESS OF THE SEVEN NARROW DOORS

Now as to Finn. He and the others went forward till they reached the Wood of the two Tents. And he sent forward the Clann Navin to make search; who went, and having made their way to the thickest part of the wood, they came to a fence which they could not cross.

For Dermat had cleared a space round his hut, and surrounded it with a fence that no man could pierce, with seven narrow doors of strong poles woven with saplings, to face seven different parts of the wood.

Then the Clann Navin climbed up to a high tree branch, and looked over the fence; and they saw Dermat with a lady. And when they had returned, Finn asked them if Dermat and Grania were in the wood. And they answered—

" Dermat, indeed, is there, and we saw a lady with him; but whether she be Grania or not we cannot tell, for we know not the princess."

" May ill luck attend Dermat, and all his friends for his sake! " said Finn. " I know he is in this wood; and he shall never leave it till he give me quittance for the injury he has done me."

And Oisin said, " Certain it is, that you, Finn, are blinded by jealousy; else you would never think that Dermat would await you on this plain, with no stronger fastness to shelter him from your wrath than the Wood of the two Tents."

To which Finn, being angry, replied, " Your words will profit you nothing, Oisin; neither will your friendship for Dermat avail him aught. Well I knew, indeed, when I heard Fergor's three shouts, that it was ye who caused him to shout, as a warning signal to Dermat; and I know also that ye sent my dog Bran to him with another warning. But these warnings will not avail you; for he shall never leave this wood till he pay me such eric[10] as I seek for the injury he has done me."

Then Oscar spoke and said, " Surely, Finn, it is mere folly to believe that Dermat would wait here for you, knowing, as he does, that you seek his head."

As Oscar spoke these words, they arrived at the fence; and Finn answered, " Who then, think you, has cleared the wood in this manner, and fenced the space with this strong, sheltering enclosure, and fitted it with these narrow doors? But indeed," added he, " I will find out the truth of the matter in another way." So, raising his voice a little, he called out, " Tell us now, Dermat, which of us is telling truth, Oscar or I."

And Dermat, who would not hide when called on, answered from within. "You never erred in your judgment, O king: Grania and I are here; but none shall come in unless I permit them."

Then Finn placed his men around the enclosure, a company at each narrow door; and he said to each company, " If Dermat tries to escape by this door, seize him and keep him securely for me."

Now when Grania saw these preparations, and overheard Finn's words, she was overcome with fear, and wept and trembled very much. And Dermat had pity on his wife, and comforted her; and he kissed her three times, bidding her be of good cheer, for that all would be well with them yet.

And when Finn saw this—for he stood with some others viewing the hut from a mound at a little way off—a flame of burning jealousy went through his heart; and he said—

" Now of a certainty Dermat shall not escape from me; and I shall have his head for all these injuries! "

Now Angus of Brugh,[1] the wisest and most skilled in magic arts of all the Dedannan race, was Dermat's foster-father. For he had raised him from childhood, and had taught him all the arts and accomplishments of a champion; and he loved him even as a father loves his only son.

And it was revealed to Angus that Dermat was in deadly strait. So he arose and travelled on the wings of the cool, east wind, neither did he halt till he reached the Wood of the two Tents; and he passed into the hut without being perceived by Finn and his men. And when Dermat saw the old man his heart leaped with joy.

Angus greeted Dermat and Grania, and said, " What is this thing thou hast done, my son? "

And Dermat answered, " The princess Grania, daughter of the king of Tara, asked me to take her for my wife, putting heavy geasa-bonds on me; and I did so, and we fled from her father's house. And Finn, the son of Cumhal, has pursued us with intent to kill me, for he sought the princess to wife for himself."

And Angus said, " Come now, children, under my mantle, one under each border, and I will bring you both away from this place without the knowledge of Finn."

But Dermat answered, " Take Grania; but for me, I will not go with you. However, I will leave this place; and if I am alive I will follow you. But if they slay me, send the princess to her father, and tell him to treat her neither better nor worse on account of taking me for her husband."

Then Dermat kissed Grania, and bade her be of good cheer, for that he feared not his foes. And Angus placed her under his mantle, and, telling Dermat whither to follow, went forth from the enclosure without the knowledge of Finn and the Fena. They turned south then, and nothing is told of what befell them till they came to the Wood of the two Sallows, which is now called Limerick.

Now as to Dermat. After Angus and Grania had left him, he girded on his armour, and took his sharp weapons in his hands; and he stood up tall and straight like a pillar, meditating in silence for a space. Then he went to one of the seven narrow doors, and asked who was outside.

" No enemy of thine is here, but Oisin and Oscar, with the men of the Clann Baskin. Come out to us, and no one will dare to harm thee."

" I must needs find the door where Finn himself keeps guard," answered Dermat; " so I will not go out to you."

He went to the second narrow door, and asked who was there.

" Kylta Mac Ronan with the Clann Ronan around him. Come out at this door, and we will fight to the death for thy sake."

" I will not go out to you," answered Dermat; " for I do not wish to bring Finn's anger on you for treating me with kindness."

He went to another narrow door, and asked who was there.

" Conan of the Grey Rushes and the Clann Morna. We are no friends to Finn; but thee we all love. Come out to us, then, and no one will dare to harm thee."

" Of a certainty I will not go out at this door," answered Dermat; " for well I know that Finn would rather see you all dead than that I should escape! "

He went to another narrow door, and asked who was there.

" A friend and a dear comrade of thine is here; Cuan, the chief of the Munster Fena, and his Munster men with him. Thou and we come from the same territory; and if need be we will give our lives in fight for thy sake."

" I will not go out to you," said Dermat; " for it would bring Finn's sure displeasure on you to act kindly towards me."

He went to another narrow door, and asked who was there.

" Finn, the son of Glore of the Loud Voice, chief of the Fena of Ulster, and the Ulster men around him. Thou and we come not from the same territory; but we all love thee, Dermat; and now come forth to us, and who will dare to wound or harm thee? "

" I will not go out to you," replied Dermat. " You are a faithful friend of mine, and your father in like manner; and I do not wish you to earn the enmity of Finn on my account."

He went to another narrow door, and asked who was there.

" No friend of thine! Here stand the Clann Navin watching for thee; namely, Aedh the Lesser, and Aedh the Tall, and Gonna the Wounder, and Gothan the Loud-voiced, and Cuan the Tracker, with all their men. We bear thee no love; and if thou come out at this door, we shall make thee a mark for our swords and spears! "

And Dermat answered, " Lying and mean-faced dogs! It is not fear of you that keeps me from going forth at this door; but I do not wish to defile my spear with the blood of your shoeless, tracking vagabonds! "

And he went to another narrow door, and asked who was there.

" Finn, the son of Cumhal, the son of Art, the son of Trenmore O'Baskin, and with him the Leinster Fena. No love awaits thee here; and if thou come forth we will cleave thee, flesh and bones! "

" The door I have sought I have found at last! " cried Dermat; " for the door where thou, Finn, standest, that, of a certainty, is the very door by which I shall pass out! "

Then Finn charged his men, under pain of death, not to let
Dermat pass. But Dermat, watching an unguarded place, rose
by means of his two spears with a light, airy bound over the
fence, and alighted on the clear space outside; and running
swiftly forward, was in a moment beyond the reach of sword
and spear. And so dismayed were they by his threatening look,
that not a man attempted to follow him.

Then, turning southward, he never halted till he came to
the Wood of the two Sallows, where he found Angus and
Grania in a warm hut, with a boar fixed on hazel spits roasting
before a great flaming fire. Dermat greeted them; and the
spark of life all but leaped from Grania's heart with joy when
she saw him.* So he told them all that had befallen him; and
they ate their meal and slept in peace that night, till the morning
of next day filled the world with light.

Then Angus arose with the dawn, and said to Dermat, "I
will now depart, my son; but Finn will still pursue you, and I
leave you this counsel to guide you when I am gone. Go not
into a tree having only one trunk; never enter a cave that has
only one opening; never land on an island of the sea that has
only one channel of approach; where you cook your food, there
eat it not; where you eat, sleep not there; and where you sleep
to-night, sleep not there to-morrow night!"

So Angus bade them farewell; and they were sad after him.


## CHAPTER V

### THE THREE SEA-CHAMPIONS AND THEIR THREE VENOMOUS
### HOUNDS ON THE TRACK OF DERMAT AND GRANIA

AFTER Angus was gone, Dermat and Grania journeyed westward,
keeping the Shannon on their right, till they reached the Rough
Stream of the Champions, which is now called the Laune.†
They rested there; and Dermat killed a salmon with his spear,
and fixed it on a hazel spit to broil on the near bank; and he

---

* Original: "It was little but that the salmon of her life fled through her mouth
   with joy before Dermat."
† The river Laune, flowing from the Lakes of Killarney into Dingle Bay.

crossed the river with Grania, to eat it on the further bank, as Angus had told him. And after they had eaten, they sought a sleeping-place further west.

They rose early next morning, and journeyed still west, till they reached the Grey Moor of Finnlia. There they met a man of great size, noble in gait and feature, but with arms and armour not befitting his appearance. Dermat greeted him, and asked who he was; and he replied—

" My name is Modan, and I am seeking a lord whom I may serve for pay."

" If I take you into my service," asked Dermat, " what can you do for us! "

" I will serve you by day and watch for you by night," answered Modan.

Whereupon they entered into bonds of agreement with one another, Modan to serve by day and watch by night, and Dermat to pay him wages.

Then the three went westward till they reached the river of Carra, and Modan lifted Dermat and Grania with the greatest ease, and bore them dry across the stream. From that, further west to Beha, and Modan bore them over this stream in like manner. Here they found a cave, on the side of the hill over that part of the sea called Tonn Toma, namely, the hill of Curra-Kenn-Ammid; and Modan prepared a couch of soft rushes and birch tops in the innermost part of the cave, for Dermat and Grania. After this he went to the nearest wood

---

The Grey Moor of Finnlia (*Bogach-Fhinnléithe* in the original) was somewhere between the river Laune and the river Caragh.

The river of Carra, the Caragh river, flowing into Dingle Bay from the beautiful lake Caragh, twenty miles west of Killarney.

Beha, the river Behy, about a mile-and-a-half west from the Caragh, flowing through Glanbehy into Rossbehy creek.

Tonn Toma, the wave of Toma (a woman). The word Tonn (a wave) was often applied to the sea-waves that break over certain sandbanks and rocks with an exceptionally loud roaring. Tonn Toma is the name of a sandbank at the head of Dingle Bay; and in the winter storms, the sea thunders on this sandbank, and indeed on the whole length of the peninsula, so as often to be heard twenty miles inland. This roaring is popularly believed to predict rain.

There is a chain of three hills, Stookaniller, Knockatinna, and Knockboy, lying between Behy bridge and Drung mountain, and isolated from the hills to the south-east by the valley of Glanbehy. These hills rise directly over Tonn Toma; and the old Gaelic name, Currach-Cinn-Adhmaid (the moor of the head [or hill] of timber) must have been anciently applied to one or all of them.

and cut him a long, straight quicken tree rod; and, having put
a hair and a hook on the rod, and a holly berry on the hook,
he stood on the brink of the stream, and with three casts he
hooked three salmon.  Then he put the rod by for next day;
and, putting the hook and the hair under his girdle, he returned
to Dermat and Grania.  And he broiled the fish, and they ate
their meal, Modan giving the largest salmon to Dermat, the
second in size to Grania, and keeping the smallest for himself.
After which Dermat and Grania went to sleep in the cave, and
Modan kept watch and ward at the mouth, till morning arose
with its abundant light.

Dermat rose early and set out for the nearest high hill, to
look round the country, telling Grania to keep watch at the
mouth of the cave while Modan slept.  Having come to the top
of the hill, he viewed the country all round to the four points
of the sky; and after a little while, he saw a fleet of black ships
approaching from the west.  When they had come near enough
to the shore, a company of nine nines landed at the very foot
of the hill where Dermat stood.  He went to them, and, after
greeting them, asked who they were, and from what country
they had come.

" We are three sea-champions from the Iccian Sea,* who are
at the head of this troop," replied they, " and our names are
Ducoss, Fincoss, and Trencoss;† and we have come hither at
the suit of Finn the son of Cumhal. For a certain chief named
Dermat O'Dyna has rebelled against him, and is now an outlaw,
flying through the country from one fastness to another.  And
Finn has asked us to come with our fleet to watch the coast,
while he himself watches inland, so that this marauder may no
longer escape punishment.  We hear, moreover, that this Dermat
is valiant and dangerous to attack, and we have brought thither
three venomous hounds to loose them on his track, and scent
him to his hiding-place: fire cannot burn them, water cannot
drown them, and weapons cannot wound them.  And now tell
us who thou art, and whether thou hast heard any tidings of
this Dermat O'Dyna."

---

* Iccian Sea (Irish, *Muir nIcht*), the Irish name for the sea between England and
    France.
† Ducoss, Fincoss, and Trencoss, *i.e.*, Blackfoot, Whitefoot, and Strongfoot.

" I saw him, indeed, yesterday," answered Dermat. " I know him well, too, and I counsel you to follow your quest warily; for if you meet with Dermat O'Dyna you will have no common man to deal with."

Then he asked if they had got any wine in their ships. They replied that they had; so he asked that a tun might be brought, as he wished to drink; and he told them he would show them a champion-feat after he had drunk. Two men were accordingly sent on board for a tun of wine. When they had brought it, Dermat raised it in his arms and drank; and the others drank in like manner till the tun was empty.

Then he said, " I will now show you a champion-feat that Dermat O'Dyna taught me; and I challenge any man among you to do it after me. And from this you may learn what manner of man you will have to deal with, should you have the ill luck to meet with Dermat himself."

So saying, he brought the tun to the crest of the hill, and set it down at the edge of a steep cliff. Then, leaping up on it, he turned it cunningly aside from the cliff, and let it roll down the smooth slope of the hill till it reached the very bottom, while he himself remained standing on it the whole time. And three times did he do this while the strangers looked on.

But they laughed, mocking him, and said, " Do you call that a champion-feat indeed? Truly, you have never in your life seen a good champion-feat! "

Thereupon one among them started up and brought the tun to the top of the hill, intending to do the same feat; and, placing it on the edge of the cliff, he leaped up on it. And while he stood on it, Dermat pushed it with his foot to set it going. But the moment it moved, the man lost his balance, and while the tun went rolling down the face of the hill, he himself fell over the cliff, and was dashed to pieces on the sharp edges and points of the rocks.

Another man tried the same thing, and he in like manner fell down and was killed among the rocks. And the end of the matter was, that before they would acknowledge themselves beaten, fifty of their men attempted the feat, and every man of the fifty fell over the cliff and was killed. So the others went on board their ships, gloomy and heart-sore.

Dermat returned to the cave, and Grania's heart was glad when she saw him. Modan went then, and putting the hair and the hook on the rod as before, he hooked three salmon; and he went back to the cave and broiled them on hazel spits. And they ate their meal; and Modan kept watch and ward, while Dermat and Grania slept in the cave, till the pleasant morning filled the world with light.

Dermat rose up with the dawn, and telling Grania to keep watch while Modan slept, he went to the same hill, and found the three sea-champions with their men on the shore before him. He greeted them, and asked whether they wished for any more champion-feats. But they answered that they would much rather he would give them some tidings of Dermat O'Dyna. Whereupon he said—

" I have seen a man who saw him this very morning. And now I will show you a champion-feat he taught me, in order that you may know what is before you, should you meet with Dermat O'Dyna himself."

When he had said this, he threw off helmet and tunic and armour, till only his shirt remained over his brawny shoulders; and, taking the Ga-boi,* the spear of Mannanan Mac Lir, he fixed it firmly in the earth, standing point upwards. Then, walking back some little way, he ran towards the spear, and, rising from the earth with a bird-like bound, he alighted softly on the very point; and, again leaping off it, he came to the ground on his feet without wound or hurt of any kind.

Then arose one of the strange warriors and said, " If you call that a champion-feat, it is plain that you have never seen a good champion-feat in your life! "

And so saying, he ran swiftly towards the spear and made a great bound; but he fell heavily on the sharp point, so that it pierced him through the heart, and he was taken down dead. Another man attempted the feat, and was killed in like manner; and before they ceased, fifty of their men were slain by Dermat's

---

* Dermat had two spears, the great one called the Ga-derg or Crann-derg (red javelin), and the small one called Ga-boi or Crann-boi (yellow javelin): he had also two swords: the Morallta (great fury), and the Begallta (little fury). These spears and swords he got from Mannanan Mac Lir and from Angus of the Brugh. He carried the great spear and sword in affairs of life and death; and the smaller in adventures of less danger.

spear. Then they bade him draw his spear from the earth, saying that no more should try that feat; and they went on board their ships.

So Dermat returned to the cave; and Modan hooked three salmon; and Dermat and Grania ate their meal and slept till morning, Modan keeping watch.

Next morning, Dermat went to the hill, bringing two strong forked poles cut from the wood. He found the three sea-champions with their men on the shore; and he greeted them, and said—

" I have come to-day to show you a champion-feat I learned from Dermat O'Dyna, that you may know what to expect if you should meet with Dermat himself."

He then fixed the poles standing firmly in the earth; and he placed the Morallta, that is, the long sword of Angus of the Brugh, in the forks, edge upwards, the hilt on one, and the point on the other, binding it firmly with withes. Then, rising up with a bound, he alighted gently on the edge; and he walked cunningly three times from hilt to point, and from point to hilt, and then leaped lightly to the earth without wound or hurt. And he challenged the strangers to do that feat.

The one arose and said, " There never yet was done a champion-feat by a man of Erin, that one among us will not do likewise."

And he leaped up, intending to alight on his feet; but he came down heavily on the sharp edge, so that the sword cut him clean in two. Another tried the same, and was killed also; and, they ceased not till as many were killed that day by Dermat's sword as were killed on each of the two days before.

When they were about to return to their ships, they asked him had he got any tidings of Dermat O'Dyna; and he answered—

" I have seen him this day: I will now go to seek him, and methinks I shall bring him to you in the morning."

Then he returned to the cave; and he and Grania ate their meal, and slept that night, while Modan kept watch.

Next morning, Dermat arose with the dawn, and this time he arrayed himself for battle. He put on his heavy armour— no man who wore it could be wounded through it, or above it,

or beneath it.   He hung the Morallta at his left hip, the sword
of Angus of the Brugh, which never left anything for a
second blow; and he took his two thick-handled spears, the
Ga-derg and the Ga-boi, from whose wounds no one ever
recovered.

Then he awakened Grania, telling her to keep watch till he
returned, that Modan might sleep.  And when she saw him so
arrayed, she trembled with fear, for she well knew that this was
his manner of preparing for battle.  And she asked him what
he meant to do to-day, and whether Finn's pursuers had found
them.  But he, to quiet her fears, put off the matter lightly, and
said, " It is better to be prepared, lest the enemy come in my
way "; and this soothed her.

So he went to the hill, and met the strangers on the shore
as before.  And they asked him had he any tidings to give them
of Dermat O'Dyna.

He answered, " He is not very far off, for I have seen him
just now."

" Then," said they, " lead us to his hiding-place, that we
may bring his head to Finn the son of Cumhal."

" That would, indeed, be an ill way of repaying friendship,"
answered he.  " Dermat O'Dyna is my friend; and he is now
under the protection of my valour: so of this be sure, I will
do him no treachery."

And they replied wrathfully, " If thou art a friend to Dermat
O'Dyna, thou art a foe to Finn; and now we will take thy head
and bring it to him along with the head of Dermat."

" You might indeed do that with much ease," answered
Dermat, " if I were bound hand and foot; but being as I am,
free, I shall defend myself after my usual custom."

Then he drew the Morallta from its sheath, and, springing
forward to meet them as they closed on him, he clove the body
of the foremost in two with one blow.  Then he rushed through
them and under them and over them, like a wolf among sheep,
or a hawk among sparrows, cleaving and slaughtering them, till
only a few were left, who hardly escaped to their ships.

## CHAPTER VI

### WHAT BEFELL THE THREE SEA-CHAMPIONS
### AND THEIR THREE VENOMOUS HOUNDS

AFTER this, Dermat returned to the cave without wound or hurt; and he and Grania ate and slept, and Modan watched till morning. Then he repaired to the hill, fully armed as before, and standing right over the ships, he struck his hollow-sounding shield* with his spear for a challenge, till the whole shore and the surrounding hills re-echoed. And Ducoss straightway armed himself and came ashore to fight Dermat single-hand.

Now Dermat by no means wished to slay his foe immediately, being, indeed, intent on worse punishment. So he closed with Ducoss; and the two champions, throwing aside their weapons, seized each other round the waists with their sinewy arms. Then they twisted and tugged and wrestled in deadly silence; and their swollen sinews strained and crackled; and the earth trembled beneath their feet; like two great writhing serpents, or like two raging lions, or like two savage bulls that strive and struggle to heave each other with horns interlocked. Thus did the heroes contend; till at last Dermat, heaving Ducoss on his shoulder, dashed him helpless and groaning to the ground; and instantly seizing him, he bound him in hard iron bonds.

Fincoss came next against Dermat, and after him, Trencoss; but he overcame them both, and bound them with like bonds; and then, leaving the three writhing with pain, he said to them—

" I would strike off your heads, but that I wish to prolong your torment; for none can release you from these bonds till you die! "

Dermat then returned to the cave; and he and Grania ate their meal and slept that night, Modan watching. In the morning, Dermat told Grania all that had happened from beginning to end; how fifty of the foreigners had been killed each day for the first three days; how he had slain a much

---

* A usual form of challenge among the ancient Irish warriors. This custom is remembered to the present day, even in places where the Irish language is no longer spoken. In the south, and in parts of the west, a boaster is called a *buailim sciach*, an expression which means literally, " I strike the shield."

greater number on the fourth day; and how he had overcome
and bound the three sea-champions in hard iron bonds.

" I have left them bound on the hill," continued he, " instead
of killing them; because I would rather their torment to be long
than short. For there are only four men in Erin that can loosen
the bonds I tie; that is to say, Oisin, and Oscar, and Mac Lugha,
and Conan Maol; and I think no one of these will free them.
Finn will doubtless hear of their state, and the news will sting
him to the heart. But he will know that we are here; so we
must now leave this cave, to escape him, and also to escape the
three venomous dogs."

So they came forth from the cave, and travelled eastward
till they came to the Grey Moor of Finnlia; and whenever
Grania was tired, or when they had to walk over rugged places,
Modan lifted her tenderly and carried her, without ever being in
the least tired himself. And so they journeyed, till they reached
the broad, heathery slopes of Slieve Lougher;* and they sat down
to rest on the green bank of a stream that wound through the
heart of the mountain.

Now as to the sea-strangers. Those of them that were left
alive landed from their ships, and coming to the hill, found
their three chiefs bound tightly, hand and foot and neck. And
they tried to loose them, but only made their bonds the tighter.
While they were so engaged, they saw Finn's errand-woman
coming towards them, with the speed of a swallow, or of a
weasel, or of the swift, cold wind blowing over a mountain-side.
When she had come near, she greeted them, and, seeing the
bodies of the slain, she asked who it was that had made that
fearful slaughter.

" Tell us first," said they, " who art thou that makest this
inquiry? "

" I am Derdri of the Black Mountain, the errand-woman of
Finn the son of Cumhal," she replied; "and he has sent me
hither to look for you."

And they said, " We know not who made this slaughter;
but we can tell thee his appearance, for that we know well. He
was a tall warrior, with a fair, handsome, open countenance,
and jet-black, curly hair. He has been three days fighting

---

* Slieve Lougher, a mountain near Castleisland in Kerry.

against us; and what grieves us even more than the slaughter of our men is that our three chiefs lie here bound by him so firmly that we are not able to loose them from their bonds."

"Alas, friends!" said Derdri, "you have sped but badly at the very beginning of your quest; for this man was Dermat O'Dyna himself. And now loose your three venomous dogs on his track without delay; and I will return and send Finn to meet you."

Then they brought forth the three hounds, and loosed them on the track of Dermat; and leaving one of their druids to attend to the three fettered chiefs, they followed the hounds till they came to the cave, where they found the soft, rushy bed of Dermat and Grania. From that they fared east, and crossing the Carra, and the Grey Moor of Finnlia, and the Laune, they reached at length the broad, heathy Slieve Lougher.

As Dermat sat by the mountain stream with Grania and Modan, looking westward, he saw the silken banners of the foreigners at a distance as they approached the hill. In front of all marched three warriors with mantles of green, who held the three fierce hounds by three chains. And Dermat, when he saw the hounds, was filled with loathing and hatred of them. Then Modan lifted Grania, and walked a mile with Dermat up the stream into the heart of the mountain.

When the green-clad warriors saw them, they loosed one of the three hounds; and when Grania heard his hoarse yelps down the valley, she was in great dread. But Modan bade her not fear, for that he would deal with this hound; and then, turning round, he drew forth from beneath his girdle a small hound-whelp, and placed it on the palm of his hand. There it stood till the great hound came up raging, with jaws wide open; when the little whelp leaped from Modan's hand down the dog's throat, and broke his heart, so that he fell dead. And after that the whelp leaped back again on Modan's hand; and Modan put him under his girdle.

Then they walked another mile up the stream through the mountain, Modan bringing Grania. But the second hound was loosed, and soon overtook them; and Dermat said—

"I will try the Ga-derg on this hound. For no spell can guard against the magic spear of Angus of the Brugh; and I have heard it said also that there is no charm that can shield the throat of an animal from being wounded."

Then, while Modan and Grania stood to look, Dermat, putting his finger into the silken loop of the spear, threw a cast, and drove the spear-head down the hound's throat, so that the entrails of the brute were scattered about; and Dermat, leaping forward, drew the spear, and followed Modan and Grania.

After they had walked yet another mile, the third hound was loosed; and Grania, seeing him coming on, said, trembling—

" This is the fiercest of the three, and I greatly fear him; guard yourself, Dermat, guard yourself well against this hound! "

Even while she spoke, the hound overtook them at the place called Duban's Pillar-stone; and as they stood looking back at him, Dermat stepped in front of Grania to shield her. The hound rose with a great spring over Dermat's head to seize Grania: but Dermat grasped him by the two hind legs as he passed, and, swinging him round, he struck his carcase against a rock and dashed out his brains.

Then, putting his tapering finger into the silken string of the Ga-derg, he threw the spear at the foremost of the green-clad knights, and slew him. He made another cast of the Ga-boi and brought down the second warrior; and, drawing the Morallta, he sprang on the third, and swept off his head.

When the foreigners saw their leader slain, they fled hither and thither in utter rout. And Dermat fell upon them with sword and spear, scattering and slaughtering them, so that there seemed no escape for them, unless, indeed, they could fly over the tops of the trees, or hide themselves under the earth, or dive beneath the water. And when Derdri of the Black Mountain saw this havoc, she ran, panic-stricken and crazed with fright, off the field towards the hill where the three kings lay bound.

Now as to Finn. Tidings were brought to him of what happened to the three sea-kings, and how they were lying bound in hard bonds on the hill over Tonn Toma. So he set out straightway from Allen, and travelled by the shortest ways till he reached the hill. And when he saw the three champions, he was grieved to the heart; for he knew of old that the iron fetters bound by Dermat slew by slow torment, and that none could loose them except Oisin, or Oscar, or Mac Lugha, or Conan Maol.

And Finn asked Oisin to loose the bonds and relieve the kings.

" I cannot do so," answered Oisin, " for Dermat bound me under geasa[12] never to loose any warrior that he should bind."

He next asked Oscar; but the young warrior answered, " None shall be released by me who seeks to harm Dermat O'Dyna. Fain would I indeed put heavier bonds on them."

And when he asked Mac Lugha and Conan, they refused in like manner.

Now while they were speaking in this wise, they saw the errand-woman, Derdri of the Black Mountain, running towards them, breathless and with failing steps, and her eyes starting from the sockets with terror. And Finn asked her what tidings she had brought.

" Tidings indeed, O king, tidings of grievous mishap and woe! " Whereupon she told him all that she had seen—how Dermat O'Dyna had killed the three fierce hounds, and had made a slaughter of the foreigners. " And hardly, indeed," she cried, " hardly have I myself got off scathless with the news! "

The three kings, hearing this, and being worn out with the straitness and torment of their bonds, died at the same moment. And Finn caused them to be buried in three wide graves; and flagstones were placed over them with their names graved in Ogham; and their funeral rites were performed. Then, with heart full of grief and gall, Finn marched northwards with his men to Allen of the green hill-slopes.

## CHAPTER VII

### SHARVAN, THE SURLY GIANT, AND THE FAIRY QUICKEN TREE OF DOOROS

Now touching Dermat and Grania. They travelled eastward from Slieve Lougher, through Hy Conall Gavra, keeping the Shannon on their left, till they reached the Wood of the two Sallow Trees, which is now called Limerick. Here they rested; and Dermat killed a wild deer, and they ate of its flesh, and drank pure spring water, and slept that night. Next morning Modan bade them farewell, and left them. And Dermat and

Grania were sad after him, for he was very gentle, and had served them faithfully.

On that same day they departed from the Wood of the two Sallows; and nothing is related of what befell them till they arrived at the Forest of Dooros, in the district of Hy Ficra* of the Moy, which was at that time guarded by Sharvan the Surly, of Lochlann.

Now this is the history of Sharvan the Surly, of Lochlann. On a certain occasion, a game of hurley was played by the Dedannans against the Fena, on the plain beside the Lake of Lein of the Crooked Teeth.† They played for three days and three nights, neither side being able to win a single goal from the other during the whole time. And when the Dedannans found that they could not overcome the Fena, they suddenly withdrew from the contest, and departed from the lake, journeying in a body northwards.

The Dedannans had for food during the game, and for their journey afterwards, crimson nuts and arbutus apples and scarlet quicken berries, which they had brought from the Land of Promise.‡ These fruits were gifted with many secret virtues; and the Dedannans were careful that neither apple nor nut nor berry should touch the soil of Erin. But as they passed through the Wood of Dooros, in Hy Ficra of the Moy, one of the scarlet quicken berries dropped on the earth; and the Dedannans passed on, not heeding.

From this berry a great quicken tree§ sprang up, which had the virtues of the quicken trees that grow in Fairyland. For its berries had the taste of honey, and those who ate of them felt a cheerful flow of spirits, as if they had drunk of wine or old mead; and if a man were even a hundred years old, he returned to the age of thirty, as soon as he had eaten three of them.

Now when the Dedannans heard of this tree, and knew of its many virtues, they would not that any one should eat of the berries but themselves; and they sent a Fomor‖ of their own

---

* Hy Ficra, now the barony of Tireragh, in Sligo.
† The Lake of Lein of the Crooked Teeth, *i.e.*, Loch Lein, or the Lakes of Killarney.
‡ The Land of Promise, or Fairyland. (See note 8 at the end.)
§ Quicken tree, the mountain ash or rowan.
‖ Fomor, a giant.

people to guard it, namely, Sharvan the Surly, of Lochlann; so that no man dared even to approach it. For this Sharvan was a giant of the race of the wicked Cain, burly and strong; with heavy bones, large, thick nose, crooked teeth, and one broad, red, fiery eye in the middle of his black forehead. And he had a great club tied by a chain to an iron girdle which was round his body. He was, moreover, so skilled in magic that fire could not burn him, water could not drown him, and weapons could not wound him; and there was no way to kill him but by giving him three blows of his own club. By day he sat at the foot of the tree, watching; and at night he slept in a hut he had made for himself, high up among the branches.

Into this land Dermat came, knowing well that he should be safe there from the pursuit of Finn. For Sharvan did not let any of the Fena hunt in Hy Ficra. And neither they nor any others dared to come near the great Wood of Dooros, for dread of the giant; so that the land around the quicken tree for many miles was a wilderness.

Dermat, leaving Grania behind in safe shelter, went boldly to the giant, where he sat at the foot of the tree, and told him he wished to live amidst the woods of Hy Ficra, and chase its wild animals for food. Whereupon the giant, bending his red eye on him, told him, in words few and surly, that he might live and hunt where he pleased, as long as he did not take and eat the berries of the quicken tree.

So Dermat built him a hunting-booth near a spring, in the thick of the Forest of Dooros; and, clearing a space all round, fenced it with strong stakes interwoven with tough withes, leaving one narrow door well barred and secured. And they lived in peace for a time, eating the flesh of the wild animals of Dooros, which Dermat brought down each day in the chase, and drinking the water of the well.

Now let us speak of Finn, the son of Cumhal. One day, soon after his return to Allen, as he and his household troops were on the exercise green before the palace, a company of fifty horsemen were seen approaching from the east, led by two taller and nobler-looking than the others. Having come near, they bowed low and greeted the king; and when he asked them who they were, and from whence they had come, they answered—

" We are enemies of thine, who now desire to make peace; and our names are Angus, the son of Art Mac Morna, and Aedh, the son of Andala Mac Morna. Our fathers were present at the battle of Knocka,[27] aiding those who fought against thy father, Cumhal, when he was slain; for which thou didst afterwards slay them both, and didst outlaw us, their sons, though indeed we were blameless in the matter, seeing that we were not born till after the death of Cumhal. However, we have come now to ask this boon of thee: that thou make peace with us, and give us the places our fathers held in the ranks of the Fena."

" I will grant your request," answered Finn, " provided you pay me eric for the death of my father."

" We would indeed pay thee eric willingly if we could," answered they; " but we have neither gold, nor silver, nor cattle, nor wealth of any kind to give."

And then Oisin spoke and said, " Ask them not for eric, O king; surely the death of their fathers should be eric enough."

But Finn replied, " Of a truth, I think, Oisin, that if any one should slay me, it would not be hard to satisfy you in the matter of an eric. But, indeed, none of those who fought at Knocka against my father, and none of their sons, shall ever get peace from me, or join the Fena, without such eric as I demand."

Then Angus, one of the two, asked, " What eric dost thou require, O king? "

" I ask only one or the other of two things," answered Finn; " namely, the head of a warrior, or the full of my hand of the berries of a quicken tree."

" I will give you counsel, ye sons of Morna, that will stand you in good stead, if you follow it," said Oisin, addressing the two strange chiefs. "And my counsel is, that you return to the place from whence you came, and seek this peace no longer. Know that the head the king seeks from you is the head of Dermat O'Dyna, the most dangerous of all the Fena to meddle with, who is well able to defend himself, even if you were twenty times as many as you are; and who will certainly take your heads if you attempt to take his. Know also that the berries Finn seeks from you are the berries of the quicken tree of

Dooros. And it is hard to say if this be not a more perilous quest than the other; for the quicken tree belongs to the Dedannans, who have sent Sharvan, the surly giant of Lochlann, to guard it day and night."

But the two chiefs, unmoved by what they had heard from Oisin, said that they would rather perish in seeking out the eric than return to their mother's country. So, leaving their people in the care of Oisin, they set out on their quest. They travelled through the Wood of the two Sallows, and from that to Dooros of the Moy, where they found the track of Dermat and Grania, and followed it till they came to the hunting-booth. Dermat heard their voices and footsteps outside, and, snatching up his weapons, went to the door and asked who was there.

"We are Aedh, the son of Andala Mac Morna, and Angus, the son of Art Mac Morna," they replied. "We have come hither from Allen of Leinster, to get either the head of Dermat O'Dyna, or a handful of the berries of the quicken tree of Dooros; for Finn, the son of Cumhal, has demanded of us that we bring him either the one or the other, as an eric for the killing of his father."

Dermat laughed when he heard this, and said, "Truly this is not pleasant news for me to hear, for I am Dermat O'Dyna. But however, friends, I am not willing to give you my head, and you will find it no easy matter to take it. And as for the berries, these are quite as hard to get; for you will have to fight the surly giant Sharvan, who cannot be burned with fire, or drowned with water, or wounded with weapons. But woe to the man who falls under the power of Finn, the son of Cumhal. And you have come, methinks, on a bootless quest; for even if you should be able to bring him either of the two things he asks for, he will not grant you the place or the rank ye seek after all. And now, which of the two do ye wish to strive for first, my head or the quicken berries?"

And they answered, "We will do battle with thee first."

So Dermat opened the door, and they made ready for the combat. Now this is the manner in which they agreed to fight: to throw aside their weapons, and to use the strength of their hands alone. And if the sons of Morna were able to overcome Dermat, they should take his head to Finn; but if, on the other hand, they were overpowered and bound by Dermat, their heads should be in like manner forfeit to him. But the fight was, indeed, a short one; for these two chiefs were even as children in Dermat's hands, and he bound them in close and bitter bonds.

Now when Grania heard of the berries of the quicken tree, she was seized with a longing desire to taste them. At first she strove against it and was silent, knowing the danger; but now she was not able to hide it any longer, and she told Dermat that she should certainly die if she did not get some of the berries to eat. This troubled Dermat, for he did not wish to quarrel with the giant Sharvan; but, seeing that harm might come to Grania if she did not get the berries, he told her he would go and get some for her, either by good will or by force.

When the sons of Morna heard this, they said, " Loose these bonds, and we will go with thee and help thee to fight the giant."

But Dermat answered, " Not much help, indeed, could ye give me, as I think, for the mere sight of this giant would be enough to unman you. But even were it otherwise, I would not seek your help, for if I fight at all I shall fight unaided."

And they said: " Even so, let us go. Our lives are now forfeit to thee, but grant us this request before we die, to let us see thee fight this giant."

And he consented to this.

So Dermat went straightway to the quicken tree, followed by the two sons of Morna; and he found the giant lying asleep at the foot of the tree. He dealt him a heavy blow to awaken him, and the giant, raising his head, glared at him with his great red eye, and said—

" There has been peace between us hitherto; do you now wish for strife? "

" I seek not strife," answered Dermat, " but the Princess Grania, my wife, the daughter of King Cormac Mac Airt, longs to taste of these quicken berries; and if she does not get them she will die. This is why I have come; and now I pray you give me a few of the berries for the princess."

But the giant answered: " I swear that if the princess and her child were now dying, and that one of my berries would save them, I would not give it! "

Then Dermat said: " I do not wish to deal unfairly with you; and I have accordingly awakened you from your sleep, and made my request openly, wishing for peace. But now understand that before I leave this spot, I will have some of these quicken berries, whether you will or no."

When the giant heard this, he rose up, and, seizing his club, dealt Dermat three great blows, which the hero had much ado to ward off; nor did he escape without some hurt, even though his shield was tough and his arm strong. But now, watching narrowly, and seeing that the giant expected to be attacked with sword and spear, he suddenly threw down his weapons and sprang upon him, taking him unguarded. He threw his arms round his body, and, heaving him with his shoulder, hurled him with mighty shock to the earth; and then, seizing the heavy club, he dealt him three blows, dashing out his brains with the last.

Dermat sat down to rest, weary and breathless. And the sons of Morna, having witnessed the fight from beginning to end, came forth rejoiced when they saw the giant slain. Dermat told them to drag the body into the wood and bury it out of sight, lest Grania might see it and be affrighted; and when they had done so, he sent them for the princess. When she had come, Dermat said to her: " Behold the quicken berries, Grania: take now and eat."

But she answered: " I will eat no berries except those that are plucked by the hands of my husband."

So Dermat stood up and plucked the berries; and Grania ate till she was satisfied. And he also plucked some for the sons of Morna, and said:

" Take these berries now, friends, as much as you please, and pay your eric to Finn; and you may, if you are so minded, tell him that it was you who slew Sharvan the Surly, of Lochlann."

They answered: " We will bring to Finn as much as he demanded, one handful and no more; and we grudge even so much."

Then they thanked Dermat very much; for he had given them the berries, what they should never have been able to get for themselves; and though their lives were forfeit to him, he had not so much as mentioned the matter, but had allowed them to return freely. And after bidding Dermat and Grania farewell, they went their ways.

After that, Dermat left his hunting-booth, and he and Grania lived thenceforth in Sharvan's hut among the branches. And they found the berries on the top of the tree the most delicious of all; those on the lower branches being as it were bitter in comparison.

When the sons of Morna reached Allen, Finn asked them how they had fared, and whether they had brought him the eric: and they answered—

" Sharvan, the surly giant of Lochlann, is slain; and here we have brought thee the berries of the quicken tree of Dooros as eric for the death of thy father, Cumhal, that we may have peace from thee, and be placed in our due rank among the Fena."

Finn took the berries and knew them; and he smelled them three times, and said: " These, indeed, are the berries of the quicken tree of Dooros; but they have passed through the hands of Dermat O'Dyna, for I smell his touch. And sure I am that it was Dermat, and not you, who slew Sharvan, the surly giant. It shall profit you nothing, indeed, to have brought me these berries; neither will you get from me the peace you seek, nor your place among the Fena, till you pay me fair eric for my father's death. For you have gotten the berries not by your own strength; and you have, besides, made peace with my enemy. And now I shall go to the Wood of Dooros, to learn if Dermat abides near the quicken tree."

After this he gathered together the choice men of the seven battalions of the Fena, and marched with them to Dooros of Hy Ficra. They followed Dermat's track to the foot of the quicken tree, and found the berries without any one to guard them; and they ate of them as much as they pleased.

Now it was noon when they had come to the tree; and the sun shone hot, and Finn said: " We shall rest under this tree till evening come, and the heat pass away; for well I know that Dermat O'Dyna is on the tree among the branches."

And Oisin said: " Truly your mind must be blinded by jealousy, if you think that Dermat O'Dyna has waited for you on that tree, since he knows well that you seek his head."

Finn answered nothing to this speech, but called for a chess-board and men.[26] And he and Oisin sat down to a game; while Oscar and Mac Lugha and Dering, the son of Dobar O'Baskin, sat near Oisin to advise him; for Finn played against them all. They played on for a time warily and skilfully, till at last Oisin had only one move to make; and Finn said: "One move more would win you the game, Oisin, but I challenge all your helpers to show you that move." And Oisin was puzzled.

Dermat had been viewing the game from the beginning, where he sat among the branches; and he said, speaking to himself: "Pity that you should be in a strait, Oisin, and I not near to advise your move."

Grania, sitting near, overheard him, and said: "It is a small matter whether Oisin win or lose a game; far worse is it for you to be in this hut, while the men of the seven battalions of the Fena are round about you, waiting to kill you."

Then Dermat, not giving heed to Grania's words, plucked a berry, and, flinging it down with true aim, struck Oisin's chess-man—the man that should be moved. And Oisin moved the man, and won the game against Finn.

The game was begun again, and it went on till it came to the same pass as before, Oisin having to make only one move to win, but that move hard to make out. And again Dermat threw a berry and struck the right man; and Oisin made the move, and won the game.

A third time the game went on, and Dermat struck the chess-man as before; and Oisin won the game the third time. Whereupon the Fena raised a mighty shout.

"I marvel not that you should win the game, Oisin," said Finn, "seeing that you have the best help of Oscar, and the zeal of Dering, and the skill of Mac Lugha; and that, along with all, you have been prompted by Dermat O'Dyna."

"It shows a mind clouded by great jealousy," said Oscar, "that you should think that Dermat O'Dyna is in that tree waiting for you to kill him."

"Which of us tells truth, Dermat," said Finn, looking up, "Oscar or I?"

"You, Finn, have never yet erred in your judgment," answered Dermat from the tree; "for indeed I am here with the princess Grania, in the hut of Sharvan, the surly giant of Lochlann."

And, looking up, Finn and the others saw them plainly through an opening in the branches.

But now Grania, seeing the danger, began to tremble with great fear, and to weep; and Dermat, taking pity on her, comforted her and kissed her three times.

And Finn, seeing this, said: "Much more than this did it grieve me the night you espoused Grania, and brought her away from Tara before all the men of Erin; but even for these kisses you shall certainly pay quittance with your head!"

Whereupon Finn, being now bent on killing Dermat, arose, and ordered his hirelings to surround the tree, catching hand in hand, so as to leave no gap; and he warned them, on pain of death, not to let Dermat pass out. Having done this, he offered a suit of armour and arms, and a high place of honour among the Fena, to any man who would go up into the tree, and either bring him the head of Dermat O'Dyna, or force him to come down.

Garva of Slieve Cua* started up and said: "Lo, I am the man! For it was Dermat's father, Donn, that slew my father; and I will now avenge the deed."

And he went up the tree.

Now it was revealed to Angus of the Brugh that Dermat was in deadly strait; and he came to the tree to his aid, without the knowledge of the Fena; and Dermat and Grania were filled with joy when they saw the old man.

And when Garva, climbing from branch to branch, had come near the hut, Dermat dealt him a blow with his foot, which dashed him to the ground among the Fena. And Finn's hirelings cut off his head on the spot, for Angus had caused him to take the shape of Dermat; but after he was slain he took his own shape, so that all knew that it was Garva of Slieve Cua that had been killed.

Then Garva of Slieve Crot† said: "It was Dermat's father, Donn, that slew my father; and I will now avenge the deed on Dermat."

---

* Slieve Cua, the ancient name of the highest of the Knockmealdown Mountains, in Waterford.

† Slieve Crot, the ancient name of the Galty Mountains.

So saying, he went up the tree. But Angus gave him a blow which hurled him to the ground under the shape of Dermat, so that the hirelings fell on him and slew him. And then Finn told them that it was not Dermat they had killed, but Garva of Slieve Cua.

Garva of Slieve Gora* next started up, and said that his father had been slain by Dermat's father; and he began to climb up the tree to take Dermat's head in revenge. But Dermat flung him down like the others, while Angus gave him for the time the shape of Dermat, so that the hirelings slew him.

And so matters went on till the nine Garvas had fallen; namely, Garva of Slieve Cua, Garva of Slieve Crot, Garva of Slieve Gora, Garva of Slieve Mucka,† Garva of Slieve-more, Garva of Slieve Lugha, Garva of Ath-free, Garva of Slieve Mish, and Garva of Drom-mor. And full of grief and bitterness was the heart of Finn, witnessing this.

Then Angus said he would take Grania away from that place of danger. And Dermat was glad, and said: " Take her with thee; and if I live till evening I will follow you. But if Finn slays me, send her to Tara to her father, and tell him to use her well."

Then Dermat kissed his dear wife; and Angus, having thrown his mantle round her, passed out from the tree without the knowledge of the Fena, and went straightway to Brugh of the Boyne.

After Angus and Grania had gone, Dermat, addressing Finn from the tree, said: " I will now go down from this tree; and I will slaughter many of thy hirelings before they slay me. For I see that thou art resolved to compass my death; and why should I fear to die now more than at a future time? There is, indeed, no escape for me, even should I pass from this place unharmed; since I can find no shelter in Erin from thy wrath. Neither have I a friend in the far-off countries of this great world to give me protection, seeing that I have from time to

---

* Slieve Gora, a mountainous district in County Cavan.
† Slieve Mucka, now Slievenamuck (the mountain of the pig), a long mountain ridge in Tipperary, separated from the Galtees by the Glen of Aherlow. Slieve Lugha, a mountainous district in the barony of Costello, County Mayo. Slieve Mish, a mountain range west of Tralee.

time dealt defeat and slaughter among them, every one, for thy
sake. For never have the Fena been caught in any strait or
danger, that I did not venture my life for them and for thee.
When we went to battle, moreover, I was always in front of
you; and I was always behind you when leaving the field. And
now I care no longer to seek to prolong my life; but of a
certainty thou shalt purchase my death dearly, for I shall avenge
myself by dealing destruction among thy hirelings."

" Dermat speaks truly," said Oscar; " and now let him have
mercy and forgiveness; for he has suffered enough already."

" I swear that I will never grant him peace or forgiveness
to the end of my life," answered Finn, " till he has given me
the eric I seek from him for the injury he has done me; that is
to say, his head."

" Shame it is to hear thee say so, and a sure mark of
jealousy," answered Oscar. "And now I take the body and life
of Dermat under the protection of my knighthood and valour;
and I pledge the word of a true champion, that sooner shall the
firmament fall on me, or the earth open up and swallow me,
than that I shall let any man harm Dermat O'Dyna! "

Then, looking upwards, he said: " Come down now, Dermat,
and thou shalt certainly go in safety from this place; for as long
as I am alive, no man will dare to offer thee hurt! "

Then Dermat, choosing that side of the tree where the men
stood nearest to the trunk, walked along a thick branch unseen,
and, leaning on the shafts of his spears, he sprang forward and
downward with a light, airy bound, and alighted outside the
circle of those who stood round with joined hands; and in a
moment he was beyond the reach of sword and spear. And
Oscar joined him, looking back threateningly, so that no man
of Finn's hirelings durst follow.

So the two heroes fared on together, crossing the Shannon;
and nothing is told of what befell them till they reached Brugh
of the Boyne, where they met Angus and Grania. And Grania
was almost beside herself with joy when she saw Dermat without
wound or hurt of any kind. And the two champions were
welcomed by Angus; and Dermat related to him and Grania
the whole story. And as Grania listened, her spirit almost left
her, at the deadly peril Dermat had passed through.

# CHAPTER VIII

### THE ATTACK OF THE WITCH-HAG

Now as regards Finn. After the departure of Dermat and Oscar, his heart was filled with anger and bitterness, and he vowed he would never rest till he had revenged himself on Dermat. And, leaving the Wood of Dooros, he marched eastward till he reached Allen. Making no delay, he ordered his trusted servants to make ready his best ship, and to put therein food and drink for a voyage. Then going on board, he put out to sea; and nothing is told of him till he reached the Land of Promise,[8] where his old nurse lived.

When he appeared before her, she gave him a joyful welcome. And after he had eaten and drunk, she asked him the cause of his journey, knowing that some weighty matter had brought him thither. So he told her the whole story of what Dermat O'Dyna had done against him; and said that he had come to seek counsel from her how he should act. " For," he said, " no strength or cunning of men can compass his death; magic alone can overmatch him."

Then the old woman told him that she would go with him next day and work magic against Dermat. Whereupon Finn was much rejoiced, and they rested that night.

Next day, they set out, Finn and his people and his nurse; and it is not told how they fared till they reached Brugh of the Boyne. And the men of Erin knew not that they had come thither, for the witch-hag threw a druidical mist round them, so that no man might see them.

It chanced that Dermat hunted that day in the forest, alone; for Oscar had gone from Brugh the day before. When this was known to the witch-hag, she caused herself to fly into the air by magic, on a water-lily, having by her spells turned the pale flat leaf into a broad millstone with a hole in the middle. And, rising over the tops of the trees, she floated on the clear, cold wind, till she had came straight over the hero. Then, standing on the flat millstone, she began to aim deadly poisoned darts at him through the hole. And no distress Dermat ever suffered could compare with this; for the darts stung him even through his shield and armour, the witch having breathed venomous spells on them.

Seeing at last that there was no escape from death unless he could slay the witch-hag, he seized the Ga-derg, and, leaning backwards, flung it with sure aim at the millstone, so that it went right through the hole, and pierced the hag; and she fell dead at Dermat's feet. Then he beheaded her, and brought the head to Angus of the Brugh; and he related to him and to Grania how he had escaped that great danger.

## CHAPTER IX

### PEACE AND REST AT LAST

ANGUS arose next morning, and, going to Finn, asked him whether he would make peace with Dermat. Finn, seeing that he was worsted in every attempt against the hero, and that moreover he had lost his nurse and many of his men, told Angus that he was weary of the quarrel, and that he was fain to make peace on whatever terms Dermat should choose.

He next went to Tara to the king, Cormac, the grandson of Conn. Him he asked in like manner whether he was willing to grant Dermat peace and forgiveness; and Cormac answered that he was quite willing.

Then he came to Dermat and said: " Peace is better for thee: art thou willing now to be at peace with Finn and Cormac? "

And Dermat answered: " Gladly will I make peace, if they grant me such conditions as befit a champion and the husband of the princess Grania."

And when Angus asked what these conditions were, he answered: " The cantred which my father had, that is to say, the cantred of O'Dyna,* without rent or tribute to the king of Erin; also the cantred of Ben-Damis,† namely, Ducarn of

---

* The cantred of O'Dyna, now the barony of Corkaguiny, in Kerry.
† The cantred of Ben-Damis, or Ducarn of Leinster, probably the district round Douce mountain, in the County Wicklow.

Leinster. These two to be granted to me by Finn; and he shall not hunt over them, nor any of his Fena, without my leave. And the king of Erin shall grant me the cantred of Kesh-Corran, as a dowry with his daughter. On these conditions will I make peace."

Angus went to Finn, and afterwards to the king, with these conditions. And they granted them, and forgave Dermat all he had done against them during the time he was outlawed. So they made peace. And Cormac gave his other daughter to Finn to wife.

Dermat and Grania went to live in the cantred of Kesh-Corran, far away from Finn and Cormac; and they built a house for themselves, namely, Rath-Grania, in which they abode many years in peace. And Grania bore Dermat four sons and one daughter. And his possessions increased year by year, insomuch that people said that no man of his time was richer than Dermat, in gold and silver and jewels, in sheep, and in cattle-herds.

## CHAPTER X

### THE DEATH OF DERMAT

Now when many years had passed, Grania said one day to Dermat: " It is surely a thing unworthy of us, seeing the greatness of our household and our wealth, and the number of our folk, that we should live in a manner so much removed from the world. And in a special manner it is unbecoming that the two most illustrious men in Erin have never been in our house, namely, my father the king, and Finn the son of Cumhal."

For indeed she had not seen her father since the night she had left Tara with Dermat, and her heart yearned for him.

" Wherefore say you this, Grania? " answered Dermat; " for though there is indeed peace between us, they are both none the less enemies of mine; and for this reason have I removed my dwelling far apart from them."

And Grania said: "Their enmity has surely softened with length of time: and now I would that you give them a feast: so shall we win back their friendship and love."

And in an evil hour Dermat consented.

For a full year were they preparing for that great feast, and when it was ready, messengers were sent to invite the king, with his house-folk, and Finn, with the chief men of the seven battalions of the Fena. So they came, with their attendants and followers, their horses and dogs; and they lived for a whole year in Rath-Grania, hunting and feasting.

It chanced one night, at the end of the year, long after all had gone to rest, that Dermat heard, through the silence of the night, the distant yelping of a hound; and he started up from his sleep. But Grania, being scared, started up also, and, throwing her arms round him, asked him what he had seen.

"I have heard the voice of a hound," answered Dermat, "and I marvel much to hear it at midnight."

"May all things guard thee from harm!" said Grania. "This is surely a trap laid for thee by the Dedannans, unknown to Angus of the Brugh: and now lie down on thy bed again."

Dermat lay down, but did not sleep, and again he heard the hound's voice. He started up, and this time was fain to go and look to the matter; but Grania caught him and kept him back a second time, saying that it was not meet for him to seek a hound whose voice he heard in the night.

A gentle slumber now fell on Dermat, and he slept through a good part of the night. But the yelping of the hound came a third time, and awakened him, so that he started up; and it being now broad day, he told Grania that he would go to seek the hound, and find out why he was abroad in the night.

And though Grania consented, she felt, she knew not why, ill at ease; and she said: "Bring with you the Morallta, the sword of Mannanan Mac Lir, and the Ga-derg, Angus's spear; for there may be danger."

But Dermat, regarding the matter lightly, and forced by fate to the worse choice, answered: "How can danger arise from such a small affair? I will bring the Begallta and the Ga-boi; and I will also bring my good hound Mac-an-choill, leading him by his chain."

So Dermat went forth, and he delayed not till he reached the summit of Ben-Gulban,* where he found Finn; and Dermat, offering him no salute, asked him who it was that held the chase.

" Some of our men came out from Rath-Grania at midnight with their hounds," answered Finn, " and one of the hounds coming across the track of a wild boar, both men and dogs have followed it up. I indeed would have held them back, but the men were eager, and left me here alone. For this is the track of the wild boar of Ben-Gulban, and they who follow him are bent on a vain and dangerous pursuit. Often has he been chased; and he has always escaped, after killing many men and dogs. Even now thou canst see in the distance that the Fena are flying before him; and he has slain several this morning. He is coming towards this hillock where we stand; and the sooner we get out of his way the better."

But Dermat said he would not leave the hillock through fear of any wild boar.

" It is not meet that thou shouldst tarry here," answered Finn. " Dost thou not know that thou art under geasa[12] never to hunt a boar? "

Dermat answered: " I know nothing of these geasa; wherefore were they placed on me? "

And Finn said: " I will tell thee of this matter, for well do I remember it. When thou wert taken to Brugh of the Boyne, to be fostered by Angus, the son of Angus's steward was fostered with thee, that he might be a companion and playmate to thee. Now the steward, being a man of the common sort, agreed to send each day to Brugh, food and drink for nine men, as a price for having his son fostered with thee—thy father, Donn, being one of the nobles of the Fena. And thy father was accordingly permitted to visit the house of Angus when it pleased him, with eight companions, and claim the food sent by the steward; and when he did not come, it was to be given to Angus's house-folk.

" It chanced on a certain day that I was at Allen of the broad hill-slopes, with the chief men of the seven battalions of the Fena. And Bran Beg O'Bucan brought to my mind, what

---

* Now Benbulben, a mountain five miles north of Sligo.

indeed I had forgotten, that it was forbidden to me to sleep at Allen more than nine nights one after another, and that the next would be the tenth.

" Now this restriction had not been placed on any of the Fena save myself, and they all went into the hall except thy father and a few others. Then I asked where we should get entertainment for that night. And thy father, Donn, answered that he would give me entertainment at Brugh of the Boyne; where food and drink awaited himself and his companions whenever he visited Angus. Donn said, moreover, that he had not been to see his son for a year, and that we were sure to get a welcome.

" So Donn and I and the few that were with us went to the house of Angus, bringing our hounds; and Angus welcomed us. And thou and the steward's son were there, two children. After a while we could see that Angus loved thee, Dermat, very much, but that the house-folk loved the son of the steward; and thy father was filled with jealousy, that the people should show fondness for him and not for thee.

"After night had fallen, it chanced that our hounds quarrelled over some broken meat we had thrown to them, and began to fight in the court; and the women and lesser people fled from them hither and thither. The son of the steward happened to run between thy father's knees, who, calling now to mind how the people favoured him more than thee, gave him a sudden strong squeeze with his knees, and killed him on the spot. And, without being seen by any one, he threw him under the feet of the hounds.

" When at last the dogs were put asunder, the child was found dead; and the steward uttered a long, mournful cry. Then he came to me and said:

" ' Of all the men in Angus's house to-night, I have come worst out of this uproar; for this boy was my only child. And now, O Finn, I demand eric from thee for his death; for thy hounds have slain him.'

" I told him to examine the body of his son, and that if he found the mark of a hound's tooth or nail, I would give him eric. So the child was examined, but no hurt—either bite or scratch—was found on him.

" Then the steward laid me under fearful bonds of druidical geasa,[12] to find out for him who slew his son. So I called for a chess-board and some water, and, having washed my hands, I put my thumb under my tooth of knowledge;[25] and then it was revealed to me that the boy had been slain by thy father. Not wishing to make this known, I now offered to pay eric for the boy; but the steward refused, saying that he should know who killed his son. So I was forced to tell him. Then he said:

" ' It is easier for Donn to pay me eric than for any other man in this house. And the eric I demand is that his son be placed between my knees: if the lad gets off safe, then I shall follow up the matter no further.'

" Angus was very wroth at this; and thy father would have struck off the steward's head if I had not come between and saved him.

" The steward said no more, but went aside and brought forth a druidical magic wand, and, striking his son with it, he turned him into a great bristly wild boar, having neither ears nor tail. And, holding the wand aloft, he chanted this incantation over the boar:

" By this magical wand,
　By the wizard's command,
　I appoint and decree,
　For Dermat and thee,
　The same bitter strife
　The same span of life:
　In the pride of his strength,
　Thou shalt slay him at length:
　Lo, Derma O'Dyna
　　Lies stretched in his gore;
　Behold my avengers,
　　The tusks of the boar!
　And thus is decreed,
　For Donn's cruel deed,
　Sure vengeance to come—
　His son's bloody doom;
　By this wand in my hand,
　By the wizard's command!

" The moment he had ended the incantation, the boar rushed out through the open door, and we knew not whither he betook himself.

" When Angus heard the steward's words, he laid a command on thee never to hunt a wild boar, that so thou mightest avoid the doom foretold for thee.

" That same boar is now rushing furiously towards us. Come, then, let us leave this hill at once, that we may avoid him in time! "

" I know nothing of these incantations and prohibitions," replied Dermat, " or if, as thou sayest, they were put on me in my boyhood, I forget them all now. And neither for fear of this wild boar of Ben-Gulban nor of any other wild beast will I leave this hillock. But thou, before thou goest, leave me thy hound, Bran, to help and encourage my dog, Mac-an-choill."

" I will not leave him," answered Finn, " for often has Bran chased this boar, and has always barely escaped with his life. And now I leave; for lo, here he comes over yonder hill-shoulder."

So Finn went his ways, and left Dermat standing alone on the hill. And after he had left, Dermat said: " I fear me, indeed, that thou hast begun this chase hoping that it would lead to my death. But here will I await the event; for if I am fated to die in this spot, I cannot avoid the doom in store for me."

Immediately the boar came rushing up the face of the hill, with the Fena following far behind. Dermat loosed Mac-an-choill against him, but to no profit; for the hound shied and fled before him at the first glance. Then Dermat said, communing with himself: " Woe to him who does not follow the advice of a good wife! For this morning Grania bade me bring the Morallta and the Ga-derg; but I brought instead the Begallta and the Ga-boi, disregarding her counsel."

Then, putting his white taper finger into the silken loop of the Ga-boi, he threw it with careful aim, and struck the boar in the middle of the forehead; but to no purpose, for the spear fell harmless to the ground, having neither wounded nor scratched the boar, nor disturbed even a single bristle.

Seeing this, Dermat, though indeed he knew not fear, felt his courage a little damped. And thereupon drawing the Begallta from its sheath, he dealt a blow on the boar's neck, with the full strength of his arm. But neither did he fare better this time; for the sword flew in pieces, leaving the hilt in his hand, while not a bristle of the boar was harmed.

And now the boar rushed on him as he stood defenceless, and with furious onset hurled him headlong to the earth; and, turning round, he gashed the hero's side with his tusk, inflicting a deep and ghastly wound. Turning again, he was about to renew the attack, when Dermat flung the hilt of the sword at him, and drove it through the skull to his brain, so that the brute fell dead on the spot.

Finn and the Fena now came up, and found Dermat lying pale and bleeding, in the pangs of death. And Finn said: " It likes me well, Dermat, to see thee in this plight; only I am grieved that all the women of Erin cannot see thee also. For now, indeed, the surpassing beauty of thy form, that they loved so well, is gone from thee, and thou art pale and deformed! "

And Dermat answered: " Alas, O Finn! these words surely come from thy lips only, and not from thy heart. And indeed it is in thy power to heal me even now if thou wilt."

" How should I heal thee? " asked Finn.

" It is not hard for thee to do so," answered Dermat. " For when, at the Boyne, the noble gift of foreknowledge was given to thee,[25] this gift also thou didst receive—that to whomsoever thou shouldst give a drink of water from the closed palms of thy two hands, he should be healed from sickness or wounds, even though he stood at the point of death."

" Why should I heal thee by giving thee drink from my hands? " replied Finn. " For of a certainty thou of all men dost least deserve it from me."

" Thou surely speakest hastily, not remembering past services," answered Dermat. " Well, indeed, do I deserve that thou shouldst heal me. Dost thou forget the day thou didst go with the chiefs and nobles of the Fena, to the house of Derca, the son of Donnara, to a banquet? And even as we sat down, and before the feast began, Carbri of the Liffey, son of Cormac, with the men of Tara, and of Bregia, and of Meath, and of Carmna, surrounded the palace, intent on slaying thee and all thy people. And they uttered three great shouts, and threw firebrands to burn the palace over our heads. Then thou didst arise and prepare to issue forth, but I put thee back and bade thee enjoy thy feast; and, leaving the banquet untasted, I rushed forth with a chosen few of my own men, and quenched the flames. Thrice we made a circuit of the palace, dealing slaughter amongst thy foes, so that we left fifty of them dead after each circuit. And having put Carbri and his men to flight, we returned to join the feast. Had I asked thee for a drink that night, gladly wouldst thou have given it to me. And yet, not more justly was it due to me then than it is now."

" Ill dost thou deserve a healing drink from me, or any other favour," said Finn, " for it was thy part to guard Grania the night we came to Tara; but thou didst espouse her secretly, and didst fly with her from Tara, knowing that she was betrothed to me."

" Lay not the blame of that on me," said Dermat, " for Grania put me under heavy geasa, which for all the wealth of the world I would not break through—no, not even for life itself. Neither did I rest on my own judgment in the matter; for well thou knowest that Oisin, and Oscar, and Dering, and Mac Lugha counselled me to the course I took.

" And now, O Finn, I pray thee let me drink from thy hands, for I feel the weakness of death coming on me. And thou wilt not gainsay that I deserve it, if thou wilt only remember the feast that Midac, the son of Colga, made for thee in the Fairy Palace of the Quicken Trees. To this feast Midac invited thee and thy companions; while to the Palace of the Island he brought secretly the King of the World with a great host, and the three kings of the Island of the Torrent, with intent to slay thee and all thy Fena.

" Now Midac caused some of the clay of the Island of the Torrent to be placed under you, with foul spells, in the Palace of the Quicken Trees, so that your feet and your hands clove to the ground. And it was revealed to thee that the King of the World was about to send a chief with a troop of warriors to slay you, helpless as you were, and to bring him your heads to the Palace of the Island.

" But at the same time, I came to thee outside the Palace of the Quicken Trees; and thou didst make known to me your deadly strait. Then did I take thee, Finn, and those who were with thee, under the protection of my knighthood and valour; and I went to the ford to defend it against the foreigners.

"And after a little time the three dragon-like kings of the Island of the Torrent came towards the palace: but I defended the ford, and, venturing my life for thee, I bore their attack and slew them all three. And I swept off their heads, and brought them, all gory as they were, in the hollow of my shield, to the palace where you lay miserably bound; and, sprinkling the clay with the blood, I broke the spell and set you free. And had I asked thee for a drink on that night, O Finn, of a surety thou wouldst not have refused me.

"And many another deadly strait did I free you from, since the day I was admitted among the Fena, always putting myself forward to the post of danger, and perilling my life for your safety; and now why dost thou requite me with this foul treachery?

"Moreover, many a king's son and many a brave warrior hast thou slain; and thou hast earned the enmity of powerful foes: neither is there yet an end of it. For the day will come—I see it even now—a day of direful overthrow and slaughter,* when few, alas! of the Fena will be left to tell the tale. Then thou shalt sorely need my help, O Finn, and sorely shalt thou rue this day. I grieve not, indeed, for thee, but for my dear, faithful companions—for Oscar and Mac Lugha and Dering, and more than all for Oisin, who shall long outlive the others in sad old age.† Alas! how deadly shall be their strait when I am not near to aid them!"

Then Oscar, moved with pity, even to tears, addressing Finn, said: "Although I am nearer akin to thee, O king, than to Dermat, yet I cannot suffer that he die, when a drink from thy hands would heal him. Bring him, then, a drink without delay."

And Finn answered: "I know of no well on this mountain from which to bring drink."

"Therein thou speakest not truth," said Dermat. "Thou knowest that not more than nine paces from thee, hidden under yonder bush, is a well of crystal water."

Thereupon Finn went to the well, and, holding his two hands tightly together, he brought up some of the water, and came towards Dermat; but after he had walked a little way, he let it

* A prophetic allusion to the battle of Gavra. (See note 28 at the end.)
† A prophetic allusion to the events related in the story of "Oisin in Tír na nÓg."

spill through his fingers, saying that he was not able to bring water in his hands so far.

"Not so, Finn," said Dermat. "I saw thee that of thy own will thou didst let it spill. And now, O king, hasten, for death is on me."

Again he went to the well, and was bringing the water slowly, while Dermat followed the dripping hands with his eyes; but when Finn thought of Grania, he let the water spill a second time. And Dermat, seeing this, uttered a piteous sigh of anguish.

And now was Oscar no longer able to contain his grief and rage. "I swear, O king," he said, "if thou dost not bring the water, that only one of us two—thou or I—shall leave this hill alive!"

Hearing Oscar's words, and seeing the frowning looks of the others, Finn dipped up the water a third time, and was hastening forward; but before he had got half-way, Dermat's head dropped backwards, and his life departed.

And all the Fena present raised three long loud cries of sorrow for Dermat O'Dyna.

Then Oscar, looking fiercely on Finn, spoke and said: "Would that thou thyself lay dead here instead of Dermat! For now indeed the noblest heart of the Fena is still; and our mainstay in battle and danger is gone. Ah! why did I not foresee this? Why was I not told that Dermat's life was linked with the life of the wild boar of Ben-Gulban? Then would I have stayed this chase, and put off the evil day!"

And Oscar wept; and Oisin, and Dering, and Mac Lugha wept also, for Dermat was much loved by all.

After a time, Finn said: "Let us now leave this hill, lest Angus of the Brugh overtake us. For although we had no hand in Dermat's death, nevertheless he may not believe us."

So Finn and the Fena departed from the hill, Finn leading Dermat's dog, Mac-an-choill. But Oisin, and Oscar, and Dering, and Mac Lugha turned back, and with tears, threw their mantles over Dermat; after which they followed the others.

Grania sat that day on the highest rampart of Rath-Grania, watching for Dermat's return; for a dark fear haunted her mind on account of this chase. And when at last the Fena came in view, she saw Dermat's dog led by Finn; but not seeing Dermat

himself, she said: " Ah me! what is this I see? Surely if
Dermat were alive, it is not by Finn that Mac-an-choill would
be led to his home! "

And as she spoke, she fell forward off the rampart, and lay
long in a swoon as if her spirit had fled, while her handmaid
stood over her, weeping and distracted. And when at last she
opened her eyes, then indeed they told her that Dermat was
dead; and she uttered a long and piteous cry, so that her women
and all the people of the court came round her to ask the cause
of her sorrow. And when they were told that Dermat had
perished by the wild boar of Ben-Gulban, they raised three loud,
bitter cries of lamentation, which were heard in the glens and
wildernesses around, and which pierced the clouds of heaven.

When at length Grania became calm, she ordered that five
hundred of her people should go to Ben-Gulban, to bring home
the body of Dermat. Then, turning to Finn, who still held
Mac-an-choill in his hand, she asked him to leave her Dermat's
hound; but Finn refused, saying that a hound was a small
matter, and that he might be allowed to inherit at least so much
of Dermat's riches. When Oisin heard this, he came forward
and took the hound from the hand of Finn and gave him to
Grania.

At the time that the men left Rath-Grania to go for the body
of Dermat, it was revealed to Angus that the hero was lying
dead on Ben-Gulban. And he set out straightway, and travelling
on the pure, cool wind, soon reached the mountain; so that
when Grania's people came up, they found him standing over
the body, sorrowing, with his people behind him. And they
held forward the wrong sides of their shields in token of peace.

Then both companies, having viewed the dead hero, raised
three mighty cries of sorrow, so loud and piercing that they
were heard in the wastes of the firmament, and over the five
provinces of Erin.

And when they had ceased, Angus spoke and said: " Alas!
why did I abandon thee, even for once, O my son? For from
the day I took thee to Brugh, a tender child, I have watched
over thee and guarded thee from thy foes, until last night. Ah!
why did I abandon thee to be decoyed to thy doom by the
guileful craft of Finn? By my neglect hast thou suffered, O

Dermat; and now, indeed, I shall for ever feel the bitter pangs of sorrow!"

Then Angus asked Grania's people what they had come for. And when they told him that Grania had sent them to bring the body of Dermat to Rath-Grania, he said:

"I will bring the body of Dermat with me to Brugh of the Boyne; and I will keep him on his bier, where he shall be preserved by my power, as if he lived. And though I cannot, indeed, restore him to life, yet I will breathe a spirit into him, so that for a little while each day he shall talk with me."

Then he caused the body to be placed on a golden bier, with the hero's javelins fixed one on each side, points upwards. And his people raised the bier and carried it before him; and in this manner they marched slowly to Brugh of the Boyne.

Grania's people then returned; and when they had told her the whole matter, though she was grieved at first, yet in the end she was content, knowing how Angus loved Dermat.

# The Chase of
# Slieve Cullinn

*In which it is related
how Finn's hair was changed in one day from
the colour of gold to silvery grey*\*

CULANN, the smith of the Dedannans,[1] who lived at Slieve
Cullinn,† had two beautiful daughters, Milucra and Aine.
They both loved Finn,[23] and each sought him for her
husband.

As they walked together one evening near Allen,‡ they fell
to talking of many things; and their conversation turning at
last on their future husbands, Aine said she would never marry
a man with grey hair.

When Milucra heard this, she resolved with herself that if
she could not get Finn, she would plan so that he should not
marry her sister Aine. So she departed immediately, and,
turning her steps northwards, she summoned the Dedannans to
meet her at Slieve Cullinn. Having brought them all together
she caused them to make her a lake§ near the top of the
mountain; and she breathed a druidical virtue on its waters,
that all who bathed in it should become grey.

---

\* This story and the two following are related by Oisin, in his old age, to St.
  Patrick. (See the prefatory note to the story of "Oisin in Tír na nÓg";
  and see also note 23 at the end.)
† Now Slieve Gullion, a mountain in the south of County Armagh, celebrated
  in legendary lore.
‡ The Hill of Allen, in Kildare, where Finn had his palace. (See note 23 at
  the end.)
§ There were several wells in Ireland which, according to the belief of old times,
  had the property of turning the hair grey. Giraldus Cambrensis tells us of
  such a well in Munster; and he states that he once saw a man who had
  washed a part of his head in this well, and that the part washed was white,
  while the rest was black!

On a morning not long after this, Finn happened to be walking alone on the lawn before the palace of Allen, when a doe sprang out from a thicket, and, passing quite close to him, bounded past like the wind. Without a moment's delay, he signalled for his companions and dogs; but none heard except his two hounds, Bran and Skolan. He instantly gave chase, with no other arms than his sword, Mac-an-Lona, and accompanied only by his two dogs; and before the Fena[23] knew of his absence, he had left Allen of the green slopes far behind.

The chase turned northwards; and though the hounds kept close to the doe, the chief kept quite as close to the hounds the whole way. And so they continued without rest or pause, till they reached Slieve Cullinn, far in the north.

Here the doe made a sudden turn and disappeared; and what direction she took, whether east or west, Finn knew not, for he never caught sight of her after. And he marvelled much that any doe in the world should be able to lead Bran and Skolan so long a chase, and escape from them in the end. Meantime they kept searching, Finn taking one side of the hill and the dogs another, so that he was at last left quite alone.

While he was wandering about the hill and whistling for his hounds, he heard the plaintive cry of a woman at no great distance; and, turning his steps towards the place, he saw a lady sitting on the brink of a little lake, weeping as if her heart would break. Never before did the chieftain see a maiden so lovely. The rose colour on her cheeks was heightened by her grief; her lips were like ruddy quicken berries; the delicate blossom of the apple tree was not more white than her neck; her hair fell in heavy golden ringlets on her shoulders; and as she looked up at the chief, her eyes beamed like stars on a frosty night.

Finn accosted her; and, seeing that she ceased her weeping for a moment, he asked her had she seen his two hounds pass that way.

"I have not seen thy hounds," she replied, "nor have I been at all concerned in the chase; for, alas, there is something that troubles me more nearly, a misadventure that has caused me great sorrow!"

And as she spoke these words, she burst out weeping and sobbing more bitterly than before.

Finn was greatly moved at this, so much so, that he quite forgot all about his hounds and his own troubles.

" What is the cause of this great grief, gentle lady? " he asked. " Has death robbed you of your husband or your child, or what other evil has befallen you? I am much concerned to see a lady in such distress; and I wish you to tell me if anything can be done to lighten your sorrow, or to remove the cause of it? "

She replied: " I had a precious gold ring on my finger, which I prized beyond anything in the world; and it has fallen from me into the water. I saw it roll down the steep slope at the bottom, till it went quite out of my sight. This is the cause of my sorrow, and thou canst remedy the mishap if thou wilt. The Fena are sworn never to refuse help to a woman in distress; and I now put on thee those geasa[12] that true heroes dare not break through, to search for the ring, and cease not till thou find it and restore it to me."

Though the chief had indeed at the moment no inclination to swim, he could not refuse a prayer urged in this manner. So he plunged in without a moment's hesitation, and examined the lake on all sides, diving and searching into every nook and cranny at the bottom.

After swimming in this manner three times round and round the lake, he found the ring at last; and approaching the lady, he handed it to her from the water. The moment she had got it she sprang into the lake before his eyes, and diving down, disappeared in an instant.

The chief, wondering greatly at this strange behaviour, stepped forth from the water; but as soon as his feet had touched the dry land, he lost all his strength, and fell on the brink, a withered, grey old man, shrunken up and trembling all over with weakness. He sat him down in woeful plight; and soon his hounds came up. They looked at him wistfully and sniffed and whined around him; but they knew him not, and, passing on, they ran round the lake, searching in vain for their master.

On that day the Fena were assembled in the banquet hall of the palace of Allen; some feasting and drinking, some playing chess, and others listening to the sweet music of the harpers.

While all were in this wise pleasantly engaged, Kylta Mac Ronan[23] stood up in the midst, and said in the hearing of all:

" I have observed, friends, that our master and king, Finn the son of Cumhal has not been amongst us to-day, as is his wont; and I wish to know whither he has gone."

This speech caused a sudden alarm amongst us; for no one knew aught of the chief, or was aware till that moment that he was absent at all; and we knew not wherefore he had disappeared or whither he had gone. In the midst of our anxious tumult, the envious and foul-mouthed Conan Maol[23] stood up, and said:

" I have never heard sweeter music than your words, Kylta! The Fena are now about to seek for their king; and my only wish is that their quest may last for a whole year, and that it may prove a vain search in the end! Be not cast down, however, O Fena; if you should fail to find the son of Cumhal, you will not be so ill off as you think; for I will undertake to be your king from this time forth! "

Though we were at the time more inclined to be sad than mirthful, being weighed down with much anxiety, we could not help laughing when we heard the loud, foolish talk of Conan Maol; but we took no further notice of him.

Inquiring now from the lesser people about the palace, we found that the chief and his two dogs had followed a doe northwards. So, having mustered a strong party of the Fena, we started in pursuit. Kylta and I took the lead, the rest keeping close behind; and in this order we followed the track, never taking rest or slackening speed till we reached Slieve Cullinn.

We began to search round the hill, hoping to find either the chief himself or some person who might give us tidings of him. After wandering among brakes and rough, rocky places, we at last espied a grey-headed old man sitting on the brink of a lake. I went up to him to ask a question, followed by the rest of the Fena. At first I thought he might be a fisherman who had come up from the plains to fish; but when we came near him, he seemed so wretched an old creature, all shrivelled up, with the skin hanging in wrinkles over the bare points of his bones, that I felt quite sure he was not a fisherman, and that he was reduced to that state more by sickness and want than by old age.

I asked the poor old man if he had seen a noble-looking hero pass that way, with two hounds, chasing a doe. He never answered a word, neither did he stir from where he sat, or even look up; but at the question, his head sank on his breast, and his limbs shook all over as with palsy. Then he fell into a sudden fit of grief, wringing his hands and uttering feeble cries of woe.

We soothed him and used him gently for a time, hoping he might speak at last; but to no purpose, for he still kept silent. Then at last growing impatient, and thinking that this might be a mere headstrong humour, we drew our swords, and threatened him with instant death if he did not at once tell us all he knew of the chief and his hounds—for we felt sure he had seen them. But he only lamented the more, and still answered nothing.

At last, after this had gone on for some time, and when we were about to leave him, he beckoned to Kylta Mac Ronan; and when Kylta had come near, the old man whispered into his ear the dreadful secret. And then we all came to know the truth. When we found that the withered old man was no other than our beloved king, Finn, himself, we uttered three shouts of lamentation and anger, so loud and prolonged that the foxes and badgers rushed affrighted from their dens in the hollows of the mountain.

Conan now stepped forward, looking very fierce; and unsheathing his sword with mighty bluster, he began in a loud voice to revile Finn and the Fena with the foulest language he could think of. And he ended by saying that he meant to slay the king that moment:

" Now, O Finn Mac Cumhail, I will certainly strike off your head; for you are the man that never gave me credit for valour, or praised my noble deeds in battle. Ever since your father, Cumhal of the Hosts was slain on the field of Knocka* by the Clann Morna[23] of the Golden Shields, you have been our bitter foe; and it is against your will that any of us are now alive. I am very glad to see you, Finn Mac Cumhail, brought down to what you now are; and I only wish that the rest of the Clann

---

* Knocka, now Castleknock, near Dublin. (See note 27 at the end.)

Baskin[23] were like you. Then should I very soon make short work of them all; and joyful to me would be the task of raising a great carn to their memory!"

To which Oscar replied with great scorn: " It is not worth while drawing a sword to punish thee, Conal Maol, vain and foolish boaster as thou art; and besides, we have at present something else to think of. But if it were not for the trouble that now lies heavy on us on account of our king, I would of a certainty chastise thee by breaking all the bones of thy mouth with my fist!"

" Cease, Oscar," returned Conan, in a voice still louder than before. " Cease your foolish talk! It is actions and not words that prove a man; and as to the noble warlike deeds done in past times by the Fena, it was by the Clann Morna they were performed, and not by the chicken-hearted Clann Baskin!"

The fiery Oscar could bear this no longer. He rushed towards Conan Maol; but Conan, terrified at his vengeful look, ran in amongst the Fena with great outcry, beseeching them to save him from the rage of Oscar. We straightway confronted the young hero, and checked him in his headlong career; and after much ado, we soothed his anger and made peace between him and Conan.

When quietness was restored, Kylta asked Finn how this dread evil had befallen him, who was the enchanter, and whether there was any hope of restoring him to his own shape. Finn told him that it was the daughter of Culann the smith who had transformed him by her spells. And then he recounted how she had lured him to swim in the lake, and how, when he came forth, he was turned into a withered old man.

We now made a framework litter of slender poles, and, placing our king on it, we lifted him tenderly on our shoulders. And, turning from the lake, we marched slowly up-hill till we came to the fairy palace of Slieve Cullinn, where we knew the daughter of Culann had her dwelling deep under ground.[19] Here we set him down, and the whole troop began at once to dig, determined to find the enchantress in her cave-palace, and to take vengeance on her if she did not restore our chief.

For three days and three nights we dug, without a moment's rest or pause, till at length we reached her hollow dwelling;

when she, affrighted at the tumult and the vengeful look of the heroes, suddenly started forth from the cave and stood before us. She held in her hand a drinking-horn of red gold, which was meant for the king. Yet she appeared unwilling, and held it back, notwithstanding the threatening looks of the Fena. But, happening to cast her eyes on the graceful and manly youth, Oscar, she was moved with such admiration and love for him that she wavered no longer, but placed the fairy drinking-horn in the hands of the king. No sooner had he drunk from it, than his own shape and features returned, save only that his hair remained of a silvery grey.

When we gazed on our chief in his own graceful and manly form, we were all pleased with the soft, silvery hue of the grey hairs. And, though the enchantress appeared ready to restore this also, Finn himself told her that it pleased him as it pleased the others, and that he chose to remain grey for the rest of his life.

When the king had drunk from the horn, he passed it to Mac Reth, who drank from it in like manner and gave it to Dering. Dering, after drinking, was about to hand it to the next, when it gave a sudden twist out of his hand, and darted into the loose earth at our feet, where it sank out of sight. We ran at once to recover it; but, though we turned up the earth deeply all round, we were not able to find the drinking-horn. This was a disappointment that vexed us exceedingly, for if we had all drunk from it, we should have been gifted with a fore-knowledge of future events.

A growth of slender twigs grew up afterwards over the spot where it sank into the ground; and this little thicket is still gifted with a part of the virtue of the golden drinking-horn. For any one who looks on it in the morning fasting, will know in a moment all things that are to happen that day.

So ended the Chase of Slieve Cullinn; and in this wise it came to pass that Finn's hair was turned in one day from golden yellow to silvery grey.

# The Chase of
# Slieve Fuad

*In which it is related how*
*Ailna, the wife of Mergah of the Sharp*
*Spears, in order to be revenged on the Fena*
*for the death of her husband, transformed herself into*
*a deer, and decoyed them till she got them into the power of her*
*brother, Dryantore, a giant and an enchanter; how*
*he threw them into a dungeon, with intent to*
*kill them; and how they were in the*
*end set free by Conan Maol.\**

FINN and the Fena went one day to hunt at Slieve Fuad.†
When they had come very near to the top of the mountain, a
deer suddenly bounded from a thicket right before them, very
large and fierce, with a great pair of sharp, dangerous antlers.
At once they loosed their dogs and gave chase; and those who
were scattered here and there about the hill gave up the pursuit
of smaller game to join the main body, for it was very seldom
they fell in with a deer that promised better sport.

She led them through rugged places, over rocks and bogs,
and into deep glens. The hounds several times surrounded her;
but she fought her way with so much strength and fury that
she always escaped, after killing many of the dogs and disabling
some of the men.

Soon she left Slieve Fuad behind, nor did she slacken speed
till she reached the green hill of Lidas, while the hunters and
dogs followed in full chase close behind. She then made her
way across the open country to a rugged and bushy hill—the

---

* This story is told by Oisin to St. Patrick.
† Slieve Fuad was the ancient name of the highest of the Fews mountains, near
   Newtown Hamilton, in Armagh.

hill of Carrigan;* and here they suddenly lost her among the rocks and thickets. They searched round the hill without avail, north, south, east, and west, till all, both men and dogs, were quite scattered; and Finn and Dara the Melodious were left alone.

At length, Finn's dog, Skolan, started the deer once more, and again the chase began. Back over the self-same course she ran, by the hill of Lidas, and straight on towards Slieve Fuad, Finn and Dara close on her track; while the main body of the Fena followed far behind, guided by the cries of the dogs.

When the deer reached Slieve Fuad, she again took cover and disappeared at the very spot where they had first started her; and the two chiefs, after beating the thickets on every side, were at length forced to give up the search.

A druidical mist now rose up, darkening the air, and enfolding them on every side; so that they lost their way. They tried many times to regain the path, but to no purpose; for they only lost themselves more and more among the quagmires and thickets. At last they sat down to rest, weary and baffled; and Dara played a mournful strain on his timpan; after which they sounded the Dord-Fian,† as a signal to their friends.

When the Fena heard the Dord-Fian sounding afar off, they felt sure that their leader was in trouble or strait of some kind; and they started to his relief, making northwards straight towards the point from which they thought the signal came. But they had not gone far when they heard it sounding from the east, and altered their course accordingly. Again it changed to the west; and no sooner had they set forward in that direction than it seemed to come from the south. In this manner were they led hither and thither, till they became quite bewildered; and they found themselves no nearer to those they were in search of, for every time they heard the Dord-Fian, it seemed as far off as ever.

Meantime Finn and Dara, after resting for a time, again started off, intent on trying once more to reach their friends; for they heard their shouts, and knew they were seeking them. As they were making their way through the thick fog, they heard a voice at a little distance, as if from one in distress; and, turning

---

* Now probably the village of Carrigans, on the river Foyle.
† Dord-Fian, a sort of musical war-cry.

their steps that way, they met a young woman, very beautiful, and very pleasing in manner, but looking weary and sore perplexed, and all over in sad plight from the bogs and brambles.

Finn accosted her in a gentle voice, asking how she came to be alone in a place so wild.

She replied: " I and my husband were journeying along over the plain, when we heard the melodious cry of hounds; and he left me to follow the chase, telling me to continue along the same path, and promising to rejoin me without delay. But this fairy fog has risen around me, and I have lost my way, so that I know not now in what direction to go."

Finn then asked her name and the name of her husband.

" My husband's name is Lavaran, and mine is Glanlua. But I perceive that you are one of the Fena; and indeed I think, from your arms and from your noble mien, that you must be the great chief Finn himself. If this be so, I place myself under your protection; and I know well that you will lead me safely out of this place to my husband; for the Fena never yet refused their help to a woman in distress."

" You are quite right, lady, for I am Finn; and this chase that has parted you and your husband belongs to me. We will certainly take you under our protection, and we will neither abandon you on this mountain, nor suffer any one to harm you. But as to leading you to your husband, it is not at present in our power to do that; for you must know, lady, that we also have been set astray by this magical fairy fog. Nevertheless, we will do the best we can; and now you had better come with us."

So the three set forward in the direction they thought most likely to lead to the open plain.

After walking for some time, they heard a low, sweet strain of fairy music; and they stopped to listen. It seemed to be near them and around them in the fog, so that Finn thought it came from the spot where the lady stood; and she thought it came from Finn or Dara: and the music was followed by shouts and noise, as if from a great company. When the noise ceased, the music began again more sweetly than before; so that they felt heavy, and as if inclined to sleep. Still more drowsy and powerless they became as they listened; and at last they all three sank on the ground, in a trance deep and deathlike.

After a time they awoke, and slowly regained their senses; though they were so weak that they could scarcely move. The fog had cleared away, leaving the air bright and warm; and when they were able to look around, they found themselves on the margin of a blue lake. The part of the lake that lay in front of them was narrow, and quite calm and smooth; but on each side, to the right and left, it opened out into two broad, green-bordered seas, with great waves tumbling wildly about, as if the waters were torn up by whirlwinds. But where they sat, not a breath was blowing. And looking across the narrow part, they saw a stately palace right before them on the opposite shore.

As they were gazing at all these strange things, silent and much astonished, they saw a warrior coming forth from the palace, in size like a giant, rough and fierce-looking, with a beautiful woman by his side. The two walked quickly down to the shore, and, plunging in, they swam straight across the middle of the lake.

And Dara and Glanlua, turning to Finn, said: " Of a surety, it is not for our good yonder strangers are approaching; but to work us treachery and mischief! "

This forecast turned out to be true. The large warrior and the beautiful lady had no sooner gained the land than they came up to Finn and his two companions; and without speaking a word, the giant seized them roughly, and led them down to the shore of the lake. For the two heroes were still so weak from the spell of the fairy music that they were not able to raise a hand to defend either the lady or themselves.

The giant and his companion, making no delay, plunged in, and swam back towards the palace, bringing the three with them; and as soon as they had reached the shore, the strange warrior, addressed Finn in a fierce and surly manner—

" For a long time," he said, " have I sought Finn Mac Cumhail, the evil-minded and crafty; and now, O Finn, now that thou hast been by a well-laid plan cast under my power, I will take good care that thou shalt not escape till I take revenge, even to the full, for all the injuries thou hast done to me and to my sister! "

Finn listened to this speech with much surprise, for he could not call to mind that he had ever seen the hero before.

" Tell me, I pray thee," he said, " who thou art; for I know thee not; neither do I know of any injury thou hast suffered at my hands. Thou art, indeed, large of body, and fierce and boastful in speech; but know that to take revenge on a foe who is unable to defend himself is a deed quite unbecoming a hero! "

The large man replied: " Do you not remember the treachery you practised on Mergah of the Sharp Spears, and on my sons, two fair youths, whom you slew by unfair means, at the battle of Knockanar?* Well indeed do I know thee, Finn, for I am Dryantore, and this is Ailna my sister, the wife of Mergah. She is left without her husband, and I without my sons, by your cruel wiles; for it was by fraud and foul play, and not by fair fighting, that you gained the battle of Knockanar, and slew Mergah and his host! "

" I remember well," said Finn, " that they all fell on the battlefield; but it was not by craft or treachery. Mergah of the Sharp Spears came with a mighty host to conquer Erin, and lay it under tribute. But they were met at Knockanar, and every man of them slain in fair, open fight, though not without sore loss to the Fena."

" You may say what you please on the matter," said Dryantore. " But it is quite enough for me that you have slain Ailna's husband and my two sons. And now, indeed, I shall take revenge—of that be sure—both on you and on all the Fena that come within my reach."

And having so spoken, he began without more ado to bind Finn, Dara, and Glanlua in strong fetters; and having done so, he threw them into a dungeon, where he left them without food or drink or comfort of any kind.

Meantime the Fena ceased not to search for their king. They knew, by the sad strain they had heard in the distance, and by the strange manner in which the music had shifted from place to place, that he was caught under some druidic spell; and they vowed they would never rest till they had found him and punished the enchanter, whoever he might be.

---

* Knockanar (the hill of slaughter), where a great battle was fought between the Fena under Finn, and the foreigners under Mergah of the Sharp Spears, in which Mergah was defeated and slain. This battle forms the subject of a poetical romance.

Next day, Ailna visited the dungeon; and Finn addressed her.

"Hast thou forgotten, Ailna," he said, "that when thou didst come to Erin after the death of thy husband, Mergah of the Sharp Spears, the Fena received thee hospitably, and, pitying thy distress, treated thee with much kindness? But for this thou hast indeed given us an ungrateful and unbecoming return; for thou hast shut us up in this dungeon, without food or drink, having, by guileful druidical spells, taken away our strength."

"I remember very well," said Ailna, "that you treated me kindly. But you killed my husband; and I am well pleased that it has now come to my turn to avenge his death. I do not feel the least pity for you; and I only wish that the whole of the Fena were with you in that dungeon, to be dealt with by my brother."

Then, casting her eyes on Glanlua, she began to upbraid her in bitter words for having been in the company of Finn and Dara. But Glanlua explained the matter, saying that she had never seen either of the chiefs before, and that it was only by chance she had fallen on them when she had lost her way in the fog.

"If that be so," said Ailna, "it is not just that you should be punished for the evil deeds of the others."

And she went and told Dryantore, who came forthwith to release the lady.

Glanlua took leave of Finn and Dara, and left the prison, grieving much for their evil plight; for she was grateful for their kindness on the mountain. Ailna led her to the palace; and, having placed food before her, bade her eat. But Glanlua, being overcome by weakness, suddenly fell into a swoon, and remained for a long time without sense or motion, like one dead. When at last she opened her eyes, she saw Ailna standing near, holding in her hand a golden drinking-horn. And Ailna gave her to drink, and immediately the spells lost their power; and she regained her strength; and the bloom and beauty of her countenance returned.

But now she bethought her of the two heroes; and, remembering their dismal plight in the dungeon, she became sorrowful, and began to sigh and weep. And when Ailna and Dryantore came to know the cause of her tears, they told her with much severity that Finn and Dara deserved their punishment; and that both should stay in prison till the time had come to put them to death.

"I seek not to release them from prison or to save them from death," said Glanlua, "but that they are left without food and drink—this it is that moves me to pity."

And Dryantore said: "If only that has caused your tears, you may, if you so please, bring them food. Besides, I do not mean to put them to death immediately. I shall let them live yet awhile, that I may decoy by them the other Fena, who are now wandering hither and thither in quest of their chief. And it is my firm belief that in a little time I shall have them all in that dungeon."

So Glanlua went to the prison, bringing food and drink, and Ailna went with her. They found the heroes sitting on the floor, sorrowing, their strength and activity all gone; for the music-spell still held them, and they suffered also from want of food. And when they saw the two ladies, they shed bitter tears. Glanlua, on her part, wept with pity when she looked on the wasted face of the chief. But not so Ailna; she was pleased at their distress, for her heart was hardened with vengeance, and she longed for the time when they should suffer death. However, Glanlua placed food and drink before them, and they ate and drank and were strengthened for the time.

When the two ladies returned, Dryantore asked Glanlua if it were true what he had heard, that Dara was a favourite among the Fena; and why it was that they loved him so.

"I only know that he is a very skilful musician," replied Glanlua, "for I never heard melody sweeter than the strains he played yesterday, when I met himself and Finn in the fog."

"I should like very much to hear this music," said Dryantore, "if it be so melodious as you say." And as he spoke these words he went towards the dungeon.

And when he had come to the door, he said to Dara, in a loud, harsh, surly voice: "I have heard that you are a skilful musician, and can play very sweet strains. I wish you to play for me now that I may know if this be true."

"If I had the Fena around me," replied Dara, "I could delight them with the melody of my timpan; but as for you, guileful and cruel as you are, I do not believe that you can take any pleasure in music. Moreover, how can you expect that I should play sweet music for you, seeing that I am shut up here in this dismal dungeon, and that all manly strength and cheerfulness of mind have left me through your foul spells?"

"I will take off the spells if only you play for me," said Dryantore. "And if your strains be as delightful as I have heard reported, I will bring you forth from your prison, and I will keep you for ever in my castle, and you shall play for me whensoever I wish for music."

"I shall never consent to be released, neither will I play any music for you, so long as my chief lies in bondage and under enchantment," said Dara, "for I grieve not indeed for myself, but for him."

Dryantore replied: "I will lift the spells from both of you for a time; but as to releasing Finn, that is a matter I do not wish to talk of now."

Whereupon Dryantore removed the spells, and the heroes regained their strength and courage.

Dara then played a low, sweet tune; and Dryantore, who had never before heard such music, listened with delight and wonder. He was so charmed that he called Ailna and Glanlua, that they also might hear; and they were as much delighted as the giant. But what pleased Glanlua most was to see the heroes restored to their wonted cheerfulness.

Now all this time the Fena were seeking among the glens and hollows of the mountain for Finn and Dara. After walking for some time over a stony and rugged way, a faint strain of music struck on their ears. They stopped to listen, breathless; and every man knew the sound of Dara's timpan; and they raised a shout of gladness, which reached Finn and Dara in their dungeon. At the same moment they came in view of the palace, and they drew their swords and put their shields and spears in readiness, as men do going to battle. And they went forward warily, for they feared foul play, and their hearts had a forecast that a foe was near. But, indeed, they little deemed what manner of foe they should meet.

When Dryantore heard the shouts, he hid himself from the view of the Fena, and forthwith betook him to his magic arts.

And again the spell fell on the two heroes, and their strength departed; and Dara's hand, losing its cunning, trembled on the strings, so that his music became dull and broken.

And when Dara's music ceased, the Fena heard a low, hoarse murmur, which, growing each moment louder, sounded at last like the hollow roar of waves. And anon their strength and their swiftness left them, and they fell to the ground every man, in a deep trance as if they slept the sleep of death.

Then Dryantore and Ailna came forth, and having bound them one by one in strong, hard fetters, they roused them up and led them helpless and faltering to the dungeon, where they shut them in with Finn and Dara.

The Fena looked sadly on their king; and he, on his part, shed bitter tears to think that he had decoyed them unwittingly into the hands of their foe.

In the midst of their sighs and tears they heard the loud voice of the giant, who, looking in on them from the open door, addressed them.

"Now at last, ye Fena, you are in my safe keeping. Truly you have done great deeds in your time, but methinks you will not be able to escape from this prison till I have taken just vengeance on you for slaying Mergah of the Sharp Spears, and my two sons, at the battle of Knockanar!"

And having so spoken, he shut the door and went his way.

When he came to the palace, he found that Glanlua's husband, Lavaran, had been there. Upon which he fell into a mighty rage; for he feared to let any man know the secrets of the palace; and he feared also that Lavaran might try to aid Finn and the others. He inquired of the two ladies whither he had gone; but they replied they did not know. He then began to search through the rooms, and, raising his voice, he called aloud for Lavaran; and the Fena, even in their dungeon, heard the roar quite plainly.

Lavaran, hearing him, was sore afraid, and answered from a remote part of the palace. And as he came forward, the giant placed him under his spells, and, having bound him, flung him into the dungeon with the others.

Dryantore's fury had not in the least abated; and, entering the dungeon, he struck off the heads of several of the Fena with his great sword, saying he would visit them each day, and do in like manner till he had killed them all.

During the time the Fena were unable to defend themselves; for, besides that their strength had gone out from their limbs on account of the spells, they found that from the time the enchanter entered the prison, they were all fixed firmly in their places, every man cleaving to the ground, in whatsoever position he chanced to be, sitting, lying, or standing. And Finn shed tears—even tears of blood in sight of all—seeing his men fall one by one, while he had to look on without power to help them.

After Dryantore had in this manner slain several, he approached Conan Maol,[23] with intent to end that day's work by cutting off his head; and as it chanced, Conan was lying full length on the floor. Now Conan, though he was large-boned and strong, and very boastful in his speech, was a coward at heart, and more afraid of wounds and death than any man that ever lived.

So when he saw Dryantore coming towards him with his sword in his hand all dripping, he shouted aloud: " Hold thy hand, Dryantore! Hold thy hand for a little while, and be not guilty of such treachery! "

But the giant, not heeding in the least Conan's words, raised his sword with his two hands and rose on tiptoe for a mighty blow. Then Conan, terrified beyond measure, put forth all his strength to free himself, and bounded from the floor clear outside the range of the sword; but left behind him, clinging to the floor, all the skin of his back, even from the points of his shoulders to the calves of his legs.

When he saw the giant still making towards him in a greater rage than ever for missing his blow, he again cried aloud: " Hold your hand this time, Dryantore! Is it not enough that you see me in this woeful plight? For it is plain that I cannot escape death. Leave me, then, to die of my wounds, and slay me not thus suddenly! "

Dryantore held his hand; but he told Conan that he would for a certainty kill him next time he came, if he did not find him already dead of his wounds. Then he stalked out of the dungeon, and, shutting close the door, left the Fena in gloom and sadness.

Though Lavaran had been only a little while in the palace, he made good use of his time, and now approaching Finn, he whispered in his ear: " There is that in yonder palace which would free us from those accursed spells if we only could get at it."

And when Finn asked what it was, he replied: " A magical golden drinking-horn of wondrous virtue. I saw it in the palace among many other precious jewels."

Finn again questioned him how he knew of its secret power.

" Glanlua, my wife, told me," said Lavaran. " For she said that, being herself at the point of death, Ailna fetched this drinking-horn and bade her drink. And when she had drunk, she was immediately freed from spells and sickness. She told me, moreover, that it would remove the spell from the Fena, and bring back their strength and heal their wounds, if they could get to drink from it."

Conan, being near, overheard this conversation; and he inwardly resolved that he would try to secure the drinking-horn, if perchance he might be able to heal his wounds by means of it.

Not long after, the giant again came to the prison, sword in hand, and addressed Conan.

" Come forward now, O big, bald man, for I am about to fulfil my promise to you! Come forward, that I may strike off your large head; for I see that your wounds have not killed you! "

But Conan, instead of coming forward, fell back even to the farthest part of the dungeon, and replied:

" You must know, Dryantore, that I, of all men alive, am the most unwilling to die any death unworthy of a brave hero. You see my evil plight, all wounded and faint from loss of blood; and, being as I am a valiant warrior, it would surely be a shameful thing and a foul blot on my fame, to be slain while in this state. I ask only one favour—that you cure me of my wounds first. After this, you may put me to death in any manner that is most agreeable to you."

To this Dryantore consented, seeing that Conan was secure; and he called to Ailna and bade her fetch him the magical golden drinking-horn. " For I wish," said he, " to heal the wounds of yonder big, bald man."

But Ailna replied: " Of what concern are his wounds to us? Is it not better that he should die at once, and all the other Fena with him? "

Conan spoke out from where he stood. " Lovely Ailna," he said, " I seek not to escape death. I ask only to be healed first and slain afterwards! "

Ailna went to the palace and soon returned, bringing, not the drinking-horn, but a large sheepskin, covered all over with a long growth of wool. Dryantore took it from her, and doing as she told him, he fitted it on Conan's back, where it cleaved firmly, so that his wounds were all healed up in an instant.

As long as Conan lived afterwards, this sheepskin remained on his back; and the wool grew upon it every year, even as wool grows on the back of a living sheep. And from that time forth, the other Fena were always mocking him and laughing at him and calling him nicknames.

As soon as Conan felt his wounds healed, he again spoke to the giant.

" It is my opinion, Dryantore, that it would be a very unwise thing for you to put me to death. I see plainly you want a servant. Now, although I am large of bone and strong of body, and very brave withal, still I am very harmless. And if you let me live, I shall be your servant for ever, and you will find me very useful to you."

The giant saw the force and wisdom of Conan's words; and he felt that he wanted a servant very much, though he never perceived it till that moment, when Conan reminded him of it.

" I believe, indeed, Conan," he said, " that your words are truth. Wherefore, I will not put you to death. You are now my servant, and so shall you be for the rest of your life."

He then led Conan forth from the dungeon towards the palace; and he was in such good humour at having got a servant, that he forgot to kill any of the Fena on that occasion.

He called to him Ailna and Glanlua, to tell them of what he had done.

" I find that I need a servant very much. Wherefore, I have made Conan my servant. And I am now about to free him from the spell and give him back his strength by a drink from the golden drinking-horn, so that he may be able to wait on me and do my work."

For Conan, though his wounds were healed, was still so weak from the spell that he was scarce able to walk.

" I do not at all approve what you have done," said Ailna. " It would be, methinks, much better to put him straightway to death along with all the others. As long as he is with us as our servant, I shall never think myself free from danger; for the Fena are treacherous all alike."

" As for the other Fena," replied Dryantore, " you need not be in any trouble on their account, for their time is short. As soon as I have got Conan free from the spell, I will go straight to the dungeon and kill them, every man. And when they are fairly put out of the way, it seems to me that we need not fear danger from this big, bald man with the sheepskin on his back."

When Ailna heard that the death of the Fena was near at hand, she no longer gainsaid her brother. So Dryantore led Conan to the palace; and placing the magical drinking-horn in his hand, bade him drink. And Conan drank; and immediately his strength and his spirits returned.

Now it so happened, while these things went on, that Finn asked Dara to play one of his sweet, sad tunes, that they might hear the music of his timpan before they died. And Dara took his timpan, and began to play; and historians say that no one either before or since ever played sweeter strains.

At the very moment that Conan had finished drinking, he and Dryantore heard the music sounding faintly in the distance; and the giant opened the door and stood on the threshold to listen. He was so charmed that he quite forgot all about Conan and the drinking-horn; and finding that he could not hear the music plainly enough where he stood, he walked hastily towards the dungeon, leaving Conan behind with the drinking-horn in his hand.

No sooner had he gone out than Conan hid the drinking-horn under his cloak, and went to the dungeon after him.

And when the giant saw him he said: " Why have you followed me; and what business have you here? Are you not my servant; and why have you come without being bidden by me? "

" I thought," replied Conan, " that you were about to put the Fena to death; and I came to look at them once more before they died."

Then suddenly Dryantore bethought him of the drinking-horn, and he said: " Where is the golden drinking-horn I gave you? "

" I left it," said Conan, " just where I found it in the palace."

The giant ran hastily towards the palace to secure the drinking-horn; and no sooner was he out of sight than Conan, drawing forth the horn, put it to the lips of each to drink, beginning with Finn. Only Finn and Oscar had drunk, when they heard the heavy steps of the giant running towards the dungeon; and now they saw that he was indeed inflamed with fury. Oscar seized his great, polished spear, and sprang to the door; and the others raised a mighty shout of joy; while Conan went on releasing the heroes one by one.

When Dryantore saw Oscar, he uttered a roar of rage and disappointment; and then called aloud to Ailna to come to him. And she came forth; and when she saw how matters stood, she was seized with such grief and terror that she dropped down and died immediately. Glanlua was standing near at hand, rejoicing at the release of her husband and friends; but when she saw Ailna fall to the ground dead, she became sad, and, stooping down, wept over her.

All this Oscar saw from where he stood; and it was with much ado he checked his tears. For though my son was the bravest of the heroes, and the most terrible in battle, he had a gentle heart, and never saw a woman or a child in distress without being moved to pity.

But Conan felt not the least pity. On the contrary, he was very glad to see Ailna dead; and he told Oscar that it was very well she was out of the way, for she was a vicious woman, and had wrought the Fena much trouble and woe.

And now Oscar, casting his eyes again on Dryantore, hardened his heart for battle, and addressed the giant in these words:

" It has at last come to pass, O Dryantore, that you are in the power of the Fena; and there is no escape for you, though you are a large and strong giant, and a druid with powerful magical spells. But the Fena never yet treated an enemy ungenerously. You indeed dealt unfairly and treacherously with us; and meant to kill us all, after having taken away our strength and valour by your black, guileful magic. But even so, we give you your choice; and we challenge you now to single combat with any of our champions you may wish to choose."

" It is very true that the Fena have prevailed over me," replied Dryantore, " and it is a just punishment for my folly in releasing Conan the Bald from my spells. I desire single combat. I will fight the Fena one after another, till I either fall myself or slay them all; and I will begin with you! "

Oscar then took his shield and made ready for battle. Meantime the giant, harbouring great wrath against Conan, approached him unawares; and when he had come near enough, he sprang suddenly on him, and aimed a blow with all his might at his head. Conan, springing aside, barely escaped the edge of the sword; and, running in great fear, called to Oscar with great outcry to save him from the giant.

Then Oscar ran between; and he and the giant fought a long and fierce fight, while we looked on with anxious hearts. The giant was furious and strong; but my son was active and watchful and fearless of heart; and Dryantore at length fell at the door of his own palace, pierced through and through by the long, smooth spear of Oscar.

When the Fena saw the giant fall, they raised three mighty shouts of joy. And Glanlua brought the magic drinking-horn to Oscar, from which he drank, so that his wounds were healed, and his strength straightway returned to him.

The Fena then went into the palace, where they found food in great plenty, with wine and mead in golden bowls and drinking-horns. And they ate and drank and made merry; after which they rested that night on soft beds and couches.

When they awoke in the morning, all was changed. The palace and the lake were gone; and the heroes found themselves lying on the heathy side of Slieve Fuad, at the selfsame spot where they had first started the deer; with the morning sun shining brightly over their heads.

# Oisin in Tír na nÓg*

## OR

## THE LAST OF THE FENA

*According to an ancient legend, Finn's son, Oisin, the hero-poet, survived to the time of St. Patrick, two hundred years (the legend makes it three hundred) after the other Fena. On a certain occasion, when the saint asked him how he had lived to such a great age, the old hero related the following story.*

A SHORT time after the fatal battle of Gavra,† where so many of our heroes fell, we were hunting on a dewy morning near the brink of Loch Lein, where the trees and hedges around us were all fragrant with blossoms, and the little birds sang melodious music on the branches. We soon roused the deer from the thickets, and as they bounded over the plain, our hounds followed after them in full cry.

We were not long so engaged, when we saw a rider coming swiftly towards us from the west; and we soon perceived that it was a maiden on a white steed. We all ceased from the chase on seeing the lady, who reined in as she approached. And Finn and the Fena were greatly surprised, for they had never before seen so lovely a maiden. A slender golden diadem encircled her head; and she wore a brown robe of silk, spangled with stars of red gold, which was fastened in front by a golden brooch, and fell from her shoulders till it swept the ground. Her yellow hair flowed far down over her robe in bright, golden ringlets. Her blue eyes were as clear as the drops of dew on the grass;

* Tír na nÓg, the Land of Youth. (See note 19 at the end.)
† Gavra, now Garristown, in north County Dublin. (For an account of this battle, see note 28 at the end.)

and while her small, white hand held the bridle and curbed her steed with a golden bit, she sat more gracefully than the swan on Loch Lein. The white steed was covered with a smooth, flowing mantle. He was shod with four shoes of pure yellow gold, and in all Erin a better or more beautiful steed could not be found.

As she came slowly to the presence of Finn, he addressed her courteously:

"Who art thou, O lovely youthful princess? Tell us thy name and the name of thy country, and relate to us the cause of thy coming."

She answered in a sweet and gentle voice. "Noble king of the Fena, I have had a long journey this day, for my country lies far off in the Western Sea. I am the daughter of the king of Tír na nÓg, and my name is Niamh of the Golden Hair."

"And what is it that has caused thee to come so far across the sea? Has thy husband forsaken thee; or what other evil has befallen thee?"

"My husband has not forsaken me, for I have never been married or betrothed to any man. But I love thy noble son, Oisin; and this is what has brought me to Erin. It is not without reason that I have given him my love, and that I have undertaken this long journey: for I have often heard of his bravery, his gentleness, and the nobleness of his person. Many princes and high chiefs have sought me in marriage; but I was quite indifferent to all men, and never consented to wed, till my heart was moved with love for thy gentle son, Oisin."

When I heard these words, and when I looked on the lovely maiden with her glossy, golden hair, I was all over in love with her. I came near, and, taking her small hand in mine, I told her she was a mild star of brightness and beauty, and that I preferred her to all the princesses in the world for my wife.

"Then," said she, "I place you under geasa,[12] which true heroes never break through, to come with me on my white steed to Tír na nÓg, the land of never-ending youth. It is the most delightful and the most renowned country under the sun. There is abundance of gold and silver and jewels, of honey and wine;

and the trees bear fruit and blossoms and green leaves together all the year round. You will get a hundred swords and a hundred robes of silk and satin, a hundred swift steeds, and a hundred slender, keen-scenting hounds. You will get herds of cows without number, and flocks of sheep with fleeces of gold; a coat of mail that cannot be pierced, and a sword that never missed a stroke and from which no one ever escaped alive. There are feasting and harmless pastimes each day. A hundred warriors fully armed shall always await you at call, and harpers shall delight you with their sweet music. You will wear the diadem of the king of Tír na nÓg, which he never yet gave to any one under the sun, and which will guard you day and night, in tumult and battle and danger of every kind. Lapse of time shall bring neither decay nor death, and you shall be for ever young, and gifted with unfading beauty and strength. All these delights you shall enjoy, and many others that I do not mention; and I myself will be your wife if you come with me to Tír na nÓg."

I replied that she was my choice above all the maidens in the world, and that I would willingly go with her to the Land of Youth.

When my father, Finn, and the Fena heard me say this, and knew that I was going from them, they raised three shouts of grief and lamentation. And Finn came up to me and took my hand in his, saying sadly: " Woe is me, my son, that you are going away from me, for I do not expect that you will ever return to me! "

The manly beauty of his countenance became quite dimmed with sorrow; and though I promised to return after a little time, and fully believed that I should see him again, I could not check my tears, as I gently kissed my father's cheek.

I then bade farewell to my dear companions, and mounted the white steed, while the lady kept her seat before me. She gave the signal, and the steed galloped swiftly and smoothly towards the west, till he reached the strand; and when his gold-shod hoofs touched the waves, he shook himself and neighed three times. He made no delay, but plunged forward at once, moving over the face of the sea with the speed of a cloud-shadow on a March day. The wind overtook the waves and we overtook the wind, so that we straightway lost sight of land; and we saw nothing but billows tumbling before us and billows tumbling behind us.

Other shores came into view, and we saw many wonderful things on our journey—islands and cities, lime-white mansions, bright grianáns* and lofty palaces. A hornless fawn once crossed our course, bounding nimbly along from the crest of one wave to the crest of another; and close after, in full chase, a white hound with red ears. We saw also a lovely young maiden on a brown steed, with a golden apple in her hand; and as she passed swiftly by, a young warrior on a white steed plunged after her, wearing a long, flowing mantle of yellow silk, and holding a gold-hilted sword in his hand.

I knew naught of these things, and, marvelling much, I asked the princess what they meant.

" Heed not what you see here, Oisin," she said, " for all these wonders are as nothing compared with what you shall see in Tír na nÓg."

At last we saw at a great distance, rising over the waves on the very verge of the sea, a palace more splendid than all the others; and, as we drew near, its front glittered like the morning sun. I asked the lady what royal house this was, and who was the prince that ruled over it.

" This country is the Land of Virtues," she replied. " Its king is the giant, Fomor of the Blows, and its queen the daughter of the king of the Land of Life.[19] This Fomor brought the lady away by force from her own country, and keeps her in his palace; but she has put him under geasa[12] that he cannot break through, never to ask her to marry him till she can find a champion to fight him in single combat. But she still remains in bondage; for no hero has yet come hither who has the courage to meet the giant."

" A blessing on you, golden-haired Niamh," I replied; " I have never heard music sweeter than your voice; and although I feel pity for this princess, yet your story is pleasant to me to hear; for of a certainty I will go to the palace, and try whether I cannot kill this Fomor, and free the lady."

---

* Grianán, a summer-house; a house in a bright, sunny spot.

So we came to land; and as we drew nigh to the palace, the lovely young queen met us and bade us welcome. She led us in and placed us on chairs of gold; after which choice food was placed before us, and drinking-horns filled with mead, and golden goblets of sweet wine.

When we had eaten and drunk, the mild young princess told us her story, while tears streamed from her soft, blue eyes; and she ended by saying: " I shall never return to my own country and to my father's house, so long as this great and cruel giant is alive! "

When I heard her sad words, and saw her tears falling, I was moved with pity; and telling her to cease from her grief, I gave her my hand as a pledge that I would meet the giant, and either slay him or fall myself in her defence.

While we were yet speaking, we saw the giant coming towards the palace, large of body, and ugly and hateful in appearance, carrying a load of deerskins on his back, and holding a great iron club in his hand. He threw down his load when he saw us, turned a surly look on the princess, and, without greeting us or showing the least mark of courtesy, he forthwith challenged me to battle in a loud, rough voice.

It was not my wont to be dismayed by a call to battle, or to be terrified at the sight of an enemy; and I went forth at once without the least fear in my heart. But though I had fought many battles in Erin against wild boars and enchanters and foreign invaders, never before did I find it so hard to preserve my life. We fought for three days and three nights without food or drink or sleep; for the giant did not give me a moment for rest, and neither did I give him. At length, when I looked at the two princesses weeping in great fear, and when I called to mind my father's deeds in battle, the fury of my valour arose; and with a sudden onset I felled the giant to the earth; and instantly, before he could recover himself, I cut off his head.

When the maidens saw the monster lying on the ground dead, they uttered three cries of joy; and they came to me, and led me into the palace. For I was indeed bruised all over, and covered with gory wounds; and a sudden dizziness of brain and feebleness of body seized me. But the daughter of the king

of the Land of Life applied precious balsam and healing herbs
to my wounds; and in a short time I was healed, and my
cheerfulness of mind returned.

Then I buried the giant in a deep and wide grave; and I
raised a great carn over him, and placed on it a stone with his
name graved in Ogham.

We rested that night, and at the dawn of next morning
Niamh said to me that it was time for us to resume our journey
to Tír na nÓg. So we took leave of the daughter of the king
of the Land of Life; and though her heart was joyful after her
release, she wept at our departure, and we were not less sorry
at parting from her. When we had mounted the white steed,
he galloped towards the strand; and as soon as his hoofs touched
the wave, he shook himself and neighed three times. We plunged
forward over the clear, green sea with the speed of a March
wind on a hillside; and soon we saw nothing but billows tumbling
before us and billows tumbling behind us. We saw again the
fawn chased by the white hound with red ears; and the maiden
with the golden apple passed swiftly by, followed by the young
warrior in yellow silk on his white steed. And again we passed
many strange islands and cities and white palaces.

The sky now darkened, so that the sun was hidden from our
view. A storm arose, and the sea was lighted up with constant
flashes. But though the wind blew from every point of the
heavens, and the waves rose up and roared around us, the white
steed kept his course straight on, moving as calmly and swiftly
as before, through the foam and blinding spray, without being
delayed or disturbed in the least, and without turning either to
the right or to the left.

At length the storm abated, and after a time the sun again
shone brightly; and when I looked up, I saw a country near at
hand, all green and full of flowers, with beautiful smooth plains,
blue hills, and bright lakes and waterfalls. Not far from the
shore stood a palace of surpassing beauty and splendour. It
was covered all over with gold and with gems of every colour—
blue, green, crimson, and yellow; and on each side were griánáns
shining with precious stones, built by artists the most skilful that
could be found. I asked Niamh the name of that delightful
country, and she replied:

"This is my native country, Tír na nÓg; and there is nothing I have promised you that you will not find in it."

As soon as we reached the shore, we dismounted; and now we saw advancing from the palace a troop of noble-looking warriors, all clad in bright garments, who came forward to meet and welcome us. Following these we saw a stately glittering host, with the king at their head wearing a robe of bright yellow satin covered with gems, and a crown that sparkled with gold and diamonds. The queen came after, attended by a hundred lovely young maidens; and as they advanced towards us, it seemed to me that this king and queen exceeded all the kings and queens of the world in beauty and gracefulness and majesty.

After they had kissed their daughter, the king took my hand, and said aloud in the hearing of the host:

"This is Oisín, the son of Finn, for whom my daughter, Niamh, travelled over the sea to Erin. This is Oisín, who is to be the husband of Niamh of the Golden Hair. We give you a hundred thousand welcomes, brave Oisín. You will be for ever young in this land. All kinds of delights and innocent pleasures are awaiting you, and my daughter, the gentle, golden-haired Niamh, shall be your wife; for I am the king of Tír na nÓg."

I gave thanks to the king, and I bowed low to the queen; after which we went into the palace, where we found a banquet prepared. The feasting and rejoicing lasted for ten days, and on the last day, I was wedded to the gentle Niamh of the Golden Hair.

I lived in the Land of Youth more than three hundred years; but it appeared to me that only three years had passed since the day I parted from my friends. At the end of that time, I began to have a longing desire to see my father, Finn, and all my old companions, and I asked leave of Niamh and of the king to visit Erin. The king gave permission, and Niamh said:

"I will give consent, though I feel sorrow in my heart, for I fear much you will never return to me."

I replied that I would surely return, and that she need not feel any doubt or dread, for that the white steed knew the way, and would bring me back in safety. Then she addressed me in these words, which seemed very strange to me.

" I will not refuse this request, though your journey afflicts me with great grief and fear. Erin is not now as it was when you left it. The great king Finn and his Fena are all gone; and you will find, instead of them, a holy father and hosts of priests and saints. Now, think well on what I say to you, and keep my words in your mind. If once you alight from the white steed, you will never come back to me. Again I warn you, if you place your feet on the green sod in Erin, you will never return to this lovely land. A third time, O Oisin, my beloved husband, a third time I say to you, if you alight from the white steed, you will never see me again."

I promised that I would faithfully attend to her words, and that I would not alight from the white steed. Then, as I looked into her gentle face and marked her grief, my heart was weighed down with sadness, and my tears flowed plentifully; but even so, my mind was bent on coming back to Erin.

When I had mounted the white steed, he galloped straight towards the shore. We moved as swiftly as before over the clear sea. The wind overtook the waves and we overtook the wind, so that we straightway left the Land of Youth behind; and we passed by many islands and cities, till at length we landed on the green shores of Erin.

As I travelled on through the country, I looked closely around me; but I scarcely knew the old places, for everything seemed strangely altered. I saw no sign of Finn and his host, and I began to dread that Niamh's saying was coming true. At length, I espied at a distance a company of little men and women,* all mounted on horses as small as themselves; and when I came near, they greeted me kindly and courteously. They looked at me with wonder and curiosity, and they marvelled much at my great size, and at the beauty and majesty of my person.

I asked them about Finn and the Fena; whether they were still living, or if any sudden disaster had swept them away. And one replied:

" We have heard of the hero Finn, who ruled the Fena of Erin in times of old, and who never had an equal for bravery and wisdom. The poets of the Gael have written many books

---

* The gigantic race of the Fena had all passed away, and their descendants looked very small in Oisin's eyes.

concerning his deeds and the deeds of the Fena, which we cannot now relate; but they are all gone long since, for they lived many ages ago. We have heard also, and we have seen it written in very old books, that Finn had a son named Oisin. Now this Oisin went with a young fairy maiden to Tír na nÓg, and his father and his friends sorrowed greatly after him, and sought him long; but he was never seen again."

When I heard all this, I was filled with amazement, and my heart grew heavy with great sorrow. I silently turned my steed away from the wondering people, and set forward straightway for Allen of the mighty deeds, on the broad, green plains of Leinster. It was a miserable journey to me; and though my mind, being full of sadness at all I saw and heard, forecasted further sorrows, I was grieved more than ever when I reached Allen. For there, indeed, I found the hill deserted and lonely, and my father's palace all in ruins and overgrown with grass and weeds.

I turned slowly away, and afterwards fared through the land in every direction in search of my friends. But I met only crowds of little people, all strangers, who gazed on me with wonder; and none knew me. I visited every place throughout the country where I knew the Fena had lived; but I found their houses all like Allen, solitary and in ruins.

At length I came to Glenasmole,* where many a time I had hunted in days of old with the Fena, and there I saw a crowd of people in the glen. As soon as they saw me, one of them came forward and said:

" Come to us, thou mighty hero, and help us out of our strait; for thou art a man of vast strength."

I went to them, and found a number of men trying in vain to raise a large, flat stone. It was half-lifted from the ground; but those who were under it were not strong enough either to raise it further or to free themselves from its weight. And they were in great distress, and on the point of being crushed to death.

I thought it a shameful thing that so many men should be unable to lift this stone, which Oscar, if he were alive, would take in his right hand and fling over the heads of the feeble

---

* Glenasmole, a valley about seven miles south of Dublin, through which the river Dodder flows.

crowd. After I had looked a little while, I stooped forward and seized the flag with one hand; and, putting forth my strength, I flung it seven perches from its place, and relieved the little men. But with the great strain the golden saddle-girth broke, and, bounding forward to keep myself from falling, I suddenly came to the ground on my two feet.

The moment the white steed felt himself free, he shook himself and neighed. Then, starting off with the speed of a cloud-shadow on a March day, he left me standing helpless and sorrowful. Instantly a woeful change came over me: the sight of my eyes began to fade, the ruddy beauty of my face fled, I lost all my strength, and I fell to the earth, a poor, withered old man, blind and wrinkled and feeble.

The white steed was never seen again. I never recovered my sight, my youth, or my strength; and I have lived in this manner, sorrowing without ceasing for my gentle, golden-haired wife, Niamh, and thinking ever of my father, Finn, and of the lost companions of my youth.

# The Voyage of
# the Sons of O'Corra*

A PRINCELY upright hundred-herd brughaidh† was born one time in the lovely province of Connacht, namely, Conall Derg O'Corra the fair-haired. And thus was this brughaidh circumstanced:—he was a fortunate, rich, prosperous man; and his house was never found without three shouts in it—the shout of the brewers brewing ale, and the shout of the servants over the cauldrons distributing meat to the hosts, and the shout of the youths over the chessboards‡ winning games from one another.

The same house was never without three measures: a measure of malt for making yeast, a measure of wheat for providing bread for the guests, and a measure of salt for savouring each kind of food.

His wife was Cairderga§ the daughter of the Erenach of Clogher. They felt no want of any kind except being without children; and it was not that they were without children being born to them, but that the infants always died the moment after birth.

Then this brughaidh said one day to his wife as she reclined near him on the couch: "It is a sad thing for us," said he,

---

* A few of the adventures in this tale are identical with those described in the Voyage of Maildun: the description of these I have omitted here. Lochan, Enna, and Silvester, the chief characters in this extraordinary fiction, are historical: they were saints of the primitive Irish church, and lived in the sixth century.

† *Brughaidh*, a sort of local officer who maintained a large establishment as keeper of a house of public hospitality.

‡ Chess-playing was a favourite amusement among the ancient Irish.

§ Cairderga: original *Caer-derg*, red berry. *Erenach*, the holder or *impropriator* of a church and its lands: usually a layman. Clogher, in Tyrone, where there was a monastery.

" that we have no children who would take our place and fill it worthily when we are gone."

" What desire is in your mind in regard to that? " says the wife.

" It is my desire," says the brughaidh, " to make a bond with the demon to try if he would give us a son or a daughter who would take our place after us, since God has not done so."

" Let us do that," said the woman.

They accordingly fasted and prayed to the demon; and the demon hearkened unto them. And in due time the pains and struggles of childbirth came upon the lady; and she bore three sons at that great birth, namely, a son at the beginning of the night, and a son at the middle of the night, and a son at the end of the night.

And they were baptized according to the baptism of the pagans (by which they were dedicated not to God but to the demon); and their names were Lochan, Enna, and Silvester. And after that, they were reared and carefully trained up till they were swift and active on sea and land; so that they were an overmatch for all the young people of their own age in every game and in every accomplishment. And they were in the mouths and on the tongues of all who saw or heard of them in their day.

One day when they were resting at the railings of the house of their father and mother, wearied after their hurling and their martial games, the housefolk said that they saw no fault or defect in these handsome much-renowned youths, except only their being baptized in the service of the devil. And the youths hearing this, said: " If it be so," said they, " that the devil is our lord and master, it is very wrong of us not to bring ruin and wrath and woe on his enemies, that is to say, we ought to slaughter the clergy, and burn and spoil their churches."

Then did these three youths arise, and collecting a band, and taking unto them their arms, they came to Tuam-da-Gualann,* and spoiled and burned the town. And after that they plundered and made dreadful havoc on the churches and clergy throughout the province of Connacht, until their wicked and bloodthirsty

---

* Tuam-da-Gualann, where was formerly a celebrated ecclesiastical establishment: now Tuam, in Galway.

ravages were noised over the four quarters of Erin. Thus did they run their evil course without ceasing for a whole year, during which time they destroyed more than half the churches of Connacht.

At the end of the year Lochan said to his brothers: "We have made one great mistake through forgetfulness," says he, "and our lord the devil will not be thankful to us on account of it." "What is that?" said the other two youths. "Our grandfather," says he, "that is our mother's father—not to have killed him and burned his church."

So they set out straightway, journeying without sparing or respite to Clogher, and this was how they found the erenach, namely, on the green of the church with a great company of his folk around him, waiting for the O'Corras, in order to attend on them and to deal out to them the choice of every food and the best of every ale. And the intention that the elder had towards them, that indeed was not the intention they had towards him, but to murder him and to burn and spoil his church.

Then the O'Corras came to the spot where the elder was standing, and they made up their minds not to kill him or burn the houses till night, when the cows and the other cattle of the homestead would be housed, all in their own proper places.

The elder welcomed them and led them to the homestead; and he now became aware of their intention. Nevertheless he put them in a goodly pleasant grianán, and they were served with food and ale till they became exhilarated and cheerful: after which couches were made ready for them on lofty bedsteads.

And now deep slumber and heavy sleep fell on them, and a wonderful vision was revealed in a dream, to Lochan, the eldest of the sons of O'Corra, in which he was carried to see heaven and hell. And after this he awoke. The other two awoke at the same time, and they said: "Let us now arise, for it is time to plunder and destroy the homestead."

"It seems to me," said Lochan, "that this is not the right thing for us to do: for evil is the lord we have served until now, and good is the Lord we have plundered and outraged.

"And last night I had a fearful dream, in which I saw a vision of heaven and hell. And first I was taken to see hell, where were countless souls of men and vast crowds of demons

suffering divers tortures, and plagues unexampled. And I saw
the four rivers of hell, that is to say, a river of toads, a river of
serpents, a river of fire, and a river of snow. I saw also a
monstrous serpent with many heads and legs, at sight whereof,
even though it were only a single glance, all the men in the world
would drop dead with loathing and horror.

"After this methought I was taken to see heaven; where I
beheld the Lord Himself seated on His kingly throne, and angels
in the shapes of white birds singing for Him. And among them
was one great snow-white bird of dazzling brightness that
excelled all the others in size and beauty and voice, chanting
strains of surpassing sweetness. Women in travail and men sore
wounded and sick people racked with pain would fall asleep if
they heard the delightful harmony of his voice. And it was
made known to me that this great bird who chanted such
heavenly music to his mild Lord was Michael the Archangel.

"And now my brothers," said Lochan, "it is my counsel
to you that you follow God henceforward."

"But," said the others, "will the Lord accept repentance
from us for the dreadful evils we have already done?"

They go to the father of their mother, namely, the erenach,
and they ask this thing of him. "He will accept your repentance
without doubt," says the erenach.

"Well then," said Lochan, "let Mass be celebrated for us,
and put us under instruction, and let us offer our confession to
God. After that we will make staffs of the handles of our
spears; and we will go to Finnen of Clonard, the tutor of the
saints and of the just men of all Erin. He is a very holy man,
and he will advise us in regard to what we ought to do."

To this counsel they agreed; and on the morrow they set
out for the place where Finnen was; whom they found on the
green of Clonard with a number of his clerics.

"Who are these coming towards us?" said the clerics. And
one said: "They are the O'Corras the robbers." Hearing this
they fled, like lightning, in a body from their master, for they
felt quite sure that the O'Corras were coming to slay them; so
that Finnen was left quite alone before the three brothers.

"It is from us the clerics are fleeing," said Lochan.

"Of a certainty it is," said his brothers.

" Let us," said Lochan, " cast from us our staffs, the only little remnant of our arms left with us; and let us throw ourselves on our knees before the cleric."

And this they did. " What is your desire? " said Finnen. " Our desire," said they, " is faith and piety, and to serve God, and to abandon the lord whom we have hitherto served, namely, the devil."

"That is a good resolution," said the cleric, "and let us go now to the homestead yonder, the place where live our brotherhood."

They go accordingly with him to the brotherhood; and after the matter had been considered, it was arranged to set apart a young cleric to teach them; and it was decreed that they should not speak to any one except their own master till the end of a year.

So they continued for a whole year till they had read the Canons through, and by the time they had come to be able to read them, the whole brotherhood felt grateful to God for their piety and their gentleness.

At the end of the year they came to Finnen; and they knelt before him, and said to him: " It is time now that we should be judged and sentence passed on us for the great crimes we have committed."

" What," said Finnen, " do ye not think it enough—the penance you have done already for a whole year among the brotherhood? " " It is not enough," said they. " What then are the greatest crimes you have committed? " says Finnen. " We have burned more than half the churches of Connacht; and neither priest nor bishop got quarter or protection from us."

" You cannot " replied Finnen, " give back life to the people you have killed; but do you that which will be in your power, namely, to build up the churches you have burned, and to repair every other damage you have committed in them. And I will give to each man of you the swiftness and strength of a hundred; and I will take from you all weariness of feet, of hands, and of body; and I will give you light and understanding which will have neither decay nor end."

So the O'Corras departed, and went first to Tuam-da-Gualann; and after that, they fared through the province, obedient to rule and working hard each day, until it came to pass that they had restored everything they had previously destroyed.

After that they came at the end of the year to speak with Finnen. "Have you been able," asks Finnen, "to repair everything you destroyed belonging to the Church?" "We have," said they, "except one place alone, namely Kenn-Mara".* "Alas for that," says Finnen. "That is the very first place you should have repaired; for it is the homestead of the oldest of all the saints of Ireland, namely, the aged Camann of Ken-Mara. And now go and carefully restore everything you have destroyed in that homestead. And the sentence that holy man passes on you, fulfil it patiently."

So they went gladly to Kenn-Mara; and they repaired everything they had ruined there.

One day when they had come forth from the homestead, they sat on the margin of the little bay, watching the sun as it went westward. And as they gazed and reflected on the course of the sun, they began to marvel greatly, pondering whither it went after it had gone down beneath the verge of the sea. "What more wonderful thing is there in the whole world," said they, "than that the sea does not freeze into ice, while ice is formed in every other water!"

Thereupon they formed the resolution on the spot to bring unto them a certain artificer who was a fast friend of theirs, and to get him to make a three-hide curragh† for them. Accordingly the curragh was made, and a strong-sided one it was. And the reward the artificer asked for building it was to be let go with them.

When the time had come, and they were about to embark, they saw a large crowd passing close by; and this crowd was a company of *crossans*.‡ "Who are yonder people that are launching this curragh on the sea?" said the *crossans*, when they saw the curragh putting forth.

The *furshore* (juggler) of the crossans said: "I know them well; they are the sons of Conall derg O'Corra the fair-haired

---

* *Kenn-Mara*, now Kinvarra, on Galway Bay.
† *Curragh*, see note 17 at end. Some curraghs were made with two—some with three—hides, one outside another, for the better security.
‡ *Crossans*: travelling gleemen: the clothes, musical instruments, &c., were the property of the company. This word is the origin of the Scotch and Irish family name MacCrossan, now often changed to Crosbie. A company of crossans had always among them a *fuirseoir*, i.e., a juggler or buffoon.

of Connacht, the destroyers and robbers, going on their pilgrimage on the sea and on the great ocean, to make search for their Lord." " And indeed," added the *furshore*, " my word for it, they do not stand more in need of seeking for heaven than we do."

" It is a long day I fancy till you go on your pilgrimage," said the leader of the band. " Say not so," answered the *furshore*, " for I will certainly go with these people on my pilgrimage now without delay."

" Upon our word," said the *crossans*, " you will not take away our clothes with you; for not a single article of the garments you wear belongs to you." " It is not so small a matter that would keep me with you," says he.

So they stripped off all his clothes, and sent him away mother naked to the curragh.

" Who and what in the world are you, good man? " asked the crew. " A poor wretch who wishes to go with you on pilgrimage," said he. " Indeed," said they, " you shall not by any means come with us, seeing that you are stark naked." " Say not so, young men," said he; " for the sake of God do not refuse me; for I will amuse you and keep your hearts cheerful with my music and singing; and your piety will not be a whit the worse for it."

And inasmuch as he had asked for the sake of God they consented to let him go.

Now this is how it was with the crew: each man of them had built a church and raised an altar to the Lord in his own district. Their number was nine; among whom was a bishop, and a priest, and a deacon; and they had one *giolla* (attendant) who was the ninth man.

" Let us go aboard our curragh now," says Lochan, " as we have finished our task of restoring the churches, and as we have, besides, each of us built a church to the Lord in our own district."

It was then they put up their prayers fervently to God in the hope that they might have fine weather; and that the Lord would quell the fury of the billows, and the might of the ocean, and the rage of the terrible sea monsters. So they embarked in their curragh, bringing their oars; and they began to question among themselves what direction they should take. " The direction in which this wind will bring us," says the bishop. And having commended themselves to God, one and all, they betook them to their oars. A great wind now arose, which drove them out on the waste of waters straight to the west; and they were forty days and forty nights on the ocean. And God revealed to them great and unheard of wonders.

They had not been long rowing when the *crossan* died; and sad and sorrowful were they for his loss, and wept much. While they were still mourning, they saw a little bird alight on the deck of the curragh. And the little bird spoke and said to them: " Good people, tell me now in God's name what is the cause of your sorrow? "

" A *crossan* that we had playing music for us; and he died a little while ago in this curragh; and that is the cause of our sorrow."

And the bird said: " Lo, I am your little *crossan:* and now be not sorrowful any longer, for I am going straightway to heaven." So saying he bade them farewell and flew away.

# I

They rowed forward for a long time till there was shown to them a wonderful island, and in it a great grove of marvellous beauty, laden with apples, golden coloured and sweet scented. A sparkling rivulet of wine flowed through the midst of the grove; and when the wind blew through the trees, sweeter than any music was the rustling it made. The O'Corras ate some of the apples and drank from the rivulet of wine, and were immediately satisfied. And from that time forth they were never troubled by either wounds or sickness.

# II

Then they took to their oars; and after a time they came in view of another island, and four companies of people in it, such as had never been seen before. Now these people had divided the island into four parts: old grey-headed people were in the first division; princes in the second; warriors in the third; and servants in the fourth. They were all beautiful and glorious to behold; and they diverted themselves continually with games and pastimes. One of the crew went to them to ask news: and though he was a comely, well-favoured youth, he seemed ugly and dark-visaged in presence of these glorious people. When he had got among them, he became in a moment beautiful like the others; and he joined in their games, and laughed, and made merry. Moreover he remembered nothing more of his companions; and he sojourned in the island after that for evermore. And the O'Corras were at length forced to depart, though much grieved for the loss of their companion.

### III

Then they set out and rowed for some time till they sighted another marvellous island. It stood up in the air high over the great sea; and it was propped up by a pillar like a single foot standing under it in the middle. And the crew heard great shouting and the loud conversation of people on the top of the island overhead; but though the O'Corras sailed round and round, they could not get a sight of them.

### IV

They rowed forward after that till they came to an island in which lived one lone cleric. Very lovely was that island, and glorious its history. Beautiful purple flowers covered all the plains, dropping honey in abundance; and on the trees were perched flocks of bright-coloured birds singing slow sweet fairy-music. The O'Corras went to ask the cleric about himself and about the island. And he spoke as follows:

" I am a disciple of St. Andrew the Apostle, and Dega is my name. On a certain night I neglected to read my Matins; and it is for this that I was sent on a pilgrimage on the ocean; and here I am awaiting the Judgment day. And yonder birds that are singing these incomparable strains on the trees, these are the souls of holy men."

### V

They took leave of the old man and plied their oars, till they reached another island, with dead people on one side of it, and living people on the other side: and many of the living people had feet of iron. All round was a burning sea, which broke over the island continually in mighty waves. And the living people uttered fearful cries when the fiery waves flowed over them, for their torments thereby were great and terrible.

## VI

After leaving this they rowed on till they saw an island formed of great flat stones for ever burning red hot. And thereon they saw whole hosts of people burning in great torment; and many had red fiery spits thrust through their bodies. And they uttered great cries of pain without ceasing. The crew called out from a distance to ask who they were: whereupon one answered:

" This is one of the flagstones of hell. We are souls who in life did not fulfil the penance imposed on us; and warn all men to avoid this place; for whosoever cometh hither shall never go hence till the Day of Judgment."

## VII

The next island they saw was very beautiful and glorious to look upon. It had a wall of copper all round it, with a network of copper hanging out from each corner; and in the centre stood a palace. The crew left their curragh on the strand and went towards the palace. And when they had come nigh unto the wall, the wind, as it rustled and murmured through the copper network, made music so soft and sweet that they fell into a gentle slumber, and slept for three days and three nights. When they awoke they saw a beautiful maiden coming towards them from the palace. She had sandals of *findrina* (a sort of white metal) on her feet, and an inner garment of fine silk next her snow-white skin. She wore a beautiful gold-coloured vest, and over all a bright-tinted mantle, plaited five-fold on its upper border, and fastened at the neck with a brooch of burnished gold. In one hand she held a pitcher of copper, and in the other a silver goblet.

When she had come near she greeted them and bade them welcome. And she gave them food from the copper pitcher which seemed to them like cheese; and she brought them water in the silver goblet from a well on the strand. And there was no delicious flavour that was ever tasted by man that they did not find in this food and drink. Then the maiden said to them: "Although we are all—you and I—of one race, yet shall ye go hence without delay, for your resurrection is not to be here."

So they bade her farewell and took to their oars once more.

## VIII

After rowing for some time they saw flocks of large birds of divers colours flying over the sea; and their number was great beyond counting. One of them alighted on the deck of the curragh.

"It would be a delightful thing," said one of the clerics, "if this bird were a messenger from the Lord, sent to give us news."

"That would be quite possible with God," said the eldest; and as he spoke he raised his eyes and looked at the bird. Whereupon the bird spoke and said:

"It is indeed to converse with you that I have come; for I am of the land of Erin."

Now this bird was crimson all over, except three beautiful streaks on her breast, which shone as bright as the sun. And after a time she said to the same cleric: "I am the soul of a woman; and I am your friend. And come ye now," says she, "to hear yonder birds; for these are the souls that are permitted to come out of hell every Sunday."

"It is better that we leave this place at once," said the same old cleric. So they departed from that place; (and the crimson bird went with them).

## IX

And as they went, they saw three wonderful streams, namely, a stream of otters, a stream of eels, and a stream of black swans. Great flocks of birds arose from these three streams and flew past the voyagers; and the black swans followed close after, tearing and tormenting the birds. And the crimson bird said:

"Marvel not, neither be ye sad of heart; for these bird-shapes that ye see are the souls of people suffering the punishment of their crimes. And the black swans that follow them, these are devils who are for ever tormenting them; and the birds scream fearfully, and are for ever trying to fly from the demons and to free themselves from their torment.

"And now as to me," continued the bird, "I am about to depart from you. It is not permitted me to make known to you what is to befall you; but in a little time another will tell you all that you need to know."

And the cleric said : "Tell us, I beseech thee, what are those three beautiful streaks on thy breast?"

"I will tell you that," answered the bird. "When I was in the world I was married; but I did not yield obedience to my husband, and when a grievous sickness came upon him I left him to die. But thrice I went in pity to him: once to see him and ask after his illness; once to bring him such food as befitted his state; and the third time when he was dead, to watch by the body and see it buried. These three good deeds are the three beautiful streaks that you see on my breast; and I should have been bright all over like these streaks if I had not violated my lawful marriage duties."

And having so spoken, the bird bade them farewell and flew away.

## X

They next discovered a very beautiful island. The grass was bright green, and it was all over intermingled with pretty purple-coloured flowers. Flocks of lovely little birds of many bright colours, and myriads of bees, flew among the trees and flowers, humming and singing harmonious music. The voyagers saw a venerable grey-headed old man with a harp in his hand. He played this harp continually; and the music thereof was sweeter than any music they had ever heard. They saluted the old man, who saluted them in return, with a blessing. But immediately he bade them to depart.

## XI

So they rowed away till they came to another island, on which they saw a man digging in a field; and his spade was all fiery, and the handle was red hot. From the sea at one side arose at times a mighty wave all flaming red with fire, which flowed quite over the island and over the man. And ever when he saw the wave coming he cried out with fear; and when the burning torrent covered him, he strove to raise his head above the flames, and roared with his great torment. Now when one of the waves had retired they spoke to him and asked: " Who art thou, O wretched man? "

And he answered: " Lo, this is my punishment for my misdeeds. For when I lived on earth I always worked on Sundays, digging in my garden; for which I am condemned to dig with this fiery spade, and to suffer the torments of these fiery waves. And now, for the sake of God, offer up your prayers for me, that my pains may be lightened."

And they prayed fervently; after which they departed from the island.

## XII

Soon after leaving this they saw a horseman of vast size riding on the sea; and the horse he rode was made of fire flaming red. And as he rode, great waves of fire came after him along the sea; and when a wave began to roll over him he yelled aloud with fear and pain. Then they asked him why he was thus tormented; and he answered:

" I am he who stole my brother's horse; and after I had gotten him I rode him every Sunday. For this I am now undergoing my punishment, riding on this horse of fire, and tormented with these great waves of fire."

## XIII

After leaving this they came in sight of another island, full of people, all weeping and lamenting grievously. Great numbers of jet-black birds with beaks of fire and red-hot fiery talons followed and fluttered round about them, tearing and burning them with their talons, and rending away pieces of flesh.

Then the crew said aloud: " Who are ye, O miserable people? "

" We are dishonest smiths and artisans; and because we cheated while we lived, we are punished by these hateful fiery birds. Moreover, our tongues are burning, being all afire in our heads; for that we reviled people with bitter words and foul taunts."

## XIV

Coming now to another place, they saw a giant, huge in size, and of a sooty black colour all over. His mouth was all on fire; and from his throat he belched forth great flakes of fire, each flake as it came from his mouth larger than the skin of a three-year-old wether. He held in his hand an iron club larger than the shaft of a mill wheel; and on his back he bore an immense faggot of firewood, a good load for a team of horses. Now this faggot often blazed up and burned him; and he tried to free himself from his torment by lying down so that the sea might flow over him. But ever as he did so, the sea around him turned to fire, and rose up in mighty burning billows, covering him all over, so that he made the place resound with his bellowings.

"Miserable wretch, who art thou?" asked the crew.

And he answered: "I will tell you truly. When I lived I used to cut faggots and bring them home on my back every Sunday: and lo, here is my punishment."

## XV

They came after that to a sea of fire full of men's heads, all black, and continually fighting with each other. And many great serpents rose up among the heads and came with fury to attack the curragh, so that at one time they pierced through the outer hide. And one of the crew who looked on cried out in great horror, and said: "It is enough to strike one dead to behold the fearful things I see!"

And the whole crew when they saw the heads and the serpents fell flat with fear. But the elder (the bishop) comforted them, saying: "Be ye not afraid or troubled on account of these things; for God is able to protect us, even though we were in a curragh of only one hide; and if He wishes to save us, these monsters cannot hurt us, however furious they may be to slay us."

And they took courage after this, and rowed out into the open sea.

## XVI

There was shown to them next another beautiful island, having in one place an open wood. The trees were laden with fruit, and the leaves dropped honey to the ground. The sides of the hills were clothed with purple blossomed heather, mixed with soft, green grass to its very centre. In the midst of the island was a lake whose waters tasted like sweet wine. They rested for a week on the shore of this lake, and cast off their weariness. And now, being about to leave the island, as they turned to go to the curragh, a monstrous reptile* rose up from the lake and looked at them. And they trembled with fear at the sight of this terrible beast; for each man thought that he himself would be the first to be attacked. But after a little time the reptile dived again into the water, and they saw no more of him.

## XVII

From this they rowed away; and after a long time they came at midnight to an island wherein was a community of Ailbe of Emly.† On the beach they found two spring wells; one foul, the other bright and clear. The giolla wished to drink of the clear well; but the bishop told him it was better to ask leave, if there was anyone living on the island.

Then they saw a great light; and coming closer, they found the twelve men of the community at their prayers; and now they perceived that the bright light they saw came from the radiant faces of the twelve; so that these holy men needed no other light. One of them, an old man, comes towards the voyagers; and he bids them welcome and asks news of them. They tell him all their adventures, and ask his leave to drink from the well; whereupon he said to them: " Ye may fill your pitchers from the clear well, if your elder (*i.e.*, the bishop) gives you leave."

---

* According to very ancient legends, which are still vividly remembered and recounted all over the country, almost every lake in Ireland has a tremendous hairy reptile in its waters. Some say they are demons, sent by St. Patrick to reside at the bottom of the lakes to the Day of Judgment.

† St. Ailbe, the patron of Munster, was a contemporary of St. Patrick. He founded his great monastery and school at Emly in County Limerick.

"Who are ye?" asks the giolla.

"A community of Ailbe of Emly," says he, "and we are the crew of one of Ailbe's curraghs. God has permitted that we live here till the Day of Judgment, praying for everyone who is drowned at sea. And now leave this land before morning, foɪ your resurrection is not to be here. And if you have not left by the dawn, so much the worse for yourselves; for if once you get a view of this island in the light of day, bitter will be your anguish of mind for leaving it on account of its surpassing loveliness. So it is better for you to go away during the night."

And they did exactly all he told them to do.

"Shall we take away some of the pebbles of the strand?" said they, talking among themselves.

"It is better to ask leave," answered the cleric. So the giolla asked leave of the same old man.

"Yes, if you have the permission of your bishop," answered he. "Nevertheless, those who take them will be sorry; and those who do not take them will be sorry also."

They pick up pebbles, some bringing away one, some two, some three. After which they row away in the dark night from the island. In the morning they drank some of the spring water of the island from their pitchers; which threw them into a deep sleep from that time till next day. On wakening up, they examined their pebbles in the light; and some were found to be crystal, some silver, and some gold. Then those who brought some away were in sorrow that they had not brought more; and much greater was the sorrow of those who had brought away none. So the words of the old man came true.

## XVIII

After leaving this they came to a lovely island on which was a church standing all alone: and when they drew nigh they heard the voice of a cleric singing the psalms with a sweet voice. They came to the door and struck it with the hand-wood; and straightway a beautiful bright-coloured bird came to speak with them. When they had told him who they were and what they wanted, he flew back to the cleric, who bade him have the door opened for the pilgrims. And when they had come in, they found the cleric—a very old man with white hair—who sang his hymns continually. And they saluted each other; and the pilgrims stayed there that night. And an angel came and brought them supper, and ministered unto them. On the morrow the old priest bade them depart, since that was not to be the place of their resurrection on the Judgment Day. But before they went he foretold all that should happen to them during the rest of their voyage.

## XIX

From that day they came to an island in which was a disciple of Christ. Glorious and beautiful was that island; and on it stood a church and a kingly shrine. As they came near they heard some one singing the Pater to God in the door of the church: whereupon one of the clerics said: " Welcome the prayer of our Father and Teacher, Jesus."

And the priest who stood praying at the door said: " Why say you so? Who are ye; and where have ye seen Him? "

And when they had told him that they were servants of Jesus, he spoke again:

" I too am one of His disciples. And when I first took Him for my Lord I was faithful and steady; but after a time I left Him and came to sea in my curragh, and rowed till I came to this island. For a long time I lived on fruit and herbs; till at length an angel came from heaven to visit me. And he said to me: ' Thou hast not done well: nevertheless thou shalt abide on this island, eating the same food without either decay or death till the Judgment Day.' And so I have lived here to this hour."

Then they all went together into one house; and being very hungry, they prayed fervently for food. And presently an angel came down from heaven; and while they looked on he placed a supper for them on a flagstone hard by the strand, namely, a cake with a slice of fish for each. And while they ate, whatsoever taste each man separately wished for, that taste he found on the food. In the morning, when they were about to bid the cleric farewell, he foretold all that should happen to them, saying:

" You shall go from me now on sea till you reach the western point of Spain. And as you near the land, you shall meet a boat with a crew of men fishing, who will bring you with them to land."

Then turning to the bishop, he said: "Immediately after leaving the curragh, as soon as you have reached the land, prostrate yourself three times to God. And the place on which you shall first set your foot, there a great crowd shall gather round you from every quarter. And they will treat you kindly, and will give you land on which they will build a church; and after this your fame shall spread over the whole world. And the successor of Peter shall bring thee eastwards to Rome. Yonder priest thou shalt leave as thy successor in the church, and the deacon thou shalt leave to be his sacristan. That place and that church shall be revered, and shall be preserved for ever. And thou shalt leave the giolla in Britain, where he will live for the rest of his life."

After this they bade the old man farewell and left the island. And all fell out just as he had foretold. And the bishop went to Rome; and he afterwards related these adventures to Saerbrethach, Bishop of West Munster, and to Mocolmoc, one of the holy men of Aran, as we have set them down here.

Thus far the Voyage of the Sons of O'Corra.

# The Fate of
# the Sons of Usna

Avenging and bright falls the swift sword of Erin
On him who the brave sons of Usna betrayed.

MOORE

## CHAPTER I

### THE FLIGHT TO ALBA

CONOR MAC NESSA, king of Ulaidh,* ruled in Emain. And his
chief story-teller, Felimid, made a feast for the king and for the
knights of the Red Branch, who all came to partake of it in his
house. While they were feasting right joyously, listening to the
sweet music of the harps and the mellow voices of the bards, a
messenger brought word that Felimid's wife had given birth to
a little daughter, an infant of wondrous beauty. And when
Caffa, the king's druid and seer, who was of the company, was
aware of the birth of the child, he went forth to view the stars
and the clouds, if he might thereby glean knowledge of what
was in store for that little babe.† And when he had returned
to his place, he sat deep pondering for a time: and then standing
up and obtaining silence, he said:

"This child shall be called Deir-dre‡; and fittingly is she
so named: for much of woe will befall Ulaidh and Erin in
general on her account. There shall be jealousies, and strifes,

---

* Ulaidh, Ulster.
† The druids professed to be able to foretell by observing the stars and
    clouds.
‡ " Deirdre " is said to mean " alarm ".

and wars: evil deeds will be done: many heroes will be exiled: many will fall."

When the heroes heard this, they were sorely troubled, and some said that the child should be killed. But the king said: " Not so, ye Knights of the Red Branch; it is not meet to commit a base deed in order to escape evils that may never come to pass. This little maid shall be reared out of the reach of mischief, and when she is old enough she shall be my wife: thus shall I be the better able to guard against those evils that Caffa forecasts for us."

And the Ultonians did not dare to gainsay the word of the king.

Then king Conor caused the child to be placed in a strong fortress on a lonely spot nigh the palace, with no opening in front, but with door and windows looking out at the back on a lovely garden watered by a clear rippling stream: and house and garden were surrounded by a wall that no man could surmount. And those who were put in charge of her were, her tutor, and her nurse, and Conor's poetess, whose name was Lavarcam: and save these three, none were permitted to see her. And so she grew up in this solitude, year by year, till she was of marriageable age, when she excelled all the maidens of her time for beauty.

One snowy day as she and Lavarcam looked forth from the window, they saw some blood on the snow, where her tutor had killed a calf for dinner; and a raven alighted and began to drink of it. " I should like," said Deirdre, " that he who is to be my husband should have these three colours: his hair as black as the raven: his cheeks red as the blood: his skin like the snow. And I saw such a youth in a dream last night; but I know not where he is, or whether he is living on the ridge of the world."

" Truly," said Lavarcam, " the young hero that answers to thy words is not far from thee; for he is among Conor's knights: namely, Naisi the son of Usna."

Now Naisi and his brothers, Ainnli and Ardan, the three sons of Usna, were the best beloved of all the Red Branch Knights, so gracious and gentle were they in time of peace, so skilful and swift-footed in the chase, so strong and valiant in battle.

And when Deirdre heard Lavarcam's words, she said: "If it be as thou sayest, that this young knight is near us, I shall not be happy till I see him: and I beseech thee to bring him to speak to me."

"Alas, child," replied Lavarcam, "thou knowest not the peril of what thou askest me to do: for if thy tutor come to know of it, he will surely tell the king; and the king's anger none can bear."

Deirdre answered not: but she remained for many days sad and silent: and her eyes often filled with tears through memory of her dream: so that Lavarcam was grieved: and she pondered on the thing if it could be done, for she loved Deirdre very much, and had compassion on her. At last she contrived that these two should meet without the tutor's knowledge: and the end of the matter was that they loved each other: and Deirdre said she would never wed the king, but she would wed Naisi.

Knowing well the doom that awaited them when Conor came to hear of this, Naisi and his young wife and his two brothers, with thrice fifty fighting men, thrice fifty women, thrice fifty attendants, and thrice fifty hounds, fled over sea to Alba. And the king of the western part of Alba received them kindly, and took them into military service. Here they remained for a space, gaining daily in favour: but they kept Deirdre apart, fearing evil if the king should see her.

And so matters went on, till it chanced that the king's steward, coming one day by Naisi's house, saw the couple as they sat on their couch: and going directly to his master, he said:

"O king, we have long sought in vain for a woman worthy to be thy wife, and now at last we have found her: for the woman, Deirdre, who is with Naisi, is worthy to be the wife of the king of the western world. And now I give thee this counsel: Let Naisi be killed, and then take thou Deirdre for thy wife."

The king basely agreed to do so; and forthwith he laid a plot to slay the sons of Usna; which matter coming betimes to the ears of the brothers, they fled by night with all their people. And when they had got to a safe distance, they took up their abode in a wild place, where they obtained food by hunting and fishing. And the brothers built three hunting booths in the forest, a little distance from that part of the seashore looking towards Erin: and the booth in which their food was prepared, in that they did not eat; and the one in which they ate, in that they did not sleep. And their people in like manner built themselves booths and huts, which gave them but scant shelter from wind and weather.

Now when it came to the ears of the Ultonians that the sons of Usna and their people were in discomfort and danger, they were sorely grieved: but they kept their thoughts to themselves, for they dared not speak their mind to the king.

## CHAPTER II

### CONOR'S GUILEFUL MESSAGE

At this same time a right joyous and very splendid feast was given by Conor in Emain Macha to the nobles and the knights of his household. And the number of the king's household that sat them down in the great hall of Emain on that occasion was five and three score above six hundred and one thousand.* Then arose, in turn, their musicians to sound their melodious harpstrings, and their poets and their story-tellers to sing their sweet strains, and to recount the deeds of the mighty heroes of old. And the feasting and the enjoyment went on, and the entire assembly were gay and cheerful. At length Conor arose from where he sat high up on his royal seat; whereupon the noise of mirth was instantly hushed. And he raised his kingly voice and said:

"I desire to know from you, Nobles and Knights of the Red Branch, have you ever seen in any quarter of Erin a house better than this house of Emain, which is my mansion: and whether you see any want in it."

And they answered that they saw no better house, and that they knew of no want in it.

---

* This inverted method of enumeration was often used in Ireland.

And the king said: " I know of a great want: namely, that we have not present among us the three noble sons of Usna. And why now should they be in banishment on account of any woman in the world? "

And the nobles replied: " Truly it is a sad thing that the sons of Usna, our dear comrades, should be in exile and distress. They were a shield of defence to Ulaidh: and now, O king, it will please us well that thou send for them and bring them back, lest they and their people perish by famine or fall by their enemies."

" Let them come," replied Conor, " and make submission to me: and their homes, and their lands and their places among the Knights of the Red Branch shall be restored to them."

Now Conor was mightily enraged at the marriage and flight of Naisi and Deirdre, though he hid his mind from all men; and he spoke these words pretending forgiveness and friendship. But there was guile in his heart, and he planned to allure them back to Ulaidh that he might kill them.

When the feast was ended, and the company had departed, the king called unto him Fergus mac Roy, and said: " Go, Fergus, and bring back the sons of Usna and their people. I promise thee that I will receive them as friends, and that what awaits them here is not enmity or injury, but welcome and friendship. Take my message of peace and good will, and give thyself as pledge and surety for their safety. But two things I charge thee to do. The moment you land in Ulaidh on your way back, go straight to Barach's house which stands on the sea cliff high over the landing place fronting Alba: and whether the time of your arrival be by day or by night, see that the sons of Usna tarry not, but let them come hither direct to Emain, that they may not eat food in Erin till they eat of mine."

And Fergus, suspecting no evil design, promised to do as the king directed: for he was glad to be sent on this errand, being a fast friend to the sons of Usna.

Fergus set out straightway, bringing with him only his two sons, Illan the Fair and Buinni the Red, and his shield-bearer to carry his shield. And as soon as he had departed, Conor sent for Barach and said to him:

"Prepare a feast in thy house for Fergus: and when he visits thee returning with the sons of Usna, invite him to partake of it." And Barach thereupon departed for his home to do the bidding of the king and prepare the feast.

Now those heroes of old, on the day they received knighthood, were wont to make certain pledges which were to bind them for life. And as they made the promises on the faith of their knighthood, with great vows, in presence of kings and nobles, they dared not violate them; no, not even if it was to save the lives of themselves and all their friends: for whosoever broke through his knighthood pledge was dishonoured for ever more. And one of Fergus's obligations was never to refuse an invitation to a banquet: a thing which was well known to King Conor and to Barach.

As to Fergus mac Roy and his sons: they went on board their galley and put to sea, and made no delay till they reached the harbour nigh the campment of the sons of Usna. And coming ashore, Fergus gave the loud shout of a mighty man of chase. The sons of Usna were at that same hour in their booth; and Naisi and Deirdre were sitting with a polished chessboard between them playing a game.

And when they heard the shout, Naisi said: "That is the call of a man from Erin."

"Not so," replied Deirdre. "It is the call of a man of Alba."

And after a little time when a second shout came, Naisi said: "That of a certainty is the call of a man of Erin!"

But Deirdre again replied: "No, indeed: it concerns us not: let us play our game."

But when a third shout came sounding louder than those before, Naisi arose and said: "Now I know the voice. That is the shout of Fergus!" And straightway he sent Ardan to the shore to meet him.

Now Deirdre knew the voice of Fergus from the first: but she kept her thoughts to herself: for her heart misgave her that the visit boded evil. And when she told Naisi that she knew the first shout, he said: "Why, my queen, didst thou conceal it then?"

And she replied: " Lo, I saw a vision in my sleep last night: three birds came to us from Emain Macha, with three drops of honey in their beaks, and they left us the honey and took away three drops of our blood."

" What dost thou read from that vision, O princess? " said Naisi.

" It denotes the message from Conor to us," said Deirdre; " for sweet as honey is the message of peace from a false man, while he has thoughts of blood hidden deep in his heart."

When Ardan arrived at the shore, the sight of Fergus and his two sons was to him like rain on the parched grass; for it was long since he had seen any of his dear comrades from Erin. " An affectionate welcome to you, my dear companions," he cried out, and he fell on Fergus's neck and kissed his cheeks, and did the like to his sons. Then he brought them to the hunting-booth; and Naisi, Ainnli, and Deirdre gave them a like kind welcome; after which they asked the news from Erin.

" The best news I have," said Fergus, " is that Conor has sent me to you with kindly greetings, to bring you back to Emain and restore you to your lands and homes, and to your places in the Red Branch; and I am myself a pledge for your safety."

" It is not meet for them to go," said Deirdre. " For here they are under no man's rule; and their sway in Alba is even as great as the sway of Conor in Erin."

But Fergus said: " One's mother country is better than all else, and gloomy is life when a man sees not his home each morning."

" Far dearer to me is Erin than Alba," said Naisi, " even though my sway should be greater here."

It was not with Deirdre's consent he spoke these words: and she still earnestly opposed their return to Erin.

But Fergus tried to reassure her: " If all the men of Erin were against you," said he, " it would avail naught once I have passed my word for your safety."

" We trust in thee," said Naisi, " and we will go with thee to Erin."

## CHAPTER III

### THE RETURN TO EMAIN

GOING next morning on board their galleys, Fergus and his companions put out on the wide sea: and oar and wind bore them on swiftly till they landed on the shore of Erin near the house of Barach.

And Deirdre, seating herself on a cliff, looked sadly over the waters at the blue headlands of Alba: and she uttered this farewell:

Dear to me is yon eastern land: Alba with its wonders. Beloved is Alba with its bright harbours and its pleasant hills of the green slopes. From that land I would never depart except to be with Naisi.

Kil-Cuan, O Kil-Cuan,* whither Ainnli was wont to resort: short seemed the time to me while I sojourned there with Naisi on the margins of its streams and waterfalls.

Glen-Lee, O Glen-Lee, where I slept happy under soft coverlets: fish and fowl, and the flesh of red deer and badgers; these were our fare in Glen-Lee.

Glen-Masan, O Glen-Masan: tall its cresses of white stalks: often were we rocked to sleep in our curragh in the grassy harbour of Glen-Masan.

Glen-Orchy, O Glen-Orchy: over thy straight glen rises the smooth ridge that oft echoed to the voices of our hounds. No man of the clan was more light-hearted than my Naisi when following the chase in Glen-Orchy.

Glen-Ettive, O Glen-Ettive: there it was that my first house was raised for me: lovely its woods in the smile of the early morn: the sun loves to shine on Glen-Ettive.

Glen-da-Roy, O Glen-da-Roy: the memory of its people is dear to me: sweet is the cuckoo's note from the bending bough on the peak over Glen-da-Roy.

Dear to me is Dreenagh over the resounding shore: dear to me its crystal waters over the speckled sand. From those sweet places I would never depart, but only to be with my beloved Naisi.

---

* This and the other places named in Deirdre's Farewell are all in the west of Scotland.

After this they entered the house of Barach; and when Barach had welcomed them, he said to Fergus: "Here I have a three-day banquet ready for thee, and I invite thee to come and partake of it."

When Fergus heard this, his heart sank and his face waxed all over a crimson red: and he said fiercely to Barach: "Thou hast done an evil thing to ask me to this banquet: for well thou knowest I cannot refuse thee. Thou knowest, too, that I am under solemn pledge to send the Sons of Usna this very hour to Emain: and if I remain feasting in thy house, how shall I see that my promise of safety is respected?"

But none the less did Barach persist; for he was one of the partners in Conor's treacherous design.

Then Fergus turned to Naisi and said: "I dare not violate my knighthood promise. What am I to do in this strait?" But Deirdre answered for her husband: "The choice is before thee, Fergus; and it is more meet for thee to abandon thy feast than to abandon the sons of Usna, who have come over on thy pledge."

Then Fergus was in sore perplexity; and pondering a little, he said: "I will not forsake the sons of Usna: for I will send with them to Emain Macha my two sons, Illan the Fair and Buinni the Red, who will be their pledge instead of me."

But Naisi said: "We need not thy sons for guard or pledge: we have ever been accustomed to defend ourselves!" And he moved from the place in great wrath: and his two brothers, and Deirdre, and the two sons of Fergus followed him, with the rest of the clan; while Fergus remained behind silent and gloomy: for his heart misgave him that mischief was brewing for the sons of Usna.

Then Deirdre tried to persuade the sons of Usna to go to Rathlin, between Erin and Alba, and tarry there till Barach's feast was ended: but they did not consent to do so, for they deemed it would be a mark of cowardice: and they sped on by the shortest ways towards Emain Macha.

When now they had come to Fincarn of the Watch-tower on Slieve Fuad, Deirdre and her attendants stayed behind the others a little: and she fell asleep. And when Naisi missed her, he turned back and found her just awakening; and he said to her: " Why didst thou tarry, my princess? "

And she answered: " I fell asleep and had a dream. And this is what I saw in my dream: Illan the Fair took your part: Buinni the Red did not: and I saw Illan without his head: but Buinni had neither wound nor hurt."

" Alas, O beauteous princess," said Naisi, " thou utterest naught but evil forebodings: but the king is true and will not break his plighted word."

So they fared on till they had come to the Ridge of the Willows,* an hour's journey from the palace: and Deirdre, looking upwards in great fear, said to Naisi: " O Naisi, see yonder cloud in the sky over Emain, a fearful chilling cloud of a blood-red tinge: a baleful red cloud that bodes disaster! Come ye now to Dundalgan and bide there with the mighty hero Cuchulainn till Fergus returns from Barach's feast; for I fear Conor's treachery."

But Naisi answered: " We cannot follow thy advice, beloved Deirdre, for it would be a mark of fear: and we have no fear."

And as they came nigh the palace Deirdre said to them: " I will now give you a sign if Conor meditates good or evil. If you are brought into his own mansion where he sits surrounded by his nobles, to eat and drink with him, this is a token that he means no ill; for no man will injure a guest that has partaken of food at his table: but if you are sent to the house of the Red Branch, be sure he is bent on treachery."

When at last they arrived at the palace, they knocked loudly with the hand-wood: and the door-keeper swung the great door wide open. And when he had spoken with them, he went and told Conor that the sons of Usna and Fergus's two sons had come, with their people.

And Conor called to him his stewards and attendants and asked them: " How is it in the house of the Red Branch as to food and drink? " And they replied that if the seven battalions of Ulaidh were to come to it, they would find enough of all good things. " If that is so," said Conor, " take the sons of Usna and their people to the Red Branch."

---

* Irish name, *Drum-Sailech;* the ridge on which Armagh was afterwards built.

Even then Deirdre besought them not to enter the Red Branch. But Illan the Fair said: " Never did we show cowardice or unmanliness, and we shall not do so now." Then she was silent, and went with them into the house.

And the company, when they had come in, sat them down so that they filled the great hall: and alluring viands and delicious drinks were set before them: and they ate and drank till they became satisfied and cheerful: all except Deirdre and the Sons of Usna, who did not partake much of food or drink. And Naisi asked for the king's chessboard and chessmen; which were brought: and he and Deirdre began to play.

## CHAPTER IV

### TROUBLE LOOMING

LET us now speak of Conor. As he sat among his nobles, the thought of Deirdre came into his mind, and he said: " Who among you will go to the Red Branch and bring me tidings of Deirdre, whether her youthful shape and looks still live upon her: for if so there is not on the ridge of the world a woman more beautiful." And Lavarcam said she would go.

Now the sons of Usna were very dear to Lavarcam: and Naisi was dearer than the others. And rising up she went to the Red Branch, where she found Naisi and Deirdre with the chessboard between them, playing. And she saluted them affectionately: and she embraced Deirdre, and wept over her, and kissed her many times with the eagerness of her love: and she kissed the cheeks of Naisi and of his brothers.

And when her loving greeting was ended, she said: " Beloved children, evil is the deed that is to be done this night in Emain: for the three torches of valour of the Gaels will be treacherously assailed, and Conor is certainly resolved to put them to death. And now set your people on guard, and bolt and bar all doors, and close all windows; and be steadfast and valorous, and defend your dear charge manfully, if you may hold the assailants at bay till Fergus comes." And she departed weeping piteously.

And when Lavarcam had returned to Conor he asked what tidings she brought. " Good tidings have I," said she: " for the three sons of Usna have come, the three valiant champions of Ulaidh: and now that they are with thee, O king, thou wilt hold sway in Erin without dispute. And bad tidings I bring also: Deirdre indeed is not as she was, for her youthful form and the splendour of her countenance have fled from her."

And when Conor heard this, his jealousy abated, and he joined in the feasting.

But again the thought of Deirdre came to him, and he asked: " Who now will go for me to the Red Branch, and bring me further tidings of Deirdre and of the sons of Usna? " for he distrusted Lavarcam. But the Knights of the Red Branch had misgivings of some evil design, and all remained silent.

Then he called to him Trendorn, one of the lesser chiefs, and he said: " Knowest thou, Trendorn, who slew thy father and thy three brothers in battle? " And Trendorn answered: "Verily, it was Naisi, the son of Usna, that slew them." Then the king said: " Go now to the Red Branch and bring me back tidings of Deirdre and of the sons of Usna."

Trendorn went right willingly. But when he found the doors and windows of the Red Branch shut up, he was seized with fear, and he said: " It is not safe to approach the sons of Usna, for they are surely in wrathful mood: nevertheless I must needs bring back tidings to the king."

Whereupon, not daring to knock at the door, he climbed nimbly to a small window high up that had been unwittingly left open, through which he viewed the spacious banquet hall, and saw Naisi and Deirdre playing chess. Deirdre chanced to look up at that moment, and seeing the face of the spy with eyes intently gazing on her, she started with affright and grasped Naisi's arm, as he was making a move with the chessman. Naisi, following her gaze, and seeing the evil-looking face, flung the chessman with unerring aim, and broke the eye in Trendorn's head.

Trendorn dropped down in pain and rage; and going straight to Conor, he said: " I have tidings for thee, O king: the three sons of Usna are sitting in the banquet hall, stately and proud like kings: and Deirdre is seated beside Naisi; and verily for beauty and queenly grace her peer cannot be found."

When Conor heard this, a flame of jealousy and fury blazed up in his heart, and he resolved that by no means should the sons of Usna escape the doom he planned for them.

## CHAPTER V

### THE ATTACK ON THE SONS OF USNA

COMING forth on the lawn of Emain, King Conor now ordered a large body of hireling troops to beset the Red Branch: and he bade them force the doors and bring forth the sons of Usna. And they uttered three dreadful shouts of defiance, and assailed the house on every side; but the strong oak stood bravely, and they were not able to break through doors or walls. So they heaped up great piles of wood and brambles, and kindled them till the red flames blazed round the house.

Buinni the Red now stood up and said to the sons of Usna: " To me be entrusted the task to repel this first assault: for I am your pledge in place of my father." And marshalling his men, and causing the great door to be thrown wide open, he sallied forth and scattered the assailants, and put out the fires: slaying thrice fifty hirelings in that onslaught.

But Buinni returned not to the Red Branch: for the king sent to him with a secret offer of favours and bribes: namely, his own royal friendship, and a fruitful tract of land; which Buinni took and basely abandoned the sons of Usna. But none the better luck came to him of it: for at that same hour a blight fell on the land, so that it became a moor, waste and profitless, which is at this day called Slieve Fuad.

When Illan the Fair became aware of his brother's treason, he was grieved to the heart, and he said: " I am the second pledge in place of my father for the sons of Usna, and of a certainty I will not betray them: while this straight sword lives in my hand I will be faithful: and I will now repel this second attack." For at this time the king's hirelings were again thundering at the doors.

Forth he issued with his band: and he made three quick furious circuits round the Red Branch, scattering the troops as he went: after which he returned to the mansion and found Naisi and Deirdre still playing.* But as the hireling hordes returned to the attack, he went forth a second time and fell on them, dealing death and havoc whithersoever he went.

Then, while the fight was still raging, Conor called to him his son Fiachra, and said to him: "Thou and Illan the Fair were born on the same night: and as he has his father's arms, so thou take mine, namely, my shield which is called the Ocean, and my two spears which are called Dart and Slaughter, and my great sword, the Blue-green blade. And bear thyself manfully against him, and vanquish him, else none of my troops will survive."

Fiachra did so and went against Illan the Fair; and they made a stout, warlike, red-wounding attack on each other, while the others looked on anxious: but none dared to interfere. And it came to pass that Illan prevailed, so that Fiachra was fain to shelter himself behind his father's shield the Ocean, and he was like to be slain. Whereupon the shield moaned, and the Three Waves of Erin uttered their hollow melancholy roar.†

---

* These champions, as well as their wives, took care never to show any signs of fear or alarm even in the time of greatest danger: so Naisi and Deirdre kept playing quietly as if nothing was going on outside, though they heard the din of battle resounding.

† The "Three *Tonns* or Waves of Erin" were the Wave of Tuath outside the mouth of the river Bann, off the coast of Derry; the Wave of Rury in Dundrum Bay, in County Down; and the Wave of Cleena in Glandore Harbour in the south of Cork. In stormy weather, when the wind blows from certain directions, the sea at those places, as it tumbles over the sandbanks, or among the caves and fissures of the rocks, utters a loud and solemn roar, which in old times was believed to forebode the death of some king.

The legends also tell that the shield belonging to a king moaned when the person who wore it in battle—whether the king himself or a member of his family—was in danger of death: the moan was heard all over Ireland; and the "Three Waves of Erin" roared in response.

The hero Conall Carnach, sitting in his dun afar off, heard the moan of the shield and the roar of the Wave of Tuath: and springing up from where he sat, he said: "Verily, the king is in danger: I will go to his rescue."

He ran with the swiftness of the wind, and arrived on the Green of Emain, where the two young heroes were fighting. Thinking it was Conor that crouched beneath the shield, he attacked Illan, not knowing him, and wounded him even unto death. And Illan looking up, said: "Is it thou, Conall? Alas, dreadful is the deed thou hast done, not knowing me, and not knowing that I am fighting in defence of the sons of Usna, who are now in deadly peril from the treachery of Conor."

And Conall, finding he had unwittingly wounded his dear young friend Illan, turned in his grief and rage on the other, and swept off his head. And he stalked fierce and silent out of the battlefield.

Illan, still faithful to his charge, called aloud to Naisi to defend himself bravely: then putting forth his remaining strength, he flung his arms, namely, his sword and his spears and his shield, into the Red Branch; and falling prone on the green sward, the shades of death dimmed his eyes, and his life departed.

And now when it was the dusk of evening, another great battalion of the hirelings assailed the Red Branch, and kindled faggots around it: whereupon Ardan sallied out with his valorous band and scattered them, and put out the fires, and held guard for the first third of the night. And during the second third Ainnli kept them at bay.

Then Naisi took his turn, issuing forth, and fought with them till the morning's dawn: and until the sands of the seashore, or the leaves of the forest, or the dew-drops on the grass, or the stars of heaven are counted, it will not be possible to number the hirelings that were slain in that fight by Naisi and his band of heroes.

And as he was returning breathless from the rout, all grimy and terrible with blood and sweat, he spied Lavarcam, as she stood watching the battle anxiously; and he said: "Go, Lavarcam, go and stand on the outer rampart, and cast thine eyes eastwards, if perchance thou shouldst see Fergus and his men coming."

For many of Naisi's brave followers had fallen in these encounters: and he doubted that he and the others could sustain much longer the continual assaults of superior numbers. And Lavarcam went, but returned downcast, saying she saw naught eastwards but the open plain with the peaceful herds browsing over it.

## CHAPTER VI

### DEATH OF THE SONS OF USNA

BELIEVING now that they could no longer defend the Red Branch, Naisi took council with his brothers; and what they resolved on was this: To sally forth with all their men and fight their way to a place of safety. Then, making a close, firm fence of shields and spears round Deirdre, they marched out in solid ranks and attacked the hireling battalions and slew three hundred in that onslaught.

Conor, seeing the rout of his men, and being now sure that it was not possible to subdue the sons of Usna in open fight, cast about if he might take them by falsehood and craft. And sending for Caffa, the druid, who loved them, he said:

"These sons of Usna are brave men, and it is our pleasure to receive them back into our service. Go now unto them, for thou art their friend; and say to them that if they lay down their arms and submit I will restore them to favour and give them their places among the Red Branch Knights. And I pledge thee my kingly word and my troth as a true knight, that no harm shall befall them."

Caffa, by no means distrusting him, went to the sons of Usna, and told them all the king had said. And they, suspecting neither guile nor treachery, joyfully threw their swords and spears aside, and went towards the king to make submission. But now, while they stood defenceless, the king caused them to be seized and bound. Then, turning aside, he sought for some one to put them to death; but he found no man of the Ultonians willing to do so.

Among his followers was a foreigner named Maini of the Rough Hand, whose father and two brothers had fallen in battle by Naisi: and this man undertook to kill the sons of Usna.

When they were brought forth to their doom, Ardan said: " I am the youngest: let me be slain first, that I may not see the death of my brothers." And Ainnli earnestly pleaded for the same thing for himself, saying that he was born before Ardan, and should die before him.

But Naisi said: " Lo, I have a sword, the gift of Mannanan mac Lir, which leaves no remnant unfinished after a blow: let us be struck with it, all three together, and we shall die at the same moment."

This was agreed to: and the sword was brought forth, and they laid their heads close together, and Maini swept off all three with one blow of the mighty sword. And when it became known that the sons of Usna were dead, the men of Ulaidh sent forth three great cries of grief and lamentation.

As for Deirdre, she cried aloud, and tore her golden hair, and became like one distracted. And after a time, when her calmness had a little returned, she uttered a lament:

> Three lions of the hill are dead, and I am left alone to weep for them. The generous princes who made the stranger welcome have been guilefully lured to their doom.

> The three strong hawks of Slieve Cullinn,* a king's three sons, strong and gentle: willing obedience was yielded to them by heroes who had conquered many lands.

> Three generous heroes of the Red Branch, who loved to praise the valour of others: three props of the battalions of Quelna: their fall is the cause of bitter grief.

> Ainnli and Ardan, haughty and fierce in battle, to me were ever loving and gentle: Naisi, Naisi, beloved spouse of my choice, thou canst not hear thy Deirdre lamenting thee.

> When they brought down the fleet red deer in the chase, when they speared the salmon skilfully in the clear water, joyful and proud were they if I looked on.

---

* Slieve Cullinn, now Slieve Gullion mountain in Armagh.

Often when my feeble feet grew weary wandering along the valleys, and climbing the hills to view the chase, often would they bear me home lightly on their linked shields and spears.

It was gladness of heart to be with the sons of Usna: long and weary is the day without their company: short will be my span of life since they have left me.

Sorrow and tears have dimmed my eyes, looking at the grave of Naisi: a dark deadly sickness has seized my heart: I cannot, I cannot live after Naisi.

O thou who diggest the new grave, make it deep and wide: let it be a grave for four; for I will sleep for ever beside my beloved.

When she had spoken these words, she fell beside the body of Naisi, and died immediately. And a great cairn of stones was piled over their grave, and their names were inscribed in Ogham, and their funeral rites were performed.

This is the sorrowful tale of The Fate of the Sons of Usna.

# NOTES

## 1.—THE DEDANNANS

ACCORDING to the old bardic legends, the first man who led a colony to Ireland after the Flood was Parthalon. Next came Nemed and his people; and after these the Firbolgs, who were conquered and succeeded by the Dedannans.

The legend relates that the Dedannans, in the course of their wanderings, spent some time in Greece, where they learned magic and other curious arts. From this they migrated to Lochlann (see Note 6), from which they came through Scotland to Ireland. From the three queens of their three last kings, Ireland got the three names, Erin, Fola, and Banba.

After the Dedannans had held sway in Ireland for about two hundred years, they were in their turn conquered by the last and greatest colony of all, the people of Miléd or Milesius, who are commonly known by the name of Milesians. The Milesians defeated the Dedannans in two great battles: one fought at *Tailltenn*, in Meath; and the other at *Druim-Lighean*, now Drumleene, about three miles from Lifford, in Donegal.

In the legendary literature of Ireland, the Dedannans are celebrated as magicians. By the Milesians and their descendants they were regarded as gods, and ultimately, in the imagination of the people, they became what are now in Ireland called " fairies."

Of this mysterious race, the following are the principal characters mentioned in these tales.

Mannanan Mac Lir, the Gaelic sea-god. In *Cormac's Glossary* (written A.D. 900), we are told that he was a famous merchant who resided in, and who gave name to, *Innis-Manann*, or the Isle of Man; and that he used to know, by examining the heavens, the length of time the fair and the foul weather would last.

The Dagda, whose name some interpret to mean " the great good fire," so called from his military ardour, who reigned as King of Ireland from A.M. 3370 to 3450.

Angus or Angus Oge, the son of the Dagda, who lived at *Brugh*, on the north shore of the Boyne, a little below Slane. Angus is spoken of as the wisest and the most skilled in magic of all the Dedannan race.

Nuada of the Silver Hand. (See Note 4.)

Lir of Shee Finnaha, the father of the four " Children of Lir," and Bove Derg of the Shee Bove, of whom we know little more than what is told in the *Fate of the Children of Lir*. Shee Finnaha is supposed to have been situated near Newtown Hamilton, in Armagh; and Shee Bove was on the shore of Lough Derg, on the Shannon.

Lugh of the Long Arms, who imposed the eric-fine on the three sons of Turenn for slaying his father, Kian. (See Note 7.)

Dianket, the great physician. He had a son Midhach, and a daughter Armedda, more skilful than himself. The old legend relates that Midhach took off the silver arm which his father Dianket had put on Nuada (see Note 4), and, having procured the bones of the real arm, he clothed them with flesh and skin, and fixed the arm in its place as well as ever " in three moments." Dianket was so enraged at being outdone by his son that he slew him. After Midhach had been buried for some time, three hundred and sixty-five healing herbs grew up from his grave, one from every joint and sinew of his body—each herb to cure disease in that part of the human body from which it grew—all which were gathered by his sister Armedda, and placed carefully in her cloak in their proper order. But before she had time to study their several virtues fully, her father Dianket mixed them all up in utter confusion.

## 2.—THE FEAST OF AGE

This was also called the Feast of Gobhnenn the Dedannan smith. It was instituted by Mannanan Mac Lir, and those who were present at it were free ever after from sickness, decay, and old age.

## 3.—THE DRUIDS

The ancient Irish druids do not appear to have been *priests* in any sense of the word. They were, in popular estimation, men of knowledge and power; they knew the arts of healing and divination; and they were skilled above all in magic.

## 4.—NUADA OF THE SILVER HAND

Nuada of the Silver Hand was King of Ireland, according to the Four Masters, from A.M. 3311 to 3330. He commanded the Dedannans in the first Battle of Moytura (see Note 11), where his arm was cut off by Sreng, the great Firbolg champion. Afterwards Credne the artificer made him a silver arm with a hand, which was fixed on by Dianket, the physician (see Note 1). Nuada was slain in the second Battle of Moytura, by Balor of the Mighty Blows (see Note 11).

## 5.—THE FOMORIANS

" Fomor," the simple form of this word, means, according to the old etymologists, a sea-robber, from *fo*, on or along, and *muir*, the sea. The word is also used to denote a giant.

The Fomorians of Irish history were sea-robbers, who infested the coasts, and indeed the interior, of Ireland, and at one time fortified themselves in Tory Island. They are stated to have come from Lochlann, in the north of Europe, but they came originally from Africa, being, according to the legend, the descendants of Ham, the son of Noah.

## 6.—LOCHLANN: THE LOCHLANNS

Lochlann was the Gaelic designation of the country from which came the people who are known in European history as Danes, i.e., the country round the southern shores of the Baltic, including the south part of Sweden. The Lochlanns figure conspicuously in our early history, and in our medieval romantic literature. In the Gaelic tales, the chief city of Lochlann is always Berva; but whether this represents a real name, or is merely an invention of the old story-tellers, I cannot tell.

## 7.—LUGH OF THE LONG ARMS: THE ILDANA

Lugh of the Long Arms was the son of Ethlenn, daughter of the Fomorian King, Balor of the Mighty Blows (see Note 9). His father, Kian, was a Dedannan; so that Lugh was half Fomorian and half Dedannan. But he always took the side of the Dedannans against the Fomorians. Lugh is often called The Ildana, the Man of many sciences, to signify his accomplishments as a warrior and a man of general knowledge.

It had been foretold that Balor would be slain by his own grandson. Accordingly, when Lugh was born, Balor sent him off to be drowned. But Lugh escaped, and lived to revenge the unnatural conduct of his grandfather, whom he slew in the second Battle of Moytura (see Note 11), after Balor had slain the Dedannan King, Nuada of the Silver Hand. Lugh succeeded Nuada as King of Ireland, and reigned, according to the Four Masters, from A.M. 3330 to 3370. It was by Lugh that the celebrated yearly assembly of Tailltenn was instituted, in honour of his foster-mother *Taillte*, after whom the place was called.

### 8.—THE LAND OF PROMISE: FAIRYLAND

In ancient Gaelic romantic tales, mention is often made of *Tir Tairrngire*, the Land of Promise, Fairyland, as being one of the chief dwelling-places of the Dedannans or fairy host. In many passages this Land of Promise is identified with *Inis-Manann*, or the Isle of Man, which was ruled over by Mannanan Mac Lir, the sea-god.

### 9.—BALOR OF THE MIGHTY BLOWS

Balor was King of the Fomorians from Lochlann in the north; his wife was Kethlend; and his son, Bres. Balor is often called Balor of the Mighty Blows; and also Balor of the Evil Eye, for he had one eye which would strike people dead or turn them into stone, so that he kept it covered, except when he wished to use it against his enemies.

### 10.—ERIC

The eric was a fine paid as compensation for murder. The friends of the murdered person might accept an eric, or they might seek instead the death of the murderer. An eric was often paid for other crimes as well as for homicide.

### 11.—BATTLES OF MOYTURA

There were two great battles, each called the Battle of Moytura.

First Battle of Moytura.—When the Dedannans came to invade Erin, they found the country occupied by the Firbolgs. After some parleying and manoeuvring, a great battle was fought between them, A.M. 3303, at Moytura, near Cong, in Mayo, lasting for four days, in which the Firbolgs were defeated with great slaughter, and their king slain; after which the Dedannans took possession of the country, leaving Connacht, however, to a powerful remnant of the Firbolgs who survived the battle.

Second Battle of Moytura.—King Nuada, who led the Dedannans in the first Battle of Moytura, had his arm cut off by

Sreng, one of the Firbolg champions. He was under cure for seven years; during which time Bres, the son of Elatha, who was a Fomorian by his father and a Dedannan by his mother, ruled Ireland as regent. But at the end of the seven years, Bres had to retire in favour of Nuada. Whereupon he repaired in anger to his father in Lochlann; and at his instigation an army of Fomorians was raised, after some years, for the invasion of Ireland, and placed under the command of Balor of the Mighty Blows.

The Fomorians landed, and were met by the Dedannan army at the Northern Moytura, or, as it is often called, Moytura of the Fomorians, situated in the parish of Kilmactranny, barony of Tirerrill, County Sligo. The battle was fought on the eve of Samhain, i.e., on the last day of October, A.M. 3330; and the Fomorians were defeated with the slaughter of their principal men and the best part of their army. In the course of the battle, Nuada of the Silver Hand, the Dedannan King, was slain by Balor; but soon after, Balor himself was killed by his grandson, Lugh. Lugh, we are told, flung a stone at him from a crann-tavall or sling, and struck him in the evil eye with so much force that the stone went clean through his head and out at the back.

## 12.—GEASA

*Geasa* means solemn vows, conjurations, injunctions, prohibitions. It would appear that individuals were often under geasa or solemn vows to observe, or to refrain from, certain lines of conduct—the vows being either taken on themselves voluntarily, or imposed on them, with their consent, by others. It would appear, also, that if one person went through the form of putting another under geasa to grant any reasonable request, the abjured person could not refuse without loss of honour and reputation.

## 13.—TIR-FA-THONN

The Gaelic tales abound in allusions to a beautiful country situated under the sea—an enchanted land sunk at some remote time, and still held under spell. In some romantic writings it is called *Tir-fa-Thonn*, the land beneath the waves. Sometimes it is *O'Brasil*, that dim land which appears over the water once every seven years—" on the verge of the azure sea "—and which would be freed from the spell, and would remain permanently over the water, if any one could succeed in throwing fire on it.

## 14.—THE ENCHANTED WELL.

Res autem sic revera evenit. Cum Angus magus equum giganteum Eochaidio et popularibus traderet, monebat homines nec stabulandi neque omnino requiescendi copiam equo faciendam; ne forte quiescendo urinam demitteret, quod si fieret exitio omnibus fore. Postea vero quam at Planitiem Silvulæ Cinereæ pervenissent, intenti adeo sarcinis ingentis equi dorso detrahendis incumbebant, ut monitorum Angi obliviscerentur; restitit autem equus, et subinde urinam demisit. Extemplo hinc fons ortus; qui cum scaturiisset, submersit omnes, sicuti in historiâ narratur.

## 15.—CONALL CARNACH OF THE RED BRANCH

The Red Branch Knights of Ulster, a sort of militia in the service of the monarch, much like the Fena of later date (see Note 23), flourished in the first century of the Christian era. Their home was the palace of Emania, near the city of Armagh; and they received their name from one of the houses of the palace in which they resided, which was called *Craobh ruadh*, or Red Branch. They attained their greatest glory in the reign of Conor Mac Nessa, King of Ulster, in the first century; and Conall Carnach was one of their most illustrious champions.

## 16.—ECCA THE SON OF MARID: COMGALL OF BANGOR.

This Marid was king of Munster about the beginning of the second century of the Christian era. St. Comgall, one of the greatest saints of the early Irish Church, flourished in the sixth century, and was the founder of the celebrated monastery of Bangor in the county of Down.

## 17.—CURRAGH

The curragh was a boat or canoe, consisting of a light framework of wood, covered over with the skins of animals. Curraghs are still used on many parts of the western coast of Ireland; but they are now covered with tarred canvas instead of skins.

## 18.—CONN THE HUNDRED-FIGHTER

Conn Céad-cathach or Conn the Fighter of a Hundred (not Conn of the Hundred Battles, as the name is generally translated), was King of Ireland from A.D. 123 to 158.

## 19.—LAND OF THE LIVING: LAND OF LIFE, ETC.

The ancient Irish had a sort of dim, vague belief that there was a land where people were always youthful, suffered no disease, and lived for ever. This country they called by various names: *Tír na mbeo*, the land of the [ever-]living; *Tír na nÓg*, the land of the [ever-]youthful; *Moy-Mell*, the plain of pleasure, etc. It had its own inhabitants—fairies; but mortals were sometimes brought there; and while they lived in it, were gifted with the everlasting youth and beauty of the fairy people themselves, and partook of their pleasures. As to the exact place where Tír na nÓg was situated, the references are shadowy and variable, but they often place it far out in the Atlantic Ocean. And here it is identical with O'Brasil, of which mention has been made in Note 13.

## 20.—ST. BRENDAN OF BIRRA

The celebrated voyage of St. Brendan of Birra (Birr) was undertaken in the sixth century. He set out from near Brandon Mountain, in Kerry, sailing westwards, into the Atlantic Ocean, and, according to the belief of some, landed on the shore of America.

## 21.—BRENDAN'S SATCHEL

The ancient Irish saints, when on their missionary journeys through the country, kept their precious books, as well as the portable sacred utensils, in leather satchels. These satchels were often highly ornamented, and, like other relics, were held in veneration after the death of the owners.

## 22.—CORMAC MAC AIRT

Cormac Mac Airt, the most illustrious of the Irish Kings, who began his reign A.D. 254, was the son of Art the Lonely, who was the son of Conn the Hundred-fighter. During his reign flourished the Fena or militia, spoken of in the next note; and the old chroniclers never tire of dwelling on the magnificence of his court at Tara, and the prosperity of the country during his reign. He was renowned for learning and wisdom, and he wrote a book called *Tegusc-righ*, or instruction for kings, copies of which are extant in the Books of Leinster and Ballymote. He also caused the records of the kingdom to be collected and written down in one great book called the Psalter of Tara; and he established three schools at Tara—one for military science, one for law, and one for history and chronology. He spent the last years of his life in retirement and study at Cletty on the Boyne, and died A.D. 277.

## 23.—FINN AND THE FENA

The Fena or "Fiana of Erin" were a sort of militia or standing army, permanently maintained by the monarch, and trained to military service. They attained their greatest glory in the reign of Cormac Mac Airt (see previous Note). Each province had its own militia under its own captain, but all were under the command of one general-in-chief. Their most renowned commander was Finn the son of Cumhal. Finn had his palace on the top of the Hill of Allen, a remarkable flat-topped hill, lying about four miles to the right of the railway as you pass Newbridge and approach Kildare.

The following are some of the principal characters celebrated in the romantic literature of the Fena.

Finn, the son of Cumhal, commander-in-chief of the Fena under King Cormac Mac Airt (see Note 22); brave, wise, and far-seeing, a man of supreme military ability. His foresight seemed so extraordinary, that the people believed it was a preternatural gift of divination, and the shanachies invented a legend to account for it (see Note 25). Like many great commanders, he had a little of the tyrant in his character, and was unforgiving to those who injured him. But in the story of Dermat and Grania, he is drawn in too unfavourable a light.

Oisin, or Ossian, Finn's son, the renowned hero-poet, to whom the bards attribute many poems still extant.

Oscar, the son of Oisin, youthful and handsome, kind-hearted, and one of the most valiant of the Fena.

Dermat O'Dyna, noble-minded, generous, of untarnished honour, and the bravest of the brave. He was as handsome as he was valiant, whence he is often styled Dermat of the Bright Face, Dermat of the White Teeth, etc. The Munster traditions represent him as a native of Kerry; but he was in reality a Leinsterman, though his descendants migrated to Munster at a very early period. This hero is equally celebrated in popular story in the Highlands of Scotland.

Kylta Mac Ronan, Finn's nephew, renowned for his fleetness of foot.

Dering, the son of Dobar O'Baskin, who was not only a brave warrior, but also "a man of knowledge," gifted with some insight into futurity.

Ligan Lumina, also celebrated for swiftness of foot.

Fergus Finnvel, poet, warrior, and frequent adviser of the Fena.

Gall Mac Morna, the leader of the Clann Morna, or Connacht Fena, one of the mightiest of all the heroes. He served under Finn, but the two chiefs bore no love to each other, for Gall had slain Finn's father, Cumhal, in the Battle of Knocka (see Note 27).

Conan Maol, or Conan the Bald, the best-marked and best-sustained character in the Ossianic romances; large-bodied, a great boaster, a great coward, and a great glutton. He had a venómous tongue, and hardly ever spoke a good word of anyone. He belonged to the Clann Morna, and was always reviling the Clann Baskin. He was the butt for the gibes and mockery of the Fena, but they dreaded his tongue.

## 24.—COOKING-PLACES

The Fena, as related in the beginning of the story of the Giolla Dacker, were quartered on the principal householders during the winter half-year; and maintained themselves chiefly by the chase during the summer months.

## 25.—FINN'S TOOTH OF KNOWLEDGE

It had been prophesied that a man named Finn would be the first to eat of the Salmon of Knowledge, which swam in the pool of Linn-Fec, in the Boyne; and that he would thereby obtain the gifts of knowledge and of divination. A certain old poet named Finn hoped that he might be the lucky man; so he took up his abode on the shore of Linn-Fec; and he fished in the pool every day in the hope of catching the Salmon of Knowledge. At this time, Finn the son of Cumhal was a boy, fleeing from place to place from his enemies, the Clann Morna. Disguised, and bearing the assumed name of Demna, he happened to come to Linn-Fec, and the old poet took him as his servant.

Finn the poet hooked the salmon at last, and gave it to Demna to broil, warning him very strictly not to taste of it. Demna proceeded to broil the fish; and soon the heat of the fire raised a great blister on its side, which the boy pressed with his thumb to keep it down, thereby scalding himself so severely that he unthinkingly thrust his thumb into his mouth.

When the salmon was cooked, the poet asked Demna had he eaten of it. " No," replied the boy; " but I scalded my thumb on the fish, and put it into my mouth." " Thy name is not Demna, but Finn," exclaimed the poet; " in thee has the prophecy been fulfilled; and thou art now a diviner and a man of knowledge! "

In this manner Finn obtained the gift of divination, so that ever after, when he put his thumb under his tooth of knowledge, the future was revealed to him. There appears to have been some sort of ceremony used, however; and it would seem that the process was attended with pain, so that it was only on very solemn and trying occasions he put his thumb under his tooth of knowledge.

## 26.—THE GAME OF CHESS

Chess-playing was one of the favourite amusements of the ancient Irish chiefs. The game is constantly mentioned in the very oldest Gaelic tales.

## 27.—BATTLE OF KNOCKA

The Battle of Knocka or *Cnucha* (now Castleknock, near Dublin) was fought in the reign of Conn the Hundred-fighter (see Note 18). The contending parties were, on the one side, Conn with his royal forces, and the renowned hero, Gall Mac Morna, with his Connacht Fena, the Clann Morna; and on the other side, Cumhal, the father of Finn, with the Clann Baskin and the Leinster forces in general, aided by Owen More, heir to the throne of Munster, with a large army of Munstermen. The Leinster and Munster armies were defeated, chiefly through the valour of Gall, who slew Cumhal with his own hand. This was the cause of the irreconcilable enmity that existed ever after between the Clann Baskin and the Clann Morna.

When Finn grew up, he succeeded to the position held by his father as leader of the Fena. But though he made peace with Gall Mac Morna, and though Gall submitted to his command, there was always a feeling of ill-concealed hatred and distrust between them.

## 28.—BATTLE OF GAVRA

When Carbri of the Liffey, son of Cormac Mac Airt, ascended the throne of Ireland, one of his first acts was to disband and outlaw the Clann Baskin; and he took into his service in their place their rivals and deadly enemies, the Clann Morna from Connacht. Whereupon the Clann Baskin marched southwards, and entered the service of Fercorb, King of Munster, Finn's grandson, in direct disobedience to King Carbri's commands. This led to the bloody Battle of Gavra, which was fought A.D. 284, at Garristown, in the north-west of the County Dublin, where the rival clans slaughtered each other almost to annihilation. In the heat of the battle, Carbri and Oscar met in single combat; and, after a long and terrible fight, the heroic Oscar fell pierced by Carbri's spear, and died in the evening of the same day. But Carbri himself was dreadfully wounded; and, while retiring from the field, his own kinsman, Semeon, whom he had previously banished from Tara, fell on him, and despatched him with a single blow.

# LIST OF PROPER NAMES
## WITH THEIR ORIGINAL GAELIC FORMS

| | | |
|---|---|---|
| Aedh | ... ... ... | a flame of fire. |
| Ahaclee | ... ... ... | *Ath-cliath*, hurdle-ford. |
| Ailna | ... ... ... | *Ailne*, beauty, joy. |
| Alba | ... ... ... | Scotland. |
| Allil | ... ... ... | *Ailioll, Ailell,* or *Oilioll.* |
| Allil Ocar Aga | ... ... | *Ailell Ochair Aga.* |
| Alva | ... ... ... | *Ailbhe.* |
| | | |
| Balor | ... ... ... | *Balar.* |
| Baskin | ... ... ... | *Baoiscne.* |
| Begallta | ... ... ... | *Beagalltach*, little fury. |
| Ben-Damis | ... ... ... | *Beann-Damhuis.* |
| Beoc | ... ... ... | *Beóc, Dabheóc,* and *Beoán.* |
| Berva | ... ... ... | *Berbhe.* |
| Borba | ... ... ... | *Borb*, proud. |
| Bran | ... ... ... | *Bran*, a raven. |
| Bres | ... ... ... | *Breas.* |
| Brickna | ... ... ... | *Briccne.* |
| Brugh of the Boyne | ... | *Brugh-na-Boinne.* |
| | | |
| Canta | ... ... ... | *Cainte.* |
| Carn-Arenn | ... ... | *Carnn-Airenn.* |
| Carricknarone | ... ... | *Carraic-na-rón*, the rock of the seals. |
| Clann Navin | ... ... | *Clann-Neamhuinn.* |
| Cloghane Kincat | ... ... | *Clochanchinnchait*, the stepping-stones of the cat's head. |
| Coil Croda | ... ... | *Cael-crodha*, the slender valiant [man]. |
| Colga | ... ... ... | *Colga.* |
| Colman | ... ... ... | *Colman*, little dove. |
| Comgall | ... ... ... | *Comhghall.* |
| Conan Maol | ... ... | Conan the Bald. |
| Conang | ... ... ... | *Conaing.* |
| Conn the Hundred-fighter | | *Conn-Céadcathach.* |

Connla ... ... ... *Connla.*
Coran ... ... ... *Coran.*
Cormac Mac Airt ... *Cormac Mac Airt.*
Corr the Swift-footed ... *Corr Cosluath.*
Cuan ... ... ... *Cuan* or *Cuadhan.*
Culand ... ... ... *Culand.*
Curnan the Simpleton ... *Curnan Onmit.*
Curoi Mac Dara ... ... *Curoi Mac Dáire.*

Dagda ... ... ... *Dagda.*
Dara Donn ... ... *Dáire Donn.*
Darvra, Lake ... ... *Loch Dairbhreach,* the lake of oaks.
Dathkeen ... ... ... *Dathchaoin,* bright-complexioned.
Decca ... ... ... *Deoch.*
Dedannans ... ... ... *Tuatha De Danann.*
Deirdre of the ... ...
    Black Mountain ... *Deirdre Duibhshleibhe.*
Dering ... ... ... *Diorraing.*
Dermat O'Dyna ... ... *Diarmait O'Duibhne.*
Dianket ... ... ... *Diancecht.*
Diuran Lekerd ... ... *Diuran Lecerd.*
Dobar O'Baskin ... ... *Dobhar O'Baoiscne.*
Dooclone ... ... ... *Dubhchluain,* dark-coloured meadow.
Dord-Fian ... ... ... *Dord-Fiann.*
Dryantore ... ... ... *Draoigheantóir.*
Ducoss ... ... ... *Dubhchosach,* blackfoot.

Eas-Dara ... ... ... *Eas-Dara.*
Ebb ... ... ... *Eab.*
Ebliu ... ... ... *Ebliu.*
Ebric ... ... ... *Aibhric.*
Ecca ... ... ... *Eochaidh,* a horseman.
Enbarr ... ... ... *Aonbharr,* splendid mane.
Encoss ... ... ... *Aonchos,* one foot.
Ethnea ... ... ... *Eithne,* sweet nutkernel.
Etta ... ... ... *Eitche.*
Eva ... ... ... *Aoife.*
Eve ... ... ... *Aebh.*

Failinis ... ... ... *Failinis.*
Fatha Conan ... ... *Fatha Chonain.*
Femin ... ... ... *Feimheann.*

Fena ... ... ... *Fianna.*
Ferdana ... ... ... *Feardána.*
Fergor ... ... ... *Fearghoir,* manly or strong voice.
Fergus ... ... ... *Fearghus,* manly strength.
Fiaca Findamnas ... ... *Fiacha Findamnais.*
Ficna ... ... ... *Fiachna,* little raven.
Fincara ... ... ... *Fianchaire.*
Fincoss ... ... ... *Finnchosach,* white-foot.
Finn ... ... ... *Finn* or *Fionn,* fair-haired.
Finnin ... ... ... *Finghín,* fair offspring.
Finola ... ... ... *Fionnghuala,* white shoulder.
Flidas ... ... ... *Flidas.*
Foltlebar, Folt-leabhar ... long hair.
Frevan ... ... ... *Freamhainn.*


Ga-boi ... ... ... *Ga-buidhe,* yellow javelin.
Ga-derg ... ... ... *Ga-dearg,* red javelin.
Gael Glas ... ... ... *Gaodhal-Glas.*
Garad Black-knee ... *Garadh Glúnduibh,* Garry Gloonduv.
Garva ... ... ... *Garbh,* rough.
Gall Mac Morna ... ... *Goll Mac Morna.*
Germane ... ... ... *German.*
Giolla Dacker ... ... *Giolla Deacair,* lazy fellow.
Glanlua ... ... ... *Glanluadh,* pure-spoken.
Glas Mac Encarda ... *Glas Mac Aeinchearda.*
Glore ... ... ... *Glóir,* a voice.


Ilbrec ... ... ... *Ilbhreac.*
Ildana ... ... ... *Ioldhanach.*
Inis Glora ... ... ... *Inis Gluaire.*
Innsa ... ... ... *Inse.*
Inver-tre-Kenand ... ... *Inbher-Tre-Cenand.*
Irann ... ... ... *Irann.*
Iroda ... ... ... *Ioruaidhe.*
Irros Domnann ... ... *Iorrus Domnann.*
Island of the Torrent ... *Inis Tuile.*


Kemoc ... ... ... *Caemhoc* or *Mochoemhoc.*
Kenn-Avrat ... ... *Ceann-Abhrat.*
Kenri ... ... ... *Caenraighe.*
Kethen ... ... ... *Cethen.*

Kethlend ... ... ... *Ceithleann* or *Ceithleand.*
Kian ... ... ... *Cian.*
Kylta Mac Ronan ... *Caeilte Mac Ronain.*

Largnen ... ... ... *Lairgnen.*
Lavaran ... ... ... *Lobharan.*
Liban ... ... ... *Liban.*
Lidas ... ... ... *Liadhas.*
Ligan Lumina ... ... *Liagan Luaimneach,* Ligan the Bounding.
Lobas ... ... ... *Lobas.*
Loskenn of the Bare Knees *Loiscinn Longhlúineach.*
Luath ... ... ... *Luath,* swift.
Lugh of the Long Arms *Lugh Lamh-fada.*

Mac-an-Lona ... ... *Mac-an-Luin.*
Mac Lugha ... ... *Mac Luigheach.*
Mac-na-Corra ... ... *Mac-na-Corra.*
Maildun ... ... ... *Mail Duin,* chief of the fort.
Manissa ... ... ... *Maighneis.*
Mannanan Mac Lir ... *Manannan Mac Lir.*
Marid Mac Carido ... *Mairid Mac Caireda.*
Mergah ... ... ... *Meargach.*
Micoorta ... ... ... *Miodhchuarta.*
Midac · ... ... ... *Miodhach* or *Mioch* (pron. *Mee-uch*).
Midir ... ... ... *Midhir.*
Midkena ... ... ... *Miodhchaoin.*
Milucra ... ... ... *Miluchradh.*
Modan ... ... ... *Muadhan.*
Morallta ... ... ... *Moralltach,* great fury.
Moyle ... ... ... *Maol,* a bare hill.
Moy-Mell ... ... ... *Magh-Mell,* plain of pleasures.
Moytura ... ... ... *Magh-tuireadh,* plain of towers.
Mumha ... ... ... *Mumha,* gen. *Mumhan.*
Muirdach ... ... ... *Muridach.*
Murthemna ... ... ... *Muirthemhne.*

Niamh ... ... ... *Niamh,* beauty.
Nuada of the Silver Hand *Nuadha Airgeadlaimh.*
Nuca ... ... ... *Nuca.*

Oisin ... ... ... *Oisin.*
Owenaght ... ... ... *Eoghannacht,* descendants of Owen.

| | | | | |
|---|---|---|---|---|
| Pezar | ... | ... | ... | *Pisear.* |

| | | | | |
|---|---|---|---|---|
| Racad | ... | ... | ... | *Rachadh.* |
| Rib | ... | ... | ... | *Ribh.* |

| | | | | |
|---|---|---|---|---|
| Sencab | ... | ... | ... | *Seanchab,* old mouth. |
| Sharvan | ... | ... | ... | *Searbhan,* a surly person. |
| Shee Finnaha | | ... | ... | *Sidh-Fionnac-haidh.* |
| Skeabrac | ... | ... | ... | *Sciath-bhreac,* speckled shield. |
| Skolan | ... | ... | ... | *Sceolaing.* |
| Slana | ... | ... | ... | *Slánach,* healthy. |
| Sorca | ... | ... | ... | *Sorcha.* |
| Sotal of the Large Heels | | | | *Sotal Sálmhór.* |

| | | | | |
|---|---|---|---|---|
| Taillkenn | ... | ... | ... | *Tailcenn.* |
| Tinna the Mighty | | | ... | *Tinne Mór.* |
| Tir-fa-thonn | | ... | ... | *Tir-fa-thuinn,* country beneath the waves. |
| Tír na nÓg | | ... | ... | land of youth. |
| Trencoss | ... | ... | ... | *Treunchosach,* strong-foot. |
| Trenmore O'Baskin | | | ... | *Treunmór O'Baoiscne.* |
| Turenn | ... | ... | ... | *Tuireann.* |

# A CATALOG OF SELECTED
# DOVER BOOKS
## IN ALL FIELDS OF INTEREST

# A CATALOG OF SELECTED DOVER
# BOOKS IN ALL FIELDS OF INTEREST

CONCERNING THE SPIRITUAL IN ART, Wassily Kandinsky. Pioneering work by father of abstract art. Thoughts on color theory, nature of art. Analysis of earlier masters. 12 illustrations. 80pp. of text. 5⅜ x 8½. 23411-8 Pa. $4.95

ANIMALS: 1,419 Copyright-Free Illustrations of Mammals, Birds, Fish, Insects, etc., Jim Harter (ed.). Clear wood engravings present, in extremely lifelike poses, over 1,000 species of animals. One of the most extensive pictorial sourcebooks of its kind. Captions. Index. 284pp. 9 x 12. 23766-4 Pa. $14.95

CELTIC ART: The Methods of Construction, George Bain. Simple geometric techniques for making Celtic interlacements, spirals, Kells-type initials, animals, humans, etc. Over 500 illustrations. 160pp. 9 x 12. (Available in U.S. only.) 22923-8 Pa. $9.95

AN ATLAS OF ANATOMY FOR ARTISTS, Fritz Schider. Most thorough reference work on art anatomy in the world. Hundreds of illustrations, including selections from works by Vesalius, Leonardo, Goya, Ingres, Michelangelo, others. 593 illustrations. 192pp. 7⅛ x 10¼. 20241-0 Pa. $9.95

CELTIC HAND STROKE-BY-STROKE (Irish Half-Uncial from "The Book of Kells"): An Arthur Baker Calligraphy Manual, Arthur Baker. Complete guide to creating each letter of the alphabet in distinctive Celtic manner. Covers hand position, strokes, pens, inks, paper, more. Illustrated. 48pp. 8¼ x 11. 24336-2 Pa. $3.95

EASY ORIGAMI, John Montroll. Charming collection of 32 projects (hat, cup, pelican, piano, swan, many more) specially designed for the novice origami hobbyist. Clearly illustrated easy-to-follow instructions insure that even beginning papercrafters will achieve successful results. 48pp. 8¼ x 11. 27298-2 Pa. $3.50

THE COMPLETE BOOK OF BIRDHOUSE CONSTRUCTION FOR WOODWORKERS, Scott D. Campbell. Detailed instructions, illustrations, tables. Also data on bird habitat and instinct patterns. Bibliography. 3 tables. 63 illustrations in 15 figures. 48pp. 5¼ x 8½. 24407-5 Pa. $2.50

BLOOMINGDALE'S ILLUSTRATED 1886 CATALOG: Fashions, Dry Goods and Housewares, Bloomingdale Brothers. Famed merchants' extremely rare catalog depicting about 1,700 products: clothing, housewares, firearms, dry goods, jewelry, more. Invaluable for dating, identifying vintage items. Also, copyright-free graphics for artists, designers. Co-published with Henry Ford Museum & Greenfield Village. 160pp. 8¼ x 11. 25780-0 Pa. $10.95

HISTORIC COSTUME IN PICTURES, Braun & Schneider. Over 1,450 costumed figures in clearly detailed engravings–from dawn of civilization to end of 19th century. Captions. Many folk costumes. 256pp. 8⅜ x 11¾. 23150-X Pa. $12.95

STICKLEY CRAFTSMAN FURNITURE CATALOGS, Gustav Stickley and L. & J. G. Stickley. Beautiful, functional furniture in two authentic catalogs from 1910. 594 illustrations, including 277 photos, show settles, rockers, armchairs, reclining chairs, bookcases, desks, tables. 183pp. 6½ x 9¼. 23838-5 Pa. $11.95

AMERICAN LOCOMOTIVES IN HISTORIC PHOTOGRAPHS: 1858 to 1949, Ron Ziel (ed.). A rare collection of 126 meticulously detailed official photographs, called "builder portraits," of American locomotives that majestically chronicle the rise of steam locomotive power in America. Introduction. Detailed captions. xi+ 129pp. 9 x 12. 27393-8 Pa. $13.95

AMERICA'S LIGHTHOUSES: An Illustrated History, Francis Ross Holland, Jr. Delightfully written, profusely illustrated fact-filled survey of over 200 American light-houses since 1716. History, anecdotes, technological advances, more. 240pp. 8 x 10¾. 25576-X Pa. $12.95

TOWARDS A NEW ARCHITECTURE, Le Corbusier. Pioneering manifesto by founder of "International School." Technical and aesthetic theories, views of industry, eco-nomics, relation of form to function, "mass-production split" and much more. Profusely illustrated. 320pp. 6⅛ x 9¼. (Available in U.S. only.) 25023-7 Pa. $10.95

HOW THE OTHER HALF LIVES, Jacob Riis. Famous journalistic record, expos-ing poverty and degradation of New York slums around 1900, by major social reformer. 100 striking and influential photographs. 233pp. 10 x 7⅞. 22012-5 Pa. $11.95

FRUIT KEY AND TWIG KEY TO TREES AND SHRUBS, William M. Harlow. One of the handiest and most widely used identification aids. Fruit key covers 120 deciduous and evergreen species; twig key 160 deciduous species. Easily used. Over 300 photographs. 126pp. 5⅜ x 8½. 20511-8 Pa. $3.95

COMMON BIRD SONGS, Dr. Donald J. Borror. Songs of 60 most common U.S. birds: robins, sparrows, cardinals, bluejays, finches, more—arranged in order of increasing complexity. Up to 9 variations of songs of each species.
Cassette and manual 99911-4 $8.95

ORCHIDS AS HOUSE PLANTS, Rebecca Tyson Northen. Grow cattleyas and many other kinds of orchids—in a window, in a case, or under artificial light. 63 illus-trations. 148pp. 5⅜ x 8½. 23261-1 Pa. $7.95

MONSTER MAZES, Dave Phillips. Masterful mazes at four levels of difficulty. Avoid deadly perils and evil creatures to find magical treasures. Solutions for all 32 exciting illustrated puzzles. 48pp. 8¼ x 11. 26005-4 Pa. $2.95

MOZART'S DON GIOVANNI (DOVER OPERA LIBRETTO SERIES), Wolfgang Amadeus Mozart. Introduced and translated by Ellen H. Bleiler. Standard Italian libretto, with complete English translation. Convenient and thoroughly portable—an ideal companion for reading along with a recording or the performance itself. Introduction. List of characters. Plot summary. 121pp. 5¼ x 8½. 24944-1 Pa. $3.95

TECHNICAL MANUAL AND DICTIONARY OF CLASSICAL BALLET, Gail Grant. Defines, explains, comments on steps, movements, poses and concepts. 15-page pictorial section. Basic book for student, viewer. 127pp. 5⅜ x 8½. 21843-0 Pa. $4.95

THE CLARINET AND CLARINET PLAYING, David Pino. Lively, comprehensive work features suggestions about technique, musicianship, and musical interpretation, as well as guidelines for teaching, making your own reeds, and preparing for public performance. Includes an intriguing look at clarinet history. "A godsend," *The Clarinet,* Journal of the International Clarinet Society. Appendixes. 7 illus. 320pp. 5⅜ x 8½. 40270-3 Pa. $9.95

HOLLYWOOD GLAMOR PORTRAITS, John Kobal (ed.). 145 photos from 1926-49. Harlow, Gable, Bogart, Bacall; 94 stars in all. Full background on photographers, technical aspects. 160pp. 8⅜ x 11¼. 23352-9 Pa. $12.95

THE ANNOTATED CASEY AT THE BAT: A Collection of Ballads about the Mighty Casey/Third, Revised Edition, Martin Gardner (ed.). Amusing sequels and parodies of one of America's best-loved poems: Casey's Revenge, Why Casey Whiffed, Casey's Sister at the Bat, others. 256pp. 5⅜ x 8½. 28598-7 Pa. $8.95

THE RAVEN AND OTHER FAVORITE POEMS, Edgar Allan Poe. Over 40 of the author's most memorable poems: "The Bells," "Ulalume," "Israfel," "To Helen," "The Conqueror Worm," "Eldorado," "Annabel Lee," many more. Alphabetic lists of titles and first lines. 64pp. 5 3/16 x 8¼. 26685-0 Pa. $1.00

PERSONAL MEMOIRS OF U. S. GRANT, Ulysses Simpson Grant. Intelligent, deeply moving firsthand account of Civil War campaigns, considered by many the finest military memoirs ever written. Includes letters, historic photographs, maps and more. 528pp. 6⅛ x 9¼. 28587-1 Pa. $12.95

ANCIENT EGYPTIAN MATERIALS AND INDUSTRIES, A. Lucas and J. Harris. Fascinating, comprehensive, thoroughly documented text describes this ancient civilization's vast resources and the processes that incorporated them in daily life, including the use of animal products, building materials, cosmetics, perfumes and incense, fibers, glazed ware, glass and its manufacture, materials used in the mummification process, and much more. 544pp. 6⅛ x 9¼. (Available in U.S. only.) 40446-3 Pa. $16.95

RUSSIAN STORIES/РУССКИЕ РАССКАЗЫ: A Dual-Language Book, edited by Gleb Struve. Twelve tales by such masters as Chekhov, Tolstoy, Dostoevsky, Pushkin, others. Excellent word-for-word English translations on facing pages, plus teaching and study aids, Russian/English vocabulary, biographical/critical introductions, more. 416pp. 5⅜ x 8½. 26244-8 Pa. $9.95

PHILADELPHIA THEN AND NOW: 60 Sites Photographed in the Past and Present, Kenneth Finkel and Susan Oyama. Rare photographs of City Hall, Logan Square, Independence Hall, Betsy Ross House, other landmarks juxtaposed with contemporary views. Captures changing face of historic city. Introduction. Captions. 128pp. 8¼ x 11. 25790-8 Pa. $9.95

AIA ARCHITECTURAL GUIDE TO NASSAU AND SUFFOLK COUNTIES, LONG ISLAND, The American Institute of Architects, Long Island Chapter, and the Society for the Preservation of Long Island Antiquities. Comprehensive, well-researched and generously illustrated volume brings to life over three centuries of Long Island's great architectural heritage. More than 240 photographs with authoritative, extensively detailed captions. 176pp. 8¼ x 11. 26946-9 Pa. $14.95

NORTH AMERICAN INDIAN LIFE: Customs and Traditions of 23 Tribes, Elsie Clews Parsons (ed.). 27 fictionalized essays by noted anthropologists examine religion, customs, government, additional facets of life among the Winnebago, Crow, Zuni, Eskimo, other tribes. 480pp. 6⅛ x 9¼. 27377-6 Pa. $10.95

FRANK LLOYD WRIGHT'S DANA HOUSE, Donald Hoffmann. Pictorial essay of residential masterpiece with over 160 interior and exterior photos, plans, elevations, sketches and studies. 128pp. $9\frac{1}{4}$ x $10\frac{3}{4}$. 29120-0 Pa. $14.95

THE MALE AND FEMALE FIGURE IN MOTION: 60 Classic Photographic Sequences, Eadweard Muybridge. 60 true-action photographs of men and women walking, running, climbing, bending, turning, etc., reproduced from rare 19th-century masterpiece. vi + 121pp. 9 x 12. 24745-7 Pa. $12.95

1001 QUESTIONS ANSWERED ABOUT THE SEASHORE, N. J. Berrill and Jacquelyn Berrill. Queries answered about dolphins, sea snails, sponges, starfish, fishes, shore birds, many others. Covers appearance, breeding, growth, feeding, much more. 305pp. $5\frac{1}{4}$ x $8\frac{1}{4}$. 23366-9 Pa. $9.95

ATTRACTING BIRDS TO YOUR YARD, William J. Weber. Easy-to-follow guide offers advice on how to attract the greatest diversity of birds: birdhouses, feeders, water and waterers, much more. 96pp. $5\frac{3}{16}$ x $8\frac{1}{4}$. 28927-3 Pa. $2.50

MEDICINAL AND OTHER USES OF NORTH AMERICAN PLANTS: A Historical Survey with Special Reference to the Eastern Indian Tribes, Charlotte Erichsen-Brown. Chronological historical citations document 500 years of usage of plants, trees, shrubs native to eastern Canada, northeastern U.S. Also complete identifying information. 343 illustrations. 544pp. $6\frac{1}{2}$ x $9\frac{1}{4}$. 25951-X Pa. $12.95

STORYBOOK MAZES, Dave Phillips. 23 stories and mazes on two-page spreads: Wizard of Oz, Treasure Island, Robin Hood, etc. Solutions. 64pp. $8\frac{1}{4}$ x 11. 23628-5 Pa. $2.95

AMERICAN NEGRO SONGS: 230 Folk Songs and Spirituals, Religious and Secular, John W. Work. This authoritative study traces the African influences of songs sung and played by black Americans at work, in church, and as entertainment. The author discusses the lyric significance of such songs as "Swing Low, Sweet Chariot," "John Henry," and others and offers the words and music for 230 songs. Bibliography. Index of Song Titles. 272pp. $6\frac{1}{2}$ x $9\frac{1}{4}$. 40271-1 Pa. $9.95

MOVIE-STAR PORTRAITS OF THE FORTIES, John Kobal (ed.). 163 glamor, studio photos of 106 stars of the 1940s: Rita Hayworth, Ava Gardner, Marlon Brando, Clark Gable, many more. 176pp. $8\frac{3}{8}$ x $11\frac{1}{4}$. 23546-7 Pa. $14.95

BENCHLEY LOST AND FOUND, Robert Benchley. Finest humor from early 30s, about pet peeves, child psychologists, post office and others. Mostly unavailable elsewhere. 73 illustrations by Peter Arno and others. 183pp. $5\frac{3}{8}$ x $8\frac{1}{2}$. 22410-4 Pa. $6.95

YEKL and THE IMPORTED BRIDEGROOM AND OTHER STORIES OF YIDDISH NEW YORK, Abraham Cahan. Film Hester Street based on *Yekl* (1896). Novel, other stories among first about Jewish immigrants on N.Y.'s East Side. 240pp. $5\frac{3}{8}$ x $8\frac{1}{2}$. 22427-9 Pa. $7.95

SELECTED POEMS, Walt Whitman. Generous sampling from *Leaves of Grass*. Twenty-four poems include "I Hear America Singing," "Song of the Open Road," "I Sing the Body Electric," "When Lilacs Last in the Dooryard Bloom'd," "O Captain! My Captain!"–all reprinted from an authoritative edition. Lists of titles and first lines. 128pp. $5\frac{3}{16}$ x $8\frac{1}{4}$. 26878-0 Pa. $1.00

THE BEST TALES OF HOFFMANN, E. T. A. Hoffmann. 10 of Hoffmann's most important stories: "Nutcracker and the King of Mice," "The Golden Flowerpot," etc. 458pp. 5⅜ x 8½. 21793-0 Pa. $9.95

FROM FETISH TO GOD IN ANCIENT EGYPT, E. A. Wallis Budge. Rich detailed survey of Egyptian conception of "God" and gods, magic, cult of animals, Osiris, more. Also, superb English translations of hymns and legends. 240 illustrations. 545pp. 5⅜ x 8½. 25803-3 Pa. $13.95

FRENCH STORIES/CONTES FRANÇAIS: A Dual-Language Book, Wallace Fowlie. Ten stories by French masters, Voltaire to Camus: "Micromegas" by Voltaire; "The Atheist's Mass" by Balzac; "Minuet" by de Maupassant; "The Guest" by Camus, six more. Excellent English translations on facing pages. Also French-English vocabulary list, exercises, more. 352pp. 5⅜ x 8½. 26443-2 Pa. $9.95

CHICAGO AT THE TURN OF THE CENTURY IN PHOTOGRAPHS: 122 Historic Views from the Collections of the Chicago Historical Society, Larry A. Viskochil. Rare large-format prints offer detailed views of City Hall, State Street, the Loop, Hull House, Union Station, many other landmarks, circa 1904-1913. Introduction. Captions. Maps. 144pp. 9⅜ x 12¼. 24656-6 Pa. $12.95

OLD BROOKLYN IN EARLY PHOTOGRAPHS, 1865-1929, William Lee Younger. Luna Park, Gravesend race track, construction of Grand Army Plaza, moving of Hotel Brighton, etc. 157 previously unpublished photographs. 165pp. 8⅞ x 11¾. 23587-4 Pa. $13.95

THE MYTHS OF THE NORTH AMERICAN INDIANS, Lewis Spence. Rich anthology of the myths and legends of the Algonquins, Iroquois, Pawnees and Sioux, prefaced by an extensive historical and ethnological commentary. 36 illustrations. 480pp. 5⅜ x 8½. 25967-6 Pa. $10.95

AN ENCYCLOPEDIA OF BATTLES: Accounts of Over 1,560 Battles from 1479 B.C. to the Present, David Eggenberger. Essential details of every major battle in recorded history from the first battle of Megiddo in 1479 B.C. to Grenada in 1984. List of Battle Maps. New Appendix covering the years 1967-1984. Index. 99 illustrations. 544pp. 6½ x 9¼. 24913-1 Pa. $16.95

SAILING ALONE AROUND THE WORLD, Captain Joshua Slocum. First man to sail around the world, alone, in small boat. One of great feats of seamanship told in delightful manner. 67 illustrations. 294pp. 5⅜ x 8½. 20326-3 Pa. $6.95

ANARCHISM AND OTHER ESSAYS, Emma Goldman. Powerful, penetrating, prophetic essays on direct action, role of minorities, prison reform, puritan hypocrisy, violence, etc. 271pp. 5⅜ x 8½. 22484-8 Pa. $8.95

MYTHS OF THE HINDUS AND BUDDHISTS, Ananda K. Coomaraswamy and Sister Nivedita. Great stories of the epics; deeds of Krishna, Shiva, taken from puranas, Vedas, folk tales; etc. 32 illustrations. 400pp. 5⅜ x 8½. 21759-0 Pa. $12.95

THE TRAUMA OF BIRTH, Otto Rank. Rank's controversial thesis that anxiety neurosis is caused by profound psychological trauma which occurs at birth. 256pp. 5⅜ x 8½. 27974-X Pa. $7.95

A THEOLOGICO-POLITICAL TREATISE, Benedict Spinoza. Also contains unfinished Political Treatise. Great classic on religious liberty, theory of government on common consent. R. Elwes translation. Total of 421pp. 5⅜ x 8½. 20249-6 Pa. $10.95

# CATALOG OF DOVER BOOKS

MY BONDAGE AND MY FREEDOM, Frederick Douglass. Born a slave, Douglass became outspoken force in antislavery movement. The best of Douglass' autobiographies. Graphic description of slave life. 464pp. 5⅜ x 8½. 22457-0 Pa. $8.95

FOLLOWING THE EQUATOR: A Journey Around the World, Mark Twain. Fascinating humorous account of 1897 voyage to Hawaii, Australia, India, New Zealand, etc. Ironic, bemused reports on peoples, customs, climate, flora and fauna, politics, much more. 197 illustrations. 720pp. 5⅜ x 8½. 26113-1 Pa. $15.95

THE PEOPLE CALLED SHAKERS, Edward D. Andrews. Definitive study of Shakers: origins, beliefs, practices, dances, social organization, furniture and crafts, etc. 33 illustrations. 351pp. 5⅜ x 8½. 21081-2 Pa. $12.95

THE MYTHS OF GREECE AND ROME, H. A. Guerber. A classic of mythology, generously illustrated, long prized for its simple, graphic, accurate retelling of the principal myths of Greece and Rome, and for its commentary on their origins and significance. With 64 illustrations by Michelangelo, Raphael, Titian, Rubens, Canova, Bernini and others. 480pp. 5⅜ x 8½. 27584-1 Pa. $10.95

PSYCHOLOGY OF MUSIC, Carl E. Seashore. Classic work discusses music as a medium from psychological viewpoint. Clear treatment of physical acoustics, auditory apparatus, sound perception, development of musical skills, nature of musical feeling, host of other topics. 88 figures. 408pp. 5⅜ x 8½. 21851-1 Pa. $11.95

THE PHILOSOPHY OF HISTORY, Georg W. Hegel. Great classic of Western thought develops concept that history is not chance but rational process, the evolution of freedom. 457pp. 5⅜ x 8½. 20112-0 Pa. $9.95

THE BOOK OF TEA, Kakuzo Okakura. Minor classic of the Orient: entertaining, charming explanation, interpretation of traditional Japanese culture in terms of tea ceremony. 94pp. 5⅜ x 8½. 20070-1 Pa. $3.95

LIFE IN ANCIENT EGYPT, Adolf Erman. Fullest, most thorough, detailed older account with much not in more recent books, domestic life, religion, magic, medicine, commerce, much more. Many illustrations reproduce tomb paintings, carvings, hieroglyphs, etc. 597pp. 5⅜ x 8½. 22632-8 Pa. $12.95

SUNDIALS, Their Theory and Construction, Albert Waugh. Far and away the best, most thorough coverage of ideas, mathematics concerned, types, construction, adjusting anywhere. Simple, nontechnical treatment allows even children to build several of these dials. Over 100 illustrations. 230pp. 5⅜ x 8½. 22947-5 Pa. $8.95

THEORETICAL HYDRODYNAMICS, L. M. Milne-Thomson. Classic exposition of the mathematical theory of fluid motion, applicable to both hydrodynamics and aerodynamics. Over 600 exercises. 768pp. 6⅛ x 9¼. 68970-0 Pa. $20.95

SONGS OF EXPERIENCE: Facsimile Reproduction with 26 Plates in Full Color, William Blake. 26 full-color plates from a rare 1826 edition. Includes "TheTyger," "London," "Holy Thursday," and other poems. Printed text of poems. 48pp. 5¼ x 7. 24636-1 Pa. $4.95

OLD-TIME VIGNETTES IN FULL COLOR, Carol Belanger Grafton (ed.). Over 390 charming, often sentimental illustrations, selected from archives of Victorian graphics–pretty women posing, children playing, food, flowers, kittens and puppies, smiling cherubs, birds and butterflies, much more. All copyright-free. 48pp. 9¼ x 12¼. 27269-9 Pa. $7.95

PERSPECTIVE FOR ARTISTS, Rex Vicat Cole. Depth, perspective of sky and sea, shadows, much more, not usually covered. 391 diagrams, 81 reproductions of drawings and paintings. 279pp. 5⅜ x 8½. 22487-2 Pa. $9.95

DRAWING THE LIVING FIGURE, Joseph Sheppard. Innovative approach to artistic anatomy focuses on specifics of surface anatomy, rather than muscles and bones. Over 170 drawings of live models in front, back and side views, and in widely varying poses. Accompanying diagrams. 177 illustrations. Introduction. Index. 144pp. 8⅜ x11¼. 26723-7 Pa. $9.95

GOTHIC AND OLD ENGLISH ALPHABETS: 100 Complete Fonts, Dan X. Solo. Add power, elegance to posters, signs, other graphics with 100 stunning copyright-free alphabets: Blackstone, Dolbey, Germania, 97 more–including many lower-case, numerals, punctuation marks. 104pp. 8⅛ x 11. 24695-7 Pa. $9.95

HOW TO DO BEADWORK, Mary White. Fundamental book on craft from simple projects to five-bead chains and woven works. 106 illustrations. 142pp. 5⅜ x 8. 20697-1 Pa. $5.95

THE BOOK OF WOOD CARVING, Charles Marshall Sayers. Finest book for beginners discusses fundamentals and offers 34 designs. "Absolutely first rate . . . well thought out and well executed."–E. J. Tangerman. 118pp. 7¾ x 10⅝. 23654-4 Pa. $7.95

ILLUSTRATED CATALOG OF CIVIL WAR MILITARY GOODS: Union Army Weapons, Insignia, Uniform Accessories, and Other Equipment, Schuyler, Hartley, and Graham. Rare, profusely illustrated 1846 catalog includes Union Army uniform and dress regulations, arms and ammunition, coats, insignia, flags, swords, rifles, etc. 226 illustrations. 160pp. 9 x 12. 24939-5 Pa. $12.95

WOMEN'S FASHIONS OF THE EARLY 1900s: An Unabridged Republication of "New York Fashions, 1909," National Cloak & Suit Co. Rare catalog of mail-order fashions documents women's and children's clothing styles shortly after the turn of the century. Captions offer full descriptions, prices. Invaluable resource for fashion, costume historians. Approximately 725 illustrations. 128pp. 8⅜ x 11¼. 27276-1 Pa. $12.95

THE 1912 AND 1915 GUSTAV STICKLEY FURNITURE CATALOGS, Gustav Stickley. With over 200 detailed illustrations and descriptions, these two catalogs are essential reading and reference materials and identification guides for Stickley furniture. Captions cite materials, dimensions and prices. 112pp. 6½ x 9¼. 26676-1 Pa. $9.95

EARLY AMERICAN LOCOMOTIVES, John H. White, Jr. Finest locomotive engravings from early 19th century: historical (1804–74), main-line (after 1870), special, foreign, etc. 147 plates. 142pp. 11⅜ x 8¼. 22772-3 Pa. $12.95

THE TALL SHIPS OF TODAY IN PHOTOGRAPHS, Frank O. Braynard. Lavishly illustrated tribute to nearly 100 majestic contemporary sailing vessels: Amerigo Vespucci, Clearwater, Constitution, Eagle, Mayflower, Sea Cloud, Victory, many more. Authoritative captions provide statistics, background on each ship. 190 black-and-white photographs and illustrations. Introduction. 128pp. 8⅞ x 11¾. 27163-3 Pa. $14.95

LITTLE BOOK OF EARLY AMERICAN CRAFTS AND TRADES, Peter Stockham (ed.). 1807 children's book explains crafts and trades: baker, hatter, cooper, potter, and many others. 23 copperplate illustrations. 140pp. 4⅝ x 6.
23336-7 Pa. $4.95

VICTORIAN FASHIONS AND COSTUMES FROM HARPER'S BAZAR, 1867–1898, Stella Blum (ed.). Day costumes, evening wear, sports clothes, shoes, hats, other accessories in over 1,000 detailed engravings. 320pp. 9⅜ x 12¼.
22990-4 Pa. $16.95

GUSTAV STICKLEY, THE CRAFTSMAN, Mary Ann Smith. Superb study surveys broad scope of Stickley's achievement, especially in architecture. Design philosophy, rise and fall of the Craftsman empire, descriptions and floor plans for many Craftsman houses, more. 86 black-and-white halftones. 31 line illustrations. Introduction 208pp. 6½ x 9¼.
27210-9 Pa. $9.95

THE LONG ISLAND RAIL ROAD IN EARLY PHOTOGRAPHS, Ron Ziel. Over 220 rare photos, informative text document origin ( 1844) and development of rail service on Long Island. Vintage views of early trains, locomotives, stations, passengers, crews, much more. Captions. 8⅞ x 11¾.
26301-0 Pa. $14.95

VOYAGE OF THE LIBERDADE, Joshua Slocum. Great 19th-century mariner's thrilling, first-hand account of the wreck of his ship off South America, the 35-foot boat he built from the wreckage, and its remarkable voyage home. 128pp. 5⅜ x 8½.
40022-0 Pa. $5.95

TEN BOOKS ON ARCHITECTURE, Vitruvius. The most important book ever written on architecture. Early Roman aesthetics, technology, classical orders, site selection, all other aspects. Morgan translation. 331pp. 5⅜ x 8½. 20645-9 Pa. $9.95

THE HUMAN FIGURE IN MOTION, Eadweard Muybridge. More than 4,500 stopped-action photos, in action series, showing undraped men, women, children jumping, lying down, throwing, sitting, wrestling, carrying, etc. 390pp. 7⅞ x 10⅝.
20204-6 Clothbd. $29.95

TREES OF THE EASTERN AND CENTRAL UNITED STATES AND CANADA, William M. Harlow. Best one-volume guide to 140 trees. Full descriptions, woodlore, range, etc. Over 600 illustrations. Handy size. 288pp. 4½ x 6⅜.
20395-6 Pa. $6.95

SONGS OF WESTERN BIRDS, Dr. Donald J. Borror. Complete song and call repertoire of 60 western species, including flycatchers, juncoes, cactus wrens, many more–includes fully illustrated booklet. Cassette and manual 99913-0 $8.95

GROWING AND USING HERBS AND SPICES, Milo Miloradovich. Versatile handbook provides all the information needed for cultivation and use of all the herbs and spices available in North America. 4 illustrations. Index. Glossary. 236pp. 5⅜ x 8½.
25058-X Pa. $7.95

BIG BOOK OF MAZES AND LABYRINTHS, Walter Shepherd. 50 mazes and labyrinths in all–classical, solid, ripple, and more–in one great volume. Perfect inexpensive puzzler for clever youngsters. Full solutions. 112pp. 8⅛ x 11.
22951-3 Pa. $5.95

PIANO TUNING, J. Cree Fischer. Clearest, best book for beginner, amateur. Simple repairs, raising dropped notes, tuning by easy method of flattened fifths. No previous skills needed. 4 illustrations. 201pp. 5⅜ x 8½. 23267-0 Pa. $6.95

HINTS TO SINGERS, Lillian Nordica. Selecting the right teacher, developing confidence, overcoming stage fright, and many other important skills receive thoughtful discussion in this indispensible guide, written by a world-famous diva of four decades' experience. 96pp. 5⅜ x 8½. 40094-8 Pa. $4.95

THE COMPLETE NONSENSE OF EDWARD LEAR, Edward Lear. All nonsense limericks, zany alphabets, Owl and Pussycat, songs, nonsense botany, etc., illustrated by Lear. Total of 320pp. 5⅜ x 8½. (Available in U.S. only.) 20167-8 Pa. $7.95

VICTORIAN PARLOUR POETRY: An Annotated Anthology, Michael R. Turner. 117 gems by Longfellow, Tennyson, Browning, many lesser-known poets. "The Village Blacksmith," "Curfew Must Not Ring Tonight," "Only a Baby Small," dozens more, often difficult to find elsewhere. Index of poets, titles, first lines. xxiii + 325pp. 5⅝ x 8¼. 27044-0 Pa. $12.95

DUBLINERS, James Joyce. Fifteen stories offer vivid, tightly focused observations of the lives of Dublin's poorer classes. At least one, "The Dead," is considered a masterpiece. Reprinted complete and unabridged from standard edition. 160pp. 5$\frac{3}{16}$ x 8¼. 26870-5 Pa. $1.50

GREAT WEIRD TALES: 14 Stories by Lovecraft, Blackwood, Machen and Others, S. T. Joshi (ed.). 14 spellbinding tales, including "The Sin Eater," by Fiona McLeod, "The Eye Above the Mantel," by Frank Belknap Long, as well as renowned works by R. H. Barlow, Lord Dunsany, Arthur Machen, W. C. Morrow and eight other masters of the genre. 256pp. 5⅜ x 8½. (Available in U.S. only.) 40436-6 Pa. $8.95

THE BOOK OF THE SACRED MAGIC OF ABRAMELIN THE MAGE, translated by S. MacGregor Mathers. Medieval manuscript of ceremonial magic. Basic document in Aleister Crowley, Golden Dawn groups. 268pp. 5⅜ x 8½. 23211-5 Pa. $9.95

NEW RUSSIAN-ENGLISH AND ENGLISH-RUSSIAN DICTIONARY, M. A. O'Brien. This is a remarkably handy Russian dictionary, containing a surprising amount of information, including over 70,000 entries. 366pp. 4½ x 6⅛. 20208-9 Pa. $10.95

HISTORIC HOMES OF THE AMERICAN PRESIDENTS, Second, Revised Edition, Irvin Haas. A traveler's guide to American Presidential homes, most open to the public, depicting and describing homes occupied by every American President from George Washington to George Bush. With visiting hours, admission charges, travel routes. 175 photographs. Index. 160pp. 8¼ x 11. 26751-2 Pa. $13.95

NEW YORK IN THE FORTIES, Andreas Feininger. 162 brilliant photographs by the well-known photographer, formerly with *Life* magazine. Commuters, shoppers, Times Square at night, much else from city at its peak. Captions by John von Hartz. 181pp. 9¼ x 10¾. 23585-8 Pa. $13.95

INDIAN SIGN LANGUAGE, William Tomkins. Over 525 signs developed by Sioux and other tribes. Written instructions and diagrams. Also 290 pictographs. 111pp. 6⅛ x 9¼. 22029-X Pa. $3.95

ANATOMY: A Complete Guide for Artists, Joseph Sheppard. A master of figure drawing shows artists how to render human anatomy convincingly. Over 460 illustrations. 224pp. 8⅜ x 11¼.                                27279-6 Pa. $11.95

MEDIEVAL CALLIGRAPHY: Its History and Technique, Marc Drogin. Spirited history, comprehensive instruction manual covers 13 styles (ca. 4th century through 15th). Excellent photographs; directions for duplicating medieval techniques with modern tools. 224pp. 8⅜ x 11¼.                        26142-5 Pa. $12.95

DRIED FLOWERS: How to Prepare Them, Sarah Whitlock and Martha Rankin. Complete instructions on how to use silica gel, meal and borax, perlite aggregate, sand and borax, glycerine and water to create attractive permanent flower arrangements. 12 illustrations. 32pp. 5⅜ x 8½.                   21802-3 Pa. $1.00

EASY-TO-MAKE BIRD FEEDERS FOR WOODWORKERS, Scott D. Campbell. Detailed, simple-to-use guide for designing, constructing, caring for and using feeders. Text, illustrations for 12 classic and contemporary designs. 96pp. 5⅜ x 8½.
25847-5 Pa. $3.95

SCOTTISH WONDER TALES FROM MYTH AND LEGEND, Donald A. Mackenzie. 16 lively tales tell of giants rumbling down mountainsides, of a magic wand that turns stone pillars into warriors, of gods and goddesses, evil hags, powerful forces and more. 240pp. 5⅜ x 8½.                            29677-6 Pa. $6.95

THE HISTORY OF UNDERCLOTHES, C. Willett Cunnington and Phyllis Cunnington. Fascinating, well-documented survey covering six centuries of English undergarments, enhanced with over 100 illustrations: 12th-century laced-up bodice, footed long drawers (1795), 19th-century bustles, 19th-century corsets for men, Victorian "bust improvers," much more. 272pp. 5⅜ x 8¼.          27124-2 Pa. $9.95

ARTS AND CRAFTS FURNITURE: The Complete Brooks Catalog of 1912, Brooks Manufacturing Co. Photos and detailed descriptions of more than 150 now very collectible furniture designs from the Arts and Crafts movement depict davenports, settees, buffets, desks, tables, chairs, bedsteads, dressers and more, all built of solid, quarter-sawed oak. Invaluable for students and enthusiasts of antiques, Americana and the decorative arts. 80pp. 6½ x 9¼.                    27471-3 Pa. $8.95

WILBUR AND ORVILLE: A Biography of the Wright Brothers, Fred Howard. Definitive, crisply written study tells the full story of the brothers' lives and work. A vividly written biography, unparalleled in scope and color, that also captures the spirit of an extraordinary era. 560pp. 6⅛ x 9¼.                    40297-5 Pa. $17.95

THE ARTS OF THE SAILOR: Knotting, Splicing and Ropework, Hervey Garrett Smith. Indispensable shipboard reference covers tools, basic knots and useful hitches; handsewing and canvas work, more. Over 100 illustrations. Delightful reading for sea lovers. 256pp. 5⅜ x 8½.                                26440-8 Pa. $8.95

FRANK LLOYD WRIGHT'S FALLINGWATER: The House and Its History, Second, Revised Edition, Donald Hoffmann. A total revision—both in text and illustrations—of the standard document on Fallingwater, the boldest, most personal architectural statement of Wright's mature years, updated with valuable new material from the recently opened Frank Lloyd Wright Archives. "Fascinating"–*The New York Times*. 116 illustrations. 128pp. 9¼ x 10¾.                27430-6 Pa. $12.95

PHOTOGRAPHIC SKETCHBOOK OF THE CIVIL WAR, Alexander Gardner. 100 photos taken on field during the Civil War. Famous shots of Manassas Harper's Ferry, Lincoln, Richmond, slave pens, etc. 244pp. 10⅝ x 8¼. 22731-6 Pa. $10.95

FIVE ACRES AND INDEPENDENCE, Maurice G. Kains. Great back-to-the-land classic explains basics of self-sufficient farming. The one book to get. 95 illustrations. 397pp. 5⅜ x 8½. 20974-1 Pa. $7.95

SONGS OF EASTERN BIRDS, Dr. Donald J. Borror. Songs and calls of 60 species most common to eastern U.S.: warblers, woodpeckers, flycatchers, thrushes, larks, many more in high-quality recording. Cassette and manual 99912-2 $9.95

A MODERN HERBAL, Margaret Grieve. Much the fullest, most exact, most useful compilation of herbal material. Gigantic alphabetical encyclopedia, from aconite to zedoary, gives botanical information, medical properties, folklore, economic uses, much else. Indispensable to serious reader. 161 illustrations. 888pp. 6½ x 9¼. 2-vol. set. (Available in U.S. only.) Vol. I: 22798-7 Pa. $10.95
Vol. II: 22799-5 Pa. $10.95

HIDDEN TREASURE MAZE BOOK, Dave Phillips. Solve 34 challenging mazes accompanied by heroic tales of adventure. Evil dragons, people-eating plants, blood-thirsty giants, many more dangerous adversaries lurk at every twist and turn. 34 mazes, stories, solutions. 48pp. 8¼ x 11. 24566-7 Pa. $2.95

LETTERS OF W. A. MOZART, Wolfgang A. Mozart. Remarkable letters show bawdy wit, humor, imagination, musical insights, contemporary musical world; includes some letters from Leopold Mozart. 276pp. 5⅜ x 8½. 22859-2 Pa. $9.95

BASIC PRINCIPLES OF CLASSICAL BALLET, Agrippina Vaganova. Great Russian theoretician, teacher explains methods for teaching classical ballet. 118 illustrations. 175pp. 5⅜ x 8½. 22036-2 Pa. $6.95

THE JUMPING FROG, Mark Twain. Revenge edition. The original story of The Celebrated Jumping Frog of Calaveras County, a hapless French translation, and Twain's hilarious "retranslation" from the French. 12 illustrations. 66pp. 5⅜ x 8½. 22686-7 Pa. $4.95

BEST REMEMBERED POEMS, Martin Gardner (ed.). The 126 poems in this superb collection of 19th- and 20th-century British and American verse range from Shelley's "To a Skylark" to the impassioned "Renascence" of Edna St. Vincent Millay and to Edward Lear's whimsical "The Owl and the Pussycat." 224pp. 5⅜ x 8½. 27165-X Pa. $5.95

COMPLETE SONNETS, William Shakespeare. Over 150 exquisite poems deal with love, friendship, the tyranny of time, beauty's evanescence, death and other themes in language of remarkable power, precision and beauty. Glossary of archaic terms. 80pp. 5³⁄₁₆ x 8¼. 26686-9 Pa. $1.00

THE BATTLES THAT CHANGED HISTORY, Fletcher Pratt. Eminent historian profiles 16 crucial conflicts, ancient to modern, that changed the course of civilization. 352pp. 5⅜ x 8½. 41129-X Pa. $9.95

THE WIT AND HUMOR OF OSCAR WILDE, Alvin Redman (ed.). More than 1,000 ripostes, paradoxes, wisecracks: Work is the curse of the drinking classes; I can resist everything except temptation; etc. 258pp. 5⅜ x 8½. 20602-5 Pa. $6.95

SHAKESPEARE LEXICON AND QUOTATION DICTIONARY, Alexander Schmidt. Full definitions, locations, shades of meaning in every word in plays and poems. More than 50,000 exact quotations. 1,485pp. 6½ x 9¼. 2-vol. set.

Vol. 1: 22726-X Pa. $17.95
Vol. 2: 22727-8 Pa. $17.95

SELECTED POEMS, Emily Dickinson. Over 100 best-known, best-loved poems by one of America's foremost poets, reprinted from authoritative early editions. No comparable edition at this price. Index of first lines. 64pp. 5³⁄₁₆ x 8¼.

26466-1 Pa. $1.00

THE INSIDIOUS DR. FU-MANCHU, Sax Rohmer. The first of the popular mystery series introduces a pair of English detectives to their archnemesis, the diabolical Dr. Fu-Manchu. Flavorful atmosphere, fast-paced action, and colorful characters enliven this classic of the genre. 208pp. 5³⁄₁₆ x 8¼. 29898-1 Pa. $2.00

THE MALLEUS MALEFICARUM OF KRAMER AND SPRENGER, translated by Montague Summers. Full text of most important witchhunter's "bible," used by both Catholics and Protestants. 278pp. 6⅝ x 10. 22802-9 Pa. $12.95

SPANISH STORIES/CUENTOS ESPAÑOLES: A Dual-Language Book, Angel Flores (ed.). Unique format offers 13 great stories in Spanish by Cervantes, Borges, others. Faithful English translations on facing pages. 352pp. 5⅜ x 8½.

25399-6 Pa. $8.95

GARDEN CITY, LONG ISLAND, IN EARLY PHOTOGRAPHS, 1869–1919, Mildred H. Smith. Handsome treasury of 118 vintage pictures, accompanied by carefully researched captions, document the Garden City Hotel fire (1899), the Vanderbilt Cup Race (1908), the first airmail flight departing from the Nassau Boulevard Aerodrome (1911), and much more. 96pp. 8⅞ x 11¾. 40669-5 Pa. $12.95

OLD QUEENS, N.Y., IN EARLY PHOTOGRAPHS, Vincent F. Seyfried and William Asadorian. Over 160 rare photographs of Maspeth, Jamaica, Jackson Heights, and other areas. Vintage views of DeWitt Clinton mansion, 1939 World's Fair and more. Captions. 192pp. 8⅞ x 11. 26358-4 Pa. $14.95

CAPTURED BY THE INDIANS: 15 Firsthand Accounts, 1750-1870, Frederick Drimmer. Astounding true historical accounts of grisly torture, bloody conflicts, relentless pursuits, miraculous escapes and more, by people who lived to tell the tale. 384pp. 5⅜ x 8½. 24901-8 Pa. $9.95

THE WORLD'S GREAT SPEECHES (Fourth Enlarged Edition), Lewis Copeland, Lawrence W. Lamm, and Stephen J. McKenna. Nearly 300 speeches provide public speakers with a wealth of updated quotes and inspiration–from Pericles' funeral oration and William Jennings Bryan's "Cross of Gold Speech" to Malcolm X's powerful words on the Black Revolution and Earl of Spenser's tribute to his sister, Diana, Princess of Wales. 944pp. 5⅜ x 8⅜. 40903-1 Pa. $15.95

THE BOOK OF THE SWORD, Sir Richard F. Burton. Great Victorian scholar/adventurer's eloquent, erudite history of the "queen of weapons"–from prehistory to early Roman Empire. Evolution and development of early swords, variations (sabre, broadsword, cutlass, scimitar, etc.), much more. 336pp. 6⅛ x 9¼.

25434-8 Pa. $9.95

AUTOBIOGRAPHY: The Story of My Experiments with Truth, Mohandas K. Gandhi. Boyhood, legal studies, purification, the growth of the Satyagraha (nonviolent protest) movement. Critical, inspiring work of the man responsible for the freedom of India. 480pp. 5⅜ x 8½. (Available in U.S. only.)          24593-4 Pa. $9.95

CELTIC MYTHS AND LEGENDS, T. W. Rolleston. Masterful retelling of Irish and Welsh stories and tales. Cuchulain, King Arthur, Deirdre, the Grail, many more. First paperback edition. 58 full-page illustrations. 512pp. 5⅜ x 8½.          26507-2 Pa. $9.95

THE PRINCIPLES OF PSYCHOLOGY, William James. Famous long course complete, unabridged. Stream of thought, time perception, memory, experimental methods; great work decades ahead of its time. 94 figures. 1,391pp. 5⅜ x 8½. 2-vol. set.

Vol. I: 20381-6 Pa. $14.95
Vol. II: 20382-4 Pa. $14.95

THE WORLD AS WILL AND REPRESENTATION, Arthur Schopenhauer. Definitive English translation of Schopenhauer's life work, correcting more than 1,000 errors, omissions in earlier translations. Translated by E. F. J. Payne. Total of 1,269pp. 5⅜ x 8½. 2-vol. set.          Vol. 1: 21761-2 Pa. $12.95
Vol. 2: 21762-0 Pa. $12.95

MAGIC AND MYSTERY IN TIBET, Madame Alexandra David-Neel. Experiences among lamas, magicians, sages, sorcerers, Bonpa wizards. A true psychic discovery. 32 illustrations. 321pp. 5⅜ x 8½. (Available in U.S. only.)          22682-4 Pa. $9.95

THE EGYPTIAN BOOK OF THE DEAD, E. A. Wallis Budge. Complete reproduction of Ani's papyrus, finest ever found. Full hieroglyphic text, interlinear transliteration, word-for-word translation, smooth translation. 533pp. 6½ x 9¼.

21866-X Pa. $12.95

MATHEMATICS FOR THE NONMATHEMATICIAN, Morris Kline. Detailed, college-level treatment of mathematics in cultural and historical context, with numerous exercises. Recommended Reading Lists. Tables. Numerous figures. 641pp. 5⅜ x 8½.

24823-2 Pa. $11.95

PROBABILISTIC METHODS IN THE THEORY OF STRUCTURES, Isaac Elishakoff. Well-written introduction covers the elements of the theory of probability from two or more random variables, the reliability of such multivariable structures, the theory of random function, Monte Carlo methods of treating problems incapable of exact solution, and more. Examples. 502pp. 5³/₈ x 8¹/₂.          40691-1 Pa. $16.95

THE RIME OF THE ANCIENT MARINER, Gustave Doré, S. T. Coleridge. Doré's finest work; 34 plates capture moods, subtleties of poem. Flawless full-size reproductions printed on facing pages with authoritative text of poem. "Beautiful. Simply beautiful."—*Publisher's Weekly.* 77pp. 9¼ x 12.          22305-1 Pa. $7.95

NORTH AMERICAN INDIAN DESIGNS FOR ARTISTS AND CRAFTSPEOPLE, Eva Wilson. Over 360 authentic copyright-free designs adapted from Navajo blankets, Hopi pottery, Sioux buffalo hides, more. Geometrics, symbolic figures, plant and animal motifs, etc. 128pp. 8⅜ x 11. (Not for sale in the United Kingdom.)          25341-4 Pa. $9.95

SCULPTURE: Principles and Practice, Louis Slobodkin. Step-by-step approach to clay, plaster, metals, stone; classical and modern. 253 drawings, photos. 255pp. 8⅛ x 11.

22960-2 Pa. $11.95

THE INFLUENCE OF SEA POWER UPON HISTORY, 1660–1783, A. T. Mahan. Influential classic of naval history and tactics still used as text in war colleges. First paperback edition. 4 maps. 24 battle plans. 640pp. 5⅜ x 8½.      25509-3 Pa. $14.95

THE STORY OF THE TITANIC AS TOLD BY ITS SURVIVORS, Jack Winocour (ed.). What it was really like. Panic, despair, shocking inefficiency, and a little heroism. More thrilling than any fictional account. 26 illustrations. 320pp. 5⅜ x 8½.
20610-6 Pa. $8.95

FAIRY AND FOLK TALES OF THE IRISH PEASANTRY, William Butler Yeats (ed.). Treasury of 64 tales from the twilight world of Celtic myth and legend: "The Soul Cages," "The Kildare Pooka," "King O'Toole and his Goose," many more. Introduction and Notes by W. B. Yeats. 352pp. 5⅜ x 8½.      26941-8 Pa. $8.95

BUDDHIST MAHAYANA TEXTS, E. B. Cowell and others (eds.). Superb, accurate translations of basic documents in Mahayana Buddhism, highly important in history of religions. The Buddha-karita of Asvaghosha, Larger Sukhavativyuha, more. 448pp. 5⅜ x 8½.      25552-2 Pa. $12.95

ONE TWO THREE . . . INFINITY: Facts and Speculations of Science, George Gamow. Great physicist's fascinating, readable overview of contemporary science: number theory, relativity, fourth dimension, entropy, genes, atomic structure, much more. 128 illustrations. Index. 352pp. 5⅜ x 8½.      25664-2 Pa. $9.95

EXPERIMENTATION AND MEASUREMENT, W. J. Youden. Introductory manual explains laws of measurement in simple terms and offers tips for achieving accuracy and minimizing errors. Mathematics of measurement, use of instruments, experimenting with machines. 1994 edition. Foreword. Preface. Introduction. Epilogue. Selected Readings. Glossary. Index. Tables and figures. 128pp. 5³/₈ x 8¹/₂.
40451-X Pa. $6.95

DALÍ ON MODERN ART: The Cuckolds of Antiquated Modern Art, Salvador Dalí. Influential painter skewers modern art and its practitioners. Outrageous evaluations of Picasso, Cézanne, Turner, more. 15 renderings of paintings discussed. 44 calligraphic decorations by Dalí. 96pp. 5⅜ x 8½. (Available in U.S. only.)      29220-7 Pa. $5.95

ANTIQUE PLAYING CARDS: A Pictorial History, Henry René D'Allemagne. Over 900 elaborate, decorative images from rare playing cards (14th–20th centuries): Bacchus, death, dancing dogs, hunting scenes, royal coats of arms, players cheating, much more. 96pp. 9¼ x 12¼.      29265-7 Pa. $12.95

MAKING FURNITURE MASTERPIECES: 30 Projects with Measured Drawings, Franklin H. Gottshall. Step-by-step instructions, illustrations for constructing handsome, useful pieces, among them a Sheraton desk, Chippendale chair, Spanish desk, Queen Anne table and a William and Mary dressing mirror. 224pp. 8⅛ x 11¼.
29338-6 Pa. $13.95

THE FOSSIL BOOK: A Record of Prehistoric Life, Patricia V. Rich et al. Profusely illustrated definitive guide covers everything from single-celled organisms and dinosaurs to birds and mammals and the interplay between climate and man. Over 1,500 illustrations. 760pp. 7½ x 10⅛.      29371-8 Pa. $29.95

*Prices subject to change without notice.*

Available at your book dealer or write for free catalog to Dept. GI, Dover Publications, Inc., 31 East 2nd St., Mineola, N.Y. 11501. Dover publishes more than 500 books each year on science, elementary and advanced mathematics, biology, music, art, literary history, social sciences and other areas.